Isolba of the Isles

The Isles

Book One

Ashley Armstrong

Isolba of the Isles

Copyright © 2026 by Ashley Armstrong.

All rights reserved. No part of this publication may be reproduced, distributed, or transmitted in any form or by any means, including photocopying, recording or other electronic or mechanical methods, without the prior written permission of the author, except in the case of brief quotations embodied in reviews and certain other non-commercial uses permitted by copyright law.

This is a work of fiction. Any characters, businesses, places, events or incidents are either the product of the author's imagination or are used fictitiously. Any resemblance to actual persons, living or dead, events or locales is entirely coincidental.

Printed in the United States of America

For more information, visit:

www.ashleyarmstrong.com

Cover illustration by Ashley Armstrong, 2026

Cover design by Ashley Armstrong, 2026

ISBN - Paperback: 978-1-972903-00-1

ISBN - Hardcover: 978-1-972903-01-8

ISBN - eBook: 978-1-972903-02-5

First Edition: April 2026

IN LOVING MEMORY OF MY DAD,
DEAN ARMSTRONG
HUSBAND, FATHER, PASTOR, ENTREPRENEUR,
SERVANT, SHEPHERD,
DESCENDANT OF CLAN ARMSTRONG,
THE SCOTTISH BORDER REIVERS

PROLOGUE

Western Isles of Scotland
Demoria, 1429 A.D.

S he stumbled amid the stony crevices in that steep mountain pass. Raw scrapes covered the palms of her hands and deep cuts splayed the soles of her feet. Wandering the crags had shred her leather shoes to ruins. Food and water stores depleted, tiny body heavy with exhaustion, she found herself in despair. Lost in a stone wilderness.

Beyond the shore, the Atlantic spread out far and wide beneath the brume. She had no method of escaping her small island. If her mother could not find her first, her father's searchers soon would.

She lacked a mantle and hat, wore men's clothing—a tattered linen tunic and wool breeks—and, with shorn hair, had no protection from the descending cold. As evening approached, she crouched beneath an overhang and shivered. She spoke to herself then.

"I am finished. I've escaped one unpleasant fate to greet another."

She contemplated going home. At least there, her death would save her people. Out here, she could not fathom what would become of her. Still, she could not turn back. The desire to live proved stronger than her dwindling resolve. She had to continue moving or risk capture.

The rhythmic waves moved undulant, unpredictable, and she pictured the earth as an awakened beast. It shuddered the waters with each breath. The fuming nostrils blew fierce gales and deluge. It held the sun captive, hoarding its vital warmth.

Would she ever again see clear sky and calm sea?

"Och, gods, perhaps there is another way."

If she could somehow reach her beloved across those harsh waters, she would be safe.

ONE

1427

Isolba stood near the cliff edge overlooking the water and watched her father's longship sail away. Two dozen oars rotated in and out of the sea from both sides of the craft. White peaks beat into frothy swells and slung back in a burst of saltwater. Even from her height, she heard the grunts of the galley slaves hidden in the lower deck as they heaved and pushed in unison.

Her father stood at the prow. Earlier, he had spoken his farewells and held her tight. Now, his colossal frame stood with a retinue of men behind him, all with a purposeful set to their shoulders. The slaves propelled the craft farther south.

A lump formed in her throat. "Do not leave me," she said to herself, but swallowed the intrusive thought. Had she not longed for this day's arrival? Yearned for it with all the passion and angst inside her?

"Manannán, protect him."

Uncle Frang stepped to her side. "Off goes your father to decide your future," he teased and threw an arm around his young charge.

She broke from her reverie to look up at him, a slight smile in the corners of her mouth. A nervous laugh escaped her lips. Her maidservant, Nareen, took her hand and squeezed it.

"'Tis not all for you, wee lass. Quiet your pride," Frang chided. "Your father desires peace more than marrying off his only child. Let us hope his meeting proves successful, or the entire voyage will be for naught."

She drew a deep breath and released it with a prolonged shudder. Her eyes fixed on the sea, her mind in a faraway place. She knew the dangers of sailing in the unpredictable waters, but her heaviest concern fell on the escalating tensions between her own Clan MacKay of Demoria and Clan McCloud of the Argarves. Her brow furrowed.

"You are afeared?" Frang asked. "My Isolba, methinks you're too old for that."

"Aye, I ken," she said in a near whisper. "Yet I fash for Father."

"You concern yourself too much. Clan McCloud has promised safe passage into their territory. There's nae threat my brother will meet an ambush on his arrival. McCloud craves amity as much as we, and why would they risk a counterattack? A fortnight ago, did we not receive their ambassador with great welcome and lay aside our arms? I expect the same reception for Escarans."

"I also fash that the marriage contract may falter," she said. "This meeting is critical."

"I don't see how it could go wrong," Frang assured. "The gods arranged this match to bring unity to these islands. You are Demoria's most valuable asset and Cormac is Argarves' future. We desire peace, to open avenues to trade, and to form a permanent alliance. The peace treaty is only possible with a marriage contract, and further disagreements could lead to violence. Neither your father nor Chief McCloud would risk that."

A chorus of shouts and pleas from behind rang in Isolba's direction. Several paces back, a row of men at arms formed a barrier between her and the outside world. Swords drawn in readiness, they held back the crowd of early-rising crofters and fisherfolk who had come to catch a glance at the chief's daughter. The commoners strained to see between the guards' shoulders and gaped at the rare sight of her.

Don't look. Cast your glance aside. Don't acknowledge them, she reminded herself, though it pained her to ignore them. In her younger years, she once handed a little girl a lace ribbon, and the sore scolding she received from her mother still replayed in her ears.

Her gaze remained fixed on her uncle, who tightened his grip on the hilt of his sword. In all his words, she heard only those that sang of her value. Warmth flowered within her to know that her father and all of Demoria held her in such distinction.

"So I *am* the key to peace?" Isolba said at last with a wide smile. Her top central teeth were longer than the others, with the framing incisors at a forward slant. With her round eyes and large ears poking out of her thick, dark hair, she appeared elfin.

Frang's brow rose, as if he realized his slip in words, and snorted in mock disgust.

"Aye, that you are," he said, chuckling. "Forgive me for attempting to dull your ego. I longed to spare you from the pressure that will come upon your first meeting with your betrothed. Everything rests on your beauty and charm. Now I must listen to you preen all this day."

Isolba's raised an eyebrow at his sarcasm. "If I'm distasteful to Cormac, he could crumble the contract and our islands will return to rabble-rousing?"

Frang produced a guttural laugh and threw his head back. After regaining his faculties, he motioned to her skirts. Isolba squinted in confusion.

"You should pray to become a woman in short time because we cannot wait for you."

The way the color drained from her face, he may as well have driven his sword through her. Heat flared up her throat and her jaw dropped. She smoothed her dress hem, bidding the telltale embroidery of her underskirt to stay hidden.

Fine, neat stitches emulating flower buds decorated the

bottom of her underskirt. Closed bluebell bulbs, orbs of corn poppies, furry red campion ovals, and dozens of other species announced her status. At her age, they symbolized her stunted, undeveloped body, and despite her embarrassment, it was island tradition to wear them. The day a lass traded her bud-trimmed skirt for one bursting in colorful blooms was a proud one. A flash of this underskirt to an intended sweetie told him she was ready for courting and prime for marriage.

Isolba and her maid had finished embroidering her new skirt a year prior, yet the day to wear it never arrived. Despite riding the cusp of womanhood, she remained small-boned, slight, and resembled a child in every way.

She blinked at Frang in disbelief and took several moments to recover from the blow. "Pray, do not speak of such a personal matter!"

Frang did not heed her warning. "Wee daughter of Demoria, your womanhood is now a public and political matter. The continuation of your single failing could collapse this treaty."

She could not tell if he spoke his cruel words in jest. If he labeled his behavior as mere play, he went too far. Still, he did not desist. It seemed he took a lusty enjoyment in vexing her.

"Though you're young yet," Frang continued, his tone lazy, as if teasing his niece bored him. "This is the final voyage of the year before turbulent waters commence, you'll have perhaps a twelve-month to amend your condition."

Isolba emitted a sharp cry and stood speechless. She longed to shove him off the cliff edge. Her maid stood silently beside her and though could not come to her defense, squeezed her palm again.

"Beauty and grace can lure any man, but only fertility and promise of great issue will hold him," he added.

Now that he exposed a nerve, his insults gained momentum. Indeed, he had too much fun, and Isolba, with her youth and hot-blooded demeanor, did not see the possibility that Frang deflected his anxieties onto her. The absolute importance of the meeting in the Argarves drew tension, and Frang found an easy distraction.

"Speak nae more of it," Isolba said and turned to her maid. "I wish to return home."

She stomped away, her excitement replaced by dread. Nareen followed at her heels and Frang sprang to escort his niece home. His brother left Isolba under his protection, and no matter the extent he assaulted her feelings, no bodily harm could come to her. He was her last line of defense.

The men at arms moved with Isolba as she walked down the slope toward home. The commoners followed and craned their necks for a proper view. They knew better than to push their way through the fortress of men to reach her. Their desperate calls begged her favor, but her refusal to even look their way made her all the more inaccessible.

They only wished to see her and ask for a blessing for their health, their crops, and their fishing expeditions. Yet, they rarely saw her face, only the back of her hooded mantle over her trailing gown of worsted wool. She strode away with small, quick steps, head down, and hands clasped at her stomach.

She wished to turn, peer into their faces, and witness their humanity. Their voices unnerved her and tapped her rib cage like tremulous fingers strumming an instrument.

As the sensation accelerated, she walked eagerly toward cover. Purple heather and yellow gorse quivered from either side of the well-worn path. Nareen knelt to pull the fabric of Isolba's skirts from reaching thorns. The greenery stirred harsher. Ripples of wind rushed through the leaves. Then, the stalks thrust sideways in the heave of an arriving gust that blew the hoods back from their faces. Isolba whipped around to view the southern sea and shivered. Her father's ship had disappeared. From the east, a vivid crimson shade surrounded the rising sun.

Frang wondered at her for a moment before he, too, cringed beneath the unseasonable chill rushing through the summer air. His green half-mantle cloak violently flapped in the gale, and only its jeweled fibula secured it from taking off.

"I do hope that doesn't mean a storm blows in the distance," he said. "Escarans plans to return in three nights' time. A delay will cause more worry."

The sky was clear and cloudless. A fine day for sailing. Yet that brought no comfort. On their remote island, storm clouds could blow into the atmosphere within minutes. Isolba whimpered.

"It's wise to move from this cliff," Frang warned, and shot her a knowing glance.

The group left the path, well away from the precipice, and continued on through the thick vegetation. Frang sang a heartfelt dirge, low at first and with rising boldness, belted out for a lost lover. The rich timbre of his voice carried down the rock face to intermingle with the whoosh of the wind and cymbal clash of the sea.

Her uncle carried his broad shoulders with pride. His long linen tunic and tartan breeks rippled in the wind. A strip of leather held back his blonde hair. A lifelong bachelor, he was twenty years younger than her father and more like an older brother to her. Yet at the moment, she could not look at him.

She seized her skirts in tight fists as the poke of thorns and woody stems stabbed the leather of her shoes. The heat of annoyance and embarrassment welled within her. Frang could pretend he had not insulted her womanhood, but she would not soon forget. An ache rose in her chest, and tears blurred her vision. She wanted Cormac to find her acceptable and for the people of the Argarves to adore her. More than anything, she longed to please her father by bringing peace between the clans.

Past the open green sat the fortress bordering the heart of Demoria. A high wall of sod and stone encircled the town. The single opening, flanked by massive iron gates, marked the entrance. A cobblestone street stretched the distance to Brochnall Castle.

When the group approached the open gate, Frang smiled broadly at the guards who allowed entry. The crofters and fisherfolk stopped, their territory at an end, but their desperate cries continued.

"Milady! Milady!" they shouted as the busy town swallowed her.

Isolba's group walked the thoroughfare between symmetrical rows of stone houses. The nobles and their slaves were about. The latter carried earthenware jugs to fetch water from an outside spring and pulled carts full of goods. When they noticed Isolba pass by, they stopped to pay her reverence. She slowed her steps and offered a fleeting nod in return.

Her pounding heart had not quieted by the time she acknowledged every noble in her path and approached the castle entrance. Its heavy iron doors yawned open, pulled with effort by the porters on each side. She walked up a gradual slope and into the wide-open court.

A stone-paved path ran between walled flower beds. Pretentious campion shamed her while butterflies danced from bloom to bloom. They flitted by statues of Lugh and Brigid, whose leering expressions drained her last ounce of confidence. As she marched with purpose toward a second doorway, she stopped short.

The still body of a common blue lay at her feet. Its delicate wings were closed, and its hair-width legs motionless.

She bent to scoop the furry body into her palms, careful not to brush her fingertips against the feathered wings. Nareen came to a stop, rested a hand on Isolba's forearm, and peered within the cupped hands.

Isolba bowed her head and closed her eyes. She heard Frang bantering with the porters, but tuned out his grating voice and focused inward. The veins in her wrists pulsed with energy, and her palms warmed as she cocooned the butterfly within her possession. She whispered to it. Her soothing words willed life into the vacant shell.

Frang's footsteps sounded behind her. "Isolba," he said. "What are you doing, lass?"

Soft movements patted her skin. She opened her hands, and a flutter of cerulean wings palpated the air as the insect flew skyward, swooped with life and lightness.

Isolba guffawed, forgetting her insecurities for only a moment. The painful lump in her throat remained as she peered up with her large blue eyes. Her maid stepped back, her mouth open and face full of wonder.

"You ken you're not to do that," Frang warned. "Isolba!"

Yet Isolba ignored him. With renewed purpose, she walked to the interior and slipped into the darkness.

Two

Rindan sidestepped along the cliff edge while the wind whistled in his ears. Wingbeats of fulmars pounded the air, their throaty trills aimed his way while he slaughtered their young with one hand. As he came upon a nest built on a jutting rock shelf, he grabbed the not-yet fledged chick around the head and shook it dead. His other hand clung to the rope tied to his waist. It stretched tautly toward the summit high above and strained beneath his weight.

A guttural yelp came from his left. He turned and found Marcus, a lad a few years younger, desperately hanging onto his rope while trying to regain his footing. One bare foot had slipped off the ledge and dangled above the churning sea while his other toed the rim of cracked gabbro. He tried hoisting himself, but his weight dragged him back. In seconds, he could lose complete purchase.

Rindan tossed the dead chick back into its nest for later retrieval. His feet quickly shuffled along the ledge as he made his way to Marcus. Though his face remained calm and expressionless, a muscle in his cheek bulged. The fervent galloping in his chest directed energy to his sinewy arms and solid legs.

"Do not fash, Marcus!" he called, his voice high and raspy to be heard over the deafening surf and sharp seabird calls. "I've got you, lad!"

He reached the smaller, fair-haired boy a moment before his foot slipped from the slick stone. He grabbed Marcus beneath one arm and yanked. The boy was heavy. In his fear-induced paralysis, he weighed heavier. Rindan strained to lift him, nearly wrenching one shoulder with the effort.

Heartbeats picked up speed. His own bare feet began to slide on the sea spray wetting the ledge. He pushed through his toes. Gripped the textured surface with his hardened soles.

"Rin!" Marcus cried. "I can't hold on!"

Rindan released his rope and clamped his hand under Marcus' other arm. His weight shifted to his well-developed thighs and calves to preserve balance. With his slim ankles and wide feet anchored to this base of support, he hoisted.

By mere fractions of measurement, Marcus slid upward. Rindan bent his knees and grounded himself deeper, heaving with all his might as his torso muscles burned. Marcus jerked his foot fully onto the ledge to pinion himself. His other leg kicked toward the cliffside.

Rindan used his entire strength to lift Marcus until his foot made the landing. Marcus held fast to his rope and, splay-kneed, pulled himself forward. Both feet planted firmly on the ledge.

Unburdened by the boy's weight, Rindan relaxed, though his pulse still raced. Hot blood surged through his veins, and haggard breaths rushed between his chapped lips.

Marcus stood on shaky legs, feet pressing into the ledge as he gripped his rope with both fists. His eyes slid toward Rindan, and a shadow of shame cast over his boyish face.

Rindan clapped him on the back with an uneasy laugh. "All is well. You were never in true danger of falling."

"I ken," Marcus whispered with shuddering words. "Yet I think I need a moment to recover."

"Aye," Rindan nodded. "Take a wee break, why don't you? Sit

on the grass awhile and drink some water. You'll be well in nae time at all."

Marcus nodded and smiled slightly. "Aye. Thanks be with you, Rindan."

"Och, there's nae need for that," Rindan said. "Go on now. I must get back to fowling."

Marcus nodded a second time and, hand over fist, gripped the rope while walking up the cliffside. Well out of danger, his gait became sure and steady as he used his prehensile toes to tread the wall of stone. Marcus was a decent climber, but had much to learn. The sea spray had made conditions perilous, and the younger lad should have stepped with greater care.

Like Rindan, Marcus had developed his skills on the cliffs and stacs within their archipelago. For two weeks, they had climbed on their neighboring island of Aonar, hunting fulmars with ten other men. Home lay four miles to the north by longboat, and as the fowling expedition came to a close, Rindan dreaded returning to his prison.

Teutatwen, his home, lay some ten or so miles west of the nearest island of Demoria, where their factor, Chief Escarans, lived. Rindan's people were not part of Clan MacKay and lived with little help from the outside world. From his overlook, he could see his island snug in its blanket of fog, suspended on the farthest edge of the world where only the open expanse of the Atlantic stretched beyond it.

Rindan worked until he came to the end of the ledge, where a sudden steep drop forced his gaze to the dark, roiling waters below. He tucked the last dead bird into his belt and began the ascent. With powerful arms holding onto the rope and hands winding its lengthening slack, he walked up the solid rock face, his angle parallel with the water.

His ear-length brown hair whipped into his eyes as the gale rippled his thin tunic. The fabric draped loosely from his broad shoulders and clung to his muscled chest that tapered into narrow hips. So narrow, he had tied his wool breeks doubly and tight with a thin cord fashioned from twisted hay strands. With his small, compact frame, his lean muscle mass quickly fired, his ligaments like rapidly uncoiling springs.

Because he had climbed from an early age, the dizzying heights bore no effect on his equilibrium nor struck the tiniest note of panic. He could hang from his fingertips alone, the pride and faith he carried in those first digits as unfailing as the tide.

For now, he used his rope for leverage. Once he crested the summit, he fell against the soft grass and inhaled the cool, salty air. Marcus had joined the other men in gathering the dead birds into baskets. When they saw Rindan, they looked up and instantly lauded him.

"I'm proud of you, Son," his father said. The small man loped near to rest his hands on Rindan's shoulders. With a squeeze, he added, "Marcus came up as white as snow. He's recovered now, but he sure gave us all a fright."

"Not I," Rindan said with a dismissive shrug. "He wasn't going to fall, and I would never let him."

"I ken. I ken. Well, so long as the rope did not snap," his father said. The bearded face creased in a wide, relaxed smile. "You did well. 'Tis all I wish to say. As soon as we process these birds and load the boat, we row home."

Dread curled in Rindan's belly. He wished the adventure to continue, to persist hunting on the steep cliffs and outlying stacs. But his mother and older sister waited at home, worried for him and his father, and their angst would endure until they sighted the longboat rowing ashore.

Late that afternoon, the boat sagged with the weight of their catch. Rindan sat in the rocking craft, helping row, and looked back at Aonar as it grew smaller in the distance. He could not know that it would be the last time he would set foot upon it for years.

CAREFUL NOT TO WAKE HIS sister, Rindan crept from the croopan he shared with her. A faint rectangle of light entered the open doorway as dawn crested the farthest line of waves beyond his village's bay. His father and mother slept in their own bed within the close confines of the blackhouse. The island of Teutatwen lay quiet, aside from the spitting of the dying fire and the endless crash of breakers.

Coleen, the cow, opened one eye to observe him pass and closed it again in disinterest. He wrapped a mantle around himself as fortification against the unusual cold and added chunks of peat to the fire. Coleen shifted her rear away from the sudden revival of intense heat before settling back into delicious slumber. Her shaggy brown fur rose and fell with each heavy breath.

In an hour, everyone would awake with Coleen standing over a jug while Rindan's sister milked her. Yet that morning, as Rindan slipped from the doorway and trod through his village, the world was his—at least the two miles in either direction he could go.

He collected a length of rope, a stake, and a hammer from one of the cleitan, and headed north. When he passed by a sheepfold, the animals within looked at him sleepily. Some bleated in response. He began his ascent up the grassy slope behind the village. A few island hounds followed. He rubbed their backs and spoke warm greetings while they panted in excitement.

His brisk walk to the highest clifftop lasted a half hour. By the time he reached the summit of Àrdaill, blood rushed through his veins and primed his leg muscles. He removed his mantle and tucked it between two rocks, safe from the gale. As he knelt on the ground, he wavered beneath the wind's push.

The endless sea stretched out to blend with the dark clouds on the horizon. Its waves rolled steadily toward the island, shattered against the base of the cliffs far below, and sent salt spray several feet upward. The scent of sulfur rose in the cool, clean gust with the heady aroma of fish and seaweed. Moisture hung thick in the air, and he took a deep, intoxicating breath.

To his left sat Dalais, home of the feral sheep. A quarter-mile-wide channel separated the isle from Teutatwen's western coast. A herd of mouflon sheep wandered across its plateau. His people used their thick, brown wool to weave the durable tweeds they gave the tacksman for rent.

To his right, Stac Worth jutted tall and solid from the sea. A natural bridge of rock connected the base of Stac Worth to Teutatwen. The island lads climbed it as a rite of passage into manhood, to show their worthiness to take a bride. Rindan had yet to accomplish such a feat.

As he wedged a stake between two boulders and pounded it with his hammer, the hounds lost interest and raced each other across the ridge. He threaded the end of the rope through the stake's hole, and once secure, tested his weight. He tied the other end around his waist, formed tight knots, then swung his legs out over the edge and turned to grip the cliffside with his widespread toes. Hanging onto the rope, he propelled himself downward. The rush of the descent drove pulses of exhilaration through his nerves.

After his feet touched the base of the smooth pediment below, he crouched and allowed himself to be. Solitude was a balm for his soul, and he craved it more than anything. In the village, folks constantly crossed into his space, knew everyone's rituals and private business. Here, he was alone, away from prying eyes and persistent tongues.

He cared little for talking. His mother spoke enough words in a day to supply the entire village with speech. He could not think with all the chatter, and thinking was what he liked to do most. To lose himself in thought and have an hour for reflection gave him the peace and calm he desired.

He remained for a long while as he watched the sun climb from its watery bed. Gray clouds wandered across its halo. Cries of gannets and guillemots filled the air, chorused by the continuous charge and retreat of the water against the rocks.

Not once had he left the archipelago. The reality of spending his life there, like many of his people before him, was a matter he never dwelled on. Now that he did, the thought unsettled him. He was once content on the island. But now that his boyish frame grew into a man's, he could not ignore the intrigue of the outside world.

The possibility of seeing what lay beyond the horizon seemed such a thrill. Where would he go? How would he make his way in such a vast, unknown world?

He stood and flung notions of escape aside. How could he leave? His responsibilities not only to his immediate family, but to all the people of Teutatwen, bound him there for life. They depended on his youth, his strength, and his unrivaled agility while capturing seabirds from the most remote and dangerous areas of the cliffs. He caught plenty for all, with enough meat and feathers to pay the tacksman.

His shoulders strained in his upward pull. When he reached the summit, he decided he had time for one more stop, a ritual to follow the sweaty exertion of a good climb. He retrieved his mantle and tools, carried them with him as he made his way southwest for about a half mile, and eventually arrived at a basin dipping into the earth. Steam hung above a clear hot spring bubbling from the earth below.

Teutatwen, though covered in freshwater springs, had one hot spring. The islanders regarded it as a place of great physical and spiritual healing—almost sacred, but never off-limits.

Rindan peeled off his clothes, stepped into the shallow pool that rose to waist level, and immersed himself in the warm, soothing water. He threw his head back, and after floating for some time, disconnected from his body. He merged with the pool, with the earth, and became part of everything, all being part of one whole, of one consciousness.

Time slipped away as he remained in this stasis, trapped between worlds. Though he longed to remain for eternity, earthly bonds called. When he left the warm water, the cool air prickled his wet skin, and he redressed.

He recalled a dream. Sometime during the night, his subconscious had formed a creature never known in waking life. A lass—

fair of skin, with hair unbleached by the sun, as if she resided in some subterranean world. He had observed the fine lineaments hanging from her person as she floated before him in wordless splendor. He had reached for her.

When he had roused to wakefulness, he found his arm outstretched, but she was gone. Now, as he replayed his dream, he stood stunned. How could his mind conjure such a being? She was nothing like the lasses of Teutatwen. Even if he took the finest features from each and pieced them together, he could not reconstruct that singular lass.

He drew in a long inhale and blew it out abruptly, shoulders sagging. The brief note of longing fizzled. She ceased to exist. Was she a captive of the faeries, snatched from her land and awaiting rescue within the hollows of the earth? He scoffed at the ridiculous thought. He did not believe in supernatural creatures, though most of the islanders did.

A faerie house stood near the scree slopes of Teutatwen—a mound built of stones circled the opening to an underground tunnel—but the island children were too frightened to go inside. The adults harbored incredible superstitions about it. They said to bother the faeries invited bad weather and ruined crops. Rindan, ever the bravest, once ducked inside the entrance as a youth. The darkness seemed impenetrable, and the air cold as ice.

He shook his head at the idea and, as he moved back across the moor, his steps lost a measure of purpose. The only lass on the island he deemed pretty was Dolag Fleming, but she was older and had married the year prior. Ellar Fleming did not deserve her, as Rindan considered him weak and plain-faced with poor hygiene. Yet Ellar had won Dolag's hand by climbing the steep incline of Stac Worth without a rope, and as a result, she accepted his offer of a blackhouse to call her own.

Rindan would not climb Stac Worth and claim a bride, not because he was physically incapable—for indeed he could climb it twice as fast as Ellar—and not because he was not yet of age. He was close. Nae, because no lass suited him.

It was no matter. Even if he thought a lass bonny, he could not speak to her. What could he possibly say to bend her ear in his direction? He was not charming like Ellar, with a knack for forming words that enticed her interest.

Rindan snickered. Charm counted for little on Teutatwen, other than as a diversion from the cruel terrain and harsh waters. Charm was not a marketable skill there, unlike brute strength, thick skin, and resilience against the severest of conditions a human being could endure.

Rindan owned all those traits, but what he wanted lay out of reach. It came to him then. He would have to discard the burden of responsibility and leave Teutatwen, his family, and all he held dear to find it.

THREE

Brochnall Castle rested on a rocky outcropping at the northern point of Demoria, its bulwark built solid against the sea. Violent waves crashed against outlying skerries and islets, and discouraged any watercraft from approaching the castle. The high walls had stood over the Atlantic for hundreds of years and had housed many great chiefs of Clan MacKay for as long as anyone could recall. Many of Isolba's ancestors uttered their first cry and later gave up their spirit within its walls.

Inside, the halls were calm after the early morning haste and scurry of seeing Chief Escarans off. On the lower level, Isolba heard the quick footsteps of kitchen slaves in their urgency to prepare breakfast for herself and her mothers. She assumed they all slept, but her only interest lay in her birth mother.

Nareen and Frang remained close to her heels. Their steps echoed as they passed through the great hall and onto the switchback stairs. Isolba clambered up the steps as Nareen hurried behind to keep Isolba's gown from tripping her. Shaking his head, Frang briskly trailed the girls and mounted the steps two at a time. When they arrived at the chief's sitting room, Frang paused by a sideboard to pour himself a drink.

The girls moved into the richly decorated chambers. Fine

tapestries hung on the walls, and broad fur rugs covered the floor. Bronze statues peered from the corners of the rooms. Escarans' varied collection of garments and robes dangled from wall hooks. Across from the massive fireplace sat the chief's bed, where he always slept alone. Empty and freshly made-up, the tasseled sashes cinched back its luxurious curtains and awaited his return.

Isolba tarried long enough for Nareen to unfasten her mantle and gather it in her arms. Then, the maid hung back while Isolba charged into her mother's private bedchamber and tugged the heavy bed curtain aside. Her mother, Moira, lay stretched out across her large feather mattress. One thin arm lay flung across her face as she breathed within the grip of sleep. Long dark hair spread about her in untidy strands, and her skin matched the paleness of her thin smock.

Isolba heaved her weight down by her mother, rousing her. Moira's maid stirred awake from her pallet near the far wall. She rose to her feet and, bleary-eyed, crossed the room to kneel at the foot of the bed. Her skin sagged from her bones as she moved with difficulty. With downcast eyes, she crouched, hands reposed in her lap, and waited.

Meanwhile, Isolba accosted her mother. Moira tried to sit up, disoriented, but the pair of hands encircling her waist forced her down. Isolba squeezed her mother's body close and burrowed her face into the warm back. Only then did the ache in her throat and tightness in her chest rise. She released the dam. Great sobs spilled out as her lungs heaved in and out with spastic force. Burning tears wet the back of Moira's smock.

"Och! Wee lass! You frightened me!" Moira said, her voice hoarse with sleep. "What's amiss? Has Escarans left?"

Isolba took a moment to respond as she caught her breath and swallowed. "Aye, he has," she said at last, her shoulders quaking. "Frang brought me to watch Father's boat depart, but he's been cruel to me this morning."

Moira turned to face her daughter, cupped the little head in her hands, and smoothed her hair with tender strokes. She shushed and cooed as gently as if Isolba was a newborn babe. The pair made a lovely set, lying side by side on the embroidered sheets. Isolba was like a small doll fashioned in her mother's likeness.

"Your father has been cruel?" Moira asked, squinting her eyes open in confusion.

Isolba jut her lower lip. "Nae! Frang has!"

Before Moira could lead into inquiries, they heard Frang's voice. When they peered around the bed curtain, they saw him leaning in the entry, sipping his drink. Nareen stood behind him.

"I've been naught but honest," he defended. "I spake truth as I see it and am not sorrowful. Escarans is on his way to approve her marriage contract. 'Tis time you have a conversation with your wee daughter about expectations."

Moira pried Isolba's fingers from their clench about her ribs and sat up to look at Frang. He showed no signs of discomfort by standing in her private chamber, as if he stormed her room every morning. Moira smirked and laughed beneath her breath.

Isolba propped herself up on her elbows to witness the nonverbal exchange between her mother and Frang. Mischievous expressions played across their faces. Isolba scowled that her mother ignored her complaints.

"Mother!" Isolba railed. "Scold him! He cannot speak to me so."

Frang smiled playfully. He shook his head and laughed, though angst subdued his amusement. This unease electrified the very air they breathed.

Moira read his aura and swung her legs over the mattress to meet the floor with bare feet. "Hush, Isolba," she said softly. She stared at Frang with curiosity, but he did not further betray his fears.

Moira's maid stood and snatched a dressing gown from a wall hook. She pulled it over her mistress's offered arms and fastened it at the front. Moira rose and strode to a table holding baubles, ornate combs, and tiny jars filled with fragrant oils and lotions. She selected a polished brash mirror from among the adornments and raised it to face level. Her maid took up a comb and began to untangle the thick, straight hair.

Isolba sat up in the bed and watched her mother, unaware of the longing in her eyes. She hoped to look like her when she became a woman. Moira bore a petite frame with slender shoulders and hips, and breasts barely pronounced beneath the bodice of her gown. A distinct widow's peak drew the focus in her mass of dark hair. Her facial features were small and delicately formed, save for her eyes, which were harsh and wide, icy blue, and cold as midwinter's night.

Moira did not look away from her mirror when she addressed Frang. "How was Escarans' mood this morning?" she asked.

"Quiet, but confident," Frang replied, his gaze fixed on her. "He appeared every bit a man who would trade his only child to the enemy for peace."

Moira issued an unrestrained cackle and clamped her lips closed. She flashed Isolba an expression of shock, but the girl had fallen into a reverie and sat motionless on the bed. "'Tisn't true!" she said to Frang, her eyes dancing.

The maid, once finished with brushing and parting Moira's hair, bent over and plaited the strands into two wide braids. Her gnarled hands trembled, fingers twisted with arthritis, but her work proved neat and sufficient.

"'Tis true if we simplify the matter," Frang said, shifting from one foot to the other.

His mockery so quickly transferred from daughter to mother, but Moira ignored his attempts to antagonize her. She did not take the bait as easily as Isolba and when she refocused on her reflection, bid the morning puffiness beneath her eyes to banishment.

"I regret not rising early to see him," she said, though no guilt hung on her words. "I wasn't abed till quite late."

The maid poured water from a pitcher into a basin and readied a linen towel.

"Is that not what you're wont to do?"

Moira did not answer. She plunged her face into the basin, and when she came up, water dripped from her chin. Her maid patted the youthful face gently with a towel that Moira took and held against her brow. The maid poured a little more water into a small cup that Moira tilted between her lips, swished away the night's staleness from her mouth, and spat into a pot.

Isolba yawned, fatigue settling in.

"Return to bed, lass," Frang instructed. "You woke before the sun and nae doubt require rest. All we do now is wait."

"But I wish to speak to Mother," Isolba whined. "In private."

"That can wait, can it not?" he said. "Nae doubt you wish to wheedle sympathy against me."

"You spake wickedly," Isolba replied. Her eyes, so like her mother's, narrowed and cooled to frosty daggers. The small, pillowed lips clamped, dimples deepening in her frown.

Frang shrugged and Moira stifled a laugh beneath her hand. Isolba ceased to breathe. As her lips pressed together even tighter, she shut her eyes, and her face distorted, grew redder by the moment.

"Isolba, enough," Moira chided.

The scrunched face turned a shade of bluish-purple. Her little fists clenched so tight that the bones showed white beneath the skin.

Frang rolled his eyes and turned away. "Again?" he said to no one.

Moira strode to the bed and grabbed Isolba's arms. "Isolba, stop!" she shouted and shook her daughter.

But it was too late. Isolba's body turned limp. The contorted muscles in her face relaxed, and her lips fell open. Moira gestured wildly to her slave, who brought a flagon of water. She snatched it and tipped it over her daughter's face. The cold liquid flowed down Isolba's chin and soaked the bodice of her dress. A high-pitched gasp tore from her throat. Her eyes snapped open and darted from side to side before she recalled where she was.

Moira's body sagged, and she drew Isolba close. "Why must you frighten me so?"

Frang gaped, incredulous, and Isolba offered a smug smile in his direction.

He guffawed. "She does so deliberately, you ken? She is getting much too old for these fits." He drew his cup to his lips and drained the rest of the wine.

"'Tis on account of her delicate condition," Moira excused. "She cannot become upset or it affects her nerves. You've teased too much."

"'Tis on *your* account she acts this way," said Frang. Annoyance flashed in his eyes.

"Now you turn on me?" Moira asked in disbelief. "'Twas not I alone who raised her. Her other mothers are equally at fault."

"Nae husband will suffer such behavior," he said, shaking his head. "Och, and I nearly forgot, she's resurrecting again."

"You cannot be serious! Isolba, you ken you are not to be practicing! What was it this time?"

"A butterfly," Isolba answered in a small voice.

"A butterfly?" Moira repeated. "Are you certain it was dead to begin with?"

Isolba, still curled in her mother's embrace, nodded.

"Do butterflies have souls?" Moira wondered.

"Who can say?" Frang said with agitation, as if he had no patience for such introspection. "Does a bird? Does a cat? I've not witnessed her revive a hound."

Moira cast a nervous look his way. "Who saw?"

"I cannot be certain, but I believe none but myself and Nareen," Frang replied. "Though the porters were present, they seemed not to pay any mind."

"Good." Moira issued a prolonged sigh of relief and shook her head at her daughter. "Whatever shall we do with you, lass?"

"I need to fetch another drink," Frang announced. "Moira, would you like a dram?"

"Aye, I would," she replied, holding a hand over her forehead. "My nerves are affray. I propose we lose ourselves in oblivion until Escarans returns and then drink more for our merriment."

"But what of me?" Isolba whined.

"A cup of wine would do you some good," Moira said in exhaustion.

Frang snorted. "A cup? May I suggest a cask?"

⚘

"YOU MUSTN'T ALLOW Frang to upset you so," Nareen said when they sat alone and breakfasted in Isolba's chamber. "He speaks in jest."

The girls perched on cushions on the floor, with trays of porridge, fish, and buttered bannocks before them. The warm glow of the hearth fire reflected on their faces.

"Aye, I ken," Isolba said with a sigh.

She reached toward the hem of her underskirt and traced the stitches with a delicate finger. She stole a glance at Nareen's underskirt, visible beneath the folds of her gown. The flowers there burst in ostentatious bloom, as if mocking the closed buds on Isolba's hem. When Nareen caught Isolba's pitiful gaze toward her underskirt, she adjusted her position, and her overskirt fell to obscure the blossoms.

"It will happen soon, milady," Nareen reassured. Sincerity showed in her down-turned eyes and warm smile.

Though almost as slight as Isolba, Nareen was now a woman, and her mistress was not. Isolba anguished over herself. Did she carry some ailment or defect? Yet, with the same worry, she wrestled with the idea of leaving her childhood forever.

"I'm not certain I wish it to be soon," she said in a whisper, weighing her words. "I want to marry, aye, but I'm frightened to leave Demoria and live amongst strange people. I fear my life will never be my own."

"Won't you have more freedom as a married lady?" Nareen wondered.

"I ken not," Isolba replied. Her breathing grew deep and caught in her throat. "I ken I should not behave the way I do, but

26

it often feels as though everyone but me is privy to a secret. I anger when Frang teases, but when Mother joins in, 'tis intolerable. It feels as though all are against me. I am discontent as of late. I despise having protection every moment I wish to go outdoors. For once I wish we could race across the moors, only us and none else."

Sobs interrupted her breathless rant, and Nareen scooted to her side. She enveloped Isolba in her arms.

"If I do go to the Argarves and marry Cormac," Isolba croaked, "I hope Father sends you with me."

Nareen seemed startled and said, "I do hope so! I couldn't imagine a life without you." She became forlorn, as if she indeed could imagine such a life and found it unpleasant.

"Nor I without you," Isolba replied, grasping Nareen's hand. "You could be a sister with how close I am to you. 'Tis a pity Father had nae other children, but with you, I don't feel lonely."

"Without you, I too would be alone," Nareen said. "If you were indeed gone from this place, I would fiercely grieve the loss of you. How could I go on in this life?"

Isolba smiled wanly, knowing that Nareen spoke the truth. The maidservant had no family to speak of. Escarans paired her with Isolba when the girls were four years old. Nareen recalled nothing beyond serving Isolba as both playmate and attendant. Isolba once requested that her father trace Nareen's parentage, yet he claimed to find nothing.

Nareen was Escarans' gift to Isolba. He found great pleasure in giving his daughter fine clothes, jewels, toys, and trinkets. Her favorite gift—besides Nareen—was a heavy necklace engraved with a triskelion, which represented the trifectas of earth, water, and sky, or the mind, the body, and spirit. The continuous curling line represented the endless rhythm of time and of life cycles. Birth, death, and renewal. From the day Escarans first placed it around her throat, she refused to remove it. She had worn the gold filigree smooth, the lines blurred by her ritual touching of it.

As she now sat in her chamber with Nareen's company, she

thoughtfully stroked the triskelion with her slender fingers. When a small child, she had perched on her father's knee and listened as he told tales of their ancestors who came to the isles centuries before. She was the lone heir to a long line of chiefs—each one powerful, brave, and fodder for legends. But Isolba was no longer a child and too old to sit on her father's knee. Her value rested in what she could bring to the clan through marriage.

"Och, I nearly forgot," Nareen said then, her hand pulling something from her pocket. "I found this washed ashore while you spoke your goodbyes to the chief."

Isolba held out her hand and Nareen dropped a smooth, round stone into her palm. She peered closely at its design of gray and white stripes and recognized it instantly as banded gneiss.

"'Tis beautiful!" Isolba gasped and held it close to her heart, willing its energy to soothe her soul. "Thanks be with you."

She closed her eyes and recalled that morning as she stood near the longship and watched her father stare pensively at the sea. He had turned to the druid priest at his side and asked if it was a fine day for travel.

The priest, Baltair, had replied, "Aye, milord. 'Tis a good day." With that blessing, Baltair spoke protection over the longship and the journey to come.

Before Escarans departed, he explained to Isolba the terms of her betrothal to Cormac. "This contract will, at last, bring a solid alliance to Clan MacKay and Clan McCloud after so long on dubious standing," he said. "Beneath this contract, the waters will belong to all and raids will become unlawful, leading to the most severe of punishments. We can, at last, lay aside our fear of attack."

With a sigh, Isolba prayed for her father's safe arrival in the Argarves. She hoped Clan McCloud welcomed him and agreed to the terms of the contract without discord. The notion of marriage blossomed and overcame her with abrupt giddiness.

"What are you thinking?" Nareen asked.

Isolba did not reply right away, but walked to her window ledge where she placed her stone among others of its ilk, a collection curated over time. Some she had found herself while others had been gifted to her by her father after one of his many travels. They all held some meaning to her, and she remembered the time and place she first held each one. How many stones would she acquire on the shores of the Argarves?

At last she replied, "I think of Father and wait most anxiously for his return home. Yet I also think of Chief McCloud's son and wonder what he is like...and what he will think of me."

"He'll be most pleased with you," said Nareen. A gleam entered her eyes, and she grinned. "Do you think he'll be handsome?"

"I doubt it not," Isolba replied. "Father will make certain I marry not only well, but to a man who pleases the eye."

Nareen giggled. The diversion pulled the focus away from everything that could go wrong with the treaty, with the journey as a whole, and with Isolba's undeveloped body. She cast aside images of the boat rocked in wind-whipped seas or attacked as it approached the Argarves, Clan McCloud having decided that they wanted no peace with Clan MacKay, or the treaty broken when Isolba failed to become a woman. Instead, she pictured everything moving forward as planned.

One year from now, she would travel to the Argarves as a woman alongside her father, birth mother, favorite co-mothers, Frang, and Nareen. When she stepped ashore, Chief McCloud would warmly greet her and introduce his son. She would gaze upon Cormac for the first time. Would he be cold and proper, take time to warm to her? Or, instead, would he show immediate affection, clasp her hands in his, and land a bold kiss on her lips?

She shivered at the thought. What sort of man was he? Did he enjoy the outdoors and sport, or prefer to remain indoors listening to the bard's poetry? She would conform to his likes and dislikes and mold herself in his image. Anything for freedom.

Her current view of the world came from behind a window, the edge of a stone wall, or a line of men at arms prepared at all costs to protect her. For once, she wished to commune with the people who adored her, to reach out to someone in want of her touch, and provide a blessing.

"Aye, all will be well and we'll thrive in our new life," Isolba said, seeking to convince herself more than Nareen.

"Aye." Nareen nodded and turned her gaze toward the open window. She frowned and said, "Behold the sky, Isolba! How dark it is!"

FOUR

Rindan scanned the water, squinting toward the horizon. An aberration materialized and shattered the day's impending monotony. A ship rowed steadily toward Teutatwen, and he recognized the sails as belonging to Clan MacKay. His legs snapped into motion, and he set forth to notify his village of the ship's arrival.

At his family's blackhouse, Rindan's father had already spotted the approaching ship.

"A second summer visit from Demoria," his father said. "We've nae need for more supplies. Wonder why they've come?"

"I do hope 'tis not ill news," Rindan's mother fretted.

Rindan walked with his parents and sister on the feather-scattered ground down to the shore, where they joined the other villagers awaiting the ship. The entire population of nearly one-hundred souls stood, wrapped in their plaids against the chill, and eagerly watched.

Rindan's mother prattled to anyone standing close enough to listen. His sister moved away to join her friends while he stood quietly and tracked the crowd. He did not immediately see his own cohorts, but noticed Dolag, apple-cheeked with a closed smile on her sweet lips. Her long blonde braid hung heavy with salt. Her dress bulged outward at her waist, the mound of her belly heavy with child. Ellar, ever unkempt, draped his arm around her lovely shoulders. Rindan looked away.

Some men readied Teutatwen's lone watercraft, a small, open longboat. They threw aside the protective layer of turf laid over its mass and pushed the craft to the edge of the shoreline. The water in the bay was too shallow for the longship to dock, so as soon as it dropped anchor, a single islander tendered the boat out to greet the ship. Two men, adorned in lavish robes as seen from a distance, transferred into the longboat and rode into the bay. As it drew close to shore, the crowd stirred with surprise. Many fell to their knees and clasped their hands. One man was a face they knew well, Demoria's tacksman and representative, but the other rarely visited Teutatwen.

"Lord Escarans!" someone called out, and the villagers charged forward.

The craft skidded ashore as some men dragged it over the pebbled ground. The chief of Demoria stood at once. His hulking mass stepped out on unsteady feet, and the islanders rushed to assist him. They kissed his jeweled hands and grasped his embroidered mantle. For him, they held all esteem and reverence. The tacksman stood behind, nodded and grinned, though the islanders focused their attention on the chief.

Escarans stayed silent for a moment as his bulging eyes surveyed the crowd. His bloated red face, with its silver and blonde beard, seemed grave and solemn, like a defeated warrior. At last he spoke, his voice gravelly and deep.

"Good morrow, fair citizens. How well it is to see you and your fine island after many years. I fear I cannot tarry here and must shortly depart. The gales are growing brutal and the waves rough."

Rindan's father stepped forward and said, "Lord, I beg of you. Come sit, rest, and have some refreshment."

"I'm grateful to you, Guidman, but I must make haste and complete my business," replied Escarans. "What's your name?"

"I'm called Saithan, milord."

"Ah, Saithan! I ken you from my last visit many years ago. I yet wear that fine cravat you knit for me and recall your bonny singing voice. Your village has year after year shown me and my tacksman great generosity."

"We merely repay your boundless kindness," Saithan said. "We want to show our devotion."

"Yet 'tis the subject I wish to address," Escarans said, clearing his throat. "I fear you will mislike the news I bring as much as I mislike it myself."

The villagers drew silent and dread etched their faces. Rindan watched the scene unfold and was like a stone sitting in the bay for all the lack of emotion about him.

"Within the last day, while in the Argarves, I signed a marriage contract between my only daughter, Isolba, to Cormac, the son of Chief McCloud."

Rindan knew well that though the Chief had nine wives, he had one daughter. Because she had never visited the island of Teutatwen, she was an object of mystery among the villagers. They often spoke her name in reverence and awe, perhaps mentioning it more than the chief's. They often referred to her as "Our Lovely Wee Lass" and even swore to her, despite knowing little about her.

Escarans continued, "This contract also serves as a peace treaty to ensure that feuds over boundary lines come to an abrupt end. However, Chief McCloud wished to take more than my daughter. He requested ownership of Demoria, Teutatwen and the outlying islands and refused to sign the contract unless I met his terms. With that note, I come to inform you that in another year, I'll nae longer be your lord. Following the marriage, McCloud gains ownership of this island. As his tenants, you will pay rent to him, beginning next summer when the marriage is expected to occur."

The islanders' keening drowned out further words. The one constant in their uncertain world—the lifeline of Clan MacKay of Demoria—ripped away. The villagers clung to their lord and wet the fabric of his garments with their tears. Rindan stood unmoved, but to look into the faces of all he held dear, to see the candid display of fear and upset, unsettled him. It was as if the banks had dissolved beneath them and the villagers writhed and splashed in dark waters, drowned in sorrow and confusion.

"Demoria and Teutatwen have been one for hundreds of years," Escarans said at last, loud enough for his voice to carry over the crying. "A great change has come upon us. We found the Argarves to be a modern society, forward-thinking, with advancements we in Demoria have attempted to hold at bay to preserve our culture and history. The Argarves may bring you an easier way of living. With that, your struggles may cease. I predict positive changes."

The lilt of his speech carried doubt. He had his reasons for holding onto the ways of the past. For one, he governed himself and answered to no one. Rindan understood that. On Teutatwen, the islanders paid only their shares of hunts, harvests, and fabrics to the lord annually. They otherwise managed themselves.

"But we do not wish that," Saithan broke in. "We want naught more but to be left alone and continue our traditions, as your clan has continued its own traditions. Our simple and secluded way of life suits us."

Rindan disagreed with his father. Though he preferred their modest way of life, some aspects could be easier. Food, for starters, depended on the weather and some years yielded slimmer than others. If they could keep their freedom, but relinquish their suffering, it would be the most welcome change. Rindan also hoped for the opportunity to travel and work outside of Teutatwen.

"'Tis done," Escarans replied with open palms to show his helplessness. "The best you can do is plead your case to your new lord and ask that your lives continue as before. He may not bother to make improvements here."

Did Escarans regret notifying the villagers of the modern ways of their new lord? Perhaps he felt responsible to apprise them of possible change to come, as if losing their familiar lord was not enough of a blow.

Having completed his business, Escarans readied to leave, but the villagers were loath to release him.

"My fine people, my faithful tenants, I must be away," he bellowed. "It's been a privilege to serve you. A more goodly, hard-working society doesn't exist. We remain bonded by our history together. Perhaps I can visit again, nae longer as your lord, but as your guest."

The weeping continued. The tacksman assisted Escarans in extricating his hands and garments from desperate fingers. As the day surged forward, the sky darkened. A storm approached, but Escarans refused to bide his time on Teutatwen. He had to outrun the blasting gales and sea swells.

"Farewell!" the old chief called a final time as the tender rowed away and returned him to his ship.

The islanders watched the longship recede into the mist. Oars whipped around in hurried synchrony and Escarans abandoned the people of Teutatwen on that distant shore, so far from civilization.

THE EWES COMPLAINED BADLY over the delay to their milking, so Rindan, his mother, and sister tended to their full udders.

They watched the weather while they worked. The storm held off for a time as it ruminated in the skies and built strength. Afterward, the family dined together on bowls of porridge prepared with milk and puffin meat. His mother and sister wiped the bowls clean with their aprons and walked to the village center in the open green. There, the islanders assembled to discuss the upcoming changes.

Rindan did not tarry to listen, his mind and legs ever restless, and left the harried chatter to the adults. The changes were out of their control and he did not see the point of worrying. He walked past the village and onto the arable land thickly bordered by yellow marigolds. Oats and barley waved in the wind. He observed the growth of the crops in his family's rip. It had been quite a fair growing season and the harvest of barley adequate, that further yield was surplus. As for the oats, the upcoming harvest would prove bountiful.

The rain began then, arriving first in soft patters, then graduated to driving pelts. The wetness hit Rindan's skin with sharp, cold spears and he ducked beneath the cover of the nearest cleit. The earthy odor of the peat stored within filled the small space and mingled with ozone. He leaned against the circular stone wall next to farming implements and coils of rope. The rain ended after a few minutes, but when he stepped back out into the open, the air blew ominously colder. He shivered and looked out toward the sea. It swelled and throbbed, bucking like the back of a wild animal. Escarans was out there and he hoped for the old chief's sake that he would make it home safely.

From the corner of Rindan's eye, two figures ran in his direction. He immediately recognized his closest friends, Angus and Duffy, the latter Rindan's second cousin on his father's side. They sprinted, faces flushed, as they raced each other across the moor.

"Rindan, you mindless lad!" called Angus, who came with jaunty strides, his long, thin legs bowed at the femurs. "Why are you out here? 'Tis cold and your sister asked for you."

As the boys closed the gap between them, Angus slammed his body into Rindan's. Though Angus was taller, he failed to topple him. Rindan held his ground. Prepared for the blow, he sent the lanky lad bouncing backward. Angus' dark eyes blazed in derision. He sprung forward and clamped his arms around Rindan's legs, attempted to unbalance him.

"Angus, you're weak," Rindan teased. "Where's your power gone to, lad?"

Duffy, slightly younger and smaller, was unsure of whose side to take and stood there, laughing maniacally. The wind whipped his sandy curls into his eyes. Angus turned toward him and playfully—albeit roughly—pummeled the boy to the ground. Duffy uttered several breathless noises as Angus beat his defenseless arms, chest, and stomach with closed fists. He yowled like a hound in pain and held up his hands in surrender, but Angus refused to show mercy.

Rindan watched, shaking his head. He vaulted toward Angus. He rolled the feisty lad onto his back and pinned his shoulders down with his hands. Angus' dark hair hung in his face, his mouth set in a firm grimace. He jerked a knee upward in aim for Rindan's groin. It landed in his inner thigh. Rindan hardly flinched, though the blow shot a bolt of pain down his leg. He was thankful Angus missed his target.

"What say you now?" Rindan taunted. "We've discovered an impasse, I fear. Do you yield?"

Angus grunted, bearing all his strength upward in his struggle to shove Rindan off. His playfulness turned to anger at the realization Rindan proved far stronger.

"Och, Rindan," he seethed between his teeth as defeat entered his voice. "When did you gain such strength?"

Rindan leaned back and took his weight off Angus. Duffy remained curled on the grass, holding his stomach in a dramatic display of discomfort.

"While you sleep, I climb," Rindan replied, with a note of pride. "I've done so for the better part of a year."

"Why?" Angus scoffed as he briskly stood and brushed the dirt from his breeks. "As it is, we squander all a summer's day on the cliffs."

Rindan could not explain that constant exercise proved the one method to calm his relentless energy. Without it, he feared he would go mad. He required an outlet for the confusing thoughts and feelings that urged him beyond the shore. He chose not to answer the question.

"Duffy, are you well then?" he asked instead.

The younger boy groaned, folding his upper body into a seated position. "Aye, aye," he said, gasping for breath. "I'll recover in a moment."

Angus stared at Rindan in puzzlement. In the last year or so, the boys had ceased to understand one another. Their only commonality was age. Angus—Rindan's junior by only a few months—constantly challenged him. Physically, Rindan was always up for the task, but mentally, it took everything out of him. He preferred to be left alone to his thoughts.

"What do you think of the surprising news this day?" Duffy asked. "'Tis quite a shock!"

"I think we can lay aside all hope of marrying Isolba," Angus quipped, chuckling to himself. "'Tis a shame. I longed to climb Stac Worth for her hand someday!"

Rindan grunted. "Well, let your hopes be forever dashed. Her new husband's father is now our lord and what a change that will be."

"Do you think she would come along with the lord to visit us?" Angus wondered. "Would that not be a sight? To at long last gaze at our Lovely Lass?"

"Why have a care?" Rindan responded as he kicked the pebbles at his feet. "Someone like her would never wish to step foot here as if we are good enough for her."

"I surely care not," Duffy broke in. "I look upon nae other lass than Una."

"Careful, lad," Angus tutted. "You ken she is meant for Rindan. His sister would have it so and nae other."

Duffy's face fell and his shoulders slumped. Angus laughed at his distress and threw his arm around the smaller boy, but Duffy pushed him away and sulked.

Rindan scowled at Angus. "She is yours to have, Cousin," he said to Duffy. "I've not set my sights on her."

The light returned to Duffy's eyes, and he grinned widely. "'Tis so? I must confess my disbelief that her beauty goes unnoticed by you, though 'tis to my benefit."

"If she'll have you," Angus said smartly.

"Why would she not?" Duffy asked. He shuffled from foot to foot, obviously irritated by Angus' teasing.

"Who then?" Angus probed, addressing Rindan. "If not Una, who *do* you dote upon?"

"None," Rindan said simply.

"Och, 'tis a disappointment, indeed!" Duffy said.

Angus crossed his arms. "Nae lass is suitable for Rindan," he said with a sneer. "He'll die alone."

"Yet I kent a time Rindan set his eyes on Dolag," Duffy declared. Rindan shot him a look of admonition, but Duffy failed to notice.

"What man on this island hasn't?" Angus said. "Too bad Ellar bested you there, lad. Want me to kill him for you?"

Rindan forced a laugh, though there was nothing humorous about it. His friends could not know they exposed a nerve with the mention of Dolag's unavailability.

By fortune, Rindan avoided a response beyond his awkward laughter. At that moment, and without warning, the rain poured down in a deluge. The rocky soil beneath their feet transformed into a network of miniature rivers. Gales tore at their clothing and sent the streams into flight; they sprayed upward and met the torrential rain. It hardly took a minute for the friends to receive a thorough soaking. With that, the boys left their banter and broke apart. Fled toward their respective homes.

FIVE

The ways of the druids were mysterious. They lived in Demoria's wilderness, among the crags, holing up in bothies. As priest, Baltair had a room within Brochnall Castle, but resided there only at night, following his one daily meal. He wore the finest of robes and jewelry and reposed on a feather mattress while the druids studying beneath him slept out in the elements. Baltair rose before dawn each day and convened with his students on the hills. From a castle window, Isolba watched their distant figures walk barefoot up the mountain path before they disappeared. Only they knew what they did up there, as they performed but few of their rituals at public ceremonies.

Baltair's chamber was on the ground level, in a wing of the castle Isolba could not frequent without permission, though she slipped into it many times throughout her childhood. Escarans used the wing to entertain guests in private when he had a small group of people. Because the castle's inhabitants used this wing the least, Baltair's chambers occupied the end of the corridor with quick access to the outdoors.

A different energy existed in that realm, as well as the smell. Musky and cold, it lacked the floral notes and liveliness of a woman's habitation. Bronze statues lined the hall, muscular men and curvaceous women in varied stages of undress. She and Nareen would duck and crouch among them to point and giggle at body parts. Some coupled together, not only men with women, but men with men; bodies intertwined, sometimes kissing. The girls thought nothing of this other than as silliness contrived by a playful sculptor.

After losing interest in the statues, they explored Baltair's antechamber, where he worked in private. As he was gone for much of the day, the girls tarried there awhile, keeping quiet to escape notice.

They found much to look at, a veritable feast for the eyes. Ornate tables against the walls held copper cauldrons and flagons filled with strange, pungent-smelling liquids, large crystals, bird feathers, candles, jewelry of silver and gold, a satchel full of precious stones, leather pouches—one holding blades of several sizes and another a pair of copper divination rods, and a massive quantity of vials and containers holding all manner of herbs and tinctures.

The most fascinating objects were the skulls resting along the window ledge. Some were crumbling with age, many had missing teeth, and a few were from children. One child's skull mesmerized the girls. Baltair had carved back a layer of bone, revealing sets of milk teeth and adult teeth tucked in neat rows along the maxilla and mandible bones, having never had the chance to emerge. A row of sawn-off skull tops turned upside down served as bowls for stones or liquids.

The girls feared touching anything, save for a light brush of a finger. They did not wish to transfer energy to or from any of the objects or spoil a spell Baltair had in progress.

Baltair did not mind when the girls explored his collection. The rare times they found him present, he watched them in amusement, his eyes glittering in the candlelight. Isolba probed his knowledge of every object, and he told her what they were. Sometimes he offered a brief explanation of what they did, but never how he used them.

"Only a druid can ken these methods," he often reminded. "You must understand that these are but objects, simple tools. They may hold energy, aye, but they do not hold the power. The power is within us. Our intention directs the energy."

Isolba longed for Baltair to take her under his wing and teach her his secrets, a veiled desire. She wished to explore her silly talent of reanimating dead creatures when she put her mind to it. Escarans forbid it. He called her an uncanny child whenever she expressed interest in anything deviating from the domestic arts. To her, nothing was more painful than displeasing her father. For this, she could only respect Baltair and his craft. In turn, the priest issued her cordial regard. But for as long as she had known, she would catch him staring at her with a look of fear in his eyes.

ON THE SCHEDULED DAY OF ESCARANS' return home, Baltair broke his routine and remained in his chamber. It was little wonder as the castle inhabitants woke to the sound of gales clawing at the shutters. Isolba peered out and noted the sea. Its choppy waves and heaving swells crashed into the shore. Her belly clenched with dread. Her father floated somewhere on those thunderous waves. Struggled to make his way back to her.

For the first time in ages, nearly all of Escarans' wives came together in the great hall. Only three lived in the castle, and the rest had homes in the village. Escarans had not visited his two oldest wives in years, and they no longer took part in family gatherings. The remaining wives waited in vigil for news of Escarans' return, hoping to welcome him home.

Some wives paced about while others sat on the floor upon skins and furs, where they busied their fingers with hand looms. Slaves fed peat to the hearth fire in a vain attempt to chase out the cold that stole through every crack and crevasse with the driving gales. Isolba and Nareen joined them in whiling away the anxious hours of waiting. One of the older mothers, Anna, held Isolba close as if she were a bairn and sang in her husky, aged voice. Nareen practiced forming intricate braids in Isolba's hair and tucked marigold blossoms between the strands. Moira dozed next to them, detached and disinterested.

"Should we perform an appeasement ritual? Can we not summon Baltair?" a middle wife spoke out, weary of doing nothing.

"Calm yourself, Fiona," another wife replied. "Baltair is at rest today. The constant prayers for Escarans' journey and on behalf of the marriage contract have nae doubt fatigued him. We must be patient."

"I cannot be patient kenning our husband is upon that sea, perhaps swallowed up by now, and we would never ken. The gods look unfavorably upon us this day."

"Do not say such a thing in Isolba's presence," Elizabeth, one of the younger wives, scolded. "You will upset her. And your words carry power that brings worries to life."

"But she must ken we are at the mercy of the gods, of their moods, and their whims," Fiona said. "Isolba, my wee darling, what are you thinking?"

"I think only for the safe return of Father," Isolba replied with a meek, shaking voice. Tears welled in her eyes.

"Och, my wee one," Anna cooed, pulling the child tighter to her breast.

Some of her mothers came to lay hands on her and whisper words of comfort, while others held back, locked into personal disquiet. Isolba basked in the attention. She soaked it up like a bannock in broth.

As the day wore on, the hours drew long and tedious. The women grew silent as night fell, and they agonized over the unknown. Was Escarans safe or not? The roar of the wind and pelting rain proved deafening enough without further spoken words.

Isolba barely slept as they waited, and by morning, the tension in her sternum stifled her breath. She spiraled into panic. Gasped for air. She was well aware of Escarans' obvious peril, and yet she also could not put the thought of Cormac aside. The idea of him had grown over the days into something within her reach. Excitement blended with fear and spurred her heart to race. She could not be sure which emotion was stronger.

As Nareen clasped Isolba's hand within hers, her fingers stroked her skin. Beckoned her to calmness. The sleeve of Nareen's dress fell to reveal her pale wrist, and Isolba lost her gaze within the familiar series of birthmarks there. Six distinct brown ovals banded down her inner wrist in single file as if purposely formed. They reminded her of a constellation, a rare nightly sight in her overcast world. She prayed for the gods' approval, to align the stars, bring her father home, and give her the promise of Cormac.

The clang of the iron doors sounded from the front foyer, startling Isolba from her reverie. "Father!" she called.

Sopping steps echoed into the hall and produced the form of a man, his clothing weighed down with rainwater. He was alone. Water dripped and pooled at his feet. But the form stood too slight to be Escarans. The man pulled the cloak's hood back to reveal Frang's exhausted face. Isolba leapt up and ran to him. Fell to her knees. She reached for his hands as tears spilled down her cheeks.

"What's become of my father?" she asked in a tremulous voice.

"The ship went down southwest on the coast. It drove against the rocks and did not have a chance. We lost all slaves to the waters, but saved those above. Escarans lives."

Isolba's body collapsed against his legs, and an audible exhale blew from her parted lips. Though grateful the Atlantic spared her father, it grieved her that so many lives had ended on her account. Her eyes shut tight, and her chin quivered as the remorse became more than she could bear.

She gulped for several moments like a fish out of water before finally asking, "Where is he?"

"Nearly here," Frang replied. "They bring him this moment. I require you to give him wide berth. I've called the healer to tend to him. You must stand back."

Isolba nodded. Frang broke from her so abruptly that she fell on her hands. He strode to the entrance and watched from within the doorway. The gales howled outside, and the frigid air raced into the warm hall. Isolba clenched her fists, overcome with helplessness.

"May we now summon Baltair?" one wife called out.

"I'll fetch him!" Isolba volunteered and scrambled to her feet.

It would give her something to do other than wring her hands, and she owed it to Escarans to make herself useful. She did not pause for Nareen to accompany her. Her feet dashed out to the hallway and weaved through the maze of corridors. The fabric of her skirts lifted in her tiny clutch as she ran, unladylike, to that remote wing.

When she arrived at Baltair's doorway, she fell breathless against the wall. The cold and damp bled through the thin fabric of her gown and made her shiver. She noticed how the thick cloth panel of his door covering wavered and whipped outward at the hem. Freezing air bit her ankles and the deafening gale whistled. Though the urgency of her task prodded, she wrapped her fingers around the panel's edge and pulled it aside to steal a cautious glance within. She saw an open window, its oilcloth cover removed, and watched the freezing wind and spitting rain pour into the chamber.

Arms outstretched toward the sky, Baltair stood before it. His copious robes and gray beard fluttered wildly. His chin lifted and his eyes shone otherworldly, but he did not pray. Instead, he whispered words, lengthy and poetic, that hissed from his tongue. His long fingers spread and swayed in dance. They gestured as if pulling an invisible cord from the heavens. Though his knowledge was a secret only to him and the druids, he appeared demented.

Her throat tightened, and she drew back. The curtain fell back into place.

"Come in, milady," Baltair's voice boomed, having lost the hypnotic whisper. "You've naught to fear."

She jumped at his voice. How did he know she stood there? She had not made a sound, and he had never peered behind him.

"Aye, you wonder how I could guess your presence," he said.

She pulled the panel aside once more, slowly, with timid movements, and wider than before.

Baltair's eyes remained focused on the sky outside. The clouds hastened, bloated, murky, and never so dark. She froze in place and could not make herself step forward. For the first time, she found herself alone with him. Why did she leave Nareen behind?

"I ken much," Baltair said. "I even ken what lies in your heart. Your heart is like that of a hound: fiercely loyal, protective, tame, but in an instant you gnash and bite. You are sensitive to others but quick to burn a relationship without thought. You are compulsive and fickle, preferring company from whoever will feed you. Because of that, your loyalty is dubious. You lurk about, unsure of yourself and your place in the world. You lap at hands, asking for favors, your desperation obvious. Your wildness sleeps—indefinitely—until it awakes."

Isolba said nothing, struck dumb. Her urgency remained, but his words were ice to her ears. She found herself insulted, but intrigued at the same time. Her head spun.

"You've come to bid me to your father. Escarans will survive," Baltair said, at last turning in her direction.

Her eyes widened in disbelief. "You ken as of this moment?" she whispered.

"Aye." He smirked, as if she should already be aware. "What a misfortune. That ship was meant to carry you to the Argarves and is now driftwood."

"That would come to pass only if the contract prevailed," she noted softly.

He beckoned her to him with offered hands, and though it took a moment to thaw herself, she stepped forward on unsteady feet. He took her little hands in his. His skin was hot to the touch, and she nearly pulled back.

"Of course it came to pass. How could you doubt it?" Baltair said as if she knew better, but his voice was like honey.

"It did?"

"But you do not truly wish to go to the Argarves, correct?" he asked. His words were gentle and even, measured to gain her trust. He spoke this way to anyone he counseled, and it was both familiar and unsettling.

Convinced he was mistaken, Isolba gaped in confusion. "Of course. I wish to be married, you ken?"

His expression showed incredulity. The gray brows knitted together, and his wrinkled cheeks moved upward in a slight wince. She could hardly see his lips move beneath the thick cover of his whiskers.

"To be traded like a possession to a rival clan?" he asked, his voice now thick with sarcasm. "To live shackled to that clan and its island for the rest of your days...which I can say with great certainty are few. You're destined to die young." He bent her wrist, exposing her palm, and pressed into it with a fingertip. "See here. Your lifeline. How short."

Isolba shrank in horror, but Baltair's grip proved too strong to break. His teeth bared in a clenched grin and his light eyes were dark, almost black.

"I must go to my father, now," she sputtered, tugging her arms to no effect. Cold seeped into her bones, despite the burning heat of Baltair's hands, and she trembled.

"Tarry but a moment longer," Baltair urged. "Allow me to ask you this. Would you prefer to remain here in Demoria as your father's heir and take his place as lord and chief?"

A collapse occurred in her head. It was as though the supports holding a carefully drawn floor-plan gave away and the walls folded inward to crash down in a cloud of dust and debris. His words rang in her ears. He attempted to rewrite a narrative she had long believed. To change her purpose now, when she had prepared her entire life for this moment, seemed absurd.

"'Tis impossible!" she scoffed and his hands loosened enough for her to at last pull away.

"Only without my help," he proposed. "Think on it awhile. I see something in you—a fire. You'll never be content trapped behind walls as you've done all these years. You're not meant to live confined as a wife and a mother, then die with little accomplished. Greatness lies in you and you cannot see it!"

"Aye, I don't," Isolba answered with shaky words. She peered again toward the window and darkness closed in, grew heavier by the moment.

"You've suppressed gifts more precious than you can ken," he said.

She brushed off his statement, and after a thoughtful gaze into the void, asked, "Why did you advise my father to move forward with the treaty if you believe an alternate future is best for me?"

Baltair folded his hands in front of him. "I told him I felt the treaty would bring an immediate end to the uncertainty and fear of war. I said my guides had warned me that though peace would come, it would come at a cost. I said it was not what was best for you, but all Escarans heard was of peace, and his mind was made up."

Isolba took a step back and shook her head in disbelief. Then she remembered why she had come. "I beseech you," she pleaded. "My father needs you to pray over him and assist the healer. He must be here by now, so I ask you to make haste."

"Ask naught of me," he spoke in admonition and turned again to face the sky. "I will come when I am ready. I ask that you bear in mind what I've told you and think much on the subject. Do not allow your life—your gifts—to go to waste."

She said nothing. How could she agree to ponder something that she did not understand? Who could she ask for counsel besides Baltair? He counseled her own father in all matters, so she should trust him, but his suggestion germinated nausea in her belly.

Isolba made her way back to the great hall, burning thoughts of a shortened life to ash. As Mother Elizabeth had said, beliefs were as powerful as words and could manifest if she provided enough energy for them.

The iron doors remained open as a half-dozen men carried Escarans into the hall upon a litter. His enormous form lay flat on his back, head turned as half-open eyes peered Isolba's way. His chest rose and fell with haggard breaths. He coughed and sputtered, yet was alive and unbroken, as Baltair had foretold.

Isolba cried out and raced toward him, but stopped when she recalled Frang's instructions. Her mothers sprang forward, bumping elbows in a chaotic tromping of harried feet. They crowded around Isolba, who hung back. Together, they watched the men carry her father to the dining table and set him down with a great heave. Small streams ran from his robes and across the table's surface as it groaned beneath his weight. The iron supports held, but the wooden top bowed where he lay.

The men worked to remove his sopping garments and cover him with blankets. Isolba turned her face away and rejoined her mothers. She nestled into the furs and bosoms, at last at ease. She found relief in her major concern, his life, as she saw he had come to little harm. Though her greatest fear of the ship sinking had come to pass, her father had not drowned with it.

The same luck was not to be had by the galley slaves. The angry gods had snatched their souls, leaving their bodies as carrion. She considered that a true waste, not her life. She would not come to ruin by marriage. Escarans had made her purpose clear: her marriage to Cormac would bring peace. She had no desire to become a chief, and she had every desire to marry and have children to dote upon. Yet doubt crawled into her consciousness. She had witnessed Baltair's predictions come true time and time again. How could he be wrong about her future? Would she truly be discontent?

"Isolba!" Escarans voice thundered across the hall.

Isolba bounded up and closed the gap between her and the chief. She could not reach him beyond the fortress of men working to dry him, but managed to grab onto his outstretched hand.

"Father! I'm here!" she shouted above the clamor.

Frang stepped around and clamped onto her arm. "Did I not tell you to keep your distance, lassie?"

"Leave her be," Escarans said. His head rolled from side to side as he looked toward the ceiling in a daze.

Frang dropped his hand but stayed at her side with a pinched expression. "We must warm you, Brother," he said. "Then you may speak."

"Damn you, Frang," Escarans bellowed and his eyes fixed on his brother. "Fetch me some whisky. T'will warm me through."

"You stubborn crock of lard," Frang retorted and clomped off in search of a whisky jug.

Escarans pulled Isolba close and the men around him moved to allow her space. He brought his hand up to her cheek and stroked her face. His head turned her way, but his glazed pupils wandered.

"You are betrothed," he said, his raspy voice slow with his breaths.

A smile played on Isolba's mouth and her eyes lit from within as she covered his hand with her own.

Before she could respond, he continued, "But Clan MacKay is done. Over time, we will be absorbed by Clan McCloud. They have taken our lands as your dowry. 'Twas the only way McCloud would agree to our peace treaty."

Isolba's jaw slackened, and she dropped his hand. She took a step back and shook her head. "Why would you agree to it?"

"Because I'm old and have lost the will to fight," Escarans answered. "A decade ago, I would've declared war and fought out our disputes. Now I'm tired and have nae heir. Nine wives, but nae heir. Only a daughter. A lass. She has cost me my entire world."

Escarans no longer looked at her as he spoke, his gaze distant.

"What of Frang?" Isolba asked as her uncle arrived with a jug in his hand. "Is he not to take over the chiefdom?"

"Aye, 'twas the plan," Escarans said in a groan as Frang lifted his brother's head and lowered the whisky jug to his lips. Escarans took an eager sip and paused to swallow the burn before speaking again. "Yet he has nae fight in him likewise. He's admitted to desiring the same outcome: a true merge of clans, McCloud and MacKay."

"You've told wee Isolba the cost of her betrothal?" Frang asked. "Peace was our aim and has come at a steep price."

"Methought unity was the entire reason for this treaty?" Isolba asked in confusion.

"Aye," Escarans answered after gulping down another mouthful of whisky. "But our name! Our name will be dashed. Demoria, Teutatwen, and all the smaller islands are nae longer lands of Clan MacKay. I'll have the title of chief for the remainder of my life, but I'm nae longer lord. When I die, the title dissolves, as does the clan. I'm the last chief of Clan MacKay and 'tis such bitterness to swallow, I can hardly bear it."

Now the words of Baltair spoken only a short time ago made sense. He had reservations about the marriage contract, had intuited a grim outcome for Clan McKay. The spinning within Isolba's head whirled faster. Was it not Escarans who wanted this contract and sought it out? Now, the blame lay on her because she was born a girl and not the male heir Escarans had longed for.

"Father, what of me?" Isolba wondered. "You have told me the stories of our ancestors time and time again so I would never forget our history. Are we not descended from female warriors and leaders whose exploits have given you so much pride as to recount? Can I not be your heir, the next chief?"

Escarans and Frang looked at one another for one empty moment before bursting with laughter. Such laughter lacked joviality. Its contemptuous and dark notes echoed from the high stone walls.

"Pride has gone to her head," Frang said. "I've warned of this many times, but none heed my words. Now she conjures fantasies."

"My Isolba," Escarans said through gritted teeth. "Those

stories are grand and fantastical because they've transformed through the generations into something little resembling reality. I enjoyed telling them to see that gleam in your eyes, but oral histories are questionable. You cannot believe yourself to ever rise to such a station and be worthy of it."

"But Baltair said I could claim the title as heir and he spoke greatness over me. He proclaims 'tis possible."

Escarans sat up, no doubt fortified by the alcohol. "'Tis Baltair's purpose to breathe possibility into everything, to manifest our desires, but we must respect the limitations of society and nature. By nature you were born a female and by society you cannot hold power."

Isolba's face fell and her large ears reddened. She thought she would please her father by saving their heritage. It was no longer clear what would gratify him other than had she been a son. Her very existence displeased him. When she looked about, the eyes of everyone were on her, witnessed her shame.

"I heard my name," said Baltair, who arrived in time to break the uncomfortable silence. He bowed to Escarans and took his hands. "Your good health brings me relief."

Frang could not help himself and clapped a hand on his niece's back. "Ah, 'tis because Isolba is confused about her purpose," he said, eyeing Baltair squarely. "It seems you drove delusions of greatness into her mind. She thinks that instead of marriage and this peace treaty, she should become the next chief and fight off the rabble-rousers and invaders herself."

Isolba flashed him a rueful expression and said, "Methought that's what Father wished. 'Tis not what I desired, but—"

"I meant only that she would find leadership in her position as the future chief's wife," Baltair said, talking over her in a firm, yet kindly voice as his gaze fixed on Frang. He bent down to be level with Isolba and continued, "I ken you mean well, but that isn't your purpose, nor your longing, ken? Focus on your upcoming marriage and making a name for yourself as Lady McCloud, mother to the first generation of two clans brought together in unity. There, you will find greatness. There lies your purpose."

Perhaps she had misunderstood what Baltair had said in his chamber. She had been in great distress at the time. How could she be so foolish? Fire burned her cheeks and she sniffled.

"I wish to be off this damned table," Escarans roared and reached out. He remained wrapped in blankets that fell away to reveal the loose, hairy flesh of his chest and arms. "Also, I desire to be clothed!"

Frang and Baltair took the chief's arms and pulled him onto his feet. Unbalanced, Escarans swayed, perhaps from his near-death experience, the whisky, or a combination of the two.

While the men attended to Escarans, Isolba allowed herself to reabsorb into the group of women near the hearth.

Moira drew her daughter into her arms. "Are you mad? Are you not happy to be betrothed?"

"Aye," Isolba affirmed. "I suppose I am. I vow to heed only your instruction from this moment forward. I've caused Father the greatest displeasure, and the burden is mine."

THE DAY FOLLOWING HIS RETURN, Escarans hosted a banquet. He wished to celebrate the peace treaty and the survival of himself and his men. He had slept the entire day, oblivious to the continuing storm outside. Upon awakening, his mood lightened, and he seemed content and prideful.

The old chief perched at the head of the dining table and feasted on fish soup laden with cream and greens, mutton pie, lobster dripping in butter, and sweetmeats. With each cup of whisky he downed, he grew more jovial and boisterous. Baltair and Frang sat nearest to him. Moira, Isolba, his tacksman, his counsel and advisers, and six of his other wives sat in honorable seats. The benches beneath the crowd of people whined and squeaked with the strain. Dishes cluttered the large table. Hounds lurked about, quick to snatch up food scraps and bones.

Isolba sipped her wine and allowed all the angst from the days before to melt away. Her father was alive with the peace treaty in place. Her only worry was her womanhood. She could not bear further shame, and a long delay in her marriage would prove the ultimate embarrassment. She turned in her seat to steal a glance at Nareen, who stood against the wall, lined up with the other slaves. The maid caught her eye and flashed a quick smile before lowering her head. She remained inconspicuous with the rest of her station.

Isolba focused her attention on her father. She enjoyed watching Escarans take the spotlight and regale the assembly. The people sat with eager eyes, prepared to listen to his tale of meeting Clan McCloud, his brief visit to Teutatwen, and the perilous voyage home.

"My daughter. My Isolba. Betrothed," he said, raising his whisky cup. The guests lifted their cups in imitation. "Upon her marriage," Escarans continued, "we unite with Clan McCloud. In a twelvemonth's time, Clan MacKay will be nae more. A new era is upon us. *Sláinte!*"

Escarans knocked back his entire cupful. "Aaah!" he emitted in satisfaction and pursed his lips. "I'll require another of those."

A slave refilled his cup in one silent and stealthy motion. He went on, but his speech proved dry and uninspired. "I found the Argarves modern. I've visited there many times in the past and discovered it bettered since I last stepped foot there. The people were amiable, and the chief welcomed me. We quickly put aside our disagreements. He made his terms concise and wouldn't yield, claiming that if I refused to meet such terms, he couldn't agree to the contract and would send me home, kenning someday we'd kill each other...or attempt to. I said I wasn't such a fool to leave without the promise of a husband for my daughter-" He cut himself short and stared out at the crowd, a vacant expression on his bearded face.

In time, he called himself back to the present and cleared his throat. "Yet you've joined me this evening not to hear of such trivialities."

Isolba's grip on her cup loosened. Her wine-stained lips shuddered. How cheated she felt. She longed to know the entire story of her betrothal and every detail of Cormac and the island he lived on. Her father wished to move to a different subject, one that painted him as the hero and not a failure.

"We departed the Argarves and traveled northwest to Teutatwen," Escarans recounted, eyes shining and faraway. "The storm that was building for days at last made landfall. I visited briefly with the tenants, who begged us to stay until the waters were safe to travel. But I longed to return to Demoria, to see my daughter, and the voyage was so fleeting that it seemed nonsensical to remain in Teutatwen."

Isolba believed the decision to continue sailing was nonsensical. After all, it had cost the lives of a dozen slaves, yet she swallowed her words and sipped her wine.

"We were nearly home," Escarans said as all eyes fixed on him. "The shoreline was in sight. The waves rose and fell beneath us. Our ship rocked from side to side and the water spilled over the deck with every roll. She wandered aimlessly, and we realized the galley had flooded with all arms drowned.

"We prayed for the waves to push us to shore. The gods heard our cries and nudged us toward home. Yet from behind us rose a swell. I watched the great watery wall hover over us and kent that to be my last sight in this life. When it fell, 'twas thunder in mine ear. It swallowed us up and drove us into the crags. The deck splintered beneath us, and I pitched forward, only to land among the rocks. There, I took hold and held on with all I had while the surge retreated and took pieces of the ship."

Escarans paused to catch his breath and coughed dramatically. He threw his head back as he poured the cup of whisky down his gullet and grunted. He slammed the cup on the table, and a slave hurried to fill it.

"Mine eyes shut to the freezing waters and opened to behold

John clutching a nearby crag. I then beheld Duncan hanging by his fingertips from a pediment into those frigid waters."

John and Duncan began to drum upon the table, their percussion adding tension.

"I reached out to him first, worried he would lose purchase and slip 'neath the waves. With one free hand, I pulled him onto his belly, and from there, he pulled himself to safety."

Escarans' face shone proud and certain. A smile formed on his lips as he prepared to tell the last of his allegory. No sound disrupted the stillness as each ear perked to the sound of Escarans' voice.

"I then heard a cry and witnessed an outstretched hand from between the swells. 'Twas Owen."

With a loud growl, Owen raised his glass. Escarans went on.

"His mouth gaped open, and the waters choked his screams. The tide sucked him into the depths, and I kent I must act or he would cross into the Otherworld as I watched. I pushed off my friendly rock and went below. I found a flailing arm in the darkness and yanked it to me. We broke the water's surface and breathed. Though I cannot swim, I can float. The tide tried to take us out to sea but decided it had enough souls and pushed us back toward shore. At that moment, the men at arms, with the help of some nearby crofters, pulled us to land. With that effort, we were saved and brought home."

Escarans' face glistened with sweat, and he collapsed on his elbows. He closed his eyes as he drank his whisky breathlessly. The guests cheered. Sounds of voices and clapping swarmed toward the vaulted ceiling and electrified the air. Cups clinked together with such exuberance that whisky and wine splashed onto the table. Isolba watched in fascination as the liquids streamed along the grain of battered wood. The amber and red met and blurred together as one. She blinked, numbness overcoming her. Would she and Cormac so easily merge their clans?

From beneath the table, a pair of wide eyes peeked up at her and startled her from her daydream. A slave child crouched amongst the food scraps. Grabbed what he could before the hounds lapped up the sheep and bird bones along with varied crumbs. He shrank beneath her notice. So moved, Isolba stealthily picked up two sweet biscuits and handed them to the wean. He smiled gratefully and shoved them inside his eager mouth.

AFTER THE HEAVY MEAL, Escarans retired to his chair near the hearth. Frang came to kneel at his side, and the wives arranged themselves on the fur rugs around him. Isolba rested her head in his lap, and Indris, the bard, came to join them with his lyre in hand.

The bard began plucking soft notes, and Escarans closed his eyes to better hear the music over the din of voices. The guests huddled around, drinks in hand, and grew quiet as they listened. Escarans opened one eye and observed his daughter peering up from her restive posture. She prompted him with her hopeful eyes, and his face broke into a broad grin.

"Your lad is eager to wed you and show you his islands," he said at last.

Escarans held out an open palm to her, and within his hand rested a beautiful necklace. Composed of colored stone beads on a leather cord, a flying kittiwake hung in gold at its center, suspended within a forged iron crescent moon. She took in a sharp breath and clapped a hand over her mouth in delight.

"He was most pleased with the painting of your likeness I brought for him and couldn't take his eyes from it," Escarans continued. He clasped the necklace around her slender throat with care.

Isolba ran her fingers across the beads, so tiny and smooth, and over the delicate lines of the gold kittiwake. Her breath caught in her throat as warmth unfurled in her belly. With such a thoughtful gift, Cormac would prove a kind and doting husband.

"He proclaimed he had never before beheld a more beautiful

face, nor eyes so expressive," Escarans said. "He commented more than once on the triskelion necklace you wore. I told him how worn it had become, and he was quick to bring this to me before my departure. He asked that you wear this around your lovely neck when you arrive in the Argarves so he can see the shine of you coming across the waves. In his mind, you're a goddess. He doesn't ken how your ears poke out, and I did not give him warning. I figured your one imperfection could wait for the day he sees you in person."

Isolba scoffed, her face flushed, but recovered after a moment. "I'm pleased, Father," she said, and laid her head on his lap again. "I'm grateful to you and to him. How does he look?"

"Och, fair. So very fair and nearly ethereal. Long yellow hair, thick with curls. His skin is like bronze, and his eyes are the palest shade of blue I've ever seen."

A dreamy expression crossed Isolba's face, and her mouth curled at the corners. She was satisfied to learn her betrothed met her father's standard of beauty.

"Also, you ken how tall the people of Clan McCloud are? What Cormac lacks in dimension, he makes up for in height. I wouldn't be wrong to call him a giant."

Isolba jerked her head up at this detail. It was bad enough she appeared so childish on her own island, but next to Cormac, she would look outlandish. What an odd coupling! Surely everyone would speak with distaste as they compared her size to Cormac's. The very idea filled her with angst.

"Do not fash, my wee Isolba," Escarans said, his voice reassuring. "You'll grow yet. Baltair is working on a concoction to aid you."

Could she trust anything created by Baltair? She would take it just the same to satisfy her father and Cormac. As she leaned against her father's knees, she fell into a reverie, thinking of her betrothed and his kindness to her and her father. Such kindness mattered more, though the details of his handsome features excited her.

Perhaps her father exaggerated Cormac's height, as he was prone to do while recounting his stories. The height difference might not be as stark as she imagined. Would she crane her neck to peer into his eyes? Unless they lied side by side. The thought sent shivers across her body.

Indris continued to strum on his lyre and took the opportunity of silence to sing a song. His steady, rich voice rose over the spectators and filled the chamber with a haunting melody.

> Hear, my lover fair
> A lost song o' undersea
> Whose notes draw me down
> And immersed I shall be
> Writhing billows drive me deep
> Arms outspread, embrace my fate
> Drowning in dark waters
> Death comes for me too late...too late

Indris' voice fell away and he moved into the instrumental part of the song.

"Truly, Indris?" Escarans belted with a sardonic chuckle. "Is that the song you wish to sing tonight? My nerves are cut too fresh for that!"

Indris smiled, embarrassed. Without breaking momentum, he switched to an upbeat but ominous tune.

> Ken you the tale of the Coin-Sith?

"Aye!" Escarans shouted as he raised his cup with such a jolt that whisky splattered across the floor. Isolba rolled her eyes at her father's drunkenness and listened.

> Child wandering the lonely moor
> Be wary, wary
> Run home 'fore darkness falls

'Fore that first loud bray calls
Run, run
With the second beastly howl
You cower and shudder
Your heart beats quicken
The Coin-Sith comes
He comes for you!
With a final terrifying bray
Howl, howl
He snatches your soul
And carries you to the Netherworld!

Perspiration of terror and delight formed at Isolba's temples. The music's vibrations traveled up her spine, prickled her scalp, and echoed inside her. A spark ignited the flame within. Awakened, she sensed a yearning at her core, though she knew not what for.

Perhaps it was for Cormac. Aye, that had to be it. Not only would she gain a husband and a place for herself in the world, but the marriage would also bring unity to the clans. Peace and prosperity lay ahead for her people, while she would assimilate into a new clan and take on their customs.

Isolba had never left the shores of Demoria, resigned to knowing little of the outside world. Yet upon her marriage to Cormac, she would take her first boat ride into the great beyond. Her belly twisted into a heavy knot.

Six

ud squished between Rindan's toes as he walked between rows of barley and oats. The limp stalks drowned. So much water and nowhere for it to go. Following each storm, the clouds dispersed long enough for a cold sun to shine, perhaps for an hour, a half-day, but never longer. Then the clouds cloaked its rays, bloated and darkened with renewed moisture, and spilled their contents.

Rain washed away the fertilizer and nutrients. It left the dirt compact and deficient. The growing season came to an abrupt end and robbed the crops of a month to ripen. Harvest would begin immediately, or the islanders risked losing their crops.

His island wilted beneath the incessant rain. With every shower, the sea level rose. He noticed this most in the bay. Their homes sat on the hill above the shore, well out of reach of the rising tide, but the paths between the blackhouses turned water-logged and difficult to traverse. Small children played with the island hounds in mud puddles and used rocks to build miniature dwellings around their own tiny bay. The air blew as cool as early spring.

The turbulent waves made the September trip to the outlying island of Aonar impossible. Rindan always looked forward to the fowling expedition, so sulked to himself. He mourned the daring adventure of crossing miles of waves and approaching the land-form as spray moistened his face. The peril of bringing the boat alongside the steep shoreline, to leap to the slippery rock face, gave him a thrill like none other. And the towering cliffs—at no other time did he feel more alive than when he hung from their heights.

He daydreamed while foraging field mushrooms. He broke them off at the base of their meaty stalks and dropped them into a woven basket. His mother and sister wandered the valley nearby, seeking herbs and greens. Their skirts gathered muck up to the knees. When they had picked all they could, they divided their hoard between Rindan's, leaving him with a basketful for his grandparents.

His father's parents had slowed down in the last few years as their arduous way of life took its toll. While Rindan, in his impatient youth, sought movement, his elders had worn to idleness, their days of travail behind them. He would perform the work they no longer could.

Rindan's soaked clothing drooped from his frame as he carried the basket of mushrooms and greens to his grandparents' black-house. Norman and Martha Lennox shared their home with Norman's sister, Mary MacDuff, and her close friend, Sarah MacGill, two widows left destitute when a squall swept their husbands into the sea.

"Good morrow, Grandfather, Grandmother," he called as he swung the basket around the doorway and heaved it on the floor. He stepped to the fire to warm his hands and then flapped the hem of his damp tunic over the flames.

"Rindan, my handsome lad!" his grandmother cheered from her bed, where she convalesced. "You brought us food! And a fair bit of mud with you!"

The wide, cheery smile betrayed her condition. Her frail body withered to skin and bones, and she lay helpless beneath the ragged blankets. Norman leaned against the half-wall separating the sleeping compartment and turned his head at the sound of

Rindan's entrance. His eyesight had degraded so much in the past year that only a dim light entered them.

"Is this my wandering grandson?" he questioned. "So full of life and vigor that I hope you've brought some to share with your grandparents."

"Shall I put some of these aside for a stew and dry the rest?" asked Rindan.

"Aye, that'll do fine," said his grandmother.

"Perhaps next time, bring your youth to share instead of food," his grandfather teased. "'Twould better serve us."

"How fare you both?" asked Rindan. He dipped a cup into a jug of water and brought it to his grandmother. He held it to her lips. Her bony hands trembled on his and she gratefully sipped.

"We are well enough, though this sudden turn of weather aches our old bones," replied his grandfather. "I long to stretch these legs. 'Twould do me good."

"Aye, I'll take you," Rindan said as he put the empty cup aside. "'Tis wet though."

"Do my ears deceive me?" his grandfather said with a feigned gasp. "You hear him, Martha? Rindan says 'tis wet. It seems, once you lose your sight, you lose all senses."

"Och! You old gannet!" his grandmother howled from her bed. "Begone with you, Norman!"

Rindan chuckled. His chin dipped as he shook his head, and his brown hair fell over his eyes. He picked up his grandfather's mantle and hat. After helping Norman into the garments, Rindan folded his hand around the crook of the thin arm and carefully led him to the doorway.

"I'll have him back shortly, Grandmother," Rindan assured. "Do you need aught before we leave?"

"By Our Lovely Wee Lass, nae! You take your time, lad!" she said. "I certainly have nae need of him."

As soon as they were out in the open, Norman lifted his face to the sky and breathed in deep. Water pooled around their bare feet. The mist soon covered their wool mantles with water droplets.

"Where do you wish to walk?" Rindan asked.

"As far away from people as I can manage," Norman replied with a smile.

"To the hot spring?"

"Och, I would like to take your grandmother there. Would ease our old bones, but being as she can nae longer walk about, I would rather not go without her."

"To the moor?"

"Ah, that'll do."

They walked on in silence. Norman's hands trembled, and he took his steps in short, jerky paces. Water dripped from the brim of his straw hat. He peered out from empty eyes, sunken, cloudy, and blinking often. Norman and his wife were not exactly elderly, but the hard way of life on the island had prematurely aged them. Rindan's maternal grandparents had passed away when he was too young to recall them. He knew his time with the remaining set was coming to a close.

Rindan guided Norman beyond the humming village and bleating sheep, an act that took an eternity, but he did not mind. A trio of hounds trailed behind as seabirds flew above, their calls filling the atmosphere. He watched them soar and float on the airstream, the wonder ever-present in his clear hazel eyes.

"I sense a sadness in you," Norman noted.

Rindan's gaze fell to the ground. "Aye?" he asked.

"Something's on your mind," Norman prodded. "You're good-natured and content on an average day, so what's bothering you?"

Rindan forced a grin, even though his grandfather could not see his expression. He was a puffin chased from his burrow, detected and vulnerable. He hesitated. How could he explain something that even he could not understand?

"I do not quite ken," he said at last.

"I was once a lad your age," Norman said. "You're of a difficult age, and our isolation here leaves you with a unique predicament."

"Aye," Rindan said, his shoulders relaxing. "I suppose you've figured me out."

"Nae. I'm only presuming. I've not gotten to the heart of the matter, have I?"

"I cannot say."

"You *can* say," Norman prompted with a light-hearted nudge, though he was quite serious.

If he told his grandfather that he desired to court, but no available lass suited him, Norman would think him too choosy. Instead, he asked, "Did you ever think to leave Teutatwen?"

"By Our Lovely Wee Lass, nae! We've all we'll ever need here, far from the evil of places like Demoria."

Rindan fell quiet and after an awkward intermission, the corners of Norman's mouth twitched. He guffawed.

"Of course I've thought of leaving!" Norman said as he clapped his grandson on the back. "I recall dreaming of it often, especially at your age. We all have. Mine own father found my mother by leaving for three years and bringing her back from the mainland. 'Twas hard for her to live here, and she never did quite settle in, though Father was content after his short-lived adventure."

"Why did he return?"

"Because there is nae place in the world like Teutatwen. Its beauty and isolation are unsurpassed. Everywhere else, men murder men. You cannot tell me that's ever occurred here in our history."

"But how could he give up his freedom after tasting it?" Rindan wondered. "There must be places more beautiful than Teutatwen."

"Freedom? Teutatwen *is* freedom! Elsewhere, men are chained to their society by greed, by ego. They desire more and more, but never find satisfaction!"

"You ken 'tis not what I meant..." said Rindan.

"'Twas duty. He had his parents to care for, and he missed them and his people. The noise and hurry of the outside world unsettled him, too. In Teutatwen, one feels safe and protected. Like you, he longed for adventure and, once he had his fill of it, came home."

Rindan nodded. They made their way across the open moor, arm in arm. The hounds ran ahead and raced one another. Seabirds swooped and darted.

"You wish to leave," Norman said. All joviality and laughter had left him.

Rindan's feet stilled, and he turned to face his grandfather. "I ken not if that's why I'm empty when I have so much," he replied honestly, released the dam and let the words spill. "A part of me is missing. Will my leaving bring me to that missing piece? I somehow believe it wouldn't, though I'm urged across the waters by something deep inside me. Even so, I cannot depart. As you suggest, my parents and sister need me." As a playful afterthought, he added, "I also cannot leave Duffy here alone with Angus."

Norman's hands found Rindan's shoulders and his vacant eyes filled with warmth. "Aye, lad. You've a duty to your family, to provide for them and to protect them, yet you also have a duty to yourself. You cannot ignore the calling of your heart. Someday, those calls will quiet, die away forever, and you will regret ignoring your one chance to find yourself."

Though profound, Rindan could not take his grandfather's words to heart. The words came from someone who had lived his life and could now lose himself in myths and fairytales. The notion that Rindan could catch the next boat was not rooted in reality. It sounded ideal, but too ideal to play out in real life. Norman's father had returned to Teutatwen. The pull of duty to the island proved far too strong for any man to entertain the thought of leaving, especially for good.

"Methinks the islanders would be loath to lose their best climber," Rindan said after a pause.

"We wouldn't," his grandfather said, a mischievous smirk on his face. "We have Angus."

"Wheesht!" Rindan spat between his teeth. "Angus does tell everyone he's the best climber, but we all ken it to be a lie."

"We do?" Norman asked.

"Aye," Rindan said, matter-of-fact. His chin lifted toward the sky to better feel the raindrops on his face.

"My Rindan," his grandfather said, a hint of caution in his voice, "your ego will end you quicker than bring you triumph."

"But 'tis the truth," Rindan said with a sheepish grin.

They walked on, but Norman did not speak after that. He appeared introspective and perhaps a little sad. The lines across his thin face seemed deeper and his mouth bore a grave expression. Rindan noticed how his grandfather's face had grown pale, a sickly shade of gray.

"Grandfather," Rindan said, angst rising in his voice. "Are you unwell?"

Norman nodded and replied, "Aye, but I think I need to lie down a spell. I'll be fine after a rest."

Rindan turned Norman around to begin the walk home. He regretted telling his grandfather of his discontent. He would never wish his family to believe he truly wanted to leave, that their love was not enough to hold him there. They *were* enough. It was something outside of him that called to somewhere deep within his subconscious, a place he could not access. Yet how could he explain that to his grandfather without seeming demented? This was no call to adventure, for he could find his thrills on the cliffs. This was something else entirely.

SEVEN

"Milady, why such a look?" Nareen asked Isolba.

They stood inside the doorway to Isolba's private balcony, watching the pulsating sea. The rain rarely ceased, and they were weary of remaining indoors.

Isolba hesitated, a wistful expression on her face. "The more I dream of Chief McCloud's son, the more I love him," she said. "When I see him for the first time, I will tell him so."

Nareen clapped a hand over her mouth and tittered. "Are you relieved to ken he's handsome?"

Isolba managed a laugh in return, though it lacked joy. "Aye, that I am. How I wish to have a painting of him, but if he gave father one, 'twas lost in the shipwreck. I could not ask. If I kent it existed, lost in the sea–"

"Let us not think of that," Nareen said. "You are fortunate your father had the necklace safe in his sporran."

Isolba touched the beads at her throat that overlaid her triskelion necklace. "Aye, I'm pleased for it. I cannot wait to tell Cormac so when I see him."

"Will you tell him that first, then?"

Isolba blushed and shook her head. "I will tell him that second, after I tell him I love him."

"Nae greeting or introduction?" Nareen asked with a playful grin. She found obvious pleasure in her lady's good fortune.

"Nae," Isolba replied. "I want him to kiss me first, with nae long, drawn-out words, so that I may tell him I love him."

An impish look crossed Nareen's countenance. "But what if seasickness plagues you on the journey and your face becomes green and your breath sour?"

Isolba's face filled with horror, and she not so gently elbowed Nareen in the ribs. "Wheesht! Do not prophesy such an event. I couldn't face him then. All romance would be lost, and I would relive the shame each day of my life if I did not die of it at once."

The maidservant laughed, but winced as she rubbed her side. "I only wish to warn you, is all. Could happen!"

"As if you could ken," Isolba said haughtily.

"Aye, I ken," Nareen said in earnest. "I kent the queasy ache in my belly on the ship here."

"You never told me that," Isolba said, her forehead wrinkling. "You remember that, but not where you came from?"

"Aye, I recall being on a ship, but not where I lived before. I must remember, being as 'twas a frightening experience coming over the waters, the ship rocking to and fro. I do believe 'tis my first memory."

"I will ask Father again," Isolba said. "He must ken where you came from."

"Nae, I bid you not pursue the matter," Nareen begged. "You asked him once, and he said he did not ken. Let it rest there. 'Tis not in this life's purpose for me to ken my true family. You are family enough for me."

"Wheesht," Isolba emitted between her clenched teeth. "I wish to help you."

"You do help me every day," Nareen said, smiling, as she took her lady's hand in hers. "You give my life more meaning than I surely had as a bairn. You are my life's purpose. Where you go, I go."

A weak smile formed on Isolba's lips. "But you do not wish to ken your mother? Father? A brother or a sister?"

"Nae, I am content."

"What of love?" Isolba asked, her eyes lost in the constellation of birthmarks on Nareen's slender wrist. "Do you wish for love?"

"And where would I find love?" Nareen asked with sarcasm, her eyebrows raised.

"Aye, I ken we are sequestered here, shut away from the world," Isolba said. "Neither of us have been within speaking distance of a lad our own age. But as you said, if freedom comes with my marriage, you shall have freedom, too. Perhaps you shall meet someone in the Argarves."

"Another slave?"

Isolba did not answer in haste and took the time to weigh her response. As Cormac's wife, she could use his love for her to ask favors. "I will free you," she finally said with confidence. "I will ask Cormac to break your bonds."

"And where would I go? What would I do?"

"Remain with me," Isolba said. "As my companion."

"Isolba," Nareen said pointedly. "I could not simply live with you without having a purpose outside of giving you company. As a slave, I remain your property and would be safe. I would have my place. If I were free, I would belong to none, and to me that is more frightening than hearing the howl of the Coin-Sith. Trust me when I say I am content here with you."

"I would ask Cormac to find you a wealthy man to marry," Isolba suggested. "We could raise our children as playmates."

"I don't wish that," Nareen said. "I don't want to marry a wealthy man and live a social life. I wish for a peaceful life at your side."

Isolba nodded, realizing how naive she had been. She could not ask such things of Cormac and appear foolish. Nae, she would look to him for guidance, remain quiet and dutiful, and allow him to lead the way in all dealings of life. She had two major fears: suffering embarrassment or rejection. These phobias often fed into each other, and both at once seemed terrifying. Would Cormac find her acceptable? How she longed for him, but would *she* be enough?

Her hands spread flat against her chest, against the ladders of her ribcage, devoid of swells. Her bottom lip trembled.

"What ails you?" Nareen cried.

"They say the more a man is discontent, the more wives he marries," Isolba began. "What if, like my father, Cormac takes many wives after me? Father hasn't spoken to his first wife in years. What if that is my fate someday? The indignity of it! To be thrust aside, cast into the midden!"

"Isolba, what's to do?"

"But nae," Isolba wailed. Her breaths came rapid and shallow. "Baltair prophesied a short life for me. I will not live happily with Cormac. I could die on the journey over. Perhaps the ship will sink, and you'll die with me. Och, to die before we've lived!"

Her words became unintelligible as Nareen pulled her inside and helped her to the bed. She turned onto her side and drew her knees into her chest. Hardly able to inhale, the sobs caught in her throat. She gasped for air.

"I...I cannot breathe," she panicked.

Nareen's gentle hand rubbed her back, making circles across the knobby spine and sharp shoulder blades. "I will fetch you some wine to calm your nerves," she said.

Isolba firmly clasped her maidservant's hand and would not let go. "Nae, I do not wish to be alone."

"Gormall!" Nareen called out toward the bower.

In a moment, Moira's maidservant was there, her eyes attentive in her pale, haggard face.

"Fetch some wine for Lady Isolba!" Nareen directed. "And if Lady MacKay is about, bid her come to Lady Isolba's chamber."

Gormall nodded, turned shakily, and hobbled away. After Isolba watched Nareen's expression fill with guilt, she quieted her spastic breaths.

"I should help Gormall," Nareen said, eyes locked on Isolba's. "The poor woman can walk but little."

Isolba cleared her throat and sat up. "Go then," she said.

Once alone, she swallowed her sobs and wiped the tears from her cheeks. Utter contempt and disgust for herself raised acid in her throat. Uncle Frang was right. She could not continue behaving this way once she married. However, she could not tell where the emotions manifested or how to control them. The groping hands of terror gripped her. Its fingers wrapped around her throat and squeezed her airway closed. Breaths eluded her. She needed someone to hold her.

Within minutes, neither Nareen nor Moira darkened her doorway. Instead, Baltair came to stand at her bedside and offered her a cup of dark, viscous liquid. No emotion registered on his face. He remained as calm and direct as always, yet Isolba feared his presence.

"Drink this," he directed. "To stimulate your appetite and growth."

She sat up in her bed before lifting the cup. The bitter contents touched her tongue. Her face contorted in disgust, but Baltair tilted the cup toward her lips and the thick, fetid tincture filled her mouth.

"Hold it 'neath your tongue awhile before swallowing."

As she gulped it down, a spasm wrenched her throat and threatened to expel the drink at once.

"If you eat straight away, the nausea will subside," Baltair explained and took the cup.

"Ugh," Isolba emitted with a shuddering gag. "'Tis excrement on the tongue."

"Wheesht," Baltair said. "You will take this before every meal. By feeding the body extra, you form fat reserves vital for womanhood. Your womb will receive the message to ripen and ready you for childbearing."

Isolba shook her head. "I do not believe I can take that. I will try to eat more during my meals."

"I give you this only by the direction of your father, who requires you ready for marriage by Bealtaine," Baltair said. He walked toward the doorway and looked about before turning back to face her. "Have you pondered my suggestion?" he asked. "Though 'twas premature to mention the plan to your father. You caused me to appear foolish and forced me to deceive him."

"Och, so you *did* say such," she said in disbelief. "'Twas I who appeared the fool."

"Aye, I did say it," he replied in his straightforward tone. "But I intended our plan to remain between us."

"You did not say 'twas a secret," she remarked accusingly.

"Nae, rather I implied your discretion."

Isolba thought of herself as more puerile and naive than she had imagined, and her hopelessness weighed heavy. Baltair loomed over her like a seabird eyeing a fish in water–commanding, intimidating. She shrank into her pillow.

"To be a great leader," he began, "you must learn the art of discretion, to speak with tact. Use your advisors to your benefit."

"But I do not desire that," Isolba said. "I will marry Cormac."

"And allow your clan to dissolve? Your lands to belong to McCloud?"

"I will become a McCloud," she said succinctly. "I will lose naught and gain everything."

"But remember, you will die, and your people will have naught. Your father and mothers must answer to Clan McCloud, to be owned by them like chattel."

The fluttering in her chest returned with the panic that strangled her words. She had to remain immutable. "The best I can do for my people is to unify them with Clan McCloud. My descendants will ken only prosperity."

Baltair's lips drew back in revulsion, revealing his clenched teeth. "You do recall how all your life, your father has ensured your virtue and innocence are shielded from all harm?"

She nodded, her fingers sinking into her mattress to stabilize herself. She sensed Baltair was testing her and so she held strong.

He paced, rechecking the doorway every so often to ensure none could overhear. "Do you ken you are an object handed off in a peace trade to a man who would in a moment break that carefully guarded virtue?"

"I ken not what you mean," she whispered.

"As of now, you are pure, and that purity makes you powerful," he explained. "You see, you've retained perfection in the eyes of the gods. If you align yourself with them and to nae man, you will be powerful. You will learn all the knowledge nae mortal should ever ken, yet because you are favored, you are blessed. You would prove a powerful leader, growing into the position beneath my guidance as ambassador to the gods."

"Your words mean naught to me," she said from quivering lips. "I only desire Cormac."

"You do not ken what you want!" he whispered loudly, struggling to keep his voice low. "You do not ken yourself, so how could you ken what's best? You do realize that as soon as you marry, your husband will snatch away that purity, expelling all the power within you? All your years of promise will be stolen in an instant. Your usefulness becomes limited to a single function: to bear children. You will spend your days appealing to others, mostly your husband, and he will remind you every day where your value lies. Is that what you want?"

"My sacrifice is good, for I love him, and that is enough," she said.

Baltair chortled. His laugh proved menacing, and it unsettled her. "Do not allow yourself to be tempted by this man, or any man in your future. Beauty attracts you, not only bonny jewels and gowns, but you will find yourself infatuated with your husband and will live only for him. That is not love. Your notion of love is jest." His impassioned voice heightened in frustration. "Do not lay waste to your power by succumbing to temptation. You will forever seek, never satisfied. I ken you. I see into your heart where you cannot."

Isolba could not look at him. She focused on a single thread of the tapestry on her wall.

"I ken all," Baltair said. "Only moments ago, you expressed your fears to your maid. Your voices yet echo within your chamber. Your hesitance fills the air. Trust me. I will allow you time to think more on my words."

She shuddered. How could he read her thoughts? His intuition made his proposal enticing. It was natural she would want to trust him, but she reminded herself of her naivety. She had to proceed with a discerning mind. Until her marriage, her father would remain the most important man in her life. The priest had no control over her. Her mistake of following his lead the first time twisted like a dirk in her heart. She knew better than to disappoint the chief. She loved him and he had chosen Cormac for her. It was the reason she loved Cormac.

"Nae, I ask you not to mention it again," she said, drawing on all the strength she had. She had never before experienced such discomfort in conversation. "I will do only what my father says. He wishes me to marry and I wish to please him. Unless he tells me otherwise, I will prepare myself to travel to the Argarves next summer. I will drink your concoctions all the morrow if it means you will rest the subject."

"Very well," he said. "'Tis nae harm to me. I only hoped to teach you all the secrets of the world. 'Tis your life you put to waste. Your people will forget their love for you once you leave. They will spit hate upon you when the Argarves' tacksman comes to Demoria to collect rent."

"And then I will die?" she asked sardonically.

"Aye, then you shall die."

"Then I die doing my father's bidding," she replied.

"Your grandfather died last night."

"What say you, Mother?" Rindan wondered in disbelief.

His mother, Beathag, had entered the home at daybreak while Rindan and his sister Cait readied themselves for the morning's work. Cait's milk jug slipped from her fingers and thumped to the floor. Her hands covered her face.

"Your father is at your grandparents' house and bid me tell you the news," Beathag stated, her words sorrowful.

"But he was not ill," Rindan said in disbelief. "We enjoyed a walk together. He did tire easily, but had high spirits."

"Aye," Beathag said. "His soul crept out while he and your grandmother slept. 'Twas unexpected."

Rindan's body weakened, and he slumped to the floor. He rubbed his fingers through his hair, self-soothing. His mother's hand fell on his shoulder and when Cait stumbled close, Beathag wrapped both her children in her arms.

When they went to his grandparents' house, the women of the family took great care in dressing Norman's body where it lay on his bed. Rindan watched his great-aunt, Widow Mary MacDuff, wind a red cloth about his grandfather's head. As she tied it, the cloth closed his slackened jaw. Like her older brother Norman, she had been born in that blackhouse and planned to die there too. With the aid of her housemate, Widow MacGill, Beathag, and Duffy's mother, she pulled a canvas sack over Norman's feet and up his body. The women turned him from side to side as they enclosed him in the sack. They brought it to his chin and left his face exposed for viewing.

Rindan's grandmother lay next to the body and spent the two-day-long wake with her husband. Martha's senses betrayed her from the moment she had woken and found him dead next to her. She refused food and accepted only a few sips of water. When she was not poring over his features, she stared into the void. Rindan's chest tightened to see his grandmother's suffering.

All the immediate family took turns sitting up with the body during the two nights before the burial. By day, the islanders visited, paid their respects, and whispered their final goodbyes to Norman. With the constant intrusion of live bodies, the blackhouse filled with heat and soon the body released a faint, unpleasant odor. No one mentioned it.

When Angus visited with his father, he proved himself a model of solemnity. He nodded toward Rindan and clamped his lips in reverence, for once not belittling or goading. He emulated his father by picking up Martha's fragile hand and held it between his palms. His eyes searched her vacant expression as he whispered condolences. Then he turned and clapped a hand on Rindan's shoulder with a gentle squeeze.

On the morning of the third day, Martha leaned over and touched Norman's sunken cheek with a tender hand. She brushed her withered lips against his and allowed the tears to drip on his still features.

"Farewell, my love," she said. "May we meet again soon."

Rindan's throat ached as he held back the flood of emotion welling inside. He blinked away the wetness on his lashes. Cait

wept openly beside him, and he cursed himself for finding annoyance in her candid display of grief. Her cries roused the sharp pangs
in his chest and he fought all the more to control his own sadness.

Widow MacDuff placed a hand beneath her brother's head
and lifted it enough to pull the canvas sack up. Rindan took in his
last gaze of his grandfather's face as the fabric drew over his features
and crown of gray hair. His aunt tied the canvas at the top with a
piece of yarn, reduced her brother to a lump inside a sack. How
strange he looked.

Saithan led the procession. He, Rindan, Duffy, and Duffy's
father slipped their hands beneath the sack and lifted the body.
Rindan cast his grandmother a mournful gaze. Her expression of
defeat wrenched his soul. She could not come with them, and
sorrow consumed his heart to leave her. The retinue carried the
body outside and made their way up the main road. The other
islanders watched them pass and then followed behind to the
cemetery.

Ancient burial sites rested on the faraway slopes within cairns.
But from the last century or so onward, the islanders buried their
dead in the village. A stone wall encircled the cemetery behind the
last rows of blackhouses. The walk lasted the funeral procession a
long length of time as the men shuffled beneath their burden.
Norman had been thin, but his dead weight resisted their efforts.
Rindan marveled at how his ancestors had once carried their dead
to the high cairns.

It seemed easier for him to ponder the past than be present
at that moment and face the pain of loss. When the procession
reached the cemetery, the men were careful to step around the
rows of stone markers overgrown with dead grass and nettles.
Two island men stood before an open hole they had dug over
the last day. Rindan nodded toward them, grateful for their
effort.

The men laid the sack on the ground next to the yawning
grave. Not a sound rang out, aside from the howl of wind whipping their mantles and shawls in the cold morning air. Saithan

stood at the head of the grave and the mourners settled into a moment of silence.

"My father, Norman Lennox, was a goodly man," he began. "None could compare in gentleness nor sincerity. In all my years, including my youth, he never imparted an unkind word. He loved as hard as he toiled…"

Rindan daydreamed. He wondered if his grandfather listened. Did his spirit stand with them and critique the ceremony conducted on his behalf? Or did his essence venture off, reveling in newfound freedom and exploring all the skies and earth offered? Or did he reunite with his ancestors in the Otherworld in a great coming-home feast, complete with enough singing and dancing to quake the spiritual realm?

When Rindan died, he would not tarry and watch his family weep for him. If his widow shed tears for his departure, he would not want to know. He could not spend a single moment in sadness, for he would be helpless in comforting his loved ones. Instead, he would rejoice at the lightness of his being, to have his earthly shackles broken. Yet more than ever, he found comfort in knowing if he never found his bonny lass in this life, he could find her in the Otherworld.

Saithan sang a mournful dirge he had composed in the days prior. The low, lingering notes plucked many heartstrings, and tears flowed freely. Rindan brushed his face dry and looked around to see if anyone had noticed his tears. His eyes landed on Cait, who sobbed, her arm linked with that of her friend Una. Una's eyes rested on Rindan and he jerked his head down, closed his eyes. Her unwelcome gaze weighed heavy.

Saithan led a prayer and afterward, the men of the family tugged at the canvas sack. They found the task of lowering the body into the grave tricky. Though they knelt as low as they could manage without losing their footing, they dropped the body into the dirt-walled tomb. The body hit the base of the grave with a sickening thud. Rindan's stomach twisted at the sound, as if it rang of disrespect, but how could they help it?

In resounding unison, the village women wailed from the deepest part of them to the highest pitch their voices could project. These moans went on as the men covered the body with cold, wet dirt and filled the hole until a neat mound existed where the earth once stretched its maw. Even as the men broke away and left the cemetery, the women remained. When the rain pattered down on their shoulders, their heads, the keens bellowed on for an hour.

THE MOURNING CONTINUED FOR A WEEK. Work rested, and the family sat about to provide Martha company in her convalescence. Rindan sat with her often and found peace by staying with her when he could. His restless soul slept as he guarded her.

He pondered in the quiet moments, of nothing in particular, yet often watched his grandmother in the light of the clach shoule at her bedside. He added more fulmar oil to the hollowed stone of the lamp, and the cinder of peat burned on as the days shortened. The darkness of the world swallowed Teutatwen as it descended into the cold season.

Martha's despondency continued, and Rindan saw his grandmother would not recover. She had lost the best part of herself. He could not comprehend that loss, nor did he try to. In his silence, he commiserated as well as he could. He did not force chatter as Beathag did or insist that she eat when she refused sustenance, but allowed her to mourn in peace.

But that peace shattered one afternoon. A series of piercing cries from somewhere within the village disrupted Martha's slumber. She peered up from her stupor, her sunken eyes wide with fear.

Widows MacGill and MacDuff sat near, and Rindan deemed it safe to leave his grandmother for a moment. He dashed from the blackhouse to seek after the sound. Villagers gathered in fervent chatter, and he avoided the throng by slipping into his house.

Within, his parents and sister hurried about. Cait and Beathag gathered blankets, crockery, and a leather roll containing medicinal herbs and knives.

"Ellar Fleming will become a father this day," Saithan explained, carrying earthenware pots in both arms.

With a curt nod, Rindan grunted in response. His family paid him no mind as they dashed toward the Fleming house. Dolag was in the throes of childbirth, and as the island's knee-woman, Beathag had to tend to her. He wanted not to care, but the familiar jealousy bubbled over like a pot of boiling water. He walked back toward his grandmother's house as he kicked at clumps of mud.

Flashes of light disturbed his vision. A rock settled in his stomach. Why was he so envious? Not quite grown, he saw fatherhood as a far-off role. Dolag seemed overjoyed to embrace family life. Yet he could not shake the thought that Ellar had taken the most favorable lass on the island before Rindan had a chance to compete for her affections. Now their age difference revealed itself in its starkness. Dolag could never look at him as her contemporary.

He moped all evening and returned home, where he attempted to sleep. The thoughts spun and ran away, wild and nonsensical. He should have stolen Dolag from Ellar before they married and asked her to wait for him to come of age, but it was too late.

At dawn, Beathag and Cait darkened the doorway, unkempt and exhausted. Cait collapsed onto the bed next to Rindan and fell asleep within moments.

"Dolag had her bairn," Beathag said as she leaned over Rindan and rested a hand on his shoulder. "She struggled through the night and the wee one was born quite early this morning. The first bairns are always the most difficult. You'll ken this when you've a wife some years from now."

After Beathag laid down next to Saithan, Rindan sat up, put on his mantle, and walked outside. His morning climbs had become rare with the advent of inclement weather, but he continued his long walks. In the distance, the low-lying mountains hid behind a thick blanket of fog. Shades of gray subdued the landscape and leeched its form and depth. As he made his way to the far side of the island, his toes sank in the boggy soil. He numbed to the utter cold and wet. The sweet smell of decay drifted from the drowned velvetgrass at his feet. At every turn, death reminded him of its grip on all living matter. Someday, death would come for him, and he wasted time wishing for what he could not have.

His mind's eye formed his beautiful ghost. She approached him on the open moor, emerged from the morning mist. Her sweet smile warmed his heart. She gazed at him with such adoration, as if she existed for him alone. He reached for her. His fingertips brushed her soft hair, but went through her. She was gone.

He scanned the periphery with wild, searching eyes, and his heart thrummed inside his chest. His breath caught in his throat. A queasy ache overcame his stomach while a fresh stream of tears burned his eyes. Out here, alone, he allowed them to flow.

If she existed, he could bear the pain of his loss. Yet she did not. Lethargy settled into his bones. Cold seeped through his skin and as he shivered, his nose dripped over his lips. He wiped away the drainage with his shirt sleeve. His grandfather would not wish him to go on as he did. Rindan squared his shoulders and turned to face a new day.

As he passed the corner of a stone wall on his return to the village, a figure darted into his path. Una. His chest smarted from the shock of her sudden presence. She stood before him, a small wisp of a girl with a tender way of being, but Rindan had no feeling for her.

"Good morrow, Rindan," she said, her inflection soft, yet bright.

"Good morrow, Una," he replied and took a step forward to continue his journey home.

She moved in his way and held out something wrapped in cloth. In her other hand was a small cup.

"I baked you some barley bread," she said.

"Thanks be with you."

He went to take the bread, but she said, "I thought we could sit and share it. I also have milk. Would that please you?"

"I must be getting home." He did not look at her, only past her.

"I won't keep you long," she promised. Her eyes shone wide and hopeful. She bent to sit on a low section of wall, careful to not spill the milk.

Rindan's throat hurt and the thought of socializing irked him, but he also did not wish to be rude. How could he let her down in a gentle way? Though his mind scrambled, he could not conceive of an escape.

He half-leaned and half-sat upon the wall with obvious reluctance. A wide gap stretched between them. Una scooted toward him and set the cup down before adjusting the plaid woolen shawl that had fallen off her shoulder. She opened the cloth bundle on her lap to reveal a flat brown loaf of bread, cut in half. Steam rose from it in the cool air.

She had planned with great care to bake it early that morning. Snatched it from the fireside when she saw him coming down from the moor. He pictured her laboring for hours at the grindstone the night before, bending to blow away the husks after they separated from the grain.

When she offered him half of the bread, he took it with a grateful nod but did not look at her as he brought it to his lips. He bit into it and tasted the warm, nutty flavor and gritty texture. When he swallowed, his hollow stomach rejoiced. With renewed hunger, he took quick bites, and soon buried the last of the bread in his mouth. Chewed with a prolonged sigh.

Una nibbled on her bread and regarded him with satisfaction. She picked up the cup and held it out. Rindan grasped it, took a hurried sip—it too was warm and fresh from the udder—and tried to give it back.

She pushed it away and said, "Nae, 'tis all for you. You're also welcome to this other half of the bread."

He drained the milk, but shook his head. "I cannot take your share."

"It pleases me to see you eat," she said, her cheeks flushing. "I observed you not eating at all during the wake. I wish to profess my sorrow for your loss. Ken that I'm here should you desire someone to provide you company. You may tell your troubles to me."

Rindan's gaze fixed on anything other than her. His hands wandered uneasily over the crevasses between the stones and rolled balls of dirt between his fingertips. A horny-gollach scuttled along a cleft in a granite slab, and Rindan watched its movements with uncharacteristic fascination.

"Or we can remain silent," she suggested with an uneasy laugh. She wound a lock of loose hair around her finger.

He scratched the back of his neck, digging for elusive words. Her eyes burned into him. He dropped his hand to rest on the wall beside him, and the light touch of her fingers brushed over it. The back of her hand was dry and cracked, and her nails ragged. He withdrew his hand. What if Duffy saw?

Rindan noticed her reaction, her eyes downcast and lips twisted in disappointment. His mouth felt dry, as if filled with sand, his tongue like a dehydrated reed. He held the cup out for her to take and stood with no other thought than of walking away.

"Thanks be with you," he said.

She quickly wound the cup inside the cloth and tucked it under her apron strap. He had already stepped away, but she leapt up to grab him, to wrap her slender hand around his arm. She tossed the errant piece of hair back from her face and slowly leaned toward him. Rindan froze in place as her wind-chapped lips came to rest on his bony cheek. They were warm. His heartbeat quickened as she stepped back.

"You are welcome to it," she said. "I would very much like to accompany you on one of your walks. If you come by my house, I'll be waiting for you."

Rindan nodded, though had no intention of following through with her request. He walked on, but his legs weighed heavy. Her hand clung to his arm as she strode at his side. He could not risk entering the village with her hanging on him. Everyone would think they courted. Duffy would never forgive him.

Rindan turned, breaking her grip. "I am sorry," he said. "I forgot my rope." And he quickly strode back up the path he had come from.

When he looked back after a moment, he saw her walking toward the village. He could not imagine what she thought of him, but he found himself not caring.

Quick footfalls came from the side of him and he turned to find Angus. A sick sensation gripped his insides. Despite his swift escape, the island proved too small, and Angus had waylaid him.

"What are you doing, Rin?" his friend asked. "Meeting in secret with Una after you told Duffy she was his?"

"Nae," Rindan replied firmly. "'Tisn't the way of it."

Angus shook his head, his eyes dark. "I saw you kiss."

Drops of sweat formed on Rindan's temple. "I did not kiss her. I feel naught for her."

"You two embraced," Angus probed as he crossed his arms in front of his thin chest. "And you feel naught for her?"

Rindan chose to omit the fact that Una actively pursued him that morning. If Duffy knew, he would despise Rindan as an obstacle to his love, their friendship broken by jealousy.

"I beseech you," Rindan begged. "You saw naught but an idle chat between friends. Speak none of this to Duffy."

"He's your cousin and you betray him in your family's time of grief?"

"I would never hurt him," Rindan said. His hands rested on his hips as he stood solid in self-defense.

Angus' eyes filled with concern. He slouched and thumped the dirt between their feet with his toes. "Your sister wishes to see you and Una together. If you long for the same, speak with honesty to me."

"Nae—" Rindan tried to explain, but Angus went on, his voice forceful and commanding.

"I can speak to Duffy for you or be with you if you wish to tell him yourself. 'Tisn't wrong to change your mind, but 'tis wrong to break a promise. Duffy's besotted with Una. You ken this! He would need much time to recover."

"Nae, I declare I've nae feelings for her," Rindan said, at last. "In fact, Una mentioned she wished Duffy would visit her house and take her walking."

The lie echoed in Rindan's head the moment it left his tongue. Why did he say it? Angus squinted at him and clamped his lips together, perhaps incredulous.

"If we tell this to Duffy, do you think there's a chance he would take her suggestion?"

Rindan smirked, relaxing. "Nae," he said with a slight chortle. "Una must approach him first."

"Aye, and did you think to tell her so?"

Rindan shook his head.

Angus emitted a heavy sigh. "You amaze me, Rindan. Little helpmate you are in procuring a wife for your cousin. We must assist our friend who cannot help himself. He's too anxious to approach her without her encouragement."

His eyes again narrowed at Rindan as he paused in thought. "Una has never displayed interest in Duffy. 'Tis puzzling she would tell you alone. As far as Cait kens, Una has uttered words of love for only you."

Rindan swallowed, his throat thick and parched. "I ken not," he said simply. "'Tis possible she has changed her feelings. I must go to my grandmother now. I'm quite late as 'tis."

"Go then," Angus said. "I'll say naught to Duffy. If Una did indeed tell you of her fondness for him, I leave it to you to speak it."

As Rindan walked away, he wondered if he should have told Angus the only lass he held any affection for was Dolag. But now that she was long married and with a new bairn, such a confession would be obscene. He clenched his fists and cursed himself for allowing Una to be noticed with him. In any case, he found relief that Angus alone saw them and no one else. Angus enjoyed banter enough, but Rindan trusted he could keep a secret.

He found the widows taking the cows outside his grandmother's blackhouse to separate them from their calves.

"Would you like me to milk them?" Rindan asked.

"Nae, lad," Widow MacDuff said. "We can manage. Have you seen my grandson yet this morn?"

"Nae, I did see Angus, but Duffy was not with him. Wish me to find him? I came to visit Grandmother."

"Och, if you do not mind," she replied. "But do say 'good morrow' to Martha first."

Rindan walked into the warm blackhouse that radiated with the heat of the fire and the bodies of the cows. The calves lay asleep on a bed of straw in the corner and all was quiet. Martha dozed in her bed and Rindan approached her. He lowered himself to her side, where he took his grandmother's hand. It was cold, despite the stifling warmth of the house.

He longed to have his grandmother back the way he remembered her. To hear her cheerful voice and watch her putter about the house, working the warp-weighted loom, kneading bread, or draining whey for cheese making. In the last few years, she may have lost the ability to perform the outdoor tasks that tested a person's endurance, yet she had remained useful in all her little ways. But now, in this state, she could not even complete her household duties.

Rindan did not wish to find Duffy. His shame burned so deep. He pretended to forget as he tidied his grandmother's house and found a pair of her stockings that required mending. Widow MacDuff might have found Duffy herself, for Duffy walked in carrying a jug of fresh water.

Rindan looked up from his needle and his heart thundered beneath his ribs. "G'morrow?" he called out, clearing his throat several times.

"Morning!" Duffy replied as he set down the jug. "How's Aunt Martha?"

Rindan looked at his grandmother. Her condition was obvious, but he replied, "The same." He watched Duffy pensively and shifted in his seat, but tried acting normal.

"Have you gone to visit Dolag and see the new bairn?" Duffy asked.

Rindan's brow knit. "By Our Lovely Wee Lass, nae! Why would I?"

"To offer blessings, of course," Duffy replied. "You must be the only person besides Martha who hasn't visited this morn."

Rindan said nothing. He wanted to think of Dolag and her bairn as much as he wanted to think of Una, which was not at all. He consciously avoided the subject of both as the cold autumn days passed.

However, when Dolag's bairn was almost a week old, the child died.

During the small funeral at the cemetery, Rindan despised himself for his thoughts. Ellar and Dolag sagged over the grave with uncanny stoicism. The harsh reality of their island claimed more bairns to the grave than allowed a long life. The cemetery devoted an entire section to cradling the island's lost babes, an area that took up nearly half of the enclosure.

Chastened, Rindan sat with his grandmother most days, even though the widows were present to tend to her. He had to maintain his virtue, take penance for his lust of Dolag, ill-wishes for Ellar, the confusion he caused Una, and her kiss that should have landed on Duffy, not him.

In his revelation, his conscience urged him to help his grandmother. He recalled his last conversation with his grandfather and at last determined what would do Martha some good. One morning, on a temperate day, while the villagers joined in their daily meeting, Rindan wrapped two blankets around his grandmother. He slipped his hands beneath her and scooped her up in his arms. She weighed light with her tiny frame as he cradled her to his chest. For the first time, she peered into his eyes and he saw recognition there.

He carried her the far way around the village and avoided

coming close to the gathering of islanders. He knew if his parents saw him, they would shriek and scold him for taking his grandmother outdoors. He passed children playing, and they stopped their game to watch him walk by. As always, the island hounds followed at his heels, but he paid them no mind.

When he reached the open moor, the sheep took notice of him and the trailing hounds. One by one, they joined, and soon, Rindan led a parade. He wanted to laugh, but the procession reminded him of his grandfather's funeral. He shivered instead.

At last, he reached the hot spring. The steam of it rose in the cool air, warm and welcoming. He carefully removed the blankets from around his grandmother and dropped them on the ground. Holding her close, he slipped his feet into the spring. Mud squelched beneath his soles. Heat enveloped them. He waded out to the center of the spring, where the water rose to his waist. Then he lowered Martha, clothed in her smock.

With his hands supporting her, Martha stretched out her arms and floated on her back. Her eyes shut and her chin lifted to the sky as her wrinkled cheeks formed a closed smile. Her gray, brassy curls darkened and hovered around her head like a crown. Rindan allowed her to lie a long time while the healing spring soaked her skin. They said nothing.

The sheep flocked about the pool while watching the pair with blank eyes. The hounds rolled their bodies over the ground, laid still on their backs, and settled into an equal stupor. Rindan closed his eyes, breathed in the sulfur mist. The steam rose and covered his skin with drops of water. His tension melted away and his burdens lifted. He emptied his mind, cast aside his ruminations.

After much time had passed, Martha finally spoke. "I feel better."

She rose slightly to place her arms around his neck and he carried her from the pool. The cold air triggered goosebumps across his skin. He secured the blankets around his grandmother, and began the walk back to the village.

Martha rested her head against Rindan's chest and spoke again.

"My dear lad, the lass that marries you shall be most fortunate indeed."

His heart burst with warmth, blooming outward like a marigold in springtime. He could not help but smile.

"There is a lass in mind," Rindan heard himself say. "But I ken not where to find her."

"You'll find her," Martha replied. "She is not far."

NINE

The Demorians endured the most intemperate winter in known history. Freezing rains forced the inhabitants to remain indoors over the months. Treacherous sea swells thundered against the cliffs as if threatening to tear the island into pieces. Gales moved like a combatant taking down their opponent with driving fists. Their punches proved merciless. High winds and scathing cold killed sheep, cattle, and any unlucky soul who wandered outside at the wrong time.

When the spring season came upon them, the weather failed to warm. The elusive sun did not stir the land into wakefulness. Crofters attempting to ready their rips for planting found the ground frozen and impossible to till. The fisherfolk also wrung their hands in helplessness. So they waited and prayed to their gods.

Like the land, Isolba's womb remained dormant, and dread captured her hopes. They sank to the bottom of the Atlantic. She had mere months before she was meant to sail to the Argarves and marry, but Baltair's remedies did not work. Her body proved as stunted and undeveloped as the prior year. She forced herself to eat an extra bannock or two at mealtimes, but her body did not put on weight.

Baltair had made himself scarce after their last conversation. Slaves brought his prepared tinctures for her to drink, and she wondered if he purposely left out the key ingredient to aid her growth, or worse, something to sicken her. Make her womb shrivel into a hard endocarp. She sometimes stole away with Nareen to his chambers, yet they always found his rooms empty. It became clear Baltair avoided her, and she realized how personally he took her rejection.

Life inside the fortress lost its luster, and the people within became languid. Outside, in the clearing above the shore, came the resonance of metallic clangs and shouts of men. Frang brought Isolba with Nareen in tow to watch the progress on the new ship. She watched with fascination as the workers reassembled the pieces rescued from the sea. They filled in the remainder of the craft with driftwood from the island's storage.

"Will it be ready in time for my trip to the Argarves?" she asked.

"Aye, it will, but must be tested on the waters first," he answered. "The true question is, will you be ready?"

Frang's voice lacked the sarcasm from the prior year. Instead, wariness had taken hold, and his question was not a taunt, but a concern. His handsome face had grown wan, and he looked older.

Isolba opened her mouth to reply, but her throat swelled, and her eyes reddened. Nareen rested a hand against her mistresses' face and offered her a sorrowful look.

"Do not fash," Frang said. "The peace treaty is in place. If the end of summer arrives and you remain a child, we will send the ambassador to the Argarves and tell Cormac the marriage must be delayed until next summer."

His words gave her no comfort. Instead, she experienced a burning shame, knowing her betrothed would wait impatiently for her. Would he know she failed to bloom?

A strange tenderness crossed Frang's face, and he said, "We will not tell him outright the true reason for the delay. We will say you need another year beneath your mother's wings and will better suit him when you're a twelvemonth older. Surely, he may suspect the true reason, but he has nae interest in marrying a child—lest he's a lecher, so will be satisfied to wait."

ONCE COMPLETE, the ship sat in the yard, the waters unsailable. The soil thawed, but its wetness prevented the crops from thriving. The sun shone so little that its rays had little chance of stirring the seeds into productive plants. Those that sprouted grew weak from incessant rain and bore little fruit.

In the spring and summer months, longships once sailed from the mainland. Carried goods—food, wine, exotic fabrics and spices—in trade for feathers, seabird eggs, and tweeds. They arrived throughout the mild season, usually a four-month span. These ships were Demoria's only lifeline to the outer world, its connection to true society. Now, these ships could no longer approach the island, lest they become caught in the thrust of a violent swell and bashed to pieces against the rocky shore. The island became destitute, and its people were without help and deprived of all hope.

Even through the Summer Solstice, the skies remained overcast. Because of the high winds, most seabirds, save for the bravest, did not return to nest on the cliffs. Islanders could no longer rely on bird flesh and fish as diet staples, but scavenged whatever sea life washed ashore. Crofters and fisherfolk collected seaweed, washed-up fish, and crustaceans. They slaughtered the surplus livestock and avoided starvation.

Summer ended with no contact with the Argarves. Though her shame had deferred another year, Isolba was not relieved. Instead, she experienced a dread like no other. She knew keenly that her people were in danger. The pitiful harvest made their situation dire. They could pass the winter eating the livestock raised on the moors. Her father owned hundreds of his own sheep and dozens of cows, but the lack of hearty vegetation caused the animals to wither.

Yet, it was the change in her father that frightened Isolba most. He turned frantic. He gave offerings to the gods: precious food, drink, and livestock, including his prized bull.

Since Samhain, their clan often walked to the open air temple on the southern summit. There, Baltair burned sacrifices on the altar stone, uttered incantations to the skies. The druids emulated his movements and danced among rain, sleet, and wind.

Isolba watched the smoke billow into the atmosphere and asked the gods to hear their plea. If they chose mercy and returned the world to a state of normalcy, she would never question them. She tested their generosity with fervent prayers. Bid the heightened energy inside her womb. Then bemoaned its failure to ripen.

She changed her course. Dropped the demands. In a private ritual, she stayed awake for half the night. Knelt on the cold, hard floor of her bedchamber and whispered remorse to the gods in a crude act of penance. Even when her legs cramped and knees ached, she remained with arms outspread. Her eyes misted at the thought of her handsome betrothed and her desire to see him. But she needed to be selfless. So, she prayed only for an end to her father's worries.

It seemed her family had forgotten her as more pressing matters held their focus. Yet Moira considered her daughter's plight and, by degrees, withdrew from her self-absorbed trance. For her, the state of their island was a temporary inconvenience, and, unlike Escarans, she chose not to dwell on it. She concentrated on the future. Perhaps she heard her daughter's desperate prayers from the adjoining room night after night, and sought answers.

"I became your mother at your age," she told Isolba one day as they reposed in the solar.

Their slaves, Gormall and Nareen, sat on the floor at their feet. Waited to be needed. Gormall wavered, and Isolba half-noticed that the old woman seemed weaker.

Isolba's eyes flicked from Gormall to Moira. "I ken. I am ill-favored, an aberration. I fear I am ill and shall die before I see marriage."

Moira shook her head but did not correct her daughter. Concern settled in her forehead crease. "Baltair's remedies have failed," she stated. "So, I've arranged a meeting with the healer. She kens more about a woman's body and fertility than Baltair. She's seen many women through the carrying of children and delivering bairns. I trust her to ken why you do not develop."

"Very well," Isolba agreed.

"We must see her in secret, as I go against your father's wishes," Moira warned. "He wants Baltair alone to attend to you, but because Baltair is married to his priesthood, he kens little of women. I've appealed to Frang, and he's agreed to take us to her tonight after your father drinks himself to sleep."

"Aye, I'm fain to go," Isolba said.

True to Moira's word, Escarans became so drunk that evening that he became oblivious to the world around him and fell into a heavy sleep. Alcohol proved one commodity not yet rationed, as Escarans had always ensured his storeroom remained well stocked. It burst with enough casks of whisky, wine, and mead to supply him for years, but he drank it as though a longship could bring a fresh stock any moment.

As Nareen readied Isolba for their short walk across town, she asked her mistress, "Milady, I beg you to take Gormall with you and allow her to see the healer. She is not well. I fear she's dying, but would like to see if she can be healed. Could you ask Lady MacKay? She cannot see for herself how her maid ails."

Isolba turned and grasped Nareen's hands. "Of course I will."

The moment they walked into Moira's chamber, Isolba entreated her mother. "May Gormall come too and see the healer? She doesn't look at all well."

Moira turned to consider her slave, who slipped a dark mantle about her mistress. Moira looked perplexed and blinked, as if noticing Gormall's weak condition for the first time.

"I must tell your father first, as Gormall is his property. We risk enough taking you to the healer. Do not fash, I will speak to him in the morning."

Gormall did not look up, but the disappointment in Nareen's face moved Isolba. "How can it be more of a risk when we are already going to the healer tonight?" she asked.

"Because we must follow a proper protocol when dealing with slaves and 'tis not my wish to interfere," Moira stated. She turned to speak to Gormall. "I ask you to rest for now. Nareen will assist me in the meantime. We'll find aid for you in the morning."

Isolba knew it to be the most words Moira had ever spoken to Gormall at one time. Their relationship was nothing like hers and Nareen's. A sisterly affection bonded the girls, so attuned that their personal desires became one another's. Because Nareen sought help for Gormall, Isolba worried for the old slave in turn.

Nareen tugged Gormall over to her pallet on the floor and the woman nodded gratefully. Isolba noticed drops of sweat form on Gormall's brow, beneath the thin, graying hair. The woman lowered her head to her pillow and trembled. Her eyelids drooped as if pulled by weights. Nareen turned toward Isolba. Her eyes bore into hers, and Isolba helplessly frowned.

"May Nareen stay with Gormall?" Isolba asked. "She should not be alone."

"Aye," Moira agreed. "Frang will keep us safe, and the fewer people in our group, the better. We do not wish to draw attention to ourselves."

"Are my lasses ready?" Frang called from the doorway.

Moira smiled warmly at his arrival and rested her hand on his forearm. "Aye, let's go."

Walking out of the castle, Isolba felt that without Nareen, she was half a person. So crucial was the maid's presence in her life that she could not imagine their separation.

Frang led their group down the cobblestone streets and to a narrow path between rows of close-knit houses. Isolba recognized the withered herb garden next to the healer's home, enclosed by a low stone wall. Looking about furtively, Frang knocked on the door. Once it opened, he pushed Isolba and Moira inside and shut the door behind them.

The small, tidy space smelled of herbs. They dangled from the rafters and brewed in pots near the hearth fire. A fresh coat of limewash covered the walls and floors. In the corner sat a small bed—clean, simple, and covered in a lone sheet. Endless rows of jars filled shelves along the walls, with labels Isolba could not read. A mortar and pestle sat on a workspace on the floor next to bowls of cottongrass and polypody.

So transfixed, Isolba startled to find herself face to face with the healer. She was a small woman of middle age with bands of silver through her braided hair. The blue eyes measured her. Looked up and down in a businesslike manner.

"We meet again, Lady Isolba," the healer said, her tone level. "Though this time I tend to you and not your father. Is Chief Escarans well?"

"Aye, in health but not in spirits," Isolba answered gravely.

"'Tis nae surprise with the state of our island," the healer commented. Then, as if bored by the idle chatter, she waved her hand impatiently. "Come, remove your clothing down to your smock and lie down."

Isolba was grateful that Frang waited outside and reluctantly pulled off her mantle, dress, and petticoat. She fumbled with the fastenings, accustomed to having Nareen's help. The pile of clothing sat abandoned in the middle of the floor.

As if embarrassed, Moira scooped the garments up and held them while she waited. The healer motioned to the bed.

Isolba's heartbeat quickened as she lowered onto it, certain the healer would inform her she was dying. She looked into the older woman's face, a kind face with intelligent eyes, and decided that she would trust whatever she said. After all, she had observed the healer work in and about the castle and knew her to be highly skilled.

The healer crouched next to the bed and squinted at Isolba in earnest. "Now," she said. "Lady MacKay tells me you've yet to bleed?"

Isolba nodded. Swallowed the lump in her throat.

The healer stretched out her hands and pressed her palms into Isolba's chest. "Do you feel any soreness when I press here?"

"Nae," Isolba said with a grimace.

The healer moved her hands down to Isolba's stomach and pressed her fingertips gently into the flesh, prodding and seeking. "Do you have any pain here now?"

"Nae."

"And have you ever experienced twinges of pain in your sides or 'neath your ribs?"

"Nae," Isolba said. Her brow furrowed.

"Have you had a wetness between your legs at any time?"

Isolba's ears turned red and heat flushed her skin. Her insides twisted and turned. "Nae."

The healer then said, "I need to look between your legs. I bid you spread them apart."

Flames licked Isolba's cheeks. She ceased to breathe. With a wince, she shifted her legs, and the healer grabbed her ankles and splayed her knees wide. Isolba's hands covered her face. But in a moment, the healer lifted Isolba's smock, looked briefly, and sat back. Isolba drew her legs back together and dropped her hands to hear her death sentence.

Not an ounce of unease registered on the healer's face. She turned toward Moira and said, "Your daughter remains a child. She has nae sign of becoming a woman anytime soon. Naught has developed to the point that I can say she is fertile. You say this is her sixteenth summer?"

"Aye," Moira said. "'Tis. But how can it be? I gave birth to her when I was her age. She was to marry this summer, as you ken, but 'tis impossible to travel or send any message to her betrothed."

The healer gave Moira an assuring smile. "Imagine Isolba as a flower. Some bloom in spring, most in summer, but then you have the flowers that wait for the cool touch of autumn before their petals emerge. She is an autumn flower, naught more. Do not fash. Give her time to enjoy her childhood while she may. She will blossom when she's ready."

Moira's shoulders relaxed as she drew out a long sigh and asked, "Is there aught we can do to hasten the process?"

The healer smiled and replied, "Nae, only time may do the work. Give her a year. She may be ready around Bealtaine when sailing is possible. Are you in a hurry to see your daughter gone away forever to the Argarves?"

Moira's jaw dropped at the healer's blunt query and it took her a moment to form words. "Och, nae, of course I do not wish that. You understand that we must fulfill the stipulations in the peace treaty before McCloud becomes restless, indignant."

"I ken," the healer said. "Yet you've nae choice but to wait as 'tis. McCloud cannot reach us. The waters prevent it, so there is nae recourse. Trust that by the time we see calm waters again, Isolba will be a woman."

"Aye," Moira responded. "You're right. We're satisfied to wait."

"You've nae other need of me tonight?" the healer asked.

"Nae," Moira said, brought Isolba her clothing. "Thanks be with you, Rhyza."

"Aye!" Isolba blurted in a near shout. "Aye, we do. We've a dying slave. Gormall, my mother's maid, is unwell. Can you see to her?"

"Wheesht, Isolba!" Moira scolded. "'Tis not our duty to find help for Gormall, as I spake." Turning to the healer, she said, "We do have an unwell slave, but I have to inform my husband first."

"I see," the healer said. "'Tis not I that care for the slaves. They've their own healer among them."

"Aye," Moira replied. "And we must apprise Escarans of a slave's condition and allow him to make his judgment. We do not meddle with his rules, Isolba. Be satisfied that Gormall rests this night and will have care in the morning."

Isolba said nothing as shame burned her skin. She was weary of being a child. Being treated as a child. She hurriedly pulled her clothing on with Moira's help, but could not look her mother in the eyes.

The women moved toward the door. Isolba marched ahead wordlessly while Moira shared parting words with the healer. Once outside, Isolba breathed in the cold air. Her pulse raced in her veins and her jaw pained from clenching her teeth. She noticed Frang waited there in the dark and dropped her gaze to the ground. He led them down the pathway back toward the main street.

"Did you find the answers you sought?" Frang asked, looked back at Moira, and then Isolba, who refused to meet his eyes.

"Aye," Moira said. "Though not the ones we hoped. Naught is wrong with our Isolba, other than she's stunted. She remains a child."

Frang smirked and laughed under his breath. "We kent that, did we not?"

"Aye, I suppose we did," Moira said. "'Twas good to receive confirmation.

"Perhaps if Isolba conducts herself as a lady and not a child, then her body will follow suit?" Frang wondered.

Isolba could not bear to stay and suffer Frang's teasing. Not again. She tore past him, ran up the cobblestone street, illuminated by the light of torches suspended from poles. The ache in her chest swelled as though her heart would burst. Tears stung her cheeks.

How unfair it all was! At that moment, she should have been with her new husband in the Argarves. Her body had betrayed her, as well as the sea. Each worked against her to keep her from Cormac. He would not treat her as a child, in that she felt certain.

When she reached the court, the porters opened the doors, and she ran within, to collapse against the cold stone wall beneath an alcove. Fetid water dripped from the eaves above, and the atmosphere smelled musty and rotten. She found the surrounding decay repulsive and longed for the crisp air of autumn, with its fragrant notes of heather, wild thyme, and sea salt.

Frang and Moira's quick steps drew near, and the pair stopped breathlessly before Isolba, but did not scold her. They looked not at her, but at each other, and longer than seemed proper. Something in their eyes unsettled Isolba. She knew not what it meant. How she wearied of the adults in her life, with their secrets and mysterious glances, while she drowned in anguish. She turned and ran to a side door leading to the kitchen, where she slipped inside.

WHEN SAMHAIN ARRIVED, the clan gathered at the summit. Isolba lost herself in the music and watched the dancers sway around a great bonfire. She remained under heavy guard, forbidden to join the throng out of fear she might come to harm in the swarm of bodies. Her view of the ceremony came from behind the panel of a small A-frame tent. She peeked out with fascination.

Baltair spiraled in circles. He conducted the rising power to greet the ancestors as they arrived to mingle with mortals. The incredible energy electrified every nerve in Isolba's body as she breathed in the combined odors of smoke and rain. Near midnight, her co-mother Anna, along with a group of men at arms, spirited her away. Protected her from the debauchery that went on in the wee hours of morning.

Because the clan reveled in a location remote from the castle, they set up camp a short distance from the summit. There, Isolba lay next to Nareen inside their tent and could not sleep, but listened to the thrumming drums and shouts of merrymaking.

Nareen said no lady should witness what occurred in the darkest hours. Revelers imbibed vast amounts of drink and acted unlike themselves. Some allowed spirits to possess their bodies. Isolba knew her father, mother, and co-mothers were among the party-goers, but could not imagine what they did. Nareen said it was best she did not know and to go to sleep.

That winter, the cold brought more misery than the clan could endure. Isolba looked on helplessly as Baltair took up an old practice. He selected slaves for ritual sacrifice. He believed he could offer them to the gods in exchange for fair weather. These ceremonies took place not at the summit, but within Spirit Hound Cave.

At the summit's edge, the earth dropped away where a cloven area within the cliff concealed an opening. This passage led inside the cave, where the druids performed the most sacred of rituals.

Isolba watched only part of the proceedings. Because she had not reached womanhood and her father wished to preserve her innocence, she could not witness the ceremony in its entirety. After the druids led a shrouded figure into the cave, toward a large altar stone, the men at arms whisked Isolba to the encampment.

The shroud was key. The sacrifice had to wear humility's cloak when partaking of such an honor. The spectators could not look upon the chosen one and see their humanity, but recognize them only as a gift for the gods. Isolba understood that even after the ceremony was over, the identity of the slave remained unknown.

She found herself not as grieved for these souls as she had been for the galley slaves lost at sea. The slaves sacrificed in Spirit Hound Cave died with purpose. Such atonement would satisfy the gods and bring warmth and bounty to the island once again. She began to feel hopeful.

Yet, one day after a ceremony, a shift occurred. Isolba and Nareen had returned to the castle, where Isolba went to bed and slept for hours. When she awoke, she discovered Nareen awake on her pallet, hugging her knees. Isolba dropped to comfort her, but Nareen stood and backed away.

"I cannot find Gormall," she said, her expression wounded. She eyed her mistress with distrust.

Isolba caught her meaning, but chose not to believe it could be true. So far, the slaves sacrificed were none that she knew. She rubbed her eyes as the fog of heavy sleep drained. "Isn't she still unwell and resting in the slave quarters?" she asked.

"Nae," Nareen said. Her tears streamed like rain off a rooftop. "I've searched and entreated. None have seen her or ken where she could be."

"She must be around," Isolba assured. Despite Nareen's visible upset, she was not worried. Gormall would surely turn up. Escarans would never allow Baltair to sacrifice a slave so close to her family. She stood and leaned against her bed, curiosity on her face instead of concern. "Where do the bodies go? Are they burned?"

Nareen shook her head. "Nae," she sobbed. "They're taken to a chamber within the cave. A tomb."

Isolba pondered for a moment. The bodies were placed in a tomb. Not burned to rise into the sky as smoke and assimilate into the spiritual realm.

Her thoughts switched back to Gormall. "Why would she be chosen?" she asked in disbelief. "She was unwell, perhaps dying. What good would she be to the gods?"

"'Tis easier to kill a sick slave than one healthy and valuable to your father," Nareen said coldly.

A pang speared Isolba's body, and she took a moment to find words in Escarans' defense. "If it were she, which it wasn't, she would have died with honor," she said matter-of-factly. "Baltair sacrificed someone else last night. Offering her would carry nae weight with the gods."

"How can you say such?" Nareen asked. Her voice strained and broke with the words. Her nostrils flared and bloodshot eyes narrowed, penetrated.

Stunned by Nareen's swift anger, Isolba said, "You misunderstand. I meant not that. Forgive me. I did not realize–"

"She was a mother to me," Nareen said. Her open palms appealed for understanding. "While you looked to your mothers, I looked to her. You miss so much by thinking only of yourself and not of others around you."

"But I do notice!" Isolba scoffed. "I do care!"

"You do not care enough, milady," her maid replied. "You fail to see what is before you."

"I do!"

"Perhaps you did at one time, but since the treaty was signed, Cormac consumes your thoughts," Nareen said.

"You don't understand." Isolba pressed a hand to her heart. "You have never been in love to ken what I feel for him."

"And neither have you!" Nareen seethed, her voice erupting into an unexpected shout. "What you feel is not love!"

Isolba's palm slid to rest at the base of her throat, and her face flushed. "'Tis!" she said, her mouth agape.

Nareen stared Isolba down with a hardened expression. She crossed her arms and stepped away. Widened her distance. Her eyes squinted as she spewed venom from her tongue. "How could a *child* ken what love is?"

The maid clenched the fabric of her skirt and shook it with a huff as she left. For the first time in all their years together, Nareen stalked off in fury. Exhibited a will apart from her mistress. Her last words hung in the air. Left a miasma of resentment and misunderstanding to haunt the chamber.

Dejected, Isolba flung herself across her mattress. For once, she failed to cry. She numbed instead. How could she bear separation from Nareen? On her own, she was an empty shell. A hollow statue without personality.

"Och, Cormac," she whispered. Her chest filled with longing. "Once we're together, I will ken myself. And you will be the only person in this life to truly see me."

Yet telling herself this brought no comfort.

TEN

Chief Escarans knew the gods were angry with him. He longed to understand what he had done to cause their fury and how to repent. With every slave Baltair sacrificed, Escarans hoped it would be the one to appease the gods.

He saw himself as a failure. He might own islands, countless slaves, hold the chiefdom, and master nine wives, but life bore no substance. His wee Isolba once gave him such joy, but she no longer belonged to him. He considered her a stranger living in his house. A pawn traded to his rival, all in the name of peace. But what peace was there to have?

The women burdened him the most. The cost of maintaining his household, along with those of the wives living apart from him, drained his funds. But the monetary depletion was the least of it, because the emotional and mental strain exhausted him, body and soul.

When he had married each wife, he developed bonds based on their individuality. He took an interest in their passions and gave them independence within reason. Yet, as their literal lord and master, he set rules that all his wives had to follow. Some strove in their obeisance, but others rebelled against his restrictions. It drove him mad.

He experienced disobedience, manipulation, and rivalries among them. To his wives, he dosed his affection in equal measure, if he displayed any at all. He believed not a single wife loved him. They may have once found him charming, but now they regarded him with disgust. He did not reprimand their cruel expressions, but met their eyes and accepted their disdain.

His youngest wife, Moira, ranked as his favorite. She had birthed his one and only heir. Her loyalty and reverence added to her value. Yet when even she shirked his advances, he lost respect for her. It hardly mattered. She, too, had ultimately failed him. She did not bear him a son.

Over the years, his impotence came to light. His anger toward his wives turned to shame. Shame for himself, shame for them. He withdrew and lost himself all the more in drink. His wives remained loyal, despite their discontent. They feared him too much to stray. Only two wives were estranged, as Escarans found them too disagreeable. He often thought he should live apart from all his wives, but longed to keep Isolba close while he could. And she needed her mothers.

The wives doted on Isolba, each in their own way, though a few involved themselves more than others. Over the years, she learned various skills under their instruction. They taught her embroidery, painting, pottery-making, weaving, history, and fashion. But Escarans forbade his wives from teaching her the art of sensuality. The world was a wicked place. He wanted his daughter innocent, but in his safeguard, he left her oblivious. He took no measures to amend this, even after her betrothal.

All her life, Escarans warned Isolba to protect her virtue at all costs. Men posed a danger to her purity. Though she could not understand what he meant by this, he enacted the desired fear within her. He barred her direct association with any man other than himself, Baltair, and Frang.

He also forbade her from consorting with the commoners, out of fear that she would become tainted by sickness, fleas, foul language, or any vile thing. He shuttered her away from the world and left her a wide-eyed bairn. Without stain, without fault. Sweet, childlike, and trusting only him.

Of late, his demeanor toward his daughter turned cold and reserved, despite her countless requests to spend time with him. The pain of her impending departure grieved him. He thought that if he distanced himself, it would make her leaving easier.

When Bealtaine approached again, the storms mauled Demoria as violently as they had for a year and a half. So far, he had ordered only the old and sickly slaves to die under Baltair's dirk. But he knew the gods asked more of him, and the deafening gales roared the sign of their displeasure.

Escarans asked Baltair to select the slaves he deemed valuable, those that would satisfy the gods. Each ritual brought hope to Escarans' heart, but then despair in the days and weeks to follow. The sacrifices lasted the summer, and again the waves proved too fierce for any ship to leave the island or approach with supplies.

The hungry crofters and fisherfolk rose against him from outside the town wall. Threatened to dismantle the fortress. As their chief and lord, they held Escarans responsible. They cried out for his resignation–his execution–but the men at arms held them back. Yet inside the walls, slaves mutinied. They refused to work. Demanded Baltair's head on a pike. Escarans ordered them whipped, some to death, but they stood proud against their master.

The wives barricaded themselves inside Escarans' apartments. Moira took shelter in the bower with Isolba, Nareen, and two of his other wives. A stand-off ensued between the men at arms and slaves in the outside halls.

Escarans remained out of the fray. He and Frang hid in the east tower with Baltair for three days, surrounded by men at arms. Shut inside that cold stone room with two men, living in filth, Escarans cried out to the gods. Baltair prayed over him. Plead for a clear solution to their woes.

On the third night, while sleeping on a dirty pallet within the tower keep, Escarans had a dream. The dream proved so vivid and unsettling that he awoke in the dark and felt as though he had not slept an hour.

When Baltair wakened with the first overcast light of dawn, Escarans said to him, "I dreamt a portent, a certain message from the gods, yet I ken not what it means."

The priest sat up, his gray hair unkempt, and looked eager-eyed at the chief. "Aye? Tell it to me, every detail you recall."

Escarans gazed into the distance and, as he told the dream, relived it. Watched it replay before his eyes. "In my dream," he began, "I see a ewe lamb wandering across a barren land without a single blade of grass, starving, as fierce gales nearly sweep her into stormy seas. A shepherd comes along and slaughters the lamb. As the lamb returns to the earth, the winds quiet, and the sea calms. The clouds part, and the sun shines. Such brilliance! It warms the earth. The soil turns fertile, and grass grows from where the lamb's body had lain. Green flora sprouts betwixt the grasses, and the land is bountiful with the harvest. Then, a ram forms from the earth where the lamb fell. He is robust and powerful. Around him, eight more rams birth from the soil. They spread about the isle. The rams multiply into great flocks of sheep. They gather about the meadows and graze peacefully. It is here the dream ends."

Baltair sat in thought, having nodded and grunted at Escarans' retelling of his dream. His thick gray eyebrows drew together, and his eyes darkened.

Frang turned his head in his slumber, roused, and opened his eyes. He raised himself on an elbow and looked from the priest to his brother and back again.

Baltair fell against the stone wall, and his eyes searched the astral for instruction. After a long while, he opened his hands, palms up. "The meaning is obvious," he said. "The ewe lamb is symbolic of the virgin Isolba, and the barren land represents the near future of our isle, inhospitable and bearing nae fruit. The shepherd represents you, leader and protector of the Demorians. By slaughtering the lamb and sacrificing her to the gods, the gods will reward you with fertile land and nine powerful sons who will father legions of people. The first son will have Isolba's spirit and will grow to be a great chief of Demoria. You will not lose your daughter, she'll simply reform. Your other wives will bear you eight more sons and your issue will be great. You will be the father of nations of people who inhabit peaceful lands of plenty."

Escarans clutched his stomach, and he quaked in horror at Baltair's words. "But Isolba is my world. How could I destroy her? I would sooner sacrifice myself."

"Because she holds the greatest value to you, her sacrifice will greatly please the gods. They will ken your allegiance. Your people will neither starve nor ken hardship again. Her sacrifice will benefit the clan. If she continues to live in her current form, her future and the future of your people will be bleak, full of suffering and turmoil. You must understand this. She *will* return to you in a new form. You will destroy only her body, not her soul."

"Nae, nae," Escarans replied. He pressed his fists to his temples and shook his head fiercely. Did he yet dream? He longed to wake from this nightmare.

Baltair said, "But 'tis what the gods have asked of you." He remained calm and his voice sounded as convincing as any other time he offered counsel.

"I cannot!"

"Why would you wish to save someone who has plotted to overthrow you for some time now?" Baltair asked in his reasoning tone.

"What say you? You lie!" Escarans cried out. He fell forward and snatched a fistful of Baltair's tunic.

"I do not lie," Baltair said between clenched teeth as he swatted Escarans' hand. "Isolba wanted the chiefdom for herself. She asked you the day you almost drowned in the sea if she could be your heir and you dismissed her. But she has held onto that desire. She has come to me personally for counsel. I told her she must follow your desires by marrying Cormac, but she often asks what she can do to take your place the moment you are unfit to lead."

Frang, at last, broke from his paralysis and interjected, his eyes bulged in anger. "She has spoken of naught else than marrying Cormac. The joy is evident in her face. Is it not against your morals as priest to tell such a lie?"

As Baltair sneered, his bared teeth resembled a provoked hound. "Isolba is an excellent performer. She has fooled everyone into believing she wants to be a wife, but she confided in me. She longs to lead. And she will, but not as Isolba. She will incarnate in the body of your son and become the next chief."

Frang continued to argue with Baltair in a manner frenzied and desperate. Escarans became quiet and reflective as he drew into himself. His mind raced.

Within a short time, Escarans pushed his way out of the tower. From behind the row of men at arms, he announced to the slaves that he would sacrifice no more of them. Then, at the city's gate, before the crofters and fisherfolk, he claimed to have the answer to their woes.

"The gods have given me a message, but I desire time to meditate on the matter," he told them. "I must go alone to the moor and dwell on this."

Dozens of men at arms held back the Demorians when Escarans left the confines of the city gate. Not only the commoners, but the nobles joined the crowd. They shouted and begged for answers, but he ignored them. He wandered across the vast meadows, full of grasses withering in various shades of browns and yellows. The ground sank beneath his heavy footsteps. In the sunless sky, clouds undulated, dark, ominous. Cutting winds beat his body, whipped through his shoulder-length hair, and twisted his long mantle about his legs.

A crowd of people followed his steps, but his men contained the throng. They watched his every move with eyes either eager or darkened with distrust. Escarans knew they loved him, but their hunger and discontent marred their loyalty. They acted more animal than human.

When at last he stopped near the foothills, he fell to his knees. He begged the gods for a sign. Did they truly ask this of him? His love for Isolba softened his anger. She had plotted against him and worked against his wishes. He saw why she craved leadership instead of marriage. Her destiny lay in the chiefdom.

At this point, the sea might never quiet enough for Isolba to travel to the Argarves and marry Cormac. The storms actively prevented her from leaving because, as Escarans realized, it went against the gods' wishes. She remained a child for that very reason. The gods had placed double barriers to impede the marriage. Isolba was meant to die.

If she lived, a bleak future stretched before him. He saw the persistence of inhospitable weather and scarce food sources. He and his people would perish. If it meant the sun would shine once more upon the land, Isolba's sacrifice would not be in vain. If it meant his daughter would return to him as a son with eight brothers to follow, and peace and bounty for his people, fulfilling the priest's counsel was no more a question. He desired sons, more than he realized, and though his daughter was his one treasure on earth, he could trade her for his legacy.

When he believed he had finally convinced himself, his chest grew heavy at the memory of wee Isolba in his lap, her large eyes full of trust. While he hesitated, an old-season lamb hobbled into his line of sight. Malnourished, bedraggled, she foraged between the stones. Her legs trembled with cold and weakness. A sign.

Escarans made up his mind. He walked toward the crowds and declared that with one last sacrifice, not of a slave or commoner, but of a noble, he promised the weather would return to normal. The majority calmed and wondered who the noble could be. Others doubted his claims that another sacrifice would appease the gods. They sought to debate him even as freezing winds pressed the people toward shelter. He asked for patience and time to prove his leadership.

Then he returned home.

The chief went to his youngest wife and told her what Baltair had advised. Moira became wild with grief and shed tears so profuse that moved Escarans to sadness. She pleaded with him for her daughter's life, but he assured her it was for the best. She would find comfort in a new babe. A son.

She drew away from him to cower against the wall. "What of the contract with McCloud?" she asked in a desperate voice. "They expect her arrival."

"'Twill break upon her death. They need not ken how she departed this life. The contract doomed our future and will bring us more misery than our current condition," Escarans replied. "Now go and tell our daughter what she needs to do. Prepare her for the ceremony on Samhain."

"Nae," Moira wept. She struggled for breath. At last, she said, "Was it not I who gave her life? Why must I present her with her death?"

"'Tis not death, but rebirth. Her honor is great. She will come to understand this, as the slaves who sacrificed their lives before understood their duty."

"She is not a slave! She's our daughter and not bound by such duty as the slaves. I beseech you, Husband, do not ask this of her!"

Moira had never once spoken out against his orders. Unused to such defiance, a boiling heat shot through Escarans' veins. He raised his hand to strike her. She dodged the blow. Her eyes flashed with an unusual fierceness, and she darted from his presence.

He did not need her approval, but he did require her cooperation. He knew his plan for Isolba was upsetting, so the fewer people privy to the upcoming ritual, the better. The shroud of humility provided anonymity. No one but those in his inner circle would know it was the jewel of Demoria who approached the altar stone. Once the ritual was complete, it mattered not who discovered her identity. It would be done.

ELEVEN

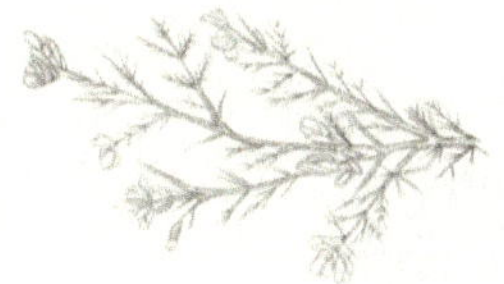

Rindan dangled from Àrdaill's rim, mesmerized by the billowing clouds and raging sea. Below him, the Atlantic pulsed and fumed. From this vantage point, he used to watch the seals as they sunned themselves on the skerries, their fat, slick bellies exposed to the skies. Dolphins and whales once visited too, and he would observe their movements for hours.

Now, turbulent waters roared, and sea creatures steered clear of the dangerous shoreline. He had only the waves to watch. Their frothy peaks formed, dispersed, and formed again.

The second summer since Escarans' visit drew to a close. In that time, no ship arrived to bring provisions or collect rent. His people were destitute and hungry. They could no more subsist on seabirds. Their numbers had plummeted. Storms flooded the puffin burrows, tore the fulmar nests from the cliff ledges. That summer, they ceased migrating. Without their presence, all seemed unnatural and eerie. A sense of doom closed in.

Despite all he had done for her, his grandmother passed earlier that year. She had fallen into a deep sleep. One day, she exhaled without taking another breath. Grew cold. The family had stored her body in a cleit, buried only when the ground thawed with a miserable, wet spring. Others died too.

He was desperate to leave the island. Something outward tugged at his soul. A great emptiness—a hollow within himself—throbbed and ached. A longing, not for adventure or to see the world—simply for something. Something profound. He could neither see it nor grasp it, but it came to him in recurring dreams. *She* came to him. But she did not exist in reality, at least not on Teutatwen.

Water swarmed the base of Stac Worth. The rising tide covered its ithsmus, and no young man could scale its height. Rindan bore no pressing need to climb it and prove his worthiness to take a bride.

Still, he longed for a woman's touch. He feared loneliness and expectations from his parents would force him into an unwanted marriage. To him, the island girls were unremarkable, and he despaired at the idea of settling for one of them. How could anyone else compare when *she* haunted his dreams?

He did not want to dwell on the thought of his ghost—his vision—so climbed to expend his restless energy. It was foolish to come out with the constant threat of storms, but he depended on the exercise and space for deep thought. A fierce gale could sweep him into the sea or throw his body against the rocks. This threat no longer deterred him, but provided a hypothetical relief from the uncertainty.

The wind blew wintery cold that morning. He pulled himself to the clifftop and collected his rope. Dashed over the open land and down to the basin. He removed his clothes and splashed into the hot spring. The sweat of the climb washed away. Heat soaked into muscle and bone. In that moment, his soul went somewhere else, and there, he held his vision, became one with her and all of time and space.

When he reluctantly pulled his clothing on, he noticed a bright shade of green along the far side of the pool. He went to investigate, and crouching, observed a crop of sorrel growing freely in the soil betwixt some stones. The plants stood erect and healthy, vibrant and lush. He pulled a broad leaf from the stem, placed it in his mouth, and tasted the crisp sourness.

The sorrel was the last of the island's vegetation. Perhaps the sloping basin acted as a natural shield from the gales and offered drainage for the torrents. But the growing season was over and winter approached. Devastating storms were on their way, with colder, wetter weather and higher sea swells.

The faint glow behind the clouds told him dawn had well passed, so he snatched the clumps of sorrel and ran toward the bay. When he reached the village, the islanders busied themselves with their daily chores. His mother and sister managed the livestock.

He had dawdled too long and made himself late. Though he needed to tend the sheep and cows, he was eager to share the late crop of sorrel. He dashed into his house, where he found his father tinkering with the loom.

"Father!" he shouted. "Some greens?"

Saithan's eyes grew wide when he saw the sorrel and took the proffered sprig. "Och, aye! Where did you find these?" He crunched down on the leaves with his teeth and threw his head back in delight.

"Near the spring," Rindan said with pride.

"We will boil these and ration the broth with everyone."

"Can we not keep them for ourselves?"

"We could, but that's not right."

"I ken," Rindan conceded. "But with another winter coming, perhaps 'tis time we think about our own family and our survival."

Saithan's eyes flashed, and he shook his head. "Nae, my son. We are together in this. The village *is* our family."

Rindan saw red. Having his father be the constant voice of reason grated on his patience. Ousted his temper. Within their crisis, how could they be entirely selfless?

"*I* discovered it!" he complained. "I may decide to use it to sustain our family where it will do much good and not divided out where it will have wee benefit."

He surprised himself. He had never raised his voice to his

parents. His father was a kindly, relaxed man, yet Rindan's own irritation goaded him. Saithan's eyes widened in his gaunt, bearded face. He looked down at Rindan's hands. They balled into tight fists and crushed the sorrel.

Rindan emitted a grunt of frustration. Dropped the crumpled leaves into Saithan's waiting palms. His agitation at last spilled its banks.

"So you are aware, Father," Rindan roared. "I will leave here when the first ship arrives. And unlike your grandfather, I will not return."

As much as he wished to storm from the house, having driven his point home, he stared his father in the face to watch his reaction. Saithan, ever calm and non-confrontational, remained silent. All joy drained from his face. He looked at the floor, and his lip trembled. He still held the sorrel in his upturned hands.

"Why do you not anger?" Rindan wondered. "Why do you say naught?"

Saithan swallowed and asked quietly, "Rindan, whatever is wrong? Why this angst? This sudden passion manifested somewhere. From where?"

Rindan imagined falling to his knees. Crying at his father's feet. To unleash his troubles in an incoherent stream of confessions. His restlessness and discontent. The angel-faced apparition who haunted his dreams and made his waking hours unbearable. How the loss of his grandparents caused him to look his own mortality in the face, a sight too ghastly to bear. Yet he remained standing, stone-faced.

"This island has become too small for me," was his simple reply.

"Your attitude will change," Saithan said. "We've kent hardship these two years and you wonder if elsewhere kens affliction or not. Anywhere else seems better than here because we suffer, but 'tis not the case. 'Tis your mindset that's wrong. We must make the best of this."

"Forgo the platitudes, Father," Rindan dismissed.

"Nae, you think yourself better than everyone and there lies your misery," Saithan said. "With your kith, you are unhappy unless you come first and best the others."

"Methinks you mistake me for Angus—"

"And Una," Saithan mentioned, breaking Rindan off. "You dismiss her so easily, without thought. She adores you, but you will not give her a single glance. She's a bonny lass, and why you do not take time to become familiar with her is beyond my ken."

"Because Duffy is besotted with her, and I respect my cousin and his desires," Rindan replied.

"But Una has made it clear to Cait that she desires you. Perhaps if Duffy found his nerve to approach her, he would find she carries nae equal feeling and will seek love elsewhere. Encourage him to approach her in the name of progress."

"I prefer not to place myself in the middle of people's relationships," Rindan said. "Perhaps Duffy doesn't approach her because he kens she will reject him. Why not allow a lad to yearn?"

"On account that his yearning has spanned years," Saithan replied. "You are nearly grown. 'Tis time to think about starting a family."

"Did you forget? I'm leaving as soon as I'm able."

"You would stay if you had a family. 'Twould give your mind a proper use than thinking about what lies beyond the sea."

Rindan shook his head. "What if I raise a family and yet long to leave? I would nae longer be able to. I would be bound here."

"Aye, and I would keep my son," Saithan said with a wry laugh.

"Have you nae care for my wishes?" Rindan wondered.

"Methinks your wishes are misplaced. Our island is in a state of crisis. In better times, you will be happier and wish to stay."

"You speak of progress, but I make none with you!" Rindan said, flustered. "I'm late milking the widows' cows."

When Rindan turned toward the door, Saithan quickly said, "Wait. I ask a favor. Samhain approaches. At the festival, I ask you to spend time with Una. Be kind to her. I realize you usually run about with the lads and take your merriment there, but if you could first tarry with her awhile. You may find you like her after all."

Rindan rolled his eyes. He wanted to end the conversation. "Very well, I will do this for you, but I will not be alone with her and upset Duffy. I will do this only if the lads and lasses come together as a group."

"'Tis fair," Saithan replied. "Now go."

With an exhale of relief, Rindan snatched up the milk jug and left the house. His pleasure from finding the sorrel was dashed. The conversation had depleted him of all energy. He loved his father, but the man simply could not understand him and refused to take him seriously. He may as well have spoken to a wall.

He walked the path between the blackhouses, headed toward his sheepfold. He saw Dolag Fleming, belly swollen with her second child. She walked in his direction. His body tensed. All her former sharp edges had rounded, and her pretty face glowed. She beamed. He nodded.

"Good morrow, Rindan," she said like a song. Even her voice had grown husky and more attractive.

His reply was barely audible as he passed. "Good morrow, Guidwife Fleming," he breathed, and held his chest as though his galloping heart would betray him. He did not follow her with his eyes, though he wanted to.

Envy took hold as he thought of her husband, Ellar, who had snagged the one favorable lass the island had to offer. The couple had been married for three years, wed when the sun still shone on the island and all was abundant and fertile–like Dolag's womb. The very thought sent him into unrest.

He banished the thought. Knew it was wrong to think of another man's wife that way. In truth, he had no infatuation. Had hardly brought her to mind, but the idea of her crushed him. Were she available, Dolag was his only suitable choice for a wife. There

was no debate if he should leave the island. He would climb Stac
Worth to prove to everyone—as well as himself—that he could.
That he was a man. And after saying his goodbyes, he would sail
away.

TWELVE

Isolba sat on her chamber floor, spinning yarn. She wondered how her father had calmed his people in such a short time. The terror of hiding in the bower behind rows of men at arms, as horrific shouts and clashing swords rang through the halls, had turned her blood to ice.

The unrest outside the fortress walls had dissipated. The slaves stood down and returned to their daily tasks, though not without tension. Neither the crofters nor the slaves trusted Escarans when he claimed to mend the frayed tether to the gods. For now, they made themselves peaceful and gave him time to come through on his word. Their peace would not last beyond Samhain.

A sickening sense of doom hung in the air. All Isolba could do was distract herself, else she would crumble. Her small fingers deftly fed wool into the tapered rod, and twirled it steadily. Focusing on the consistency of her grist, she pinched the fibers from her clump of wool down, down until they caught the spin. Nareen sat nearby and twisted her own spindle. Their heads bent together in the hearth fire's glow.

During the unrest, their torn sisterhood had mended. Fearful, hysteric, they had clung together for support. While Isolba's mothers kept her calm, she consoled Nareen. She held her tight, rubbed her quaking back, and stroked her hair. They rocked together as Isolba sang soothing songs. Nareen worried that Escarans would sentence all the slaves to death, even those innocent of insurrection. Isolba promised she would come to no harm. Trust returned to Nareen's eyes.

Isolba wished to erase her careless words, but could not. Instead, she did her best to move forward and learn from her mistake. With so much uncertainty in their world, she depended on the security of their friendship.

And so they spun their yarn. They had dropped all mention of their argument. Those long, fearful days sheltered in place seemed distant now. But, as they whiled away the hours in silence, Isolba's nervous fingers caused one too many snags in the filaments.

She whispered curses while Nareen offered glances of pity. The sound of approaching footsteps turned their attention to the doorway. Isolba dropped her spindle. It rolled off her lap, untwisting the wool. Frang stood before them, his face colored gray.

"Isolba," he said. "Your father requests your presence at once."

"Och, what's this?" Isolba uttered. "'Tis late for a meeting. Must be of importance."

Frang gave no reply to quell her curiosity. His mouth formed a grim line, his eyes dark and deep set.

Isolba stared at him with a puzzled expression, stood, and smoothed her rumpled skirts. Nareen laid aside her spindle. The girls followed Frang as he led them through the bower and into the chief's apartments.

When Isolba walked across the threshold, she beheld her father. The gold torc around his neck reflected the braziers' glow. Her mother and Priest Baltair flanked Escarans. Frang stopped to stand near Moira.

The air felt thick and eerie. The expression on her parents' faces shook her. She appeared smaller, waif-like and delicate, the planes of her skull apparent beneath the pale skin. Light cast gruesome shadows across her visage, a predictor of her fate.

With tiny hands clenched, knuckles white, and blue veins

branched across taut tendons, she stepped toward her father. Her head bowed in reverence as she stood submissive. He brought his meaty paws to both sides of her head, kissed her forehead, but no warmth flowed from his lips. An unbearable cold gripped her, and though she had adapted to the lower temperatures of late, this cold was different. It manifested in her core.

Escarans rested his broad hands on his daughter's shoulders as if fitting her with a yoke. She peered into his face and struggled to meet his eyes.

"My daughter," he said with unusual softness. "The time has come for you to save our people. A great honor will be yours to have, but not without strife. I've instructions for you to follow precisely. If you waver, our mission will fail, and you will lose all honor."

"Father, I do not understand," said Isolba. "Does this concern my marriage to Cormac?"

She looked to Moira for placation, but she did not lift her head. Only the neat part in her hair showed, secured with jewel-encrusted combs. Her arms hung before her, hands clasped tight, and shoulders rigid. Her thick lashes blinked fast.

"Och, nae, my darling child," Escarans whispered. He broke his gaze to look at the floor. "The marriage is canceled. You've a greater calling than to live as a wife, a mother, as a woman."

Isolba's stomach dropped. Her eyes widened. "Canceled?" she repeated. Her focus so singular, she had heard nothing else, and the dash of hopes carved deep. She was oblivious to the burden her father's words carried.

"Forget the Argarves. Forget Cormac. You will rule nations, but not in this body. You will die a daughter and return a son."

Her breath caught in her throat. She made a guttural sound and shook her head in incomprehension.

"Priest Baltair prophesied your fate after the gods gave me a dream foretelling the way to save our people. You, Isolba, are the key to our salvation. Baltair will give you the instructions."

Baltair came to stand before Isolba, his face stoic. His priestly robes hung long on the floor. A feldspar stone dangled from his neck by a braided leather cord.

"When you wake in the morning," he began, "you will cease to speak and will fast for three days to purify your body. Your hair will be shorn for humility's purpose and you'll be dressed in simple garments in preparation for your transition. On the third day of your fast, we will secret you to Spirit Hound Cave. Your face shall be shrouded from view, and at nightfall, a ceremony of druids will take place. You will be offered up to the gods in appeasement of their anger.

"Your sacrifice will greatly please the gods. The storms will cease and the sun will shine once again, allowing the crops to grow, livestock to multiply, and seabirds to thrive in their nests. Following the death of your body, your soul will return to your mother's womb as a son. When you are born, you will grow to be a powerful chief in a land that prospers, abundant with riches; a land that will ken nae hunger or hardship."

Isolba trembled. Her narrow shoulders shuddered, then her entire being convulsed. Spasms seized her insides. Sobs tore from her throat. At last, Moira took her in her arms. But Isolba had retreated to an internal place. Could not feel the soft caresses, nor hear the words of comfort. She felt broken then, torn in two, and all the grand plans she had for her life–of marrying Cormac, bearing his heirs, living in comfort, and in a position of great respect–crumbled to dust.

She held her breath and darkness closed in. Her knees buckled, her body drooped, but Frang caught her. With Moira's help, he held her up.

"Have you nae control?" Baltair admonished. "Do not dishonor your father."

He snapped his fingers toward the guards near the door. "Take this one," he ordered, motioning toward Frang. "I see doubt and dissent in him. Ensure he does not leave his chambers until the ceremony is complete."

Escarans gaped at his brother. Said nothing, but nodded at the guards to proceed.

The guards approached Frang and set their hands upon him. He shrugged them off. "Nae, that is not necessary. I am a man of honor and shall walk as one."

He looked at Isolba, who did not meet his eyes. To Moira, he issued a prolonged scowl. She refused to return his gaze. Instead, she held up Isolba, who leaned her entire weight into her. As the guards walked Frang from the chamber, their footsteps faded in the hall. Isolba doubted she would ever see him again.

"Her as well," Baltair said to Escarans, placing a hand on Moira's shoulder. "She cannot leave your chambers. You must remain with her. Do not let her leave your sight."

Escarans grunted in agreement. He had become Baltair's puppet, completely under the priest's control.

Baltair said to Isolba, "Go forth to your chambers and rest this night. When you awake, let your mind find sense and follow the instructions set for you. That is your duty and your honor."

Isolba broke from Moira's arms and, trailed by Nareen, sought refuge inside her rooms. Fear strangled her throat. She craved fresh air and ran to the balcony.

"Gods, save me from this fate," she cried out, head tilted toward the skies, her hands folded, wet by the tears spilling from her eyes. "I do not wish to die! Allow me to disappear so the blade cannot find me. Put light in Father's eyes so he may see reason before it's too late!"

Nareen knelt to meet her mistress on the floor of the balcony, dimly lit in the gloaming. The sea crashed against the bulwark beneath them. She touched one slim, quaking shoulder, extended her other hand toward the pale face, and blotted it with a handkerchief.

"Milady," she said, gentle, subdued. "'Tis not your burden alone to bear, but mine as well. My life's purpose is to serve you, and my life will end with yours. How will I carry on? You are everything to me. Without you I am wretched."

The maidservant's breath hitched, and faint wails escaped, rose from her depths. The wails joined the mournful cries of her mistress. Together they bleated, animal-like, their rueful song echoed in the foundation, through the granite, through the sea.

Could their gods hear them? If only they could intervene and break the waves, split the clouds, allow the sun to shine upon the land, the very fruitless soil that carried death toward the sole heir to the clan throne. They cried together on the floor, held one another for a long time, and in that hour, Isolba shed her self-preservation. She knew what she should do.

"We are cursed," she said, composed herself, and narrowed her wide eyes. "Our land is cursed. We've angered the gods, and I have to surrender. I must save my people. 'Tis the only way. You will forget me in this form and submit to your new life, one of bounty. My sacrifice will appease the gods, and you will ken nae more hunger and cold. The sun will shine again. You will bask in it and ken I bring it to you."

"Oh, milady," Nareen wept. "How can I? I'm devoted to you completely. I would rather throw myself into the sea than live without you."

Isolba replied, "Do not dare! We need to end this cycle of sadness and look toward the beauty ahead. When my soul departs, I promise to come and comfort you."

"But your soul will transfer to your brother's body. You will nae longer be Isolba, but someone completely new, with nae memory of this life as a faithful daughter and beloved friend."

"My soul will bide for some time bodiless, and that is when I shall come to you. Weep nae more, as I've shed my last tear."

Isolba passed a sleepless night staring into her dark bedchamber. Though she had resigned to show obedience and strength, she did so only for Nareen's sake. Inwardly, her chest ached in consternation, and her stomach roiled from the strain on her nerves. She retched into the chamber pot.

Nareen abandoned her pallet on the floor to lie next to her mistress in the bed filled with seabird feathers. It might as well have contained pebbles. It brought no comfort.

The fire in the hearth cast little warmth upon the two small bodies and threw distorted shadows across the stone walls. Twining shadows formed faces. They grinned and gaped in mockery, their eyes empty, horrifying.

With the morning light, Isolba's silent fast began. A pair of druids came to her room, both female. They did not announce their presence. They began their work, their faces stoic. The shears cut with steady, deliberate snips near the scalp. Its crossed-blades slid closed with a metallic clip, then scraped open.

The rhythmic noise reverberated in Isolba's ears. Vacant-eyed, she sat before the hearth while they chopped her long, thick hair. Nareen mourned the silken tresses as they fell, piece by piece. She knelt on the floor, fists full of strands, crying.

Isolba caught one of the druids shaking her head. "Poor child," she whispered. "Why would he ask this? I nae longer recognize our priest."

"Wheesht," the other warned. "They'll hear us."

Isolba pretended not to notice.

As instructed, she spent her first two days in reflection or locked in guided meditation with Priest Baltair. In these sessions, she rehearsed her soul's path upon release from her body.

He repeated, "You are not a body with a soul, but a soul with a body."

Not man, not woman. Not body. Only spirit. Genderless, her soul simply discarded one earthly shell for another—like a hermit crab. No different from the constant cycle of life and death already in motion.

"Your entire consciousness is a soul," he pressed. "Your body is temporary. The ceremony only works if you cut all attachment to your mortal body. You will have nae memory of this life. The sooner you begin thinking of herself as a roaming spirit and not flesh and bone, the sooner you will shed the pain of losing this body."

For two days, Isolba could ingest only wine, but on the third day, her body could take no sustenance. The hunger pangs did not trouble her. Food was the last thought on her mind. One glance at her shorn head in the mirror brought tears. Her large ears stuck out comically from either side of her round head, and she understood why they had cut her hair. It had held so much of her ego, her identity. Her crowning glory! Now it was gone.

The morning of the ceremony, in the hour before dawn, Isolba startled from a fitful sleep. A pair of ice-cold hands gripped her arms. She was certain a specter had entered the room to worry her. Lifting her head, her eyes adjusted to the dark chamber, lit only by embers from a dying fire. She made out the features of her mother's face.

She sat up, nearly cried out in surprise, but remembered the terms of silence. Moira brought her hand to Isolba's head and tenderly stroked the bald crown.

"This is the first moment I could come to you in secret," said Moira. "Escarans imbibed too much. He was awake most of the night, but sleeps at last. I must tell you something."

Isolba nodded and took her mother's hand. Beside her, Nareen sat up. Moira regarded the maidservant briefly, then turned back to Isolba.

"I urge you to go away from this place and hide," Moira said. "Your sacrifice will be in vain, and the ceremony will fail."

Isolba emitted a sharp gasp but did not form words on her tongue.

"You may speak, my child," Moira urged. "This is foolishness. Your father had a dream of a fruitful land with many sons only because that is what he desires most, not because it's a prophecy.

Baltair prizes his position as a counselor so greatly that he will go to any length to prove his power and direct connection to the gods."

"H...how?" Isolba whispered. Her voice sounded strange and foreign to her. "How are you so certain the ceremony won't work?"

"Because Escarans is incapable of fathering children," Moira said. A look of shame crossed her bonny face. "He isn't your true father. Before he took me as his ninth wife, I shared the bed of another man whom I loved. You yet grew in my womb when Escarans wed me. He believes he is your father, but out of nine wives, he's fathered nae children. It would be impossible for him to father nine sons. So you see? You cannot die. You'd never return to me."

Shock rushed Isolba's nerves. The revelation shattered the long-held belief of her paternity. She thought of Escarans' face and compared it to her own. Not a single physical trait matched. She recalled the countless hours sitting on his knee, hearing the stories of ancestors she could no longer call kin.

She had felt Escarans' betrayal by forcing her to the altar stone. Now, she tasted the bitterness of her mother's secret. All were against her. Perhaps death could offer her a peace not felt for years.

"'Tis possible yet for the gods to bless him once he offers me to them," Isolba said.

"Speak not in ignorance like him and Baltair," Moira scolded. "My child, I tell you this so that you may escape."

"But how?" Isolba said, her voice catching. "The druids are coming to take me away at first light."

Her thin back shook with terror. Though Moira and Nareen sought to comfort her, time quickened and dawn approached.

THIRTEEN

The Teutatwens celebrated Samhain on the last day of harvest. Their paltry yields hardly seemed worth the effort. They had nothing to offer the gods in thanks, but their festival went forward. They built a bonfire with piles of peat upon the village green, which had turned a sickly shade of brown. Though the sky misted, they struck iron to flint and sparked flames to life. As darkness descended, firelight filled the village.

Despite everything, they still had their music. They danced around the fire, played lyres, flutes, and drums. Hounds yipped and children screamed as they ran among the dancers and musicians. Voices joined and filled the air with energy. The merrymakers called to their ancestors. Bid them from their barrows.

As famine gripped their bellies, they could give the dead no food, and hoped the ancestors were forgiving. Instead, they left other offerings at the gravesites–trinkets made with bird bones or shells tied with bits of string, and pieces of broken pottery painted with images of the dead.

Rindan was not one to believe his grandparents' spirits could awaken from their tomb to mingle with the crowd. Soberly, he lurked on the periphery and watched the festivities. Finding joy seemed impossible when doom lay at their feet. He did not brighten when Angus and Duffy came to his side. So consumed with besting one another, the two boys lost themselves in nonsensical chatter.

Dolag sat on the sidelines. Her condition made her too cumbersome to dance. Ellar was at her side, and together they clapped and sang. Evidence of their love shone in their eyes. A boastful, proud love. Rindan forced himself to look away.

Cait pranced around the fire, hand in hand with Una. Rindan saw nothing extraordinary about his sister's friend. She jerked in her movements as though stuck to air. The lass in his dreams floated in stride and moved delicately like a choreographed dance. This comparison to Una wrenched his heart. How could he lower his standards to be with such an insipid lass?

His cousin's gaze rested on Una, and her actions clearly delighted him. Duffy quieted in her presence, his eyes downcast while his feet shuffled. He had hinted at his affection for years, but she acted coldly toward him, her romantic intent focused on Rindan. Duffy noticed Rindan's lack of response, his complete absence of interest in any of the girls, and never wavered in his suit.

Angus dominated the conversation between the lads, and Rindan tired of the silly jests. He stepped back, clapped a hand on Duffy's arm, and drew him near. "You wish to dance with Una?" he asked.

Duffy's face went red. With a wince, he said, "Aye, but I've not the nerve."

Though quiet, no one could accuse Rindan of shyness. He pulled Duffy along into the crowd of dancers and walked up to Cait. She wore a wide smile. Her lungs battled for breath. When Una saw Rindan before her, her face lit up, but when they fell on Duffy, she looked away.

"Una, how fare you?" Duffy asked nervously, his upper lip sweaty.

"Fair," she flatly replied. "You?"

"Very well!" he said with unrestrained enthusiasm.

Her eyes hardened toward him, but when she looked back at

Rindan, she softened. "And Rindan, how fare you?" A warm smile played on her lips.

He shrugged. "Well."

The girls continued dancing. Their arms lifted high above their heads and pulsed within the tendrils of acrid smoke. Rindan had no desire to join, so he walked alongside them with Duffy in tow as they circled the bonfire. The drizzle ended, and the blazing heat prickled his skin. Smells of burning peat and sweat mingled in the air. He caught sight of his father and nodded at him, assured he saw him conversing with Una.

Saithan nodded back in approval. He strummed a lyre as his rich voice belted out a joyous tune. Beathag stood near him, clapping her hands in rhythm to the music.

Rindan had to make a true show for Cait, who would surely complain to his parents if he did not fulfill the expectations made of him. But he was not one for idle chatter and had no words. A topic of conversation eluded him as his mind chased subjects. They dodged and hid from reach. His mouth opened as if to speak, and he was certain he looked absurd—all this to appease his family when he wanted no part of it.

Duffy's equal silence proved deafening. He continued to walk awkwardly along. Stole glances at Una at every opportunity. Her hurried looks toward Rindan were not lost and Cait peered around at them, growing flustered.

"Will you lads not dance with us?" she asked.

"Sister, you ken I do not dance," Rindan said with a hollow laugh.

Drops of perspiration spotted Duffy's forehead as he clumsily reached out for Una's hand. "I'll dance!"

Una let him take her hand, though she clasped as limply as a dead fish. She grabbed Rindan. Her palm was slick. He wriggled his fingers to release them. She gripped tighter, and with a jerk, pulled him along. Duffy struggled not to lose her. Cait moved ahead, captured his free hand, and took the lead. Together, the four formed a chain. Rindan, the aft, was the uncooperative link.

Bored and disinterested, he allowed the others to string him along.

Angus bounded in, his tall, wiry frame comical. He raised his arms, swung them from side to side, jumped against the rhythm, and emitted loud whoops in Rindan's ears. Cait laughed at his antics. Rindan cowed, his ears ringing.

Fool, Rindan thought. *Fools, the lot of them.*

"I need water," he told Una, prying his fingers from her grasp.

"Me, likewise," she said breathlessly. "I'll go with you."

Rindan rolled his eyes but could not deny her human need simply because he was uncomfortable. She tried to take his hand again, but he swished his arms back and forth and took long, purposeful strides.

"Wait!" she called. She strove to keep in step as writhing bodies blocked her path.

He did not wait. By the time she caught up with him, he had bent over a large jug of water. Held a ladle to his lips and slurped. Lowered the ladle back into the water, raised it again, and took another hefty gulp before handing it to her.

She plunged the ladle into the jug. He tried to walk away, but she called him back. "Do not leave me!" Her voice sounded high and desperate.

Rindan halted and crossed his arms. He watched her bring the ladle to her mouth, but her jerky motions splashed half the contents down her dress front.

"By Our Lovely Lass, confound it!" she exclaimed and frantically wiped her hands down her bodice.

He chuckled under his breath.

"Does my mishap amuse you?" she asked with a sharp edge to her voice.

Aye, he wished to say. Instead, he said nothing and set his face to stone.

Una's chest rose, and she exhaled a heavy breath with a prolonged *whoosh*. A pout formed on her lips. "Rindan Lennox, you are the most vexing lad I've ever kent!" she declared.

Rindan smirked. He did not care what she thought of him. He wanted her to drink her water so he could return her to Duffy's company, where she was most wanted.

Her hand came to rest on his forearm. He looked around in embarrassment and caught sight of his mother. Beathag noticed him standing with Una and clasped her hands to her breast. Her eyebrows drew together as her mouth formed an O. She sought to encourage him with expression, but he wanted none of it.

"Rindan," Una said, attempting to pull his attention to her. "*Rindan.*"

He turned back toward her, blinking, but fixed his gaze on the ground, on the yellow blades of dead grass and sickly brown mud. A broken fulmar feather stuck out partially from the muck, a remnant of a time when bird hunting filled his world. He longed to cling to a cliffside full of nests, collecting eggs or twisting bird necks, not standing dumb and uncomfortable. He would rather throw himself into the frigid sea than be there.

Una's hand weighed heavy on his arm. Her eyes penetrated his, but he refused to meet them. He sought an escape. The sooner he could extricate himself, the better.

"Rindan," she said again, in a coaxing tone. Now her hand firmly clamped down. She pulled him, stepping back.

She wished to get him alone. That fact was clear. He knew well of couples sneaking away on such nights to find some dark rock crevice, to love each other in their hiding place. Rindan and his lads used to seek them out, to spring upon them, frighten them half to death, and embarrass them. It was the only opportunity for privacy on the island, and Rindan had to ruin it while young and ignorant. Only after Angus bragged about catching Ellar and Dolag in an embrace did Rindan advise the lads to stop.

"Nae, I cannot," Rindan said to Una, his voice firm.

"Do you dislike me?" she asked in a way that expected him to proclaim the opposite.

Yet he wondered if he should go with her for the fun of it. For the distraction of it. He did not wish to lead her on. Not all the couples that ducked behind the view of a crag were serious lovers. But he knew that with Una, she would take the smallest bit of affection and run with it. She would tell Cait who would tell his parents. All three of them would insist he climb Stac Worth in Una's honor and take her as his wife.

"N...not in that way," Rindan stuttered. "You are a friend to me, ken?"

Her face darkened, and she dropped her hand. "'Ello, Duffy," she greeted, looking past Rindan without enthusiasm.

Rindan spun around and found his cousin standing there watching, appearing dejected. He wondered how much of the exchange Duffy had witnessed. Improvising, he pushed Una toward Duffy and she went obediently, confusion writ on her features.

"Will you return to dancing with Duffy?" Rindan proposed.

Una blinked at Duffy, her frustration clear. "Where's Cait?" she asked.

"I ken not," Duffy said, shrugging. "I lost sight of our group and came to find you."

He glared at Rindan, who shook his head and waved his hands in self-defense. He had made the right decision to reject Una, for he would have answered to Duffy. He was not afraid of his cousin —to be pummeled by him would be nothing—but their close family ties and friendship meant far too much to break.

"Go dance," Rindan prodded. "I need to make water and will find you shortly."

It was a lie, but it gave him an easy escape. He bounded into the darkness. His legs rejoiced to the motion and ran faster, making long, easy strides past blackhouses, sheepfolds, and toward the slopes. Giggles echoed from the direction of the open moor where children played night tag.

As he made his way farther from the bonfire and torches, his eyes adjusted to the dark. A faint moon glow throbbed behind the clouds, but the darkness was all-consuming. He slowed his steps, lest he run directly off a cliff.

Instead, he stilled and allowed himself to disappear into that space. He could hear the children's shrieks and laughs, yips of hounds, lows of cows, bleats of sheep, and, most profound of all, waves crashing against the shore. Now part of the island, he fused with the earth, and wondered if this was how death felt.

A series of bellows tore from his throat. The screams lengthened until the notes faded to a pained rasp. His knees kissed the dead grass. He pounded the soft, cold ground with closed fists. Then sat back in exhaustion.

Light footsteps approached, and a furry tail brushed his arm. A warm, soft body leaned against him, and its weight told him it was a large hound. A friend. He put his arm around the beast and lost his fingers in the thick fur. The wetness of a warm tongue lapped at his other hand. They remained there a long while until the hound rose and trotted away. He suddenly felt alone, a foreign emotion for him.

Eventually, he would stumble his way home. When he awoke the following morning, the familiar dread of facing another empty day coiled inside, but sprang away. Something was different. A promise within told him something was coming. *Someone* would come.

FOURTEEN

When Demoria unfolded from its nightly slumber, light flowed in dim and bleak like every day before. The clouded skies stubbornly concealed the sun, and Isolba would not be spared.

Chief Escarans walked to his daughter's chamber and paused by the window. He said to the dark sky, "This day, you will give up the sun. Our standoff ends this day, and you will part the clouds and return our land to its glory."

He trusted his dream. Steadfastly believed in his budding prescience and Baltair's prophecy. He would not entertain the notion of giving up his greatest treasure only to receive nothing in return.

Walking deeper into the space, he found Isolba sprawled before the hearth, her face ashen and drawn. Tracks of tears webbed her cheeks as she lay with her head in her hands. Two druids stood over her, waiting.

Escarans knelt, took her little face in his hands, and kissed the top of her shorn head. She broke from her reverie and shrank from him. Distrust flashed in her eyes like those of a hound beaten by its owner.

"My daughter, today you do a great honor for our people. The gods regard your faithfulness as pure and unerring. Tomorrow, Father Sun shall shine once again. When we see him, we will greet him with unbridled joy, and ken 'twas you who returned him to us."

Isolba closed her eyes so tightly that a new stream of tears flowed. Her dark lashes wet and matted, she brought the tips of her delicate fingers to meet them and shuddered. Despite her look of fragility, Escarans appeared unmoved.

"Goodbye, my dear one," he whispered, his expression serene and hopeful. "When we meet again, you will have taken a new form. Do you remember the journey you must make at your departure and what you will say when you meet the gods face to face?"

Escarans unclasped the last pieces of adornment from her neck. First, the beaded necklace with the engraved kittiwake from Cormac. Then, the triskelion necklace she had worn in constant upon her throat, the very one he had gifted her as a child. Escarans laid the necklaces aside, and a druid handed him a shroud. Spreading the fabric open, he pulled it over her head. Concealed her.

The druids each took one of her arms and led her from the chamber. From behind the fabric, she could faintly make out shapes. Her father's heavy footsteps followed close behind.

As Isolba walked upon the damp stones of the corridor, the shroud hung on her like a veil. It flowed over her shoulders to blend with her white smock. She saw herself as a ghost, a white wisp trailing through the halls. With great care, the druids led her down the stone steps, steep and closed-in, the descent akin to wandering into the depths of the world of the dead.

Upon reaching the main floor, the group went outside into the dark dawn. The gray sky pulsed with the threat of a storm. The druids stood in their dark robes before a large throng, ready to begin their pilgrimage to Spirit Hound Cave. Their shadowy figures were almost menacing, and it was just as well that Isolba could barely see them.

Baltair stepped forward and led the way, followed by Escarans, Isolba and her guides, and the group of druids. Their journey would take a quarter day's travel up steep and rocky terrain as they navigated the mountain path toward the southeastern end of the island.

An hour in, the sky misted, and Isolba soon shivered from the dampness permeating her thin smock. Whipping gales pummeled her as they walked the narrow pass. The crashing waves far below grew fearsome. Her leather shoes turned sodden, and her stockings became sopping wet. Toes chafed, rubbed raw with each wet, squishy footfall.

The druids, protected by their heavy woolen robes and hoods, showed no care for the well-being of their sacrificial lamb and continued at the same brisk pace as before.

By late morning, they reached the high, flat ground above the entrance to the cave. A group of slaves had arrived earlier with three clansmen to oversee their work. The slaves set up tents for the group to enjoy a meal before the day-long ceremonies commenced. They had carried bundles of food, fuel, and earthenware pots on their backs. An open fire burned a short distance from the tents. It wavered and hissed in the wind and rain. The slaves fed it with peat. Joints of meat boiled in a cauldron suspended from poles.

When Isolba felt the warmth of the fire, she tried steering toward it to melt the cold numbness in her limbs, but the druids pushed her to the main tent and forced her to sit. Flat stones covered the ground, and though they were cold and hard to sit upon, her legs found relief after the long walk. The druids at last abandoned their grip on her arms and sat nearby to guard her. They rubbed their weary feet.

Trembling with spine-wracking cold and dread, Isolba awaited the moment of her escape. Moira had promised she would find some way. She and Nareen would formulate a plan. Whatever the method, Isolba prayed it would work.

Her fingers grazed a loose pebble on the ground and clasped it. When she brought it beneath her shroud, she rubbed away the dirt and examined its surface. Though she required sunlight for a proper look, she believed it was a piece of quartzite, its gray and glittery composition a gentle weight in her hand. She squeezed it in her palm and brought it to her chest, allowing the earth's energy to absorb into her.

Isolba meditated while the druids took their meal out in the open, under the misting sky. Clansmen built the fire until it crackled and spat, impervious to the light rain. She heard the druids begin their rituals, speaking in turns to beseech the sun and ask the gods to be merciful, to accept the offering that night, and release the land from its sodden captivity. Focusing inward, she pictured Baltair's dirk missing her flesh and striking the altar stone where the metal crumpled.

As the day wore on, she found it difficult to immerse herself in her meditations. Clan members arrived to join in the ceremony and observe the druids as they sang and chanted. Musicians brought out their drums and pipes, and when they played, the tones vibrated through earth and air, and an eerie sensation rose.

They went through such trouble for her, hoping the gods would save them in exchange for her life. Her position was one of great honor. To escape would shirk her duty to her people, and she could not claim to be part of them. If she was no longer one of the clan, what then was she a part of, and what was her identity?

Losing Clan MacKay seemed far worse than losing her life. Perhaps the prophecy could come true after all, even if Escarans was sterile. Or, it could half realize, and though she would not return, the clouds would break, the sun would warm the isles, and crops could at long last thrive.

Her mind buzzed with confusion, and the hunger and dehydration further muddled her thoughts. She bargained with her ego, her sense of self, and her sense of community and decided that if an escape could not be possible, then she would give herself up to the will of people, to the gods, to the land.

When the sun began its descent toward the horizon, hidden as it was behind thick, black clouds, the island plunged into true darkness. The druids grabbed her arms. Pulled her up and led her to the opening in the cliffside. Another druid stood at the mouth of the cave with a long horn and blew into it so fiercely that a deep, foreboding wail bounced from the cliff face to echo through the chambers of the cave. The sacrificial ceremony was starting, and all were invited to join.

The ceiling of Spirit Hound Cave was as high as three and a half men. The terrain sloped and twisted. Pools pockmarked the floor, made slippery by small streams. Isolba stumbled many times in the pitch black as the glow of torches shone through her shroud. The druids attempted to guide her every step, but they, too, were quite hopeless in navigating the uncertain path.

They walked through a winding corridor for some time until at last the air opened up and they arrived at the Great Room, a wide, yawning chamber. Its smooth walls sloped up into a recessed alcove that formed a natural circular balcony. Braziers sat around this crevasse, illuminating the chamber like the grandest of cathedrals.

Isolba remembered well what existed within the chamber. The altar stone sat in the center, a wide slab of sandstone stained a rusty shade. Staked to the rear of the chamber, an enormous skull watched over the premises. It bore double rows of teeth and incisors as sharp as knife-points.

Escarans once told Isolba that the skull remained from an individual belonging to an ancient race of giants. Long ago, the great flood wiped them out, but legend said some either survived or reanimated. She supposed it could be true. As old as the skull was, it could not have coexisted with the time of the flood. No one knew where the skull had come from. It served as a proud relic of the mystical world.

Drummers pounded a slow and haunting beat in the back of the chamber, sending vibrations across every surface. The druids laid Isolba down on the altar and, as her body met the cold stone, she trembled violently. Her stomach flopped, and the precious piece of quartzite fell from her open hand.

The sacrificial ceremony had begun, yet she had received no sign from her mother. She began to panic, her senses sharpening. She lay for an eternity as the druids and clanspeople filed into the room. When space became too cramped, many lined the corridor.

She might have run at any moment that day, only to meet easy recapture. Her unbound hands and feet dangled and would remain free until the very last, when the druids would secure her to poles. As honorable as the position of sacrificial lamb was, self-preservation usually kicked in the minute a sharp blade met skin. She stayed dutiful and complicit, hoping against hope that Moira's plan for an escape was already in motion.

The time came to summon the gods. Moira and the other wives danced in a circular formation around Isolba. Their bodies swayed, arms lifted as they beckoned the gods to join them. Bid them to notice the gift on the altar. The air filled with energy, grew heavy with vibrations. Voluminous dresses and robes whipped about in every direction.

But as the room spun with spiritual force, the lights snuffed out. One by one, they extinguished in rapid order. As though someone ran along the upper crevasse with superhuman speed. The Great Room plunged into absolute darkness. Shrieks of surprise filled the chamber and echoed from the walls.

Among the noise and distraction, her mother's voice whispered in her ear. "Come. Under my skirts!"

In one swift motion, Moira cast the fabric of her dress over her daughter like a fishing net. Isolba rose from the stone slab and dove against her mother's legs. The skirts fell around her. Enveloped her with warmth, though her teeth chattered. Moira moved her legs in small steps. Concealed her daughter beneath its folds.

Isolba tore off the shroud. All was black. She moved with her mother in a crouched position. Her bones ached, the cold sweat of fear slick on her skin.

Bodies jostled against one another in the chaos while Moira worked her way out. She moved between dancers and spectators. Groped until she found the sloping cave wall close to the exit. She bent and took hold of Isolba with such force that her arm nearly wrenched from its socket.

They wove through the dark corridor and bumped into bodies as they clawed their way to the opening. Isolba reached with one searching hand. She clung to her mother with the other. When her knee struck a jutting rock, she yelped.

"Don't stop!" Moira whispered.

Isolba hissed between her teeth. Hobbled forward. Her knee throbbed and her heart pained with every beat. When they neared the exit, they saw no more people and quickened their pace. At last, the shift to dim moonlight revealed the craggy hillside.

"My child," Moira said briskly. "You need to change your clothes, and quick."

A shadowy figure slid from the cave opening. "Milady!" the figure whispered. It was Nareen.

Isolba threw her arms around her. Held her tight. "You put out the lights?"

"Aye, with help," Nareen said, breathless. With urgency, she pushed a bundle of garments into Isolba's hands. "Put these on."

Isolba asked no questions. With Moira and Nareen's help, she lifted the wet smock from her body. Pulled on a pair of men's breeks and a tunic. Darkness made their efforts clumsy. Nareen placed a rucksack on Isolba's shoulder and coaxed her toward the cliffside.

"Make your way down with care," Moira instructed. "Find the southern shore. I'll meet you there."

Isolba panicked. She would have to escape on her own, with no sense of direction, and somehow arrive at a specified meeting place. "Can Nareen come with me?"

Nareen faltered. "Nae...Isolba—"

"She cannot," Moira interrupted. "Isolba, run! We've nae time. Go far from here. Go!"

Isolba looked toward her mother in terror, then at Nareen. The maid's wide eyes held not only warmth and earnestness, but sadness too. Their years together had ended, but time did not allow for goodbyes. Isolba embraced her again, squeezing, unwilling to release her. But she broke away and briefly hugged her mother. As she turned and made her first stumbling steps down the rocks, she looked back. The pair watched with mournful gazes.

"Daughter, you're the beat of my pulse," Moira whispered. "I shall see you soon."

They disappeared inside the mouth of the cave.

FIFTEEN

In the pitch-black chaos, a clansman climbed to the alcove and relit the braziers. He was unwieldy in the dark and struggled. Several minutes passed while the chamber refilled with light. A second clansman ignited the torches in the corridor.

Dismayed cries erupted from a few of Escarans' wives upon noticing the empty stone slab. The old chief sought to calm his people. They had forgotten the music and dancing for confusion and upset. The throng looked at him for an explanation, but he had none to give. He stood, perhaps more perplexed than the lot of them. His shock briefly lasted as fire licked his sternum. Swelled through his crown in boiling waves of rage.

"Everyone, I ask for your attention," his gruff voice boomed. "Cover the exit. Find our sacrifice, else our ceremony cannot continue."

Moira stood near the exit. His eyes narrowed with suspicion, and he quickly closed the gap between them.

"Wife, where has she gone? I've nae doubt you're responsible for this disorder."

"I ken not. I've taken nae part in this," she responded coldly. "Perhaps others who stand against you have caused this."

He grunted, dismissing her with irritation. He whipped about in fervent search. His hopes, plans, and his very world fell away. The disarray surrounding him fueled his rancor all the more, the questioning expressions on his people's faces an embarrassment to his leadership. They had primed for a sacrifice, eager to see blood spilled in the name of saving their island.

Then, shouts of surprise echoed through the chamber. The crowd parted. In their midst stood a slight form cloaked in a white smock and shroud, shivering there alone.

Escarans collected his faculties. Straightened. He said loud and clear, "Our sacrifice has returned. Let us continue our ritual."

The druids closed in. Surrounded the shrouded figure and led her to the stone slab. Spread her across its breadth. They bound her hands and feet and tied them to four poles driven into the rocky soil at each corner of the rock. Whimpers sounded from behind the shroud.

A steady rebirth of drum tapping drowned out the cries. Horns and pipes joined the rhythm, slow at first, and picking up speed, remitted waves of excitement through every witness. The wives sidestepped, swayed with combined fluidity, and circled once more around the sacrifice. This time without the youngest wife.

Moira stood frozen at the mouth of the cave. Escarans remained beside her while he watched the ceremony unfold, transfixed. He was at ease once again, though perplexed by the events. It was not as though he could punish Isolba further for her insolence. Had she not recanted her error of attempted escape, found reason, and returned?

The druids convulsed their bodies in ardent dance, used their motions to summon the deities and welcome them to join the ritual. Priest Baltair watched over them, stone-faced, breathing heavily, and offered his body for total possession. His eyes rolled back, and the whites of them blazed in the torchlight. Peat smoke churned thick and heady in the damp cavern air.

The wives dispersed as Baltair walked slowly toward the sacrifice. He gripped a staff topped with a carved hound's head, its eyes wild, its tongue rolled from the snarling mouth. Two druids followed. One carried a dirk sheathed in sheepskin, and the other a bowl formed from a sawn-off skull.

The dancers stopped and cleared the floor around the sandstone slab. The music faded to the beat of a lone drum. It pounded. *Badum. Badum. Badum.* Slow, steady, and haunting. *Boom!*

Escarans came forward, pressed Moira alongside him, and they stopped at the foot of the altar stone. Moira stood like a statue, rigid and cold, mouth parted. With eyes alight, the chief smiled and beckoned his other wives to stand with him. They formed a circle.

The drumbeats quickened. *Badum. Badum. Badum.*

Baltair chanted deep and guttural. The tones echoed through the chamber and divided into many voices. The assembly repeated his chants, and the damp air hummed with the haunting melody. Arms swung like pendulums, souls surrendered to the gods and welcomed all spirits to commune. Baltair handed his staff to a druid, who laid it aside, unsheathed the dirk, and placed it in the priest's open palms.

He held the blade over the sacrifice. At last, they reached the point of no return. Escarans closed his eyes. Licked his lips in anticipation.

Baltair grasped the handle and bent toward the sacrifice's extended arm. The vulnerable veins throbbed beneath the skin. His blade pierced the line of birthmarks dotting the flesh. With one expert cut, long and deep, shrieks of agony erupted from the sacrifice.

Blood rushed from the opening. A druid placed the skull bowl beneath the wound and began filling it. Baltair stepped toward the other wrist and repeated the motion. They filled a second bowl. Moira closed her eyes as screams filled the air. She had witnessed the ritual so many times she had numbed to it. But something within her broke.

"The blood is the life," said Baltair, and all repeated the words.

The blood is the life.

He drank first from the bowl. Handed it to Escarans, who freely gulped as if in trance. Moira and the wives each had their turn. When she brought the bowl to her lips, she did not drink.

The second bowl was passed among the spectators. The druids refilled the skull bowls, sipped. Lips stained, the sharp, metallic odor filled the chamber. Lingered on breath. In time, the screams of the sacrifice quieted as her poor, withered body drained. Her heartbeats slowed and languished. Baltair dealt the fatal blow. He took up the dirk and drove it into the heart. Ended her life and ended the ceremony.

Revelry ensued. The islanders departed the cave and returned to the summit, where the slaves had built the bonfire high and bursting. Fought the spitting sky and fierce winds.

Cold no longer pervaded nerves fortified by alcohol. They drank casks of mead and wine. So certain that the land would return to its abundant state by morning, they ate the remaining stores of food. Consumed the dried flesh of fish, lobsters, and seabirds with abandon.

Escarans seemed pleased. He ate and drank with relish. His eyes, beady in the gold firelight, followed the dancers as they pranced about the flames, wild, without thought or care.

Moira had no stomach for eating and hung back from the revelry. With a shiver, she pulled her woolen mantle closed. She had to return to the cave, but would need help. She found a slave boy and bid him follow. They traversed the corridor leading into the great room. The lights within had dimmed, the peat nearly burned through. The sacrifice lay alone on the stone slab. Blood saturated the white smock and shroud.

Together, they untied the ropes and released the limbs. They knelt to pick up the body, their burden light with the combined effort and small size of the dead girl. When they slipped into a narrow passage that went deeper into the cave, no light reached there, and they stumbled on uneven ground. Moira returned to the Great Room for a torch. After prying the bundle of reeds from its fastening, she turned and saw a face. Escarans loomed before her. She shrieked.

"Wife!" he said with unexpected gentleness. "Have you moved her so soon? I wish to say farewell to our daughter."

Moira's breath left her. With a strained inhale, she explained, "I could not bear her lying there and wished to move her to the burial chamber."

"'Tis nae matter, as 'tis finished." He eyed her with distrust and pushed her from the path. Walked swiftly through the corridor where he found the boy.

"Away," he ordered, and motioned for him to leave.

The chief knelt to pick up the body and cradled it to his chest. Moira followed him as he walked with care along the narrow way. Her heartbeat thrummed in her ears.

"If you could hold up the light," Escarans instructed.

Moira lifted the torch to better illuminate the corridor ahead, which opened into a small enclosed room. A horrifying stench wafted from within. Moira covered her nose with her free hand and gagged. Corpses in various stages of decomposition lay piled inside. Some had curdled blood crusted on their clothing. Others had reduced to near bone, with dried bits of flesh attached to skulls, their jaws wide in silent screams.

Moira choked back the stomach acid welling in her throat. Escarans seemed much unaffected and laid his burden among the remains with care.

"'Tisn't right to leave her amongst the bones of slaves," he said. "But we must equalize her body with those of low birth. This is nae longer our daughter."

Moira said nothing. Wanted badly for him to return outside and lose himself in inebriation. Then she could slip away and flee.

"Our wee daughter is on her way to her transformation. At this moment, she convenes with the gods and bargains for Demoria's return to prosperity. You will lie with me tonight and conceive a son. Isolba's soul requires a new body when she completes her task."

She stood in silence. Her mind raced. Did he plan to lie with her straight away or after the celebrations when she would have made her escape long before? In any case, it was imperative to move him far from the body. He knelt with his hands over the bloodied shroud and tugged at the fabric.

"Stop!" she cried. "Let us not look upon her!"

Escarans did not heed her, and Moira stepped back. She had to flee at once.

Escarans called out, "Return with the torch. I cannot see her!"

She skittered backward. He indignantly raised himself, a difficult task with his size. He stumbled into the corridor, found Moira before she retreated, and wrested the torch from her grasp. She fled into the darkness. Rapid footfalls faded.

Escarans turned back to the burial chamber and shone the light within, illuminated the floor where he had left his daughter. With his opposite hand, he peeled the shroud away. He expected to see Isolba in her eternal slumber, with her sweet, heart-shaped face reposed. Instead, peering up at him were the glazed eyes of the slave girl, Nareen, fixed in death's clutch.

Sixteen

Through the night, Isolba huddled between two boulders and waited for her mother. She had descended the perilous cliffside in near-perfect darkness and groped her way downward. Her feet slipped and slid on the damp, unstable rock surface. The moon, though obscured behind clouds, lit the night with a faint, phantasmal glow. By this dim light, she had found the rocky foreshore, crawled over stones and sand, and made her way to the southernmost point of Demoria.

Though tired and weak, she forced herself to remain awake. She watched for the light of a torch and pricked her ears for the sound of Moira's voice. It rained no more that night, and for that, she was mortally thankful. Her tunic remained dry, and though she trembled in the cool night air, it retained enough body heat to preserve her until morning.

She waited for Moira as the sun ascended behind the murky clouds and waited yet as it climbed to a midpoint in the sky. While digging inside her rucksack for the waterskin, her hand closed around a familiar shape. She pulled out her triskelion necklace and ran her fingers across its engraved surface. Reaching in again, she discovered the kittiwake charm from her betrothed.

Either her mother or Nareen had thought to drop her most

treasured possessions into the rucksack as they planned her escape. She clasped the jewelry around her neck and reclaimed some of her former self. The old necklace held a fragment of her lost identity. The new one promised her a future with Cormac.

As the day wore on, Isolba depleted the small store of food and water in her rucksack. She looked for a spring but found none. Thirst gripped her throat as she stared longingly at the waves crashing against the shore. She knew well the danger of drinking seawater. It could fell a hardy man with an unquenchable thirst and drive him to madness.

A pit formed in her stomach. By degrees, she accepted that her mother could not come. Moira could not complete her plan, and Isolba feared her father had detained or harmed her. For her preservation, she had to move on, though the fear of facing whatever lay ahead–alone–paralyzed her.

She decided that the southwest side of the island would be far enough away from the settlement that she could find a fresh spring and forage for food, though the success of finding the latter seemed futile. She needed to find shelter, ideally a den far from Spirit Hound Cave.

Perhaps if she bided her time, nature would right itself, allow the sun to shine, and she could return home. Then, she would be certain of any harm made to her mother, a thought she refused to entertain. The very idea broke her.

Instead, she walked the shoreline in search of a cave opening while also watching the incoming tide for sea life to scrounge. Yet as the turbulent waters rolled into shore and drew back, no spoils remained, not even seaweed. Soon, she lost the shoreline completely to ragged cliffs. Then she came across an inlet marring the coast and walked its perimeter, steering clear of the steep drop-offs where the waters had eroded the rocks in a vertical cut.

She moved in, intent on staying low and out of sight, but the lower inland soil was incredibly boggy. So she walked an uncertain line between high slopes and sinking muck. Oft times, a flock of bedraggled sheep dotted a hillside. Their noses pushed between rock clusters as they sought rare vegetation.

White mist overlaid the varied shades of browns and grays of the landscape, and despite her misery, she could not deny its beauty. Acres of stone wilderness stretched far and wide, and the distance to Brochnall Castle measured too far to make out its shape.

No homes of crofters or fisherfolk sat here, the terrain too inhospitable to support life. Bedrock strata built up the outlying cliffs with horizontal rows of red and brown. The soil lay thin in most places and nonexistent in others. Ancient volcanic formations stretched upward with jagged pillars or yawned open with deep chasms where seawater carved underground channels.

The coastline reappeared with a thin trail of stony sand and low, rocky outcroppings, but a swift temperature drop announced a storm. The tide swelled higher, encroached on the shore. She maintained high ground and sought shelter from the oncoming rain. Traversing a stony embankment, bones aching and muscles straining, she pondered the absurdity of it all. Why prolong inevitable death? If she did not freeze to death first, she would surely starve. Either way, she would suffer.

"I am finished," she said to herself. "I've escaped one unpleasant fate to greet another."

The thought of going back to meet Baltair's dirk caused her to shudder. She wanted to live. She only needed to reach Cormac. Somehow survive. "Och, gods, perhaps there is another way."

When she came upon an overhanging rock that formed a crude shelter, at least from the rain, she slipped beneath it. She leaned out and lifted her head, open-mouthed, toward the sky. As the rain plummeted onto her tongue, first in patters, then in thick droplets, she swallowed away the parched, sandy sensation in her throat.

Though the rain addressed the dryness of her mouth, the droplets did not slake her extreme thirst. Soon the rain funneled over the rocks and created tiny rivulets that waterfalled over the edge of her shelter. She held out her waterskin and began filling it.

She regularly pulled it away to gulp an inch or two of collected rain before pushing it back for more.

At last, collapsing to rest within her shelter, she ran her fingers over the limestone walls and found irregularities in the grainy texture. She marveled at the fossilized seashells suspended in stone. Shooing away fears and worries, she daydreamed of Cormac. If she could reach him, he would set her situation right and offer her protection. Soon, she would return to her cozy existence.

Would Clan McCloud seek revenge for her father's decision to break the marriage contract? Once they discovered the truth, nothing would stop them from declaring war on Demoria. She could not bear the thought of harm coming to her people, but who else could save her mother and Nareen?

After her anxious thoughts cycled for several rounds, she fell asleep to rain thrumming stone. Rain infiltrated her dreams, becoming the steady succession of drumbeats leading her to slaughter. Her heart pulsed to the rhythm of the drums. Throbbed as if readying to burst. As her body lay pinned atop the sacrificial slab, dancing bodies undulated around. They twisted and turned, legs and arms swirling through the air as if made of thick mud. The heads were faceless where a smear of skin supplanted all identity. Her body convulsed with horror.

Hot breath hit her cheek. She awoke abruptly to a large, wet nose and broad snout. Shrinking, she fought the film of broken sleep to discern the shape of a huge black hound standing over her.

Was it the Coin-Sith? She lay still, elbows drawn down with fists clenched upward, and braced for attack. When she tried to suppress her breathing, it rattled in her throat. Her eyes squeezed shut.

He sniffed and snorted. His warm exhale brushed her face. She reopened her eyes. The great hound stood panting. His amber eyes gleamed as he observed her, the curiosity that she was. She deliberated whether he thought of her as a meal—his sharp teeth and massive paws mere inches away—or if he belonged to someone and explored the rock crevasses in search of mice. Her breathing hitched at the thought another person could be nearby. She longed for her mother.

The storm had ended, and though Isolba sat in a pool of damp, the fur on the large hound remained dry, smooth, and unlike the tangled mats of other island hounds. He also appeared much larger and with a coloring that did not match any breed of mutt manufactured on Demoria. His ears stood erect, rounded slightly at the tips, and his fur grew long and thick. His eyebrows twitched as he regarded her with intelligent eyes and then looked away, turned his head toward the sea, and sniffed the air.

The hound tensed, hackles raised. From a distance, the sound of barks and yips carried on the breeze. The black hound bared his teeth and growled low in his throat. Shivers tickled Isolba's spine. He stayed that way for some time while she remained still, curled under her shelter. All at once, deep bellows tore from his throat. He took off, ran toward the ridge, and frantically paced.

Curiosity took over, and she emerged from her shelter. She crouched several feet behind the hound to see what caused his unrest. Movement from beneath the ridge caught her eye before she made sense of the far shapes. A pair of hounds climbed the rocky terrain, heads down, sniffing. Each went one way, stopping to smell the air, before doubling back toward one another. They seemed to follow a scent trail, and it took her far too long to realize it was hers. They homed in on their target.

Several heads emerged from behind the ridge as a group of clansmen crested the hill. She did not wait to find out if her father walked among them, but fled. Vicious snarls rang out behind her as the black hound headed off the pair of search hounds. When she heard their yowls and yips, she assumed they pulled back, matchless against the black hound. Why did the strange creature desire to help her? Neither had she fed him, sheltered him, nor earned his protection in any way.

She clambered down the exposed outcropping of the western shore. Once she reached the shoreline, she determined to run as far from her pursuers as possible. But her lungs burned with exertion.

A crick in her side stopped her short, yet she could not afford to linger.

The waves of the Atlantic lapped at her feet, and when she looked across the lurching swells, she noticed a blot upon the sea. She squinted, and as she focused, discerned low-lying mountains and a craggy shoreline within a small landmass. A few scattered stacs reached from the water at various points around the land-form and puzzled her. Where was she?

She did not know geography. She had spent her life in and around the castle and only traveled to the far summit now and again. Never had she trod this side of the island, and could not say what lay nearby. The Argarves sat to the southeast of Demoria, but she was so turned around and exhausted, she knew not what was north and what was south. She wanted to believe she looked at the Argarves where her betrothed lived. If Cormac knew of her predicament, he would offer her safety. She looked about in vain for a boat but saw none. Even if she did, the swells bucked so high they would swallow a small craft in an instant. It was useless. She would have to keep following the shore.

The black hound tore down the cliffside, deftly jumping clefts, and raced toward her. Yipping hounds gave chase on the flatland above. Clansmen followed. She tried to run again, but the black hound rushed her, nipped her ankles. Forced her into the surf. Her numbed nerves barely sensed the frigid water soaking her shoes. The hound sloshed ahead through the ripping tide, and she turned back. The search hounds charged down the slope. She whipped around and peered desperately at the black hound. He directed his snout toward the far island. She understood then, but could not grasp why he asked it of her.

"Nae, you mindless beast!" Isolba shouted. "I cannot swim, and you want me to go in that? I will drown for certain if you have a care!"

He slanted his eyes toward her in reproof. She stubbornly shook her head, and he forged through the tide. He reached deeper water and paddled furiously against the waves. His eyes beckoned.

She looked back again, observed the approaching clansmen. She had no choice. Death by waves or death by dirk, she preferred the path of lesser pain.

As she dove into the water, the icy shock pierced through her core. She tumbled feet over head beneath the force of the waves. The powerful sea pulsed with life and strength. It did not ask for respect, but demanded it. Swept her into its mercy.

Struggling to keep her mouth above the surface, she startled from a touch on her ankle. Fingers wrapped around her leg and tugged. With a half-realized yelp, she sank into the murk. Shapes circled. Humanoid figures darted in and out of her vision. More icy fingers grabbed. Jerked her about. Pulled her deeper. They moved in close, and when her eyes adjusted, she saw their faces.

The drowned galley slaves. They stared with hollow eyes and gaping mouths. They clawed her limbs with harried desperation. Did they seek revenge? Intend to steal her soul, as the sea had taken theirs? In terror, she inhaled a burning gulp of saltwater.

All senses vanished. She became one with the black. Cradled and comforted with a sudden lack of existence. The groping fingers withdrew. Fear abandoned her. She had no urge to breathe nor impulse to push upward. She remained there, weightless in her new form. Her past, her person, mattered no more. All motivation, desire, and ego dissolved. She blended with the waters. Diminished to salt crystals.

If time passed and at what rate, she had no way of knowing. The sea had snatched her away. Perhaps the gods had at last taken their sacrifice by any available means. She could not outrun fate, and the helpful beast had driven her into the surging mass of seawater. Would her soul now begin the journey toward her next life? She waited, at last at rest, her battle over.

The sensation of solid ground startled her. Her eyes opened. She knelt on the shoreline of a vast island. Before her spread a meadow, lush green and dotted with small pink and purple flowers. The clear blue sky stretched out brilliantly, and in the distance, a shining city sprouted. Mansions of silver and gold stood solid behind a fortress, its curved marble walls receding in the distance at left and right. The city appeared endless and melted into the horizon.

A crystalline body of water lay at her back. When she turned to peer within its depths, she saw sea creatures teeming within. Schools of fish darted betwixt one another while blooms of undulating jellyfish throbbed and swayed in the dark. Lobsters and crabs scuttled lazily along the bank. Turtles sunned themselves on the flat rocks edging the sand. Fat seals broke the surface to stare at her with their large, liquid eyes. A pair of sleek dolphins popped up, dousing her with salt spray, and chattered as if beckoning her to tarry. She watched with breathless wonder for several moments, hardly able to pull away, but refocused on the grand city and her obligation to her people.

She took her first step into the meadow, expecting to feel weightless, but the cuts on her feet sent ripples of pain up her legs. Her haggard lungs rattled with aspirated seawater, and she coughed. She once imagined death to be freeing, to arrive at a place and forget all pain, hunger, or sadness. She appeared to be herself, as far as she could tell. Her men's clothing hung wet and heavy from her body and a slight breeze brushed across her naked head. She strode through the heather, feet sinking in the spongy soil, headed for the great city to plead the case of her people.

Her eye caught a slight figure standing far into the grassland. When she drew closer, her breath cut short. Nareen. The maid bore a serene smile on her face as she knelt to smell the wildflowers. Her long brown hair hung loosely down her back and she wore a white linen dress finer than anything she had donned in Demoria. Why was Nareen here in this place? She did not belong anywhere but home.

"Nareen!" Isolba called, her voice gripped with panic.

Nareen turned and, seeing her mistress, smiled wide and waved at her, but said nothing. Isolba picked up her pace and tried to run toward the maid as quickly as her pained feet would allow. The sound of hoofbeats thundered nearby. She froze. As if he emerged from the mist, a figure of a man astride a white horse moved toward her. Such an animal she knew only from drawings, never witnessed in life. Mesmerized, she watched its muscular flanks ripple with each graceful motion as its white mane and tail flowed in the breeze.

The man wore a blonde beard and his long hair tied back, secured with a small gold band. His blue linen tunic hung long on his fit, muscular frame. A deep indigo mantle fastened at his shoulder with an elaborate brooch, inset with amber and jewels. The straps of his leather sandals wrapped across his bare shins and the footwear bore gold clasps and decorations. A gold torc shined from his throat with matching bands on his biceps and wrists.

As he rode closer, Isolba noticed his eyes, such a pale shade that they blended with his sclera. He halted the horse before her and stared, his blonde brows furrowed. She peered up at him with hope.

"Why do you trespass here?" he asked. His deep voice shook her tiny frame.

Fear entered her heart, and she looked at Nareen, who remained several yards away, content with the flowers. The maid was not herself, but Isolba had no time to dwell on that. Nareen's presence had not been part of the plan the druids had outlined for her.

Her voice trembled. "I am Isolba, daughter of Lord Escarans, Chief of Clan MacKay, and I come to offer my soul for the salvation of Demoria."

"You need to leave at once," the man barked. "I fathom not how you came here, but you cannot stay."

Isolba nearly shouted with desperation. "Nae. Priest Baltair sent me and I cannot leave until I speak with the gods and ask them—or perhaps you—to reverse the blight on our island and send my soul into the body of a bairn conceived within my mother's womb."

She did not know if this man was himself a god, as he had not taken the time to introduce himself, but he became more irritated by her words.

"You spout nonsense when I demand you leave!" he shouted with such vociferation that she shrank into the heather. "No mortal may trespass here. Go now!"

Her throat ached. Tears stung her eyes. Something was not right. "But Nareen is mortal," she said, "and you've not asked her to leave. I cannot go until I speak with the gods."

The man sneered. "That lass isn't mortal. 'Tis you who are flesh and unwelcome here!"

His voice cracked with his last words, and Isolba grasped his severity. She could not understand what he meant, but had no time to dwell on why the maid would be there. She had to lay her case before him.

"I'm a sacrifice, a gift to the gods, so I may convene with them," Isolba babbled. "I–"

"You humans with your sacrifices," he interrupted, shaking his head. "Who do you believe you sacrifice to? The gods?" He snickered and continued, "Allow me to assert that your sacrifices only give power to the darkness and drive your sorrows deeper."

"But Baltair said..." Isolba began, her words fumbling.

"You must turn back now," the rider demanded. "I waste enough breath on you. Go!"

Isolba reached out a hand for her maid. "Nareen! Help me!" But the maid did not look her way.

The man charged the horse toward her, and the clopping hooves stomped the grass at her feet. Her heart whacked her ribcage. Hot blood surged through her veins. She walked backward but tripped on the underbrush. Fell roughly to the ground. Flipped onto her hands and knees. Crawled to shore. Flinched from each massive hoof as they landed behind her. Their crushing force barely missed her. The terror did not end until she fell into the water.

She screamed. Her body plunged into the crystal clear abyss and the sand bank fell away. She sank deeper and deeper. The world overturned and she had no sense of what was up and what was down.

A hot, wet head emerged from beneath her and pushed. The water's surface broke over her head and she gulped a sharp breath. Through bleary eyes, she could tell she drifted once more in murky seawater, with the hound's body keeping her afloat. She threw her arms around him and clung to his wet fur.

Certain that her weight would pull him under and drown them both, she could not be sure if she was alive. Nothing she had experienced since first entering the water made sense. Where had she gone? Who was this hound and where did he take her?

She held on tighter as he forged ahead. If she still lived, she had to remain so. According to the horseman, her sacrifice was useless.

The hound's muscles tensed, and he persisted. Isolba had not realized how big and heavy he was. He used his broad and powerful paws to paddle against the whitecaps. Though the waters relentlessly pushed them back, the hound thrust forward. When the swells came at them, the waves rushed over their heads, but the hound's strength steadied them. Between each surge, she breathed precious air. When a new wave approached, she held her breath, shut her eyes, and held on with all she had.

How far out at sea were they? Did they remain in the Atlantic or in foreign waters? Its familiar color and smell told her it was. She tried to focus on each swell and manage her breaths. Her legs kicked wildly behind her. The slick bodies of fish brushed past. She watched their silvery shapes swim with them, against them. Slimy seaweed tangled around her ankles and draped over her ears.

Her body grew inept, drained of all energy, but the hound maintained his strength. Her grip loosened, fingers slipped through wet fur, but the hound nipped and urged her awake. They continued this pattern. Bore through the swells. When she wearied, his teeth gnashed. Forced alertness.

Then she saw it. In the distance sat the island she had first noticed from Demoria's shore. It had to be the Argarves. They were closer now. If they continued as they were, they could reach it.

What a marvel she was alive, though any of the swells could drag her under for good. Could the hound lose traction? Surely, he could not keep going against such resistance, carrying his burden. Yet, he powered on. She found herself too far gone to further ponder his motive, but fought the pulling darkness. She retained enough faculty to hold on, but could no more kick up momentum. Her body weighed as heavy as stone. To let go would mean dropping to the bottom of the Atlantic—or back to that strange land.

She discarded the thought, uncertain if the experience had been real. Perhaps she had inhaled water and lost consciousness before the hound brought her up again. It may have been a dream, one she dared not dwell on. They drew closer to the Argarves and closer to Cormac. She could think only of him and the safety within his arms.

The mountains sloped above her, and through blurred eyes, she could see wide open moors dotted with sheep, huddled in groups against the driving gales. Simple stone houses rested in the valley. No grand city nor large castle occupied this land. The Argarves defied her expectations. Where lay the modernity her father spoke of? And where were the numerous smaller islands forming the archipelago of the Argarves?

The hound swam her past a massive stac rooted only a hundred feet from the stony shore. They had survived. But before they reached land, the hound's solidity left her.

Seventeen

"Och, you poor wee lad," a man's voice said, so gentle and with no sense of alarm.

Isolba stirred awake. She lay against the rocks of the shore, halfway in the water as the tide sought to drag her out to sea. A pair of hands pulled her up by her elbows and onto land. Her teeth chattered between blue lips, and she shivered violently. Cold settled into the marrow of her bones.

"I want my mother!" she cried. Her breaths whooshed in and out, fast and deep, and crackled in her lungs. Her jaw clenched and her fingers clutched the man's arms as though the waters would reclaim her.

"Och...hush, hush," the man whispered.

She fought the urge to descend into darkness. Her eyelids seemed too heavy to open, and she weakly asked, "Where am I?"

"You are in Teutatwen, lad," the kind voice replied. "'Tis a miracle you made it here alive."

"Teutatwen?" Isolba repeated and forced her eyes open. They burned from the saltwater, and as she rubbed them with trembling fingers, whimpered in pain.

"Here," the man's voice said. Pulling up a corner of his mantle, he dabbed the salt from her eyes.

She shrank from him, her distrust of the male gender too deep to hide. He withdrew and sat back on his haunches to give her space.

After she blinked away some of the pain, she squinted at her rescuer. He sat before her, a very average-looking man approaching middle age. Deep laugh creases framed soft eyes in a calm face. He wore a short beard, a loose shirt, mud-covered checkered breeks, a wool mantle pinned with a bent nail, and a fitted sheepskin hat. He leaned his elbows on his knees, observing her, and waited for her to catch her bearings.

"This is Teutatwen?" she repeated in confusion.

"Aye, Teutatwen." He removed the mantle from his shoulders and draped it over her. "Nae wonder you've never heard of us. We are a far way from the mainland."

Isolba cringed at this gesture, too. She knew of Teutatwen, but it was so far and remote from Demoria that she could not see it with bare eyes. Teutatwen belonged to Escarans, who rented the island to crofters. It was a distance of ten miles at least. She shook her head in disbelief.

"Nae, 'tis impossible," she wheezed. "Teutatwen is three or four thousand rods from the nearest land."

"I imagine the ship you were on lost its way in the storm. You came a very far distance to be sure."

She clenched her eyes shut, but no matter how deeply she scoured her thoughts, she could not make sense of it. No hound could swim such a distance in turbulent waters and especially one with a human clinging to its back. She had seen the land from Demoria's shore before she went into the water, but perhaps it was an illusion.

"My hound..." she said, looking about for the creature who had saved her, but found him nowhere.

"Your what?"

"I came with a great black hound, who brought me to this shore. Where is he?"

"I saw nae hound," the man replied. "You were alone when I found you."

"Och, aye," she uttered. She felt lost and exposed without her new protector.

She was now sure the gods had sent the hound to come to her aid. It proved to be the only sensible explanation. He was a spiritual vehicle, carrying her to safety. But what if the place he had taken her did not exist in the mortal realm? Perhaps she was dead? Though she sensed the cold and weakened state of her body, she felt it to a lesser extent than if she had physically traveled ten miles through stormy waves.

"Am I in the afterlife?" she asked the man in a serious tone.

The man laughed then, a deep rolling sound that erupted from his lungs like music. "Nae, lad. You are as alive as I."

She could not make sense of it. Her journey defied all explanation. She despaired then. She had come all this way thinking she had reached the Argarves, yet she remained in her father's territory, even farther from Cormac's protection.

The man assumed from her clothing and shorn hair that she was a boy, a sensible judgment. She would not correct him. It was better if he thought her a boy, shipwrecked and washed in from the storm. She hoped to evade detection at all costs. If these people identified her as Isolba, they would surely return her to Demoria.

"If you are able, do you think you can walk with me to the village? You look in need of dry clothes and a fire to warm you."

Isolba nodded, and the man helped her to her feet. Her boneless legs wobbled. He held her steady as she worked to regain the use of her feet, and together they walked up a sloping hill covered in drowned grass. Their steps sank in the mire.

She found herself within a circular bay at the mouth of a valley. Low-lying mountains sloped upward at a sharp angle to her left, her right, and in the distance ahead. A small village rested in the dell between these mountains, with blackhouses dispersed on either side of a cobblestone street. The houses, with their stacked stone walls and turf roofs, resembled the croft houses in Demoria.

A multitude of small cleitan dispersed between the houses, and a drystone wall encircled a broad area of arable land. Beyond that, more cleitan, sheepfolds, and pastures fanned out in the distance. The moor extended to the ridgetops, so high as if the world would fold over. Her head spun, her equilibrium unbalanced, and she fell against the man.

He held her up. "Woah, lad."

She fought the urge to shrink from him. He seemed harmless, but how could she trust him?

Then, materializing from all angles, many figures walked toward them with questioning shouts.

"A shipwreck survivor," the man replied. "He's unharmed. A wee bit cold, but I'm remedying that."

A flurry of words and faces beat against her like a flock of seabirds. Now, she completely listed into the man, overcome.

"Give us space," he said. "This lad is weary. He can answer questions later. I suggest you all watch the tide for driftwood or other survivors, though I noticed nae flotsam. I must get him warm."

Some of their followers turned on their heels and headed toward the bay where they would search for nonexistent ship debris. The rest tracked close, their hungry eyes feeding.

Isolba trained her gaze to the ground and asked, "You are certain I'm not dead?"

The man coughed awkwardly and said, "Aye, I'm certain." After a pause, he cleared his throat and continued, "While we remain in our introductory phase, I am Saithan. Saithan Lennox."

Isolba said nothing but bid her vertigo to depart. They did not speak further, and Isolba was glad for it, too cold and weary to answer more questions. They reached the cobblestone street that ran westward.

A group of friendly hounds swarmed to greet the pair as they walked up. The mutts sniffed and licked Isolba's hands with wet noses and warm tongues. A hollow pit formed in her stomach at the loss of the black hound, and she decided when she had strength, she would search for him.

"Get on now," Saithan said to the hounds. "Let us through, mongrels."

The hounds parted to make way and followed with profound curiosity. Children, drawn from the warm houses by the commotion of yipping hounds, came to join them, and soon Isolba and Saithan had quite a procession parading at their heels.

"My home is over here," he said, pointing to a blackhouse nearby. "I've a change of clothing for you. My son grew out of his and sewed a new set, so we are nae longer in need of them. Though mind, they are wee more than rags, but they are warm and dry."

She nodded, eager to reach shelter and a fire.

"Beathag!" Saithan called, and as they stepped into the blackhouse, the startled face of a lone cow reared up at them.

The cow stood inside the entryway, blocking the way with her shaggy-furred body while chewing monotonously on a clump of hay. She looked at Isolba with disinterest. A fire roared behind her, and the sweet scent of peat drifted up with the smoke.

"That's not Beathag," Saithan said, chuckling. "This is Coleen, our best milker. Beathag is my wife."

The heat of annoyance flushed Isolba's cold skin. The man lacked urgency in finding her the comfort she desperately needed. Her teeth clacked in protest against his lackadaisical manner.

"What's to do, Saithan?" a woman's voice erupted from behind the cow.

"Coleen, move aside," Saithan ordered, pushing the great beast with his shoulder, and guided Isolba into the blackhouse.

A woman was standing behind the cow, feeding the central fire, and when she looked up, her eyes widened in surprise.

"By Our Lovely Wee Lass! Who's this?" she said, her voice loud and brusque.

Isolba's insides lurched. Did the woman deem her a lass?

"A poor soul washed in from a shipwreck," Saithan replied,

guiding Isolba to the fire where she dropped like a sack of rocks before it.

"Och, you poor wee lad!" Beathag cooed.

Isolba's tense shoulders relaxed, content that the woman, too, could not see beyond the veneer.

"Aye, he's suffered an ordeal." Saithan rubbed Isolba's mantle-covered shoulders to warm her. "He's in need of dry clothing. Where's Rindan's old set?"

"Here in the rag bin," Beathag said. She hastily rummaged through a woven basket. "You want help to put them on?"

"Nae!" Isolba shrieked, louder than she intended, as she grabbed the garments. "Nae...I shall do it on my own. In private."

"Very well." Beathag flashed a bewildered frown toward Saithan, and together, they left the blackhouse.

The dwelling had no doorway covering and Isolba's self-consciousness weighed upon her, tightened her chest with panic. She wished to change before the warm fire, but so fearful that someone would walk in on her, she moved behind Coleen. Keeping Saithan's mantle wrapped around her shoulders, she removed her tattered shoes and stockings, peeled off her wet tunic and breeks. She hurriedly pulled the dry breeks over her legs. The fabric had a faded blue tartan weave, similar to Saithan's, and was threadbare at the knees. The loose homespun shirt hung too long on her slight frame and was badly discolored, patched at the elbows.

She heard Saithan speak to his wife outside.

"I saw him swimming in from fairly far out. He was unconscious when he washed in. The ship surely went down somewhere nearby. He couldn't have survived in those waters for long."

"They must've had an outbreak of lice onboard," Beathag's voice said. "His hair is shorn clean off."

"Aye, you may be right," Saithan replied.

After several moments more, Beathag called, "You finished, lad?"

"Aye!" Isolba called back and seated herself before the fire.

The pair reentered the house. Saithan picked up the pile of wet clothing Isolba had left on the floor behind Coleen. He spread them out on the packed earth beside the fire to dry. Holding the hopeless remains of her shoes, he examined them with curiosity.

"You are fortunate," Beathag said. She bent over a crock before the fire as she ladled a spoonful of hot broth into a cup and handed it to Isolba. "The sea took a dislike to you...spit you out 'stead of swallowing you whole."

Beathag abruptly guffawed, startling Isolba, who nearly spilled her broth. The woman's toothy grin spread wide on her face, and Saithan chuckled, his eyes shining toward his wife. He rubbed the thighs of his dirty breeks to warm himself as he crouched before the fire.

Isolba sat in silence, eyebrows raised, and slowly sipped the broth. An oily film floated on the surface and tasted watery, but was warm and coated her insides with a comforting heat. After a moment of weighing Saithan's words, Isolba became aware of something he had said.

"I was not swimming," Isolba corrected. "I ken not how. 'Twas a large, black hound that carried me, the one I'm searching for."

Beathag flashed a questioning expression Saithan's way and he shrugged.

"My lad," Saithan said, hesitating. "As I spake before, I saw you wash into shore alone—whether swimming or floating, I'm uncertain. You had nae hound with you. You are the only survivor I've seen. I was in search of seaweed when I spotted you and saw nae debris from the ship either."

Beathag asked, "What ship were you on, lad? 'Twas foolish of your captain to sail a boat on these waters. He surely paid for his folly with his life."

"Aye," Isolba began, thinking fast. "Our ship took sail from the Hebrides. We were set for the Argarves. I had hoped this to be it."

"Nae, this belongs to Clan MacKay, at least for now, but that is a complicated tale to tell. The Argarves, owned by Clan McCloud, are to the southeast, though I've not traveled to Demoria nor the

Argarves. My feet have not left this ground since I breathed my first breath, and I've nae plans to change that before I breathe my last."

"I must go to the Argarves. Do you have a boat that would take me there at once?"

Saithan laughed, a deep, jovial sound that shook his short, thin frame. Insulted at this slight to her ego, she lifted her head haughtily and narrowed her eyes.

"Were you knocked on the head, lad?" he said, his eyes blazing. "Were you not but shipwrecked in these dangerous waters and you deem a wee boat could survive such a treacherous sea? We've but one boat, our greatest possession, that is shared by all. We do not use it to travel to any distant landmass, but for fishing and going to the outlying islands for seabirds. And we've not brought it out on the water in two years."

Isolba sensed a burn rising in her throat. She choked it down, willing her temper to lie fallow.

"Even so," Saithan continued, "none here could find the Argarves. You have to wait until the tacksman comes in the summer and sail back with him. But I'm afraid even then he cannot come, for the storms of the past two summers have isolated us from everyone. You are the first nonnative we've seen in years."

Isolba despaired. As soon as the sea calmed, her father's tacksman would come and, if he knew her to be on the island, would return her to Demoria. For that reason, she needed to keep her identity a secret and await another vessel. However, if she could convince the islanders to allow the use of their boat, she could find the Argarves by steering toward Demoria but bearing to the southeast. If nowhere else, she would come upon the Hebrides.

"You're such a wee lad to be out on a large ship," Saithan commented, breaking her thoughts. "Were you passenger or crew?"

She deliberated her response. If he believed her to be a child beneath her years, perhaps he would not blame her ignorance. The voices of boys her age were deeper, so she should present herself as younger. She was the size of a preadolescent boy, too young for a crewman, and also lacked the rough, calloused hands gained in the seafaring life.

"Passenger," she replied. The shorter her answers, the better.

"I'm sorry for your troubles and I'm sorry to have laughed at you," he said. "We've had a fair amount of trouble ourselves and have reached a point where we cope with humor. Well, I speak for myself, as I suppose we all manage our sorrows in different ways. Your mother, was she on the ship as well?"

"My mother?" Isolba asked in surprise.

"Aye, you asked for her when I first found you."

"Och, nae...nae she was not." Her voice grew thin and weak while her eyelids drooped.

"You need rest," Beathag said. "Lie by the fire awhile and warm through."

"I'll go speak with my aunt, Widow MacDuff, and her house-mate, Widow MacGill," Saithan said. "They have room for you."

Fog filled Isolba's mind. Her memory fragmented, and she questioned everything. She knew the hound to be real. Solid. If it had not been for him, she likely would have died after the searchers captured her or drowned in the Atlantic. She determined Saithan could not see the hound because he had been beneath her, holding her up. Perhaps he was mortal after all and succumbed to the waves at the very last.

Her stomach clenched at the thought, and she shook her head, discarding the notion. He had to be from the spiritual realm, and his aim was merely to get her to safety. With his task fulfilled, he moved on. He was no Coin-Sith as the legends described, but something else.

Saithan stepped out, his eyes full of concern, and walked with a hunch to his bony shoulders. People stood outside, peering in with unbridled curiosity. He said to them, "I beg you, leave him be for the evening. He needs rest."

Most departed, shuffled away with dramatic reluctance. A few stragglers remained to eavesdrop, but eventually turned away.

Beathag knelt next to Isolba before the fire. Her face was kind, but not comely. She had a prominent overbite, and the lines on her face revealed the travails of a hard life. A bright red headscarf trimmed with a white ruffle hid her hair. She wore a long gray dress of worsted wool, tied with a piece of rope around the waist and another beneath her breasts and armpits. A plaid shawl covered her shoulders, pinned with a small metal brooch.

"Poor wee lad," Beathag cooed, looking Isolba over. As soon as she noticed the cuts on Isolba's feet, she rushed to gather some items from a basket.

"I did not hear your name," she said. With a rag, she wiped the dirt from Isolba's feet.

"I am Indris," Isolba replied, wincing. The name belonged to the Demorian bard and came to her fast.

From a container, Beathag coated her fingers with a thick, oily substance and spread it over the cuts.

"We've two children older than you," she said. "A daughter, Cait, and a son, Rindan. We had many others, but they did not survive as bairns, you ken. Cait is gathering peat, and Rindan is tending to the sheep. They shall be great company to you while you're here."

Beathag finished by wrapping Isolba's feet in scraps of fabric, and Isolba did not thank her. Instead, a faraway expression lay on her face.

"I cannot stay," Isolba said firmly. "I must go to the Argarves."

Beathag frowned and stirred the fire with an iron poker, rousted the flames. "That isn't possible."

"Your husband said you've a boat here. I need someone to take me there."

"We do not take our boat into such waters. It simply has never been done as long as we've lived here. We ken better than to test the sea. Those who fail to respect it deserve to perish."

"Well, you have your first exception," Isolba said, refusing to stand down. "I make nae request. It must be done."

Beathag's chest rose, and she drew her shoulders back. "Listen here." Her voice gained an edge. "You sit on our island, in our home, wearing our clothes and having our food in your belly, and you are not gracious. I do not ken exactly who you think you are, but I will not have you making demands of us. You need to rest and come to your own good senses if your mother raised you to have any. I will leave now before I give you a proper throttling so you can have some quiet, and before nightfall, we will get you to the widows' house."

Isolba's stomach dropped, and her bones quaked. She glared into the fire ruefully as Beathag heaved herself up and marched out the doorway, leaving Isolba alone with the cow. Coleen produced a plaintive low after her master, and Isolba threw a hard look at the beast. The cow's eyes watered in the peat smoke, but she otherwise appeared content in the warm house. Fit enough for a cow, perhaps, but Isolba longed for her feather mattress and the roaring hearth fire of her cozy chamber at Brochnall Castle.

She peered around and took in the sad atmosphere with meager belongings. Two croopans attached to the wall of each corner of the back side of the house for sleeping purposes. The crude wool blankets covering the stiff straw mattresses lay neatly smoothed. A warp-weighted loom rested upright against a wall, and a quern stone for grinding grain sat near it. Upon the wall ledge sat crockery, tools, and baskets, while dried herbs hung from the rafters.

Coleen's byre sat on one side of the house, with a low dividing wall to contain the straw and animal mess. Manure littered the ground there, its odor mixed with the scent of peat and produced a sickly sweet pungency.

Isolba wrinkled her nose. How anyone could live in such a place among animals, without fine clothing, furniture, and other comforts, she could not comprehend. She supposed she could understand why they would not wish to risk their single boat on the rough sea, but still thought of herself as worth the chance. Her life and happiness were at stake, but she could not explain that to these people, whose loyalty was to their lord, her father.

Isolba lay down on her side near the fire and adjusted Saithan's mantle to cover her. Her bandaged feet burned against the close flames, so she folded her knees into her chest and curled her arms around her shins. Sleep quickly took her into a blissful, dreamless unconsciousness while her body repaired.

UPON WAKING, Isolba lifted her head and took a moment to remember where she was. Her bones ached. When she took in a sharp breath, her lungs crackled. She found Coleen curled up beside her, providing extra warmth.

"Morning, lad," Beathag said, stoking the fire.

Isolba coughed. "Morning?"

"Aye, you slept the night through. I suppose you needed it. My children came in, and we tiptoed around. We didn't dare wake you."

A girl wearing a plaid shawl walked through the door. She carried thick cuts of peat and regarded Isolba before throwing the fuel into the fire. She was several years older, nearly grown. Her dark blonde hair hung loose, her skin tanned and wind-chapped, and her eyes a beautiful shade of honey. Isolba thought her lovely, despite her rough appearance, with the delicate bone structure Isolba hoped to have.

"This is Cait, my daughter," Beathag said.

"Good morrow," Cait said in a friendly way, though a hint of wariness hung on the words.

"Good morrow," Isolba replied, self-conscious after a night spent sleeping on the floor. She brought her hands to her head to smooth her hair. With a pang, she remembered it was completely gone, and she had to continue the pretense of being a boy. A boy would not care how he looked upon waking.

"Father went to the morning meeting," Cait said, directing her words toward her mother. "I ken not where Rindan is."

"Perhaps he ran off with his kith?" Beathag suggested.

"Nae," said Cait. "Angus and Duffy are at the meeting, along with the others."

"Ah, wandered off alone again," Beathag said, shaking her head.

Isolba turned toward the open doorway, looking down the slope into the bay where waves crashed against the shoreline. Was it only yesterday those waves bore her in on the back of a hound? She pushed herself up to stand on unsteady feet and went to peer outside. Observing the sky, it remained overcast, the dark clouds billowing in the wind, a fierce wind that wicked moisture from her skin. She pulled the mantle tight about her. Her bald head prickled with the cold, and she longed for a hat.

"If you are checking the weather, lad," Beathag said from behind her, "I'm sorry to tell you, winter is upon us. Even before the blight of the sun, the largest of ships could not brave these waters in the winter. You are stuck with us until spring, and even then, there's nae telling if the land will return to how it was."

Isolba turned to look the older woman in the face and said, "But what if it never ends and we all die here? Why not take the chance to sail to the Argarves and ask for a ship to come and take us all?"

"Why leave our home?" Beathag asked. "We survived last winter without provisions, and we shall survive this coming one—without help. I wager Demoria and the Argarves are in as poor a condition as us. Trust me when I say we'll not risk our lives or our boat to get you there. You will wait for the tacksman to come in the summer–*if* he comes. Meanwhile, the sooner you go seek your shelter with the widows, the sooner I will be at peace, the thorn in my side you are!"

Isolba stood fuming in the doorway while Cait stifled a laugh with one bony hand.

"I'll go then," Isolba said and stomped out the entrance. She walked behind the house, toward the sound of voices.

Ahead, in a large opening between the cobbled road and paths, she found a gathering of men and women. A pair of small children running about stopped and stared at her, dumbstruck, but she paid them no mind. She stumbled, nearly blind with rage, over the stony ground and merged into the back of the crowd, a group of about sixty souls.

"Our only chance of surviving this winter is to slaughter much of the sheep," a man near the center of the group told the crowd.

"That is the unpopular opinion of the masses, but we must continue to be selective and heavily ration what we do take," another man said. "We cannot cull the population of our sheep by more than what we can spare. We rely on that wool."

"What use is the wool if none are here to shear it and weave it?" a woman broke in, voice heavy with sarcasm. "I'd rather us be naked with nae textiles to pay the tacksman with when he comes than for him to arrive and find naught but our bones."

Several of the islanders chuckled, leaving Isolba to wonder at their morbid sense of humor.

"I say we take one quarter, leave the yearlings and the two-year-old females," someone suggested.

As they took turns speaking, Isolba noticed no one led the meeting. Each person said their piece, and no one mediated or spoke for the crowd. They reached agreements only when the bulk of the islanders nodded their approval and none objected or voiced their dissatisfaction. It was a remarkable way of conducting business, entirely different from how her father lead Clan MacKay.

Saithan stood near the center, and when she caught his eye, he beckoned her. Everyone had focused so much on the discussion that they had failed to notice her presence. Now, the crowd gaped at her with obvious curiosity and parted, made way for her. As she walked through the sea of tartan plaid shawls and knit cravats, the islanders laid hands on her. They smiled, their faces shy but friendly, and spoke paradoxical words of pity and gratitude over her.

After a long while, the crowd at last settled, and she came to stand next to Saithan, exposed and out of place.

"This here is Indris," Saithan announced. "He is the lad much talked about today. My wife tended to his wounds, but we find him in fair health, considering his hardship. I spoke to my aunt, Widow MacDuff, and also Widow MacGill, and they agreed to take him into their home where they've the space. They also are needing a strong young lad to help them with their croft."

Isolba flashed a cold glare Saithan's way at the last part of the arrangements. So that is what they meant her to do—to work like a slave? He and the widows would be sorely mistaken if that is what they had in mind.

Saithan read her expression and added, "But he is eager for the next ship to come so that he can return home, hopefully in the coming summer."

He smiled at her and patted the top of her bald head, but she maintained her grimace, unable to accept her lot. Her mind's voice cursed the hound for bringing her here instead of the Argarves.

As the group turned to other business, she stood silent. Her heart sank deeper in her stomach. She longed for her mother, for Nareen, and for Cormac—a man she had never met but who owned her heart. If she could only find a way to him, she knew he could bring both her mother and Nareen to her.

At the close of the meeting, the islanders divvied up the day's tasks. The women and children would climb the hillsides and shores in search of vegetation and seaweed to dry and add to the winter stores. The men would make repairs to the blackhouses, fill in any gaps between the stones with earth, and add fresh thatch to the roofs.

Despite the day's work ahead, the crowd lagged in dispersing. They surrounded Isolba with searching eyes. Most appeared too shy to speak, especially the children, but their curiosity drove them closer. One small child leaned from his mother's arms and pointed. Two girls, nearly her own age with wild, curly hair, gawked with vacant expressions.

Saithan turned to Isolba and said, "I shall walk you to the widows' house so you can get settled."

Isolba nodded. Her chest burned with anger, but she could not speak to Saithan with the harshness she had his wife. Perhaps it was because he was a man and she feared him in the way she feared and respected her father and Priest Baltair, at least before they turned on her.

"Here," she said, unpinning the mantle from her shoulders and pushing it toward him. "You should have this."

He shoved it back into her arms and said, "Nae, lad, you need it. I can make another."

They walked on. From the distance, a figure rushed toward them. A lad with a wide smile. Isolba stared, her legs heavy, her gait slowed. He bounded over the stony soil, his bare feet greeting the ground with ease. Her eyes widened with recognition.

"Ah," Saithan said. "Here comes my son, Rindan."

The lad stopped before them and held out a handful of limp lovage to Saithan. Isolba perceived the bright hazel eyes and the wild brown hair that swung across his forehead. A tremendous weight came down on her. Drumbeats pounded. The spaces between the tones shortened, the rhythm quickening in her ears. She wavered, gripped by neurosis, and transported.

Those eyes stared up at her as she held him in a verdant gully, surrounded by thick vegetation, and her tears wet his face. Her hand pressed against his heaving chest as hot blood spurted from between her fingers. His open mouth gasped for air. Her lips greeted his forehead, and a sob tore from her throat.

Yet in that fleeting sense akin to memory, her feet remained planted on the ground as she stood next to Saithan. It did not matter that they had never met. In innate response, she knew this strange boy more than she knew herself. She breathed through her racing heartbeats, willing calmness, and struggled to maintain a stoic expression. A sensation unknown to her—perhaps empathy—cast from her to him. She could not explain why she cared, but it was as though someone lost to her was now found.

EIGHTEEN

Rindan regarded the lad. Their eyes met for a moment, and his heart skipped. He had seen the face before, but could not place it. Perhaps he had dreamt of him? If so, he could not recall it. The shock froze him in place.

The younger boy's eyes were too large and wide for his little face, a face pale and heart-shaped. He looked quite young, though Rindan could not be sure of his age, and frail and delicate, like a boy who had spent his childhood indoors, coddled by his mother. An overwhelming urgency to protect the lad came over him. It was as if an eerie sense of responsibility for the stranger anchored him. But why?

"This is Indris," Saithan said.

The lad, Indris, said nothing, but stared back with his disarming eyes. Rindan shrugged off the notion of familiarity. He had surely never met the lad before and nodded in his direction before turning his gaze back to his father.

"He's to live with the widows," Saithan said. "We're on our way now."

"Very well," Rindan replied. "I wish to take this lovage to Mother."

"Get on then," said Saithan. "We've much work today and mustn't tarry."

Rindan nodded and ran down the road toward his blackhouse, imagining Indris' gaze burning into his back. The child disturbed him, so he busied himself by dropping off the lovage to his mother and walked to fetch some turf. He found the pile nearly depleted, and when he brought the remaining turf back to their house, he informed his mother of the dwindling supply.

In time, Saithan came from the widows' house and joined Rindan in hauling turf to the roof. They whiled away the morning patching the village roofs. Near midday, Rindan sighted Ellar running down the lane. He shouted for Beathag.

"She's on the slope digging turf," Saithan informed him. "What's the matter?"

"'Tis Dolag," Ellar said, his voice high with angst. "The bairn is coming."

Rindan's insides twisted at the reminder of his lost object of affection. He hopped down to the ground, wiped his dirt-covered hands on his breeks, and said without looking at Ellar, "I'll fetch her."

His feet made quick progress through the dell. Numbness and disinterest consumed him. He wished not to think of the bairn or of Dolag, a lass he used to chase on these very slopes. Their childish laughter rang in his ears. The memory haunted those hills. She had never returned his affection other than acts of friendship, yet he had quietly continued to pursue her.

Like Duffy, he had remained too discreet and left his suit dubious. He had allowed Ellar to slip in and take her from him before he had a chance. He wondered then if it would be easier if she died in childbirth instead of seeing her as a wife and mother, not belonging to him, not wanting him. Once again, he cursed himself for thinking such a thought.

Instead, his mind turned to the shipwrecked soul whom his father had taken to live with the widows. Times were hard enough with their scanty food rations. To feed another mouth seemed unsustainable. His father should have left the lad to drown. But something within the lad spoke to his very soul, something uncanny. It was not the lad's arrival that proved so strange—for every several years, the island received a shipwrecked survivor or two—but the child himself unnerved him.

He found his mother, tusker in hand, digging chunks of fresh turf from the slope. Her bright-red cheeks bled from windburn and her teeth chattered as she bent over her work.

"Mother!" he called out. "You must see to Dolag. Her bairn's coming, and Ellar is nearly in fits."

"By Our Lovely Wee Lass!" she emitted. "I will hurry to her. He need not fash so."

Her plaid laid out on the ground was nearly full of turf, so Rindan said, "Go on, I will carry this down for you."

"That's my dear lad," she said, smiling at him with a quick stroke of his hair, and with tusker in hand, hurried down the slope as fast as the uneven terrain allowed her.

Rindan rolled the turf up within the plaid and placed it on his back. The wind blew fiercely on the slope. He thought of opening his arms and allowing the gale to take him, his body flying off into oblivion.

DOLAG SAFELY DELIVERED A BABY GIRL, and Beathag's excited retelling of the news bruised Rindan's heart. His mother described the child as healthy, with a robust cry and eyes of an elder who stared into her soul. She told how she wiped the afterbirth from the thrashing body, severed the umbilical cord, and applied a rag soaked in fulmar oil to the stump. Beathag said she then wrapped the child in a soft plaid and laid her in her mother's arms.

"Dolag is a natural mother," she commented. "Tender, affectionate. She soon forgot the entire ordeal of childbirth and doted on that bairn as though she were the most precious possession one could ever hope for."

Rindan hung his head and ruminated.

But a few days later, Beathag announced, "I've visited Ellar and Dolag. The bairn is unwell. She refuses to nurse and grows weaker by the hour."

Before the week's end, the bairn passed away. Rindan and his father removed the earth from the first child's grave, the bundle of cloth within still intact, but diminished. At the funeral, they laid the fresh bundle upon the old and cast dirt over the bodies. On Teutatwen, death snatched away the newly born quicker than the elderly. By this rule, Rindan lacked the brothers and sisters he should have, having only Cait.

His relationship with his sister was once close, but lately, he noticed her putting distance between them. She adopted a manner of secrecy and grew quiet and withdrawn. As a child, she had talked much like their mother, but now she spoke only to her friends and far from his earshot. Una often tried to impose herself on Rindan, but Cait would pull her away to continue their girlish chatter elsewhere.

Rindan lost himself in work, both to distract himself from thoughts of Dolag and to avoid Una's advances. The islanders' efforts in repairing and fortifying the blackhouses and cleitan came undone when a terrific storm blew through, carrying away large pieces of the roofs. The winds roared so loudly that Rindan's ears rang for days afterward. He set about repairing the damage, knowing he would repeat it after the next storm, which was rarely far behind.

It seemed the more he tried to forget Dolag, the more thoughts of her chased him. He wondered if a mismatch between Ellar and Dolag doomed their children to death. Perhaps they lacked the unification of true love and therefore their progeny missed some element vital to life. How many bairns would die before Dolag realized Rindan made a better partner?

As the weeks progressed, the island grew colder and the winds fiercer. His people spent more of their time indoors among the peat smoke and soot-stained walls, leaving to tend to the livestock once in the morning and once in the evening, and collect spring water and fuel. They whiled away their days weaving fabric, knitting, sewing, and in the evenings played instruments while singing lively tunes. Spirits lifted and even Rindan experienced an inner warmth, a spark of hope among the darkness and gloom.

But by morning, that spark extinguished. His daydreams of Dolag or leaving the island, two impossibilities as they were, brought him to despair. Winter settled in, but he and the men had not slaughtered enough seabirds that summer. They could not survive the winter on the dried carcasses hanging in the cleitan. Instead, as discussed in their meetings, they would kill more sheep than usual for meat on an as-needed basis. The villagers decided they would wait until they had consumed all other stores of dried meat before slaughtering the sheep.

Their crops that autumn had withered as they sprouted, and the yield, so rotted with wet, was hardly worth harvesting. They had collected every edible part, conscious of hungry bellies, as the pangs of famine gripped them.

After each storm, Saithan, Rindan, and the other men repaired the blackhouses. They saw to all the needs requiring a man's efforts, and helped the widows with many a chore. Sarah MacGill and Mary MacDuff were getting older and struggled to perform even the most menial tasks, such as fetching water from the spring or milking their cows. All hope rested on Indris to take over their more strenuous duties and put in his share of work.

However, Indris lied in the croopan Widow MacDuff had given up for his comfort. After his near-drowning, he suffered from a terrible cough and congestion. The illness hung on for too many weeks to count. At first, they wondered if he would survive the sudden, severe symptoms that gripped his body. His breathing became labored, and he shook with chills, burned with fever.

Beathag visited Indris daily. It seemed she felt responsible for him in a way, like an adoptive mother, and nursed him through his illness. Rindan watched the way she fretted over the child. She would hand-feed Indris broth, tipping an earthenware bowl between the chapped lips. At other times, she would prop the tiny body up to breathe in the steam from a crock of hot water infused with chickweed and eyebright.

When he eventually improved, he remained weak by all appearances. He refused to get up and walk about, except to see to bodily functions outside.

The widows felt sorry for him and made excuses to Saithan and Rindan, offering reasons why the little lad barely budged from his bed. Mary especially fussed over the newcomer. She offered him much of their daily rations, but he often shook his head in refusal. She constantly stoked the central fire to assure Indris never felt a moment's chill, lest the illness take hold of him again.

The lad did little but sleep and take in meager sustenance here and there. When awake, his eyes were glazed and distant. The widows' patience endured as the weeks turned into months. Everyone agreed Indris needed time to rest and repair after his ordeal, and did not coax him from his bed.

The islanders found extreme interest in the shipwrecked child. The lad rarely spoke and volunteered little information about himself or where he came from. Some would often stop in at the widows' blackhouse under the guise of a certain errand, while others arrived more boldly, wishing to visit with the newcomer.

None received much of a reaction or more than a word or two from the lad, and they gossiped amongst themselves. Perhaps he was a stowaway or a criminal and did not wish for trouble. Or, maybe he was a refugee or spy from a distant place. But daftness seemed the likely reason for his silence. Someone suggested he had suffered a hard blow to the head when the ship went down. Knocked him dumb, with no memory of his prior life.

Rindan silently laughed at their speculations, disagreeing that Indris was anything more than a spoiled lad homesick for his mother. Like the other islanders, he continued to observe Indris out of great curiosity, but kept his scrutiny discreet. He regularly visited the widows' house with Saithan or Beathag to help with chores and see how he was getting along.

Widows MacDuff and MacGill were good people, though they kept to themselves. With Rindan's visits, he gleaned how well their housemate was working out. Despite the passage of time, the newcomer never lifted a hand to help with basic everyday tasks.

Beathag admitted her frustration with Indris now that he was back from death's door. "'Tisn't right for a lad to lie abed all day," she told Rindan with a shake of her head. "Nae matter what horrors he witnessed during the shipwreck, lying about will do naught for his mind."

Rindan could not agree more. Used to constant movement and hard work, he ardently disdained laziness. But Indris' sloth proved not his only fault. Rindan accompanied his mother the day she brought the lad the clothing he had arrived in, scrubbed clean and mended, but she received not a word of thanks. On another day, Rindan watched Widow MacDuff present Indris with a sheepskin hat she had sewn for him. The gift went unappreciated.

Instead, the lad would stare at Rindan with wonder. The haunting eyes tickled the hairs on the back of Rindan's neck—made them stand on end—and he looked away in discomfort. He did feel sorry for the lad. What if Indris desired friendship, but lacked the social skills to carry a conversation?

Yet it was Saithan he spoke to more than anyone else, though it was often the same question. "Can you take me to the Argarves now?" Indris asked nearly every visit.

Saithan, ever sparing the long explanation, would issue him a firm, "Nae."

"I only hoped so because the sea looks much calmer today," Indris said stoically, surely knowing it was useless to even ask. He continued to ask anyway.

"'Tis nae calmer, lad," Saithan said, chuckling. "You would see for yourself if you left your bed."

"Och, aye. Perhaps tomorrow then," Indris often replied with a wistful sigh. He would bite his lower lip pensively, wring his little hands, and vacantly watch the fire.

He continued this performance. Acted languid and morose at each visit, until one day when Saithan brought something in hopes of cheering him up.

"I have these for you," the older man said and set a pair of shoes near Indris' feet.

Indris regarded them quietly. His fingers ran over the tiny stitches that held the pieces of torn leather together. The shoes had somehow remained on his feet while he had kicked afloat in the ocean, no doubt due to the ankle straps. He neither smiled nor spoke.

"They required a great deal of mending," Saithan went on, fishing for gratitude, but the lad produced none.

The widows sat in silence by the fire, listening to the conversation inertly, having long before given up pressing their charge. Their eyes sparkled in the firelight. Their arms stretched out between them with fingers intertwined.

Rindan looked around the room as he shifted his weight from foot to foot. He grew more and more irritated, thoroughly fed up with the lethargic dawdling and quiet thanklessness. Saithan, despite having a soft spot for the lad, seemed to feel it, too.

"Up," Saithan ordered, his voice loud and firm. "You must get up and move about. You require exercise to restore your strength."

Rindan stood stunned. He rarely saw his cool-headed father incited to shout, and burned with glee.

"Nae, I think not," Indris replied and looked down at his hands.

"You have nae choice!" Saithan said, reaching to pull Indris up by an elbow. "Put on your shoes if you need them, but you are getting up and coming with us."

Indris stared at their feet. Despite their warm mantles and the thick cravats wrapped around their necks, neither Saithan nor Rindan wore shoes. They preferred to feel the earth with bare toes.

Widow MacDuff arose, fetched the leather hat so lovingly

made for the child, and pulled it over the short regrowth of hair. She patted Indris' head with a wordless smile and returned to her seat on the floor.

"Up!" Saithan repeated, hoisting Indris to stand on unwilling feet.

The blue eyes blazed, and the small, round nostrils flared in and out with steady, angry breaths.

Rindan gripped Indris' other arm and nearly pulled back with shock. Beneath his fingers, he felt bone under the slip of loose skin. It repulsed him. Indris shot a stern look at him, but the anger seemed to dissolve, as if a sudden tenderness eased out defiance. Growing uncomfortable, the older boy withdrew his gaze and motioned to the shoes at Indris' feet. Indris obediently bent to slide them on, secured the straps, and stood, at last prepared for the excursion.

They made it but a little way across the moor before Indris stopped to catch his breath. Rindan and his father looked at one another in silence and shook their heads. The sky spat, and gales whipped their clothing, so after a moment, they pulled Indris into action. The boy stumbled along until they eventually made it to the basin carved into the moor. Indris stood before it, as if taking in the beauty of the hot spring. Sulphuric steam rose from its placid surface.

"Go on in," Saithan instructed, pushing Indris forward. "You will feel much better when you do. 'Tis healing, you ken. It tends to reverse most ailments."

Indris stepped out of his shoes, dipped a toe into the pool, and sighed with apparent pleasure.

"You'd best remove your clothes first," Saithan said, beginning to peel off his own shirt. "You need a proper bathing."

Indris stiffened and without turning to look at Saithan or Rindan, said, "Leave me."

Saithan stopped undressing and said, "We require bathing as well, lad."

"I bathe alone," Indris said firmly.

"Get over yourself," Saithan said with derision, though he laughed in the same breath. He finished pulling off his shirt and began untying the rope holding up his breeks.

Rindan shook his head, chortled low in his throat, and followed his father's lead by pulling off his own shirt. Indris withdrew from the pool and walked past them before stopping several yards off to stand with his back turned. Rindan wondered what caused the lad's restraint. Was it shyness? Prudishness?

As he and Saithan finished undressing, he noticed two forms appear in the distance and run toward them. When they moved closer, he saw they were Angus and Duffy, their faces bearing wide smiles. They dashed past the still form of Indris and tore off their clothing, which they dropped haphazardly across the moor. Angus bounded forth, slammed his body into Rindan's, and sent them both crashing through the water's surface. Duffy hollered jovially as he ran, launched himself into the spring, and sent a wide spray of water in all directions.

Rindan shoved Angus off, choking, sputtering, and holding back all the unholy words he wished to say. He wiped the water from his eyes and looked sidelong toward Angus, who grinned with clenched teeth. Duffy watched them, chortling as he tread water. Saithan pulled his breeks back on and shook his head in disapproval.

"You did not think to leave us out of a swim, did you?" Angus asked, laughing and coughing. He ran his fingers through his wet hair and smoothed the long strands back from his face.

"Our purpose here isn't for merriment," Rindan replied. "'Twas to see to bathing yon lad."

Angus and Duffy turned to look at the small form of Indris, shivering alone on the moor, his back turned to them.

"Nae improvement with him?" Duffy asked as he regarded Indris with amusement.

"Nae," Saithan said. "'Twould be a help to us if you lads would offer some assistance in the matter."

"What's to do?" Angus asked.

"Invite him in your merriments," Saithan replied. "Perhaps friendship will draw him from his shell."

Angus looked back with skepticism and said, "But the lad refuses to do aught. Has Rindan not lured him out?"

"You ken that hasn't happened," Rindan said with a wry chuckle. "He's odd and I do not desire his company."

Angus and Duffy laughed at this, looking again at Indris, who they hoped was out of earshot. A flicker of guilt quivered in Rindan's conscience, and he wondered if Indris had indeed heard his unkind words. Saithan offered his son a critical glare, though he seemed aware Rindan was right in a way, albeit callous.

"Then take him by force," Angus suggested. Mischief glinted in his eyes.

Rindan looked at his father uneasily, and Saithan shrugged, throwing his palms up. Rindan understood his father had given up and left him in charge.

With consent given, the three boys emerged from the water, naked and dripping. Rindan regretted leaving the warmth of the spring as the icy chill prickled his skin. The wind had picked up, and he worried another storm would soon be upon them. They would have to hurry.

Angus quietly stepped behind Indris. He sprung into action. His arms wrapped around the boy. Took him by surprise. Indris yelped as Angus picked him up. Rindan took hold of the kicking legs. Duffy helped pinion the clawing hands, though Angus and Rindan could manage fine without him. Their victim proved small and easily overtaken. They carried Indris toward the pool while Saithan stood back, arms akimbo, and snickered under his breath.

As they reached the edge of the spring, the boys succeeded in removing Indris' hat and mantle, but he began to shriek and thrash even more violently when they tugged at his shirt. The little face winced in terror. His eyes clenched tight as inhuman sounds escaped from his gaping mouth.

Waves of guilt returned, and Rindan began to question their

actions. "Just put him in," he said. "His clothing needs a washing as well."

Angus and Duffy nodded, and with Rindan's help, drug the boy into the water, soaking his clothes through. Rindan and Duffy loosened their hold, but Angus pushed Indris completely down beneath the water. A gurgling sound rose to the surface.

Rindan's chest tightened with worry. "Stop!" he ordered.

"Why have a care?" Angus asked, looking back darkly while releasing his grasp.

Rindan silently shook his head.

With a great splash, Indris' head emerged from beneath the water. He stood up in the pool, sputtered and choked, the sound of sobs strangling his throat. Streams of water ran off his clothes. His hands covered his face, trembling, as he wiped his eyes.

"Perhaps now we can tolerate the smell of you," Angus mocked.

"Wheesht!" Rindan scolded.

The boys watched as Indris crawled from the water. He shuddered and sobbed. He retrieved his mantle and draped it around himself. With shaking hands, he attempted to put his shoes on. Saithan took pity and knelt to assist him. As soon as the leather hat was in place, Indris left. Plodding toward the village, he trembled inside his mantle.

"You were too rough," Rindan said to Angus. "You've set back the trust we've sought to build with him."

"Wheesht," Angus said, chuckling. "You ken perfectly well you've made nae progress."

"But we have, lad," said Saithan. "Like the wild sheep of Dalais, we must show patience, step lightly, and approach slowly."

"Aye, up to the moment we slit their throats," Angus remarked cynically.

"You ken 'tisn't what I meant," Saithan huffed.

"And why have such a care?" Angus asked. "He'll be taken by the next boat that docks here."

"Aye, but who kens when that time may be?" Rindan retorted.

"You had nae right to do what you did. 'Tis our duty to keep him safe 'til that time may come, nae matter if we dislike him."

"Perhaps he'll catch his death of cold, and we can rid ourselves of him," Angus said sardonically.

"Enough," Saithan scolded.

"He is weak and will not survive here," Angus added.

They said nothing more, knowing that Angus was right.

NINETEEN

Isolba crept into the widows' blackhouse. When her guardians saw her, their eyes widened in alarm. They quickly leapt from their seats by the fire.

"Och! You poor lad!" cooed Widow MacDuff, coming to meet Isolba and pull her toward the fire's warmth.

Isolba's shoulders quivered, and the chattering of her teeth produced a clacking shrill against the soft popping of the fire. Her breath shuddered thickly in her throat, and as she warmed, tears streamed down her cheeks. She wept openly, without shame, but her face held anger instead of sadness.

"What's happened?" asked Widow MacDuff, concern welling in her eyes, but Widow MacGill looked away, her mouth pinched and thoughtful.

"I must leave this island," Isolba said through haggard breaths. "I cannot stay here a moment longer."

"'Tis impossible, you ken," Widow MacDuff said kindly. "You have to bide your time here, for as long as that may be, and make the best of it."

"Nae, I need a boat, else I will attempt to swim it."

"And end your life, then? By Our Lovely Wee Lass, are you mad?" Widow MacDuff asked, eyes wide with alarm.

Widow MacGill shook her head, a sour expression crossing her face, and she adjusted her folded hands in obvious discomfort. "Do not fall for his dramatics, Mary," she said to Widow MacDuff. "Perhaps 'tis time we've a talk with the lad."

"Wheesht, let it wait," Widow MacDuff replied. Wariness cast across her visage. "Let us step out a moment so the lad can change into dry clothes."

Widow MacGill stood and adjusted her plaid shawl. "Aye, I suppose we can address it a wee bit later, but we must resolve the matter without delay."

Once the widows left, Isolba stared after them in stupor. She had reached a point of crisis, had pleaded for help in leaving, shed tears even, and her anguish had not stirred them. Though she could not convey the full account of her ordeal, they knew enough to sympathize. Overshadowed by despair, she wallowed in melancholia. She was uncertain which was worse: death or being trapped in this prison with these hardened people.

She changed into her extra set of clothes. Sniffled and sobbed. What was the use of telling the widows what happened at the spring? Recounting her recent ordeal would hardly fetch her the compassion she craved. She recalled the nude bodies of the lads as they lifted her, and burned with the shock of having seen unclothed men. Though she had shut her eyes, the experience evoked deep shame.

These people were brash and uninhibited, disrobing completely in the sight of a stranger before attempting to drown her. She reminded herself that they viewed her as a fellow lad and not a lady to treat delicately. How could she go on pretending to be one of them, especially when they asked her to strip down? They would shortly discover her identity and return her to Demoria the minute the tacksman docked his boat.

The widows called in and she allowed them back inside. They reseated themselves before the fire, settled in comfortably, and joined hands in their usual pose.

"You saw to your bathing then?" Widow MacDuff asked

cheerfully, as if there could be another reason for the drenched clothing.

Isolba looked back blankly. Whistling breaths punctuated by light sobs escaped her lips. She rubbed her arms before the fire, unable to release the chill from her bones. Widow MacDuff retrieved a wool blanket from Isolba's bed and covered her with it.

How did two widows so unlike one another get along so well? Widow MacDuff showed gentleness, caring, and sensitivity, while Widow MacGill bore a brusqueness in her speech and manner. Widow MacDuff stood short and plump, while lanky Widow MacGill stood at an impressive height.

Widow MacGill preferred to wear breeks in and around the immediate outside of the house. She said it was more comfortable, and did not hide her fondness for men's clothing. She would wear a dress when attending morning meetings—something the widows did only on occasion—or the rare visit to a neighbor.

Before that day, Isolba had spoken some two dozen words to the widows, having spent so much of her time ill and lost in sleep. In her convalescence, she had watched the widows at their daily tasks: weaving, sewing, cooking, and tending to the cows that took residence in their blackhouse. By remaining quiet and out of the way, she had hoped to seem too dull to face further inquiries. She ate little, allowing the widows to serve her and clean up after her. She knew no other way.

"'Twas good of Saithan to see you out of the house for a spell and breathing fresh air, aye?" Widow MacDuff asked.

Isolba nodded warily.

"'Tis good to be clean too," Widow MacDuff went on.

Isolba said nothing. It was easier to remain silent. The cold, dead sensation of hopelessness consumed her. After a lengthy spell of awkward stillness, she decided she had adequately warmed and made her way to the croopan. She fell onto the stiff mattress, folded her legs to her chest, and shut her eyes tight.

She wanted to forget what the lads had done, but could not hate Rindan for it. He had acted in her best interest and sought to carry out the instructions Saithan gave him. He seemed quite goodly in her eyes, and well composed for a boy his age, unlike his friends. She wished to push the tall one off a cliff.

Eventually, the widows blew out the oil lamp and made their way to the other croopan. The straw within the mattress crunched beneath their weight. When all grew dark and silent, besides the glow and crackle of the fire, Isolba heard their whispers, soft and comforting.

Their nightly ritual soothed her in a way because it gave her something to depend on in her unpredictable world. Sometimes, one of the island hounds would come in to seek respite from the cold and lie beside the fire. It would rest its head on its front paws with a heavy sigh.

Nearly every evening, music and singing from the other houses drifted in on the night breeze. Together, these noises formed her lullaby, nudging her into the deep abyss where nightmares played.

Isolba slept in late, partly hearing the morning movements of the widows as they fed the fire and prepared a meager breakfast. She had half a mind to spend the day in bed, attempting to stay within the unconsciousness of sleep, but her dreams proved more frightful than waking life.

Each time she drifted off to sleep, she fell into the same allegory. Again and again, the blade of Baltair's dirk pressed into her skin. She watched as a line of red trailed its path before a thick globule of crimson oozed out. It flowed slowly at first, but as it gained momentum, streamed in vast pools around her, draining her body until she lay as empty as a clay vessel. Then Nareen was before her, falling to her knees and weeping.

The maid would choke back a sob and say, "You are safe now."

Isolba sat up in bed, Nareen's voice echoing in her ears. Her heart frantically thumped against her chest wall. With every painful whack against her ribs, she felt sure it would burst, lest it dislodge itself entirely. She sucked in a deep breath, and nausea crept into her belly. What did Nareen's words mean? From the hollow of her wame came a wrenching—a worry—that Nareen and her mother were in danger. They had to be rescued.

"You are awake!" Widow MacDuff said cheerfully. "How about some porridge now for your strength?"

Isolba nodded, squinting, and peeled herself from the croopan. She stumbled across the floor, in need of emptying her bladder. She made her way outside and to the midden, where, after ensuring no one was nearby, she pulled down her breeks and squatted. The islanders did not use chamber pots or proper holes in the ground outside for human waste. Isolba was appalled the first time the widows directed her to the midden to relieve herself among the piles of rubbish and food scraps, but she had grown used to it.

So far, she was fortunate that her true sex remained hidden. She had little privacy while tending to her bodily functions. She drank as little water as possible and lived in a permanent state of dehydration. Nighttime was the only interval she deemed perfectly safe to use the midden, the cloak of darkness hiding the fact that she crouched instead of stood. Any other time, she found a stone wall to hide behind and prayed no one came upon her.

Once relieved, she walked toward the widows' house, and her trained eye caught the smooth sphere of a pebble sitting atop the mud. She snatched it up and returned inside. The widows sat at the fireside, immobile, neither making an effort to grab Isolba's breakfast. She warmed her hands with the pebble secured in her palm and joined the women near the fire. Her legs folded beneath her as she sat in wait to be served. Widow MacGill cleared her throat, and Isolba peered up to see the aged woman cast a prodding look toward Widow MacDuff.

"Och, aye," Widow MacDuff said, as if recollecting something. She nodded and nervously stirred the fire. "We need to speak with you."

Isolba turned her face away and said nothing. Dread settled in.

Widow MacDuff opened her mouth, but hesitated, and after

an encouraging nod from Widow MacGill, gently began, "Dear lad, this is the way of it. We had a discussion and have come to an agreement. We believe you've returned to health and implore you to get on your feet. You must begin to do for yourself. We cannot allow you to mope about doing naught. 'Tisn't right at all."

The pebble launched from the little palm and landed in the fire. The heat of anger brimmed in Isolba's chest, and she stared into the flames, unable to look at the widows. Why did everyone stand against her, careless of her plight and her desperate need to get to the Argarves?

Her silence did not diffuse the widows' case against her, and Widow MacGill spoke in her curt manner of speaking.

"We do not ken who you are, but when you live on Teutatwen, every man and woman is equal, and those who are capable do the work for those who cannot. You, young lad, are capable."

The widows looked at her expectantly, but Isolba sat, glowering into the void, nostrils flaring. Her eyes grew menacing, and her lips clamped shut. In her silence, she delivered clear defiance to the widows.

"This is the way of it," Widow MacGill continued. "If you do not work, we will turn you out. You will shelter elsewhere as we'll nae longer suffer this laziness and entitlement."

Isolba remained silent. Her eyes reflected the glowing fire. Its flames wavered then. The tendrils wildly licked the air, sputtered, and crackled.

The widows watched in alarm, and Widow MacDuff peered toward the doorway. "A storm is approaching," she announced.

"I feel nae wind coming in," said Widow MacGill. "But it must be so."

Isolba's breaths drew in and out. Grew heavier and in rapid succession. *Crack! Whoosh!* The blaze combusted outward, flickered with blatant violence, and spit sparks and ash at the trio. The widows beat the flaming embers from their skirts, stood, and backed away. Fear showed in their faces, but Isolba sat, nearly catatonic, eyes fixed on the fire.

"'Tis the work of Caorthannach!" Widow MacDuff screeched, as her back pressed into the sooty wall behind her.

"Out!" Widow MacGill roared. She grabbed one of Isolba's thin arms. "Out with you!"

She flung the child out the doorway. Isolba landed on her knees. Fingers sinking into the cold, wet earth, she came back to herself. What had happened? It felt as though she had left her body and went away, to somewhere dark and distant. Her chest throbbed and burned. She beat the ground with closed fists. As she roared deep in her throat, she released the fury in a prolonged emittance until her vocal cords strained.

She clambered to her feet, walked with shaking steps, and all the while refused to turn around to see if the widows watched. Villagers stood about, halted in their steps to witness her outburst. Their faces registered a stunned vacancy, and they blinked with shy stupor. No one came forward to ask of her trouble. She ignored them and stalked down the slope toward the sea. The water in the bay lapped at the shore. Smacked and sprayed the rocks. When she reached the water's edge, she stared at the Atlantic. Dark mist merged the sky and sea into a muddy interfusion of black clouds and roiling swells.

Somewhere in the distance lay Demoria, her dangerous home. Surely, the gods were punishing her. Should she return on the next ship and greet her fate? At least then she could see her mother and Nareen one final time. Tears misted her eyes at the memory of their love. Sickness gripped her insides. Their situation was grave. If they were both gone from the world, then she could no longer live in it.

Sinking beneath the waves and drowning would prove a quicker route of dispatch than beneath Baltair's dirk, but there had to be a reason she had made it safely across the waters the first time. Did the black hound know something she did not?

She longed for him then, a friend in her friendless world. The hound, her mother, and Nareen had all risked their lives to guide her to safety. But why end up there? Why Teutatwen? Perhaps, as Nareen had said, she was now safe.

She walked along the water, skirted the edge of the bay, and put distance between herself and the village. Near the southern end of the island, she crouched beneath a stone wall, obscured from view, and found reprieve from watchful eyes. She breathed deeply. Sobs caught in her throat as the cold wind abraded her cheeks. Her stomach soured as utter wretchedness consumed her. It was as though a great fish had swallowed her and squeezed her inside its gullet.

To shake the feeling, she stood and stumbled along the wall a ways before it notched inward, cornered to straight for several feet before turning back to meet the original line. This notch in the wall surrounded a pile of turf, the crude squares forming some type of covering as they would upon a roof, but this proved too shallow for a building. From the center, a tall post loomed. It looked strangely like a mast.

The shock of discovery enthralled her, and she tore the turf away. Flung it aside to reveal the structure beneath. What took form was the rare sight of wood curving into a familiar shape. A longboat.

As soon as she had cleared the turf, she saw how the islanders had filled the boat with rocks to weigh it down against the powerful gales. She had quite tired herself as it was, but forged ahead in her excitement. Scooped the rocks up one by one and threw them to the ground to mix with the turf. Her palms and fingers became raw, the fingernails tore, and drops of blood emerged from the dry, tender skin around them. Her arms soon grew unbearably heavy and ached with exertion. Sweat rolled off her temples despite the chill in the air.

With the boat emptied, Isolba collapsed against its side and at once viewed its position in relation to the sea. The vessel sat high on the slope, placed far enough from the bay for its secure hibernation. She would have to push it, though surely gravity would assist her and make the remainder of her work light. Soon, she would be on the waters, heading for the Argarves—wherever that was.

She shrugged off the doubt. It was no matter. The Argarves

could not be far, and as long as she stayed due east, she would sight one of the islands and not become lost at sea. She could not think about the heaving swells that could toss her from the boat with ease. She would chance it.

She thought again of Cormac and how he would welcome her when she arrived. He would pity her predicament and immediately secure the safety of her mother and Nareen—if they were still alive. She closed her eyes and banished the thought, forbidding herself to believe they were dead. Perhaps they too made their escape and were hiding somewhere among the rocks of Demoria.

She positioned herself behind the boat and pushed with all her might. It did not budge an inch. She heaved all her weight forward and strained what little muscle she had. Willed the boat to move. It sat undisturbed by her efforts, and she fell to the ground. The outstretched tentacles of despair tugged at her. She screamed in frustration. Her head fell into the open palms of her hands, and her fingers splayed across her scalp.

Below, the breakers bellowed like a groaning beast. The waves crashed violently into the craggy shore, and she peered out to witness their rage. The angry water churned and boiled, black and rabid, as foam collected on its surface.

"My gods!" she cried out toward the sea. "I ask of you: what do you want? My body or my soul? If I give myself to you, would you lift the blight? Would you alas be content? If there's a way for me to save my people without losing my life, make it kent! If your answer is 'aye', that I may have my life, then I ask you to dislodge this boat!"

Again, she bent with renewed force. Every bone, tendon, and muscle fiber burned. The friction of her energy scorched the very marrow of her bones. Her efforts proved useless. The boat remained too heavy and settled to release from its muddy nest.

The gods had not helped her. If they had, it meant they had use for her life as it was, but since they had not, they still insisted on a sacrifice. They demanded the spilling of blood. Then, she would be reborn as a son. But her mother had said Escarans could not father children. Perhaps the divine will of the gods could change that.

She peered into the frothy waves. Was it time to give herself up? *Nae, not yet.*

Frozen stuck for months, the gears of her mind began to turn. Self-pity and fantasies of Cormac had long consumed her thoughts, but now, with the fresh air and exercise, the fog cleared and her synapses fired. Formed notions and joined ideas.

If Escarans' dream was only a dream and nothing more, why would Baltair name it as a prophecy, knowing it could not come true? Or perhaps Baltair carried great faith in his abilities and acted in the best interest of Escarans and the clan as a whole?

The more she pondered, she realized that by rejecting Baltair's counsel, she had insulted him. He wanted to teach her his ways, to make her powerful, and raise her up to inherit the chiefdom. But she had wanted only Cormac. While Baltair sought to preserve the clan, she sought peace through marriage and a new life in the Argarves.

Nausea bubbled in her stomach as she realized Baltair had taken the opportunity to murder her. With her gone, the contract with Clan McCloud would crumble. Demoria, Teutatwen, and the smaller islands would remain in the possession of Clan MacKay. He had chosen tradition over peace.

Baltair had won, had he not? Isolba was gone, surely presumed dead. Escarans would have punished her mother and Nareen for helping her escape. Demoria would likely be an island of great unrest and danger. Isolba could not return there without Cormac and his army.

Her breathing hitched at the thought of her betrothed, and she touched her fingers to her lips. *Och, Cormac!* If he could only dream of her troubles.

"Indris!" an annoyed voice shouted behind her.

Isolba whirled around to find Rindan standing there, his eyes ablaze. Her jaw fell as she peered down at the mess of tossed rocks and turf scattered at her feet. Shame enveloped her. She carried herself like a blameworthy child who could not look at him due to her disgrace. How low she had fallen, and to see Rindan—whom she liked best of all—in such disgust of her, seemed unbearable.

"What's to do?" he said, shaking his head in disappointment. "Have I not stood by and witnessed your laziness? Your dismissal of the kindness given to you by my father, mother, and the widows? Watched you offend every soul on this island? But this blatant disrespect done here, to our most cherished possession...I cannot be silent."

Isolba grimaced and bowed her head. She peered down at her hands and picked at the torn cuticles. His words triggered that familiar heat in her chest, but only because they bore correction to her fault.

"What plan have you?" Rindan continued. "Take our boat out on these waters, having nae oars and nae sails, and sink beneath the waves? Although we would be quite sad for the loss of you, we would be sadder yet for loss of the boat, for without it we cannot travel to the stacs and gather eggs and birds to live on."

She opened her mouth to speak, but he continued, his words bitter and picking up speed. "But why would you care? You care only for escaping, to be away and done with us. Nae matter how you hurt us, aye? 'Tis only about you, isn't it? But what worth are you to us? I have not seen you accomplish little more than pumping blood and sucking air. You're a burden, that's all. Nae help for us or care for us. You ought to go back in that water. I wish you had never come. If you only kent how much my mother and father care for you–the widows too, along with all of us here–but you've nae heart. I'm done with you."

Isolba emitted a low yelp as she looked up at him. She did not know that they cared so much. When Beathag had nursed her back to health, she assumed it was out of duty. She believed that everyone merely tolerated her until they could be rid of her. Though Rindan had not said it aloud, perhaps he cared for her too. His words stung, and the sensation surprised her. For so long, she had felt nothing, numb completely through, and lived as an empty vessel. But that day brought anger, shame, and now an unnamed sensation stirring within.

Was it possible for anyone to love her now that she was no longer the jewel of Clan MacKay? The islanders knew her as a shipwrecked lad with a dubious origin and until now, they did not see her as a burden, but someone to care for and look after.

Rindan's honey-colored eyes had turned from dark and wrathful to melancholy. His thick eyebrows drew together and his lips formed a sour expression, no longer of disgust, but one of deep pain. He turned and walked away. His feet crunched the salt on the brown grass.

Isolba followed in his pace, reached out, and tugged at his mantle. She alas spoke, choked on the word. "Nae."

He turned, brought both hands to her shoulders, and pushed her to the ground. It hardly took much force, as she was a feather-weight. He continued walking. She lay stunned by the blow, her absolute weakness defined in the act, and without picking herself up, called after him.

"What shall I do?"

He swung around and marched a few yards back in her direction, feet splayed slightly outward in dominance. In that moment, she found his beauty profound. Her anger could not hold up against the subtle power he held over her.

"You should begin caring more for others than for yourself," he suggested. "But you can start by putting the stones and turf back in the boat."

She nodded, shoulders sagging. Rindan left her then, producing a feeling in her of discard. Though her energy had depleted, all frustration abandoned her, and left her determined. She would do anything to right her wrongs and win his favor.

TWENTY

Before Rindan discovered Indris trying to make off with the island's boat, Saithan visited the widows' house and inquired about the source of the commotion.

He scoffed when they described the events leading up to Indris' outburst, but after he comprehended the fright and anger in their eyes and voices, he attempted reassurance. He told them Indris could stay with him for the interim while they sorted out the lad's emotions.

Saithan hoped the widows would decide to take the boy back when they were ready, for their blackhouse had the room to spare. He pointedly made a case for Indris, telling them he was certain the lad had suffered much trauma prior to his arrival. They should be patient with him, for they had no other choice, short of throwing him off the island, and that would never happen so long as Saithan had a say. He did not believe the natives wished the lad harm, but the widows were direct when they told him their reserves of patience had dried up.

Saithan met Rindan coming home for the midday meal and related to him what the widows had said. "I fash they are spreading rumors to the other islanders and everyone will fear the lad. It does not help his case, that much is certain. 'Tis up to me to go find the lad and learn his side of the story. You ken he speaks the most to me."

Rindan's lips clamped in thought and, after a moment, said, "Nae, Father, allow me to go. I will find him. I feel poorly for yesterday and wish to make matters right."

"Aye," Saithan agreed. "I too am much bothered. If it were not for Angus and Duffy coming along, perhaps it wouldn't have ended so badly. It's been hard enough trying to earn the lad's trust, and now he may never open himself to us."

"'Twas all Angus' doing," Rindan said, shaking his head in disgust. "He has too much vigor and desire for domination."

"Aye, I've noticed," Saithan said through gritted teeth. "But why did he have to hurt the lad? If you could talk to Angus—"

"Angus refuses to heed any word I say," interrupted Rindan. "I've tried long before Indris landed on our soil."

"Then I will speak to him," Saithan suggested. "Or better yet, to his father."

"I wish you luck then, Father," said Rindan with a prolonged sigh. "I'm off now...I'll find Indris and resolve the matter."

RINDAN RETURNED HOME after his altercation with Indris in the bay, red-cheeked and breathing heavily. Despite the irritation sensed so hotly moments before, his eyes danced and a wide grin spread across his face. Beathag handed him a bowl of food, and he began eating in haste.

"You returned home without Indris? You did not find him?" asked Saithan.

"Nae, I did," Rindan answered, pausing from his dinner to issue his father a sidelong glare. "Found him trying to make off with our boat, but the puny lad could not push it to the water."

With an abrupt peal of laughter, Beathag buried her face in Coleen's side. Saithan appeared unsure whether to laugh in turn or spit in fury, but he shook his head and waited for Rindan to continue.

"I asked him how he expected a successful voyage without oars and sail, never mind the rough waters."

Saithan finally chuckled.

"Father," Rindan began, growing serious. "Happen you to ken if the widows ever gave Indris instructions? Did they ask him to help, expecting him to ken what to do?"

"I do not ken," Saithan replied. "Why?"

"Methinks Indris requires instruction. He never volunteered to help or asked what could be done. We do not ken his background, so perhaps he doesn't ken how to croft or do much of aught for that matter. I wonder if he is wont to having all done for him, based on his inaction. His entitlement and such."

"Aye," Saithan said, nodding. "I do believe you've unlocked the mystery of the wee lad. I do partly blame the widows for never coaxing or encouraging the child. And the way they believed him too weak to get up for months, but suddenly threw him out. Seems an extreme force of egos at play. But where's the child? I thought you would bring him back."

"Well, that's the argument I am reaching. You ken, I told him to set the boat to right, and indeed he is on the task that I asked. Therefore, he is able. 'Tis guidance he requires."

"Seems to make quite a bit of sense," Beathag chimed in. "The widows have clearly forgotten what it takes to raise a child, to direct their path. They probably sat in expectation that Indris would get up and begin doing chores like that's that."

"Very well," said Saithan. "'Tis time to put the lad to good use then. He may've had a comfortable upbringing, but he's on Teutatwen now for nae telling how long and will work like the rest of us."

"Aye, he must," Rindan agreed. "I fear, though, that I did not sort out the incident with the widows, having lost my course by Indris meddling with the boat."

"Och," Saithan muttered. "Should I check on the lad and ensure he does a proper job of securing it?"

Rindan shook his head. "Do not help him. He must do it on his own if he is to form any appreciation of hard work."

"I've brought you up well," Saithan said, smiling.

Twenty-One

The first night after Isolba's falling out with the widows, she tried to curl up against the boat for shelter, teeth chattering and bones aching from the cold. Saithan had come by earlier to invite her for a meal and a warm place to sleep, but she did not think she could face the islanders. She also felt ashamed of her exchange with Rindan and wondered what he thought of her.

In time, the driving gales proved too brutal and forced her to humble herself. Lured up the hill to the blackhouses by a growling stomach, she came to stand outside the Lennox home. The merry refrain of music came from within, and she heard Saithan's voice belting out a pleasant tune.

She stood just beyond the opening, an outsider, longing to be within and a part of the gaiety. These islanders had nothing, and yet they remained optimistic. She thought she had known happiness at Brochnall Castle with Nareen by her side, but she had lived a life shut away from the real world. Every need had been met and nearly every desire fulfilled without exertion on her part. She did not know how to be an active part of a family or society.

She did not know herself, not wholly. Her existence up to her departure from Demoria was superficial. Did she have any thoughts of her own? Of course she had, but to voice or act upon those thoughts usually caused a stern look or punishment. So she had been but a statue, a fixture in the castle. Her only real desire was to marry Cormac, but that was because it was her father's desire first. Cormac was no more real to her than the gods she was meant to worship.

In despair, she understood she had no dreams of her own and certainly no personality. Who was she? She was nothing. Stripped down to bare bones...an offering to the skies. She had to prove her worth as more than a sacrifice. It was time to become someone. For now, she would be Indris.

Holding her breath, she stepped into the house. It was warm and smoky and smelled of peat and stew. She first locked eyes with Rindan, who sat around the fire with his family and the ever-present Coleen. His sincere smile welcomed her. Saithan beamed at the sight of her but did not break from his song. Beathag and Cait reached out and pulled her down to sit with them. Their warmth and energy swept around her and through her. For the first time, she experienced gratitude.

Later, when the household slumbered, Isolba settled beside Coleen. The warmth from her full belly curled up to greet the heat emanating from the animal and the fire they rested near. She had never felt more exhausted, as though she had used every muscle fiber and measure of energy. Her heavy eyelids slid downward, and she peered off into the corner where Rindan reposed next to his sister. When she met his open eyes shining in the firelight, she stiffened and shut her eyes tight.

AT DAYBREAK, Beathag nudged Isolba awake, and she, along with Cait and Rindan, left the warm cocoon of their blankets to begin the morning's work. Isolba could barely bring herself to stand. Her entire body ached from the previous day's lifting of turf and rocks. Stiff and sore, her tender muscles and strained tendons protested their overuse.

As she stood, she brushed at the wrinkles in her breeks and tunic but gave up in futility. She pulled her ragged shoes over her knit stockings while the others remained barefoot, their hardened feet impervious to the elements. As Isolba tugged her wool mantle over her shoulders, she looked with envy at Saithan curled up in his bed.

"Have you ever milked a cow?" Beathag asked with a toothy smile.

Isolba shook her head and stared at the ground. The idea of work seemed alien and unimaginable. Beneath her guise, she remained a lady, bred to sit weaving or embroidering by a fire and charm the court with her humor and grace. But now she would be Indris, an obedient lad who had to survive, biding his time before the ships could sail.

"'Tisn't difficult," Beathag said. "We will have you help tend the widows' livestock. This will be your task every morn and eve."

Isolba sighed and took the jug Beathag offered her. With their mantles pulled closed and jugs in hand, the four left the warmth of the blackhouse. The icy air outside sent an instant shock to their systems.

As they climbed the hill behind the rows of blackhouses, a group of island hounds followed close behind. Their ribs jutted beneath their short fur coats, expanding and contracting as wet noses sniffed the ground in search of mice. Isolba looked for her savior among them, as was her habit, but he was never there.

If he lived, he tested the mortal boundary and was not bound by its laws. On Demoria, her clan deemed hounds as sacred because they carried the reincarnated souls of men. Perhaps her hound was an ancestor, a protector.

Children drew out of the houses, watching the outsider from a distance, and gathered to whisper of the strange creature that could manipulate fire. They regarded Isolba for a long while before losing interest. She saw them skip away, chasing and shoving one another across the moor.

Beathag led the group toward the sheepfolds that were composed of stones loosely stacked to form a crude circular fence. The sheep huddled together in each fold and bleated in welcome. They rushed forward within their enclosure, their wool coats thick and matted with muck. Beathag and Cait moved a large, flat stone aside to reveal an opening in the fold from where they coaxed the sheep out onto the grassland.

"Come with me," Rindan said, motioning for Isolba to follow him up the slope toward another sheepfold. "The widows' sheepfold is up there."

He walked briskly, with ease and surety, up the embankment. Isolba struggled to keep up with his long strides. She slipped on the partially frozen mud and stumbled on slick, jutting stones. When they reached the sheepfold, he set down his jug, and she set hers next to his before he moved the stone aside. When they entered, the sheep scurried around them. Isolba froze in place as they pushed against her. Their long tongues licked the frost clinging to her mantle.

Rindan laughed. "You've nae experience with sheep?"

"Nae," Isolba whispered.

"Spent your life within walls?" he probed, a grin lighting up his face.

The warmth of his eyes put her at ease, and she reached out to touch the coarse wool of their backs. "Aye, I suppose I have."

"You must be strong to survive here," he said. "On this island, the lads your age have scaled cliffs for years. My father allowed me to begin climbing in my fifth summer."

"Whatever for?" she asked.

"To help in the collection of eggs, of course," he replied. "Later, I learned how to kill birds with a single hand. You will soon learn that our entire world is sheep and birds. Without either, we die. And for however long you remain here, they will be part of you as well. Each able one does the work for themselves and those who are not able. Those who are very young or very old are not able. You aren't among them, therefore you must do your part."

Isolba nodded. He was a curious lad, taking charge and telling her what to do. The lads she watched from a distance in Demoria were impish and full of mischief. In the short time she had known Rindan, she had not witnessed him act foolish or playful like other youths his age. The sober lines of his face revealed his tough upbringing.

"The sheep must be let out to graze each morning and then placed back within their fold in the evening," he instructed. "It doesn't matter which sheep end up in the fold as we collectively raise them. You are in charge of the ones that go into this fold. Releasing them is a matter of ease, but fetching them…"

"What do they have to graze upon?" Isolba asked as her eyes scanned the bleak moor.

"Whatever they can forage," Rindan said. "We give them hay, of course, but must ration it. They wander the entire island and are able to find some vegetation between the rock crevasses and such. I've managed to collect sorrel and fescue in hidden areas, away from the wind. Every bit helps keep us alive."

Rindan drew the closest sheep from the fold and the others clumsily followed.

"Help move them out," Rindan instructed.

Isolba's hands fell on the back of a sheep and she pushed it toward the opening. It bleated in protest, startling her, and as it hurried away, she plunged forward and tumbled into the cold, stinking muck. She rolled away from the trampling hooves, leapt to her feet, and brushed the mud off her clothing.

Rindan shook his head, his expression blank. He did not need to speak for her to know exactly what he was thinking. She was aware of how feeble and pathetic she looked. With an exhale, she returned to coaxing the remaining sheep from the fold. They followed their comrades to the barren pastures.

"Take your jug," Rindan ordered as he picked up his own.

"The widows' cows are this way. At one time, they belonged to my grandparents who are... gone."

His voice faded as he turned his face from her. A lilt of sadness hung on his tone, and she grasped his meaning. She had not read him as sentimental, but she had never taken the time to dissect the layers of Rindan's personality. She found him intriguing, a mystery behind a somber countenance.

In a short time, they found the cows tied near a drystone wall, munching the dead grass along its base. She recognized them as the ones that dwelled in the widows' house. The two cows were small, shorter than Isolba, with dark, shaggy coats. Rindan placed his hand against the side of one and stroked its fur. A smile formed on his face. Isolba could not help but notice how incredibly handsome he was when he smiled.

"Good morrow, Min," he said in a soft, soothing voice. Turning to the other, he petted her forehead in greeting. "Good morrow, Brìde."

Though Isolba cringed at their wet noses and the large, drooling mouths chewing absent-mindedly, their soulful eyes entranced her from behind wavy strands of fur. She reached a trembling hand out to touch the one Rindan called Min. Its long fur proved incredibly soft, the body warm as she felt every breath.

Rindan looked back at her with his hazel eyes and flutters quickened in her chest. Why did his gaze strike familiarity in her? All this time, she had pushed aside the memory of him, believing it had manifested from her trauma. Yet she continued to experience a connection, even then as he prepared to milk a cow.

"Watch," he said simply.

She struggled to concentrate as a strange feeling washed over her. She should not think of him as anyone other than a crofter, a tenant of her father's, a nobody she would leave behind when she sought shelter beneath Cormac's wings. She watched Rindan squat beside Brìde and set his jug beneath her udder.

"They're nearly dry, but we must take what we can," he said.

Rindan reached out with his strong hands. The prominent veins roped beneath his thick skin. With his thumb and forefinger about one teat, he began to stroke downward. Milk flowed into the jug in a straight stream. Brìde stood unfazed, peering at Isolba curiously. The first few squirts seemed productive, but in a short time, Rindan's tugs induced only a weak spray. The light in his eyes dimmed.

"Continue to strip the milk down from the udder in this way," he said, all surety in his voice diminished.

The result in the pot was little more than a puddle.

"'Tisn't much," Rindan said. "They are malnourished and will soon produce naught at all. They calved in autumn, so should've continued to give milk through to summer."

Isolba sensed the wave of doom that flowed from him, but did not fully comprehend what it meant.

"But we must persevere and get what we can," he said. "You try the next one."

She placed her jug below Min's udder and crouched low. Rindan knelt and held the jug's rim steady.

"In case she kicks it," he explained. "We cannot afford to lose a drop."

With timidity, she pulled downward on a teat as she had watched Rindan do, but moved clumsily. Her efforts proved inept and unproductive. The cow shifted her weight, and Rindan placed a calming hand against her flank.

"Here," Rindan directed. He moved alongside Isolba and covered her hands with his calloused ones.

His touch sent a current up her arms, the vibrations branching out through her nerves. Heat bloomed up her throat and her stomach clenched in a strange sensation that caught her off guard. Her entire body tensed with the closeness of his body to hers, and the visceral reaction was as new and foreign as the island and its inhabitants.

Again, a memory flashed before her. She ran next to him in an open, desolate land as her feet landed on dry sand. Incredible heat thickened the air as she saw nothing but sand edged against a blue sky for eternity. This memory provided her with calm and happiness, unlike the first memory where he bled in a gully. He bore a wide smile, his teeth white against deeply tanned skin. A long, colorless tunic hung from his thin frame, a wrap covered his head, and leather sandals clasped about his narrow feet. He was laughing and so was she. They owned not a single worry.

The memory left her. Surely, she had too vivid an imagination, though she had hardly daydreamed in her youth, other than of Cormac. Remembering to breathe, she forced herself to refocus on the task at hand.

Rindan took her fingers and showed her where to latch them at the base of the teat, and with quick motions, pulled tautly. Within seconds, streams of milk began to spurt into the jug.

He withdrew his hands and moved back. "Aye, that's it. Not too bad. It will soon come easy to you with each milking. Methinks she likes your soft hands. They are like the skin of a bairn."

He laughed again, this time louder, and Isolba's cheeks flushed.

"You got more milk out of that one," he said when she stripped all the milk from each teat.

Without realizing it, the corners of her lips curved upward, and when they did, Rindan's eyebrows raised in surprise.

"Do not tell me 'tis so," he said. "The lad can smile? Blessed day! Wait till Mother and Cait hear of this and you will not find a more shocked pair."

She managed a chuckle in return and the weight in her stomach, present since the beginning of her ordeal, lightened a little.

"Now to the widows' to deliver their milk."

Isolba stiffened. "Must I go?" she asked, her voice not more than a whisper.

Rindan lifted his chin to the sky and issued her a sidelong glance. "'Tis a small island with few people and we live so closely.

You are bound to see them again, and soon. 'Tis better to look them in the face and set matters right. After all, we would like for them to invite you back into their home, to be a help to them."

Isolba's legs grew heavy, but she fought the stubborn urge to set down her jug and run. Rindan was right, and his presence would buffer the reunion between her and her guardians. She watched his jaunty stride, examining the way his strong legs moved with purpose, feet pointed slightly outward, and attempted to emulate it. If she were to have a boy's image, she had to be one in more ways than hair and clothing. She had to act like a boy.

Her gait was awkward and unsure on the unfamiliar terrain, while Rindan walked with confidence and certainty with each footfall. His arm remained rigid as he carried his jug with one hand and the milk within trembled gently with each step. Isolba clutched her jug close to her chest, cradling it with both arms, and watched her feet to ensure she would not trip. Between the slippery mud and protruding stones, any one obstacle could send her tumbling to the ground.

"Here we are," said Rindan when they arrived near the widows' blackhouse.

They walked around to the front of the house and Rindan announced, "Good morrow!" into the doorway. Isolba followed in fevered anticipation. Her heart errantly trounced with fear.

"Come in, lad!" Widow MacDuff's voice called out.

When Rindan entered ahead of Isolba, they found the women in their common pose, hands linked as they sat beside the fire. The minute the widows saw Isolba walk in behind Rindan, they stood and backed away.

"Do not be bringing the evil spirits in here!" Widow MacGill barked. Spittle sprayed her chin with the fervor of her words.

Isolba remained in the doorway and, with shaking hands, knelt to set her jug of milk inside. She shrank back then, ears burning with shame. How could she explain the fire combusting the day before? She could only think of it as a coincidence, nothing more, yet the widows in their ardent superstition attributed the phenomenon to her.

"There are nae evil spirits within these," Rindan reassured, setting down his jug next to Isolba's. "Only milk. He helped me milk your cows this morning. I'm afraid there's less than yesterday. They're drying out, you ken."

"'Tis he that causes them to ill-produce!" Widow MacGill continued. "He's been a blight to our island ever since he arrived here. We would rather milk them ourselves, aching bones or not. We'll not suffer his cursed hands to touch our animals."

"Nae," Rindan said. "'Tis because they are malnourished and there is little to forage upon these hills. We must pray for spring to come this season or we all die. You think this wee lad has control over the weather?"

"He very well could if he were in commune with a demon," Widow MacDuff said.

"Wheesht!" Rindan uttered, shaking his head in disbelief. "My father has appointed Indris as steward of your livestock and to tend your croft. Will you refuse his help?"

"As I spake," Widow MacGill said. "We will do it ourselves."

"But did not you ask for assistance last year, seeing you've found your daily tasks most difficult?" Rindan questioned.

"Aye, we did," Widow MacGill admitted. "And we were fine so long as it was you or Saithan or Cait helping, but not this lad. We would rather do it ourselves."

"But he needs to do the work and requires the experience. 'Tis good for him," Rindan argued. "He's an able body and you must put him to task."

"Aye, that's for certain, but how long did he live with us and prove himself useless?" said Widow MacGill.

"Did you instruct him? Guide him on what to do and show him how he could be of help?" Rindan probed.

"Beg pardon?" Widow MacGill. "You accuse us and defend him?"

"Nae, not at all!" Rindan replied, his voice full of passion. "I speak of inaction itself, of the lad's ignorance and his need for guidance. 'Tis clear you were not aware before, but now you are."

"Aye, I suppose we now ken, but it doesn't change matters. We do not want him near us, our home, or our livestock."

"But he has done nae wrong, and I'm prepared to show him how he can be of service to you."

"Nae wrong?" Widow MacGill repeated, incredulous. "Do our singed eyebrows not give testament to the fact our fire was provoked by his will? As we told your father yesterday, the lad has evil powers of sort and we want naught to do with him."

"He's but a simple lad," Rindan said, defeat in his voice. "He means nae harm." It was plain he could not win against two women who had their minds made up. He turned to look at Isolba, and she backed outside in hopes he would leave.

Though she was grateful Rindan had fought her case so ardently, she knew she was an unwanted fixture on the island. No matter how hard she worked and proved her worth, she would never belong. But she had little choice but to endure. She was becoming Indris, and Indris would not accept defeat as easily as Isolba.

"I will tend to your cows for now," she heard Rindan say within the house. "Yet I do hope you have a change of mind."

Widow MacGill grunted in response, and Isolba saw Rindan's face appear in the doorway as he stepped outside. He offered a reassuring smile, but his face quickly turned business-like and he made off down the slope.

"Let us eat some breakfast and then it's time for the morning meeting," he said as she followed him toward the Lennox's blackhouse. "Worry nae more of the widows. They need time to come down from their fear and superstition."

Isolba walked on in silence, her chest tight and heavy with despair. She knew the widows misunderstood her, but their reaction to her presence struck a melancholy chord. She certainly had not cared in all the months she lived with them, yet she longed to be accepted and be part of something. She had no place to call home. She could not step foot on the shore of Demoria ever again and become a sacrifice.

Her intended home was in the Argarves, but she knew nothing about it or its people, only the notion of her betrothed. He was only a thought and her a thought to him. He would not know she was dead. The waters had inhibited travel and communication along with it. He probably waited for the day his bride would arrive, not knowing that the first ship able to dock would bear news of her death.

When they entered the cozy confines of the home, they found Saithan seated on the floor, knitting. Cait poured some of the precious milk into a pot that Beathag stirred before the fire. At their entrance, she spooned a small portion of porridge into bowls and handed it to them.

"I fear this is the last of the porridge," Beathag said with a frown. She then asked cheerfully, "How did the milking go? Get along alright, Indris?"

Isolba took the bowl and nodded. "Aye," she whispered.

"He's a true milker!" Rindan commented. "A fine job he did, I do say. Though the cows are drying up."

"Aye," said Beathag. "We only managed half a jug from Coleen this morn. It will only get worse."

"Spring isn't so far away if it does arrive this year," Saithan said, not looking up from his knitting. "If it comes, we can manage till then. If not..."

"We eat more of the sheep," said Cait.

Rindan shook his head. "It cannot come to that," he said. "We must pray for the return of the birds."

"And the sun even sooner," Saithan added.

The family fell quiet, consuming their meager breakfast in silence, but Isolba could not eat. Despite all her travails and need for sustenance, a rock sat in the pit of her stomach. She held out her bowl to Rindan in silent offering, but he shook his head.

"Eat, lad," Beathag said, pushing the bowl's rim toward Isolba's lips. "After breakfast, you are to go with me and Cait up the hill to cut peat. Have you experience with a tusker?"

Isolba shook her head and poured a bit of porridge into her mouth. It tasted gamey and sticky on her tongue, but she swallowed it down in a hard lump.

"You will learn easily enough," the woman replied with a reassuring smile. "'Tis a risk to harvest peat so early in the year, but we have wee more than a month's supply and it will take twice as long to dry in this damp."

Isolba nodded, holding her head up to meet the woman's eyes, and reminded herself to be Indris, agreeable and eager to work. She read Beathag's expression. Kindness set deep in the creases of her face, along with a hint of surprise.

"My, you are a comely wee lad," Beathag remarked. "Such delicate features. 'Tis a pity you've washed up here, on this island, the thief of youth's fairness."

Isolba's cheeks grew hot, and she ducked her head, wary of having her face examined. Rindan and Cait laughed with mouthfuls of porridge. Such a strange sort of people to find amusement as they ate the last of their porridge and contemplated their doom. The heaviness that pervaded the atmosphere could not enter this home. So long as they had one another, outside forces, weather included, seemed to wield no control over their happiness.

After Isolba choked down the last bite of porridge, Saithan took her bowl and pressed the softness of knit wool into her hands. She looked to see what he had made and found a pair of thick mittens, the threads woven tightly together to keep out the cold. She slipped them over her hands, hiding the cracked and bleeding skin. Her stiff fingers rejoiced inside their warm cocoon, and she looked up at the man with tears in her eyes.

The bearded face smiled at her. The corners of his eyes crinkled in pleats of leathery skin. His face reminded her of her father's, only this face held pure kindness. His smile did not mask deep cruelty and betrayal like Escarans' had, a face turned from doting father to selfish murderer.

"I made them for you," he stated. "They are yours to keep."

Isolba began to smile, but a surge of emotion forced her lips into a frown. She tried to suppress the swelling ache in her throat that spread to her chest, but she wept. She concealed her face behind her mitten-covered hands, unable to bear the concerned look everyone wore.

"Och, poor wee lad," Beathag cooed and cloaked Isolba in her embrace. "'Tis a gift and naught to weep at. Saithan has nae better task than to work a needle."

Beathag could not know that her embrace reminded Isolba of the last touch of her mother. Though Beathag did not compare in looks to the beautiful, lithe Moira with her clinking jewels and perfumed hair, a mother's touch was all the same, warm and all-enveloping. Isolba muffled her sobs with her hands, and in her shame, ran outside.

Out of the safe walls of the blackhouse, dozens of islanders stopped their daily ministrations to stare. With fear on their faces, some backed away while others leaned toward one another and whispered. She saw the widows' work before her, the fear, doubt, and superstition woven into the minds of the people. She was not only an outsider, but an aberration.

She swallowed her sobs and wiped her face, ducking back into the blackhouse to face the Lennox family. They seemed surprised to see her so soon, sure she would go off on her own once more. Isolba knew they were possibly the only family that did not believe her to be in line with the forces of evil.

"I regret how I've behaved since coming here," Isolba began, her voice sounding strange. "I can never truly express my gratitude for all you've done for me. I'm prepared to work to repay your kindness."

"We've done nae different for you than we've done for any other shipwrecked soul who's landed here," Saithan said.

It caught Isolba by surprise every time someone mentioned she was a shipwreck survivor. If they knew where she had come from and how she arrived, then they would certainly believe she had uncanny powers. Truly, she could not explain the hound whose back she arrived upon or the visit to the Otherworld. Besides her silly, suppressed gift of reanimating small creatures, her old life seemed ordinary and uneventful in comparison. It was as though the gods had descended upon the earth and a supernatural stirring arose.

TWENTY-TWO

Nearly a mile's distance from the village, on the high slopes of Teutatwen, rich deposits of peat compacted in thick swaths. Women and children trod the hills, worked their tuskers into the soft moss, and cut the peat into a grid-like pattern. Children scooped the chunks of peat onto old plaids, gathered them in bundles, and carried them on their backs for the long return.

As Beathag drove the sharp edge of her tool into the earth, it created a wet scraping noise. In one skilled movement, she brought up a rectangular hunk of peat, earthy and fragrant in the cold air. Cait spread out a threadbare plaid, and with each shovelful Beathag excavated, she stacked the peat in neat rows upon it.

Isolba observed the muck along with the stench of decayed plant matter and wrinkled her nose. Beathag handed her the tusker, and she took it with resignation. Her mittens slipped while trying to grip it, so she reluctantly removed them, tucking them beneath her rope belt. She wrapped her burning palms around the handle, pressed and twisted, but her muscles ached so formidably that she had no strength to pierce the soil. Beathag reclaimed the tusker and determined that Isolba would not help with the digging, but the carrying.

Cait helped load the first full plaid onto Isolba's back and sent her on her way. She struggled under the weight of peat and walked bent-kneed with staggered steps. Children half her size breezed past her while carrying their enormous bundles with ease. Beathag and Cait shook their heads and smirked at her pitiful attempt.

"Careful, Indris!" Beathag called. "You do not want to hurt yourself. Take less peat if it makes the trip easier. You've a long way to go."

Isolba did not wish to lighten her load. She was already carrying less than even the smallest child and felt foolish. She could hear their mocking laughter around her as she walked, her head bent to the ground. The weight of her burden and the angle of the slope nearly pitched her forward. She stopped many times to rest as great, shuddering breaths swelled her ribcage. The others soon outpaced her, but she plodded onward.

In Demoria, slaves performed this task, and Isolba never once thought of who obtained the fuel for her hearth fire. The dense peat weighed heavy with moisture. Bred to carry out such hard work, the Teutatwen children were sturdy, hard-muscled, and full of stamina. She could not imagine such an upbringing, but they never once complained and set about their task with not only a sense of duty but a sense of urgency.

What a mellifluous existence had been hers! She longed for the days spent with Nareen by the fire or in the garden, weaving, painting pottery, or experimenting with different hairstyles. Now, the state of her hair nearly made her weep. Every night as she fell asleep, she ran her fingers over the short regrowth, willed it to speed its progress.

As much as she wanted to reach the Argarves in haste, she also did not want Cormac to see her this way. Would he be furious to learn how she lived and toiled on this strange island? Of course, such information was trivial when compared to her intended slaughter on the altar stone. It seemed strange to be alive, knowing she should be dead, and every movement of muscle and tendon, every heavy breath, and every beat of her heart surprised her, as if living rebuked nature's will.

When she finally closed in toward the village with her large burden, she stumbled along, watching the heels of the other children far ahead for guidance. Beathag and Cait soon caught up to her as they bore their own bundles and hollered words of encouragement.

She did not know how close she was to the flat ground where they piled the peat for footing. As she continued forward, weak muscles about to give way, her shins slammed into something solid. She tumbled headfirst onto the ground. When her torso hit the soil, all the air left her lungs. The bundled plaid burst open. Aromatic, wet peat rolled out and broke apart. She heard deep, guttural laughter from a lone male voice. Titters from the children swiftly joined the cruel notes.

Dazed and faint, she pushed herself up with her forearms and turned her head to look behind and witness the jester who thought himself so clever. It was the boy from the hot spring, the one who had nearly tried to drown her in his zeal. His leg remained splayed across her path, and he threw his head back in laughter. His hands clutched his chest as though he found her situation unbearably humorous. His little friend was at his side, smiling and chuckling, though his eyes would not look at her.

"Silly wee lad," her tormentor said. "You need to take care and watch where you walk."

A rush of fire lapped up her sternum, and she longed to scream, to shove him, but she held back and as soon as she found her breath again, she rose to her knees. Beathag and Cait rushed to her side.

"Angus!" Beathag called out. "Look what you've done!"

But Angus had walked away and made it several strides out with his friend at his heels. The children with their sacks of peat immediately stopped laughing and turned somber.

"And wee Duffy! You should ken better, lad!" Beathag continued, though the boys made off without acknowledging her.

Beathag sighed and laid down her bundle. Cait, glaring after Angus, followed suit, and they began picking up the fallen peat and placing it back into Isolba's plaid. Isolba swallowed the knot in her throat and helped gather, so that in time, they salvaged her bundle.

"I shall have Saithan speak with the lads' fathers," Beathag said in a comforting tone.

"Beg pardon, Mother," Cait interjected. "But what good has that done before? You ken when Angus threw gannet guts on Marcus Keenan? The day after Father spoke to Paedrus Gorrie, Angus came around with a black eye and meaner than ever. He would not let Marcus be for weeks. Made his life a misery. Even now, Marcus will not go near him."

Beathag's shoulders sagged in defeat, though the anger in her voice refused to fade. "Indris, lad, do not go near Angus if you can help it. When he speaks to you, ignore him. Give him nae reaction and soon he will tire and look elsewhere for trouble."

Cait looked doubtful. Her windburned face scrunched up. "You do not ken Angus, do you, Mother?"

THE FOLLOWING day passed with the family footing their share of the peat. They worked next to their neighbors, carrying peat into the cleitan. Isolba watched as Saithan, Beathag, Cait, and Rindan each took bricks of wet peat and stacked them on the floors of the cleitan, two by two, crisscrossed. Saithan explained that the air would come through the gaps in the drystone walls, flow between the empty spaces of each stack, and dry out the peat evenly.

"'Tis imperative they dry completely," Saithan instructed. "A damp hunk of peat is nae use at all. It will not burn. It will not keep us warm nor cook our food. The stacking must be done proper. With care."

Isolba's back ached from the carrying and constant bending.

Peat caked in the folds of her breeks and tunic. It encrusted her fingernails where soreness dwelt in the quicks. She longed to lie in a warm bath before slipping between cool linen sheets on a feather mattress.

As much as she wanted to prepare a thorough statement for Cormac listing every machination done to her during her stay in Teutatwen, she failed to anger. The incredible sense of purpose drowned out any irritation of unfairness that rang in her skull. She worked alongside these people, all performing the same task and all of equal rank.

What did irritate her was Angus. He would dash to Rindan's side, make some critical remark about Isolba's work, and dart away before anyone had a moment to respond. He continued his running commentary for what seemed like hours. Sometimes he was gone so long that the Lennoxes believed he had grown bored or made to fear his father, but he never failed to reappear just as they forgot his antics.

Isolba saw the sandy-haired lad, Duffy, who had laughed when Angus tripped her. He worked nearby with his parents and chatted to Rindan whenever the boys visited the peat pile. Rindan responded with clipped words, too focused on his task to waste time in conversation. Every time Angus visited, Duffy paused his work and tittered in amusement. It came to pass after another of Angus' visits that Saithan mentioned this to Duffy's father.

"Cousin Askill," Saithan said. "I must tell you, only because you would equally warn me on account of my son, but your Duffy is learning shameful behaviors from that Angus."

Isolba noticed Duffy drop all gaiety and look to the ground, his ears reddening.

"That so?" Askill remarked and eyed his son with disappointment. He stiffened and pointed at Duffy in accusation. "You mind yourself, lad. I will not stand for foolishness. If I catch you laughing nigh, I'll smack you so hard you'll never wish to laugh again."

Duffy hurried back to stacking peat. Isolba caught him

narrowing his eyes at her as if he blamed her for his tongue-lashing. She felt sickened to know how many hated her simply for existing. If she presented as a lass, would they treat her better? Perhaps, but she was much safer as Indris.

When their piles of peat diminished and their neat stacks formed rows of miniature towers within the cleitan, Angus burned through their remaining patience. He arrived with mischief in his mien, knelt next to Isolba, and scrutinized her stacked bricks. She paused and issued a pleading glance toward Saithan.

"Not wide enough," Angus commented, and with the forceful shove of his fingers, nudged one brick so that her entire arrangement shifted askew.

Isolba shouted in dismay, and Angus jumped from the cleit to sprint off. Rindan bounded behind him, lifted one foot, and drove it into Angus' rear. Angus dropped like a sack of rocks. Landed forward on knees and elbows.

"Rindan!" Beathag scolded.

Askill gaped at the sight and his mouth twitched with humor. He turned to address Duffy while motioning to Angus. "That lad had it coming."

As Angus rose to his feet, he laughed uneasily and offered a playful smile at the Lennoxes. Rindan glared at him in a clear warning.

"Be off with you, Angus," Beathag ordered. "Is your father not looking for you?"

Angus took a moment to reply. His gaze landed on Cait, who never once stopped bending and stacking. Finally, he said, "He is home ill this day."

"Ah, give Paedrus my well wishes," Saithan said. "But leave us now. We will not stand for foolery."

Angus' mouth drew tight. His eyes still rested on Cait. She continued ignoring him and at last, he departed and stalked back to his work.

Rindan shook his head and returned to the task. A flame flickered in Isolba's core and for a moment she forgot to breathe. Once again, he had come to her defense. Was not Angus his friend and Rindan had opposed him?

She stood frozen and stared. He looked up to notice her and furrowed his brow. His lips twisted in confusion before he motioned toward her stack. Breaking her reverie, she hurried back to the footing, aware of the heady sensation stealing her breath.

Isolba completed her work in a dreamlike state. The haze of disbelief and wonder clouded her vision. Then, when Beathag instructed her to follow Rindan and collect the sheep, she gladly complied.

Rindan led her over the moor and up to a brae. A freshwater spring spilled from a rocky partition in the hillside. He plunged his arms into the stream and washed away the layers of muck. He cupped water in his palms and splashed the grime from his face.

Isolba went to his side and held her hands in the rushing water. The shock of cold paralyzed her, but the clean coolness refreshed her senses. Alone with Rindan, thoughts of Angus vanished.

She bent her head to wash her face, and her fingers grew numb. Beneath the spray of water, she caught a shimmer. She reached and plucked a geometric stone from the ground. Its flat, notched planes sparkled in the dim light. Feldspar. She clasped it in her palm and examined it in awe. Noted its intricate pattern and luster. She called to mind the little information Baltair had once told her about this stone. It acted as an aid for travel, but she knew not exactly how.

"If you like that one, I can show you where we have many stones of interest," Rindan volunteered, breaking the silence.

She looked up at him and fought to suppress her excitement. Still, her eyes widened, and her jaw went slack. "Aye, if we've the time."

"We are going in that direction anyhow, but you must ken that most islanders avoid that area, particularly the elders," he warned. "I will tell you why when we get there."

Though weariness and discomfort wracked her body, glee fluttered within her, and she followed him higher up the slope, northward. She could watch him without conscience as she traced his steps. His small, thin body navigated the crags with ease. His strong back rose and fell with steady breaths while muscled legs powered through boggy soil and up vast inclines. The dark mud clinging to his tunic and breeks gradually dried and blew away in particles.

Her heartbeats accelerated until she became nearly out of breath, though the exertion caused only part of the physiological effect. She had deemed Rindan handsome at first sight, but the rush of blood in her veins told her she saw more in him than beauty. Isolba saw him as her safety, her protector, and longed to curl within his shelter and absorb his warmth, his calm energy. He was not an idea, a hypothetical notion, like Cormac, but flesh and bone before her.

She had never known true desire, only the pining away for a betrothed yet to meet, but she was besotted. Though she meant to bide her time until she reached Cormac, she could not fight the pull toward Rindan. How could she remain fixated on Cormac, whom she had never met, and after all these long months, no longer seemed real? Yet she could not act on her emotions. They would remain fettered within the body of Indris and never freed.

Yet when Rindan halted and waved his hand ahead to a dark hole in the ground framed by large drystones, it was Isolba's personality that reacted. She squealed and clapped a hand over her mouth. Numerous tiny stones glittered about the mouth of the entryway, specimens of quartz, gneiss, feldspar, and brown olivine all placed there with intent by human hands. The heaviness in the air weighed on her as if composed of sand. The earth held a palpable charge and the shining stones hummed with energy and force. She knelt to reach for one.

"Nae," Rindan said abruptly. "Do not do that."

She pulled her hand away and peered up at him, quizzical. Why did he bring her into the temptation of all these stones only to dissuade her touch?

His stoic face broke into a slight grin and he chortled. "'Tis the house of the faeries and the stones are our offerings."

"Och, I did not ken," she whispered and marveled at the gaping hole.

"I do not believe in it," Rindan said, and placed his hands on his hips. "'Tis all superstition to me. I do not have a care if you touch them, but if others see them moved, they would react badly."

I believe, she thought to herself and set her shining piece of feldspar among the other stones.

"Our people lived up on these slopes at one time," Rindan explained. "We've only dwelled in the bay perhaps one or two hundred years. You can see the cairns all about. There are nae ruins of houses as we took all the stones to build our homes in the bay."

"But why has the faerie house remained untouched?" she asked.

"None will enter it or take from its foundation because they believe harm will come to one who does," he replied. "So we leave offerings instead. We do not ken how long it's been here or why 'twas built, but we've kent it as the house of the wee ones for as long as anyone remembers."

Isolba closed her eyes in reverence and splayed her hands over the ground. Tremors entered her fingertips and toes, crawled up her arms and legs, and reverberated across her body until her skin crawled with gooseflesh.

"You cannot feel it?" she asked him bravely. *Can you feel how I care for you?*

"I feel naught but a gale," he answered and shook his head with a slight smirk. "We ought to collect the sheep."

"Need help?" a voice rang out behind them.

Isolba turned to see an unkempt lass walking up the slope, and blanched at the imposition to her and Rindan's moment of solitude. The girl carried a basket in one arm while her long, wavy hair tangled with elflocks over her plaid shawl. Her features were ordinary, but she could not be called plain.

"Good evening, Una," Rindan said with a heavy sigh. "We need nae help. I only wished to show Indris the faerie house on the way to collect our sheep."

"Aye, Cait said I would find you this way. Angus is searching for you."

"Aye?" Rindan uttered warily. His bare feet shuffled upon the matted grass. "I've nae wish to see him."

"I saw what you did," Una said with a giggle. "What a sight! I'm amazed you tolerated him for as long as you did."

Isolba disliked how this lass pretended she did not see her there as she kneeled on the grass before the faerie house. Una regarded Rindan alone and smiled sweetly at him, her chatter light and flirtatious.

"I've a gift for you," she said, holding the basket out to him. "A wee bit of barley bread and some dried seaweed."

"Nae," Rindan rejected and pushed the basket away. "I cannot take your rations. 'Tis a wonder how you've barley left."

"'Tis the dust left from the last of it, not much," she said. "I've noticed how thin you've become, and I ken you'll need your strength for the bird season."

Isolba bristled. Una's boldness and affection toward Rindan made her ill. Fever overcame her, a response to the hate brewing beneath her skin. Nae, Una could not have him. But Isolba, as Indris, was utterly helpless in stopping her.

"Take it," Una goaded.

"I cannot," Rindan replied. "We're fetching the sheep."

"Then eat it now," she said. Her lips drew up in a silly, coquettish beam.

Isolba's mouth fell open in disgust. Her hands pressed harder into the earth, her fingertips dug into the soft soil. The vibrations quickened along her nerves. A gust of wind blew through the vicinity and curled into the entrance of the faerie house. A howl echoed within the dark tunnel. The lonesome sound grieved the earth, the air, and faded in prolonged lament.

Una shivered and terror distorted her features. She furrowed her brow at Isolba, at last acknowledging her. Isolba slowly rose to her feet and her expression appealed Rindan, asked to depart.

"I ken why many do not visit here," Una commented, wide eyes staring into the abyss. "What a fearsome sound."

"'Tis only the wind," Rindan said.

"I've never heard the wind to sound like that," Una said.

THEY MOVED on after Una stumbled away, basket in hand. Together, they sought sheep from the northern point of the island and coaxed them into a herd. Isolba, no stranger to shepherding, had observed flocks steered to their folds many times. When chased, most of the sheep naturally merged into a pack, and from there, were directed toward an intended location.

From the high point of Àrdaill, Isolba watched the other youths fetch sheep from opposing ends of Teutatwen and marveled at the evening dance of human and animal. Some of the trained island hounds assisted in the work and cut off any rogue sheep attempting to run in the wrong direction. The task was not easy, nor light, especially on stony, boggy, or steep terrain, and descending darkness added to the anxiety of collecting every stray.

Running in the cool gloaming with Rindan sent electricity through her veins. At times, his face cracked into a whisper of the handsome smile she so adored. Out on the lonely lip of Teutatwen, discourse came naturally to him. He pointed out the separate islet of Dalais and the mouflon sheep they could not access. The sloping plateau sheared off to cliffs where the exposed faces of weathered granite stood tall and looming.

They departed the summit as they herded the sheep deeper into the valley below. They passed within sight of the hot spring, and Isolba watched the steam billow above it in the cold night air. At last, they guided the gaunt animals into the sheepfolds. Isolba's body sagged with fatigue, and her mind turned foggy.

But as the pair pulled the stone block in front of the sheepfold's entrance, a familiar, grating voice shouted from the near dusk. "Rindan!"

They watched Angus charge forward. He backed Rindan against the drystones of the fold, jaw clenching as he set his face within inches of his friend's. Isolba shrank to the ground. Made herself small against the base of the fold.

"You dare humiliate me?" Angus growled.

Rindan held up his hands in surrender and chortled nervously. "Och, that wee kick was enough to humiliate you?"

"All of Teutatwen watched. Why did you do it before your parents...before Cait?"

"You disturbed our work," Rindan reasoned. "You continuously insulted Indris, who's worked hard to prove himself useful."

Isolba froze and wished she had words to use against Angus, to defend Rindan as he defended her. She despised her weakness and wished she had the gumption to throw herself between the lads. Knowing she would not, she instead longed to disappear. Because of her, Rindan and Angus had turned from friends to enemies. What good did she provide anyone on the island by being there? All confidence and purpose gained in the prior days drained from her spirit.

Angus looked down at Isolba and curled his upper lip. "He would prove his use better if he were dead, and we took his rations."

Pain entered Isolba's soul. Angus' words triggered the sacrificial ceremony and brought to life the horrific nightmares where Baltair cut her open, again and again. An animal sound erupted from her throat, projected unwillingly. She covered her head, collapsed deeper, and wailed.

Angus drew back, and Rindan knelt at her side. He touched her gently. "Indris!" he called. "He isn't serious."

She closed her eyes tight and clamped her mouth to stop the sound, and when that failed to work, she acted the only way she could. She stopped breathing.

Quick footsteps trod the damp ground. "What's to do?" Cait called.

Angus issued a dismissive grunt.

Isolba last felt Rindan's cool fingers lightly smacking her face as she slipped into darkness. The stench of the muck beneath her hung in her nostrils, and as she faded, despair ate a cavity within her.

TWENTY-THREE

Instead of spring, a historic snowstorm arrived in Teutatwen. It froze the edges of the Atlantic in the bay and piled snow several feet against the blackhouses. The islanders tacked sheepskin across their open doorways to barricade the blowing drifts.

As the storm rushed in, they herded the sheep into the cleitan and provided them hay. The animals warmed within the round stone structures, huddled together. Their bewildered eyes peered out at the incoming snow. The hounds also sheltered in cleitan or scurried into the houses with their tails between their legs. They whined with fright and shivered as they sought the cows' companionship.

"Poor creatures have never seen such snow before," Beathag said, as she and the rest of the family carried dried peat from a cleit into the blackhouse and piled it along the inside wall. "Neither have we. Beira has bestowed her winter's bounty, that's certain."

After they brought in plenty of fuel, the family hunkered down to wait. With the constant wind and snow that blew through the doorway's cracks and mixed with peat smoke, the family could not adequately warm. They quaked together near the fire, wrapped in plaids, and drew heat from one another.

Coleen added her warmth to the mix. With the first whistling snow squalls, her eyes rolled in terror, and she stomped her hooves. She wandered from her byre to the doorway and back again. Beathag tried coaxing her to her corner, but she stubbornly stood and dropped her manure. It permeated the air and froze into hard bricks. Rindan rose to scrape up the mess with a shovel and tossed it into the byre. When it happened again, Cait reluctantly unfolded herself to take on the task.

In time, Isolba learned to spring up before them and tackle the work without being asked. She would hold her breath and choke back her disgust, all the while maintaining a stoic expression. When she saw how her efforts pleased them and the way Rindan's mouth curved and eyes danced in appreciation, she followed every cue and put in her share.

"We have fertilizer enough," Beathag commented dryly. "All we need now is spring."

Spring. When it arrived, ships could sail the waters. Isolba could find Cormac. Save her mother and Nareen. Hear their laughter upon learning of her experiences shoveling cow excrement. Then, she would look at the faces of the family so dear to her, and a twinge of guilt snatched her back from her daydream.

The snowstorm added difficulty in attending to bodily needs. Wintry winds howled for three days, and they could not brave the elements each time they had to empty their bladders. Beathag partitioned off a corner of the house with an old plaid hung from the reed rafters. Behind it, the family used an old clay pot for their private business. It needed emptying twice daily, but Saithan insisted he do the job. He stumbled into the frozen abyss to toss the contents into the midden.

He tried to cheer the household. Would play his lyre and sing, but only for a short while. With their slight rations, he had little energy for merrymaking, and his company not roused to gaiety. He lamented how the chill stiffened his fingers and made his plucking unwieldy.

When not on his lyre, Saithan was slow and languorous, often lost deep in thought. Isolba had yet to see him angry or excited. He went about his days in a calm, unhurried manner. He wove a bit here and there, carded wool, and knitted. The cheeks of his bearded face sank deep, with smile lines imprinted around his eyes and mouth. His long, calloused fingers deftly worked a sewing needle through fabric. He had a habit of stopping to stare into nothingness and could not easily be called back.

Beathag bore issue with keeping still and fidgeted through her confinement. Accustomed to the usual preoccupation with some task or another, her days stretched long and monotonous. She also could not bear silence, and so, restless and fretful, she spoke any thought aloud.

"Those widows only demonize you, Indris, because they are miserable and wish to share their misery with the rest of us," she said, as if she worried over the island's gossip. "And Angus has naught else to do than pester you because he has found merriment there."

Isolba had ignored the gossip at first. Why call more attention to herself—other than the unavoidable curiosity she, an outsider, invited? Yet Angus' incessant bullying had put her on alert. Before the snowstorm, she made a routine of looking over her shoulder when leaving the house, but he had not bothered her since their last altercation.

Most of the islanders had given up asking questions because she answered with silence. Her prudence did not help the case of superstition against her. Lately, new gossip arose that she convened with the faeries and called darkness forth from the tunnel. Also, her fit at the sheepfold invited talk that an evil spirit possessed her.

It did not matter how she acted. The majority did not want Indris, the strange child, in their midst. The sooner she could reach the Argarves and resume her former identity, the better for her, her mother, and Nareen. But the thought of leaving the Lennoxes, especially Rindan, broke her heart. They were the only family to show her kindness. They did not treat her as an aberration and had especially warmed to her after her willingness to work.

Though inwardly she fretted, she adopted Rindan's attitude of cool and calm. Rindan and Cait had inherited their father's wistfulness, allowing their mother to do all the talking and saying little themselves, unless impassioned. She was in good company as she continued her plan to speak little.

Cait remained aloof and had a restrained manner of speaking to Isolba. She often seemed distracted. The older girl would sometimes sit apart from her family and peer into the void, her expression contemplative, sometimes troubled. Her brow knitted as if working through some problem. Like her mother, she could not hide her restlessness, and paced along one wall, her fingers slid over the stones and grew black with soot.

And then there was Rindan. Despite the cold, Isolba's cheeks flushed with heat from the nearness of him. She snuck far too many glances at his pensive mouth, the thick lashes of his downcast eyes, and over his folded arms. How often she wondered what it would feel like to be enveloped by those arms. Those broad, gentle hands showed such strength. Their corded veins twisted over knuckles and wrist bones. She longed to interlock her fingers with his and feel the warmth, the vigor. To smooth back that shock of brown hair that hung over his eyes.

Isolba caught herself in a longing sigh and swallowed the yearning. It swelled in her throat and ached. In those moments, she forced herself to close her eyes and attempt to sleep. *Cormac*, she had to think only of him. Yet the vision of her betrothed now wavered, blurred, and was replaced with the lad who had unknowingly stolen her devotion.

In those long, dark days, Rindan turned particularly quiet. No one could know what he thought or if he worried. His empty expression seemed set in stone. Isolba thought back to the rare times he had smiled and wanted more than anything to see him happy.

When Rindan did speak, he mentioned going out to check on the livestock.

"Do not dare!" Beathag said. "You will lose your way and

freeze to death. 'Tis impossible to see aught out there. You could not see your hand if you held it before your face."

Rindan would gently argue, but Beathag had the louder and firmer voice that demanded obedience. So, he hushed into brooding silence, his lips clamped together and eyes faraway.

Beathag and Cait prepared all the meals, though their food supply diminished. Only mutton remained, and they were careful to stretch their portions. Like everyone else, Beathag had lost weight through the winter months and no longer carried her soft, round appearance.

"We are withering away," Beathag said, maintaining good humor. "Soon we will disappear altogether. When the tacksman alas docks his ship on our shore, he will find none here, not a trace of us."

"Surrounded by more fish than we can eat in our lifetime, yet we cannot reach a single one," Saithan said, looping yarn around his needle.

"Indris, why not use those powers to dry up the sea?" Beathag asked, and laughed at the absurdity of her request. "Then we can reach all the sea creatures and fill our bellies to bursting."

Isolba's face flushed, and with a smirk, showed that despite everything, she had a sense of humor, too.

Saithan chuckled, but grew introspective. "Thousands of years ago, this was all dry land and there was nae sea and nae fish."

Isolba's face filled with wonder, and when he saw her interest, he continued. "Land once existed between Teutatwen and the Hebrides, connecting us to Demoria, the Argarves, and all the smaller islands. In that land, our ancestors coexisted with the giants and other great fearsome beasts who regularly struck terror in the hearts of men. In that land called Perottia, our ancestors lived as a great society of people."

Rindan twisted his fingers in boredom. Cait sighed and rolled her eyes. No doubt the siblings had heard their father tell the story many times.

Saithan's voice rose, rich and engaging, a voice that spoke little in everyday life but proved to be in its element when storytelling.

"Perottia's last leader was the great King Adaidh who had nine hundred wives," Saithan went on. "Our people lived in a fertile land filled with riches beyond our imagination. They had massive temples and statues dedicated to the king and his family. They treated them like gods. Yet these monuments were built by slave labor, slaves who were once everyday people stolen from neighboring societies. They were poorly treated and given little food. Their shelters were unfit for even the lowest animal. Disease and unsafe working conditions caused many to perish. It did not matter when their numbers dwindled, as the Perrotians kidnapped from other lands at will and forced their victims into slavery."

Isolba's ears perked up. The slaves were kidnapped?

"The giants terrorized the land, and the people fought against them in battles and built the city walls high for protection. These giants and other beasts devoured humans. They had nae morality nor value for life."

Isolba trembled in horror. She disliked gruesome stories, but could not cover her ears to drown out Saithan's words.

"To seek favor with the gods against the giants, King Adaidh and the kings before him regularly sacrificed slaves as offerings. For ninety days before a ritual, a slave kent all the riches and comforts like a member of royalty, growing fat from the bounty of food. He wore fine robes and was visited by people bearing gifts, hoping the slave would ask the gods to favor them when he passed over the threshold from life to death.

"Because of this practice, the slaves sought sacrifice and competed against each other, hoping to be chosen. Their poverty had pushed them that low. It meant that for ninety days, they would experience comfort and how it felt to have a full stomach."

Isolba's own stomach clenched with unease. Her fingers rested on her throat, where she rubbed her necklaces beneath the cover of her blanket. She had never pondered the plight of the slaves, instead viewing them as everyday fixtures in her life. They had existed to serve her and her family. Though Nareen was her dearest friend in the world, she had no choice but to stay at Isolba's side. Was it likely Nareen had not been born into slavery, but abducted?

Her soul might have crushed under the weight of the possibility. She had once trusted her father in all things, even when he could not recall Nareen's origins. Had Escarans stolen Nareen from her homeland to become his daughter's companion?

Saithan went on, "When the great flood arrived, seawater covered this land. As the water washed into the palace and temples, the people panicked, and all was chaos. A group of slaves murdered the king and his family. Thousands of people attempted to escape the floodwaters in search of higher ground, but many drowned. The beasts and their evil ways perished in the flood, never again to harm humans."

Isolba recalled the giant's skull within Spirit Hound Cave. By that evidence, it seemed some giants survived, but she dared not share the knowledge with her company.

"Survivors escaped to the mountaintops to wait for the waters to recede," Saithan said. "But that day never arrived. These high points became the islands of Teutatwen, Demoria, and the Argarves, and the people of the great nation of Perottia were forever separated. The people of Demoria and the Argarves established clans and began life anew as a primitive race. They faced many deprivations. When they established connections with the Hebrides, they returned to a life closely resembling what they had before, and that included keeping and sacrificing slaves."

Isolba sucked in a great breath and drew it out in a prolonged, tremulous exhale. She glanced at Saithan, but he did not notice her distress. Beathag, Rindan, and Cait stared into the fire with indifference.

"But our ancestors in Teutatwen took a different path. They believed the flood happened for a reason: because of the evil ways of the wealthy, because of the poor treatment of the slaves, and how they slaughtered them in rituals. Nae more would we have separation between the classes. Nae man would be better than another, and all would be equal, including women. We formed a pact to always remain peaceful people and have lived this way ever since."

The knot in Isoba's stomach twisted tighter. Then, she tensed when her people became the direct subject of Saithan's story.

"When Clan MacKay of Demoria claimed ownership of our island six hundred years ago, it was for our benefit. Each summer, the tacksman of Clan MacKay docks his boat. We feed him and his retinue for days and give a portion of our meat, feathers, and fabric to the tacksman as payment. It is a small price to pay to live in complete peace. In return, we receive protection, food, and other goods we may need, but most importantly, a lifeline to the outside world."

Saithan paused, and his story took a turn. With his next words, Isolba's eyes opened further to the truth about her people.

"Some years ago, a man washed ashore. The waves carried him in, and our people pulled him to safety." His eyes flicked to Isolba and with a light laugh, he added, "Like you, Indris!"

Isolba peered back, bashful, and Saithan took a moment to restrain his smile. With a hard swallow, he continued, "He was lifeless when they found him, beaten and strapped to a wooden panel. Yet, he lived to tell his story. He was an Ovate from Ireland who came to Demoria with his Filid. They had traveled all over the highlands, lowlands, and isles of Scotland, seeking other active druids who performed their rituals in secret in a land where their religion was banned. They were glad at first to find the Demorians, their island so remote that they could openly practice their religion. But the Filid were shocked by the ritual of human sacrifice, something they had thought was only a rumor from the past.

"The Filid sought to turn the Demorians from their ways. They denounced their holding of slaves and said nae god of lightness would ask for human sacrifice. They admonished them, telling them that by sacrificing human souls, they offered dominion to the serpent. The serpent would see all humans dead because he fell from favor and we took his place as sons and daughters. The Demorians did not want to hear their way of life was wrong, so they beat the Ovates nearly to death before throwing them into the sea."

Isolba's jaw slackened. This history was nowhere in the stories Escarans used to tell as she sat upon his knee, eager-eared. Her people had ignored this new knowledge. Trusted their history instead of a wandering group of druids. A shiver rushed through her. Though she had not witnessed the full ritual of human sacrifice, she was close enough to Baltair's blade to know they occurred. It had always been part of her people's culture. How could it be so wrong?

The grounding of her roots, once planted so firmly in Demoria, had withered with the news of her sacrifice. Now, those roots drew up from the soil and left her with a complete loss of identity.

"This lone survivor was carried in on the waves to Teutatwen. He remained here for one year until another boat traveling to Ireland passed through, and he departed. In that year, he taught us that long, long ago, in the beginning, our world was populated by the Fomorians. Their leader was Balor. Those were the darkest of days, days of evil and strife.

"And so, the Earth Shapers, artists of creation, threw out the Fomorians and created beautiful green lands and blue waters and gave the deities of antiquity dominion of this new earth, to act as stewards of the land and overseers of us, their children. We ken one of these deities only as the serpent, as his name was burned from history. He sought to expand his kingdom and refused to listen to the Shapers' advice. His ways turned evil. He tricked the other deities into giving up their power to him. When Balor was slain by his grandson, Lugh, the serpent took his throne. The Fomorians backed him and formed a great, evil army.

"Seeing how the world was returning to the dark days, the Shapers withdrew all dominion from the deities and gave the earth to humankind. The serpent was so angry that we, the new stewards, took over his dominion that he seeks to steal it back from us at every turn. He doesn't use force, but is a trickster who tempts and beguiles. He uses false promises to turn the hearts of kings black. When the earth ran over with evil, when the giants and beasts numbered too many, the Shapers created the flood to cleanse the world."

On Isolba's accidental visit to the Otherworld, the guard had mentioned how the sacrifices empowered a being of darkness. She wondered if he meant the serpent. It made sense. How did Baltair so calmly lead the Demorians into wickedness? How had her father allowed it? Her body tensed with contempt for them both.

"Now it's us humans who give the deities their power. Without our calling them, they wouldn't have the energy to exist on our earthly plane. We give them reverence, and they provide us with their ancient wisdom. 'Tis a cycle, but all are parts of one whole, all being the Father, the Mother, the Son, the Maiden. All operating in good and light and love."

Isolba understood then. All moved seamlessly and as it should, so long as humans caused no harm to one another. By disregarding human life, their actions told the serpent that people were weak, and he used their hatred for one another to bring about their destruction. Humans were highly valuable and powerful, but the serpent did not want them to know that. *She* was powerful. Baltair had been right in that regard, but he had aligned with the powers of darkness, and she could not trust him.

As night descended on the island, she settled in and concentrated on sleep. Instead, her mind spun. Saithan went on.

"Though we disagree with their rituals, our loyalty to Clan MacKay remains unbroken. We depend too much on them for our survival, but Teutatwen and Demoria may as well be a world apart instead of a day's journey across the water. Clan MacKay of Demoria, who yet practices sacrificial ceremonies, is in great peril, for the serpent has a firm foothold there and will destroy all they hold dear. There must be a reckoning...another cleansing, lest that evil overtake the world. I believe this current blight is a symptom of a deeper problem."

Isolba buried her face in her hands. What would happen to her mother and Nareen? What of her co-mothers whom she loved and missed, too? Even hopeless Frang. She could not bear for him to suffer beneath the leadership of Escarans, who was fed lies by Baltair. They were all innocent, led astray.

"Here in Teutatwen," Saithan said, winding down, "we ken our land belongs to the Shapers. This island is a vast sanctuary. We feel spirit alive in the grasses, in the waves, and in the wind. It's all around us and within us, all working together as one. If we could only spread such peace through all of earth…"

His voice trailed off, the thought unfinished, and left suspended in the air. Isolba prayed the gods heard his plea.

SILENCE GREETED Isolba when she woke in the morning. For so long, the wind had howled and drove its message of torment into her soul. Now that she heard nothing, the emptiness proved deafening.

But Beathag's voice broke into that dead space as she declared, "The snowstorm is over at last! Come see the island! I've not witnessed such to compare to in all my days!"

Isolba sat up abruptly, loath to leave her warm cocoon of blankets. The others stirred awake around her, groaned at the interruption of their dreams, far from the nightmare of reality.

As they readied themselves for a day of repairs and to salvage what remained, Saithan presented her with his latest creation: a pair of warm woolen stockings. After she pulled them on, softness enveloped her feet, and she wished to wear them always.

Wearing also the mittens, mantle, and leather hat, she picked up a large jug and walked outdoors. Such brightness nearly blinded her. A crisp white blanket covered everything, from the high slopes behind the village to the bay in front. The hard lines of the blackhouse eaves indented the snow to hint at the structures hidden beneath. Only the tall planes of vertical rockfaces with their muted tones of black and tan remained naked. Even the cleitan sat disguised as mounds of snowy hillocks.

The edges of the sea crusted with ice, and farther out, churned waves of angry black. The sky remained dark, as if threatening to dump another cloud of heavy precipitation. Such lack of color dulled her senses, while the frosty air pricked her lungs. She frowned.

"I must see to the sheep," said Rindan, stealing her attention. "The widows surely need water as well," he said. "I will join you at the spring as soon as I fetch their crockery. We also need to bring water to the livestock."

"Aye," Isolba replied with a nod.

Rindan ran up the hill, his feet now covered in stockings that sank in the snow with every step. His strong legs barreled through the drifts with ease, and after some time, she realized she watched him too long, so transfixed on his movements.

Other islanders walked about, on their way to check on the cattle and sheep, fetch water from the freshwater springs, and gather supplies from the cleitan. Some men already brushed away the snow from the roofs, set to repair the holes the wind had made in the turf and thatch.

When the islanders noticed Isolba, they all stopped to stare and gave her wide berth when they passed her walking to the spring. She held her head down.

A voice barked out into the snowy silence. Startled her. "What curse have you laid on our land, wee lad?"

She peered up to notice another islander standing before her in his ragged plaid mantle. He bore the same hollow cheeks and unkempt beard that every other Teutatwen man possessed. His eyes were vacant, the eyes of someone starved, suffering, and desperate for reprieve.

It took a moment for Isolba to realize he addressed her. "What?" she meekly asked and squinted in confusion.

"You are responsible for this," he replied. At first, it seemed he jested, but his solemn expression made his seriousness plain.

"Nae..." Isolba said, shaking her head and refusing to look him in the face.

He glared at her so intensely, she could feel his eyes bore into her like an auger. "We have witnesses to you bending nature to your will...said you drew up flames to burn the widows in their house. 'Tis also said you called up unearthly sounds from the house of the wee ones."

Isolba did not stay to listen and continued toward the closest spring. Strangely, she was unbothered by his words. They were nothing more than superstitions wrought by a primitive mind.

"I speak to you. Do not walk away when I call you!" he shouted.

"Grigor!" Beathag's voice called out from a distance behind Isolba. "Leave the lad be!"

Isolba whirled around, relieved to see Beathag tracking her. Perhaps the woman had left the house after noticing the man engage her young charge. Beathag warily regarded the man and swiftly closed the gap between her and Isolba.

"You defend him?" Grigor shouted back to Beathag.

"Aye, I do," Rebecca replied defiantly. "I consider him another son to me, and those that render ill to him must deal with me and Saithan."

Isolba's heart blossomed at the word 'son'. The reality that Beathag regarded her as her kin and thus came to her aid warmed her through.

"He ought to be cast into the sea from where he came," Grigor said to Beathag. "'Tis nae lad but some creature from the ocean depths. A soul eater seeking to destroy us all."

"Do not speak of him in that manner!" Beathag said firmly. "He's only a wee lad, can you not see that?"

"I see a stranger. An outsider," Grigor replied. "An odd lad who doesn't speak and holds his identity secret."

"His name is Indris, as you well ken," the woman barked. "And how would you act in a strange land after suffering the trauma of a shipwreck...losing all kin and possessions and nearly your life?"

Grigor threw up his hands in defeat, blowing the air from his lungs in a heavy sigh. He looked as though he wished to form another rebuttal, but he turned to shuffle away, and peered back but once.

Beathag placed her hands upon Isolba's narrow shoulders. "Give nae mind to fools," she said. "He cannot see the spirit that I see in you."

She stared into Isolba's eyes in the way only a mother could with her child. Isolba swallowed a great lump in her throat. A bond of trust cemented between them, and Beathag could not know how grateful Isolba was for this life-worn woman with her bold tongue. At that moment, Isolba welcomed a rash thought to tell Beathag everything and opened her mouth to speak.

A stinging crack exploded on Isolba's cheek as snow spray burst across her face and clothing. Her cheek burned, and she placed her mitten-covered hand over it. She heard a cackle and turned to find Angus standing on the sloping ground above. He pointed in her direction, his mouth spread wide in laughter.

Beathag's face turned deep red, and she drew her lips back in a snarl, "Angus! Nae more!"

Ignoring her, he scooped up another handful of snow and began packing it between his palms. When it formed into compacted ice, he took aim. Before he could hurl it, Rindan appeared behind Angus. He locked his arms around the taller boy's waist and threw him to the ground. Angus sprang up and pushed Rindan backward with such force that Rindan lost his footing and fell into the snow. He rolled back and grabbed Angus by the ankle. Dragged him down and pinned the boy with his full weight. Angus picked up a wad of snow and stuffed it into Rindan's face, but the lad did not lose his hold even as he growled in irritation.

"Stop! Stop!" Beathag screamed. She ran up the hill and pushed the boys apart.

Angus pulled himself up and backed away, amusement set in his features, though he had no air left in his lungs to laugh. He coughed and took a breath. "'Twas but a lark," he said and ran off before Beathag could give him a harsh dressing down.

Isolba's heart pounded in her ears as she watched Rindan brush the snow off his clothing. Beathag spoke to him sternly.

"I do not approve of fighting," she said. "That isn't how we solve our quarrels."

"How would you have stopped Angus?" Rindan asked, his voice strained. "With words? Threats to talk to his father? Angus cannot be handled with words."

Beathag seemed at a loss and turned to look at Isolba. A pained expression crossed her face. "You poor lad, you're bleeding!"

The ball of ice had broken the soft skin of her cheek. A purple bruise developed as pin-drops of deep red blood seeped from the white surface. Rindan shook his head in anger and bit his lower lip as if holding back from chasing after Angus.

"Let's get back to work," Beathag said. "We will dwell on this later. For now, we've far too much to do."

"I came to tell you we lost four sheep in the first cleit I went inside," Rindan said in a near whisper. "And the others hardly look long for this world. I had nae chance to view the full extent of the losses, but I did see Askill and Duffy walking out of another cleit looking somber like."

A tragic expression crossed Beathag's face. She sighed and cleared her throat. "Myself and Cait will be along to dress the dead ones. For now, we will not starve. You and Indris fetch the water and see to the widows."

"Aye, Mother," Rindan said. He regarded Isolba briefly with a look of concern and went away.

Isolba and Beathag walked in separate directions, Isolba toward the spring and Beathag to fetch Cait. Isolba's legs were heavy and uneasy as despair gripped her being. She struggled to make sense of the accusations against her. It seemed she was under attack from anyone who was not of the Lennox household. Unwanted and regarded as a bad omen, she was blamed for the islanders' turmoil.

The Lennoxes treated her as a family member, one they were

quick to protect, and that baffled her. Yet when she thought of how Rindan fought Angus in her defense, heat braised her face. He did not hesitate to shield those in his circle, and it was clear he considered her within it.

She fell on her knees at the spring, held the jug beneath the gurgling gush of fresh water, and filled it. When it was nearly full to the brim, she set it aside and placed a cupped palm into the stream. She slurped the cool water from her hand and swallowed gratefully. With splashes to her face, she washed away days of grime and longed to immerse her full body in the clean pool, freezing or not.

Footsteps crunched the snow behind her. She hurriedly picked up the full jug and stood, nearly bent over with the weight of it. She could not bear another meeting with a superstitious islander. But when she turned, she almost bumped into Rindan, who stood holding the widows' jug.

His face shone raw with cold, and he eyed her skeptically. He sniffed. The dry, colorless lips parted to exhale his steaming breath.

Her legs instantly grew weak. Her stomach flopped. All air left her, and the depths of her viscera swelled with a strange sensation—perhaps overwhelming gratitude, perhaps longing. So ensnared by his male beauty, she forced herself to look away.

"What is it?" he asked. Even the soft sound of his voice sent tremors through her nerves.

Still, she fixed her eyes to the ground, and with effort, managed a shy smile. "Thanks be with you," she whispered, and brushed past him.

Twenty-Four

Whether it was Angus' horrible behavior or the three-day imprisonment with his family, Rindan's restlessness rose within him and he grew on edge. It did not help that the sheep were dying and served as nourishment for his family's survival. Those that perished would feed them for a long time if they sensibly rationed the meat and bones.

Dozens of livestock had died, and those that remained suffered. The cows ceased to produce milk. Even Coleen, their best milker, went dry.

The blankets of snow eventually melted down into thick sheets of ice that made walking the slopes treacherous. Rindan could not burn his excess energy climbing the cliffs, and so remained close to the village, where he helped repair the damage caused by the storm.

The islanders held their breath, waiting for spring, but Rindan doubted it would come in its true form with warmth and greenery pushing through the soil. Instead, rain beat down in heavy sheets, melting the snow and forming muddy freshets that flowed down the bay to merge with the sea. Then the rain abruptly ended, and the soil dried, but the clouds never broke apart to reveal the sun.

One day at noontime, Rindan left home and found himself curious about the sheep. He had already released them in the morning, but noticed they had returned to their enclosures and refused to come out.

While traversing the slope toward his family's sheepfold, he found Cait and Una sitting atop the enclosure's stone wall. The girls looked up when they heard his approach and ceased their chatter. Normally, his stomach pained at the sight of Una, but he was too distracted to recall their last awkward exchange.

"What's the gossip of this day?" Rindan inquired dully, though he had not a care.

Irked by his interruption, Cait scowled. "None we would discuss with the likes of you, Wee Brother."

Una smiled his way, but he continued to pay her no mind. His thoughts remained on the sheep behind her. Her cheeks and nose were flushed red from the cold and burned brighter at the sight of him. He looked away with disinterest.

"Must be a secret if you've come up here," he commented, entering the enclosure where the weary sheep greeted him with mournful bleats.

He rubbed their velvety snouts, and their wet tongues lapped at the palms of his hands. Chills rushed across his skin as the hair on his exposed wrists stood on end. He could feel the sheep's ribs beneath their thick wool coats. They barely clung to life and would all eventually die, taking with them the wool required to weave fabric, one of the island's staple commodities.

Sheep were not known for their intelligence. But their eyes were as soulful as a human's, and in that moment, seemed to roll anxiously. They recognized his voice, and he considered that a sign of awareness. Not only that, but their decision to return to the sheepfold at midday proved telling. Despite the mild weather the day had shown so far, if their behavior was any indicator, a storm brewed in the distance.

These sheep were not so daft as to wander near the cliffs during a storm when the gales blew so viciously they could pull an aimless animal into the sea. It had happened countless times before, but these sheep had been through the most unpredictable weather the island had ever seen, and possibly sensed incoming disaster.

"Rindan Lennox!" a familiar voice called out from a distance and broken from his thoughts, Rindan turned to see Angus, trailed by Duffy, as he walked in from the moor.

Rindan groaned in disgust. Angus was in one of his usual moods, ready to incite conflict where there was none to be had. His long, bowed legs walked forward with lengthy strides. He stopped several feet away from Rindan and the girls as he tucked his dark hair behind his ears and licked his lips.

"Angus Gorrie!" Rindan mocked in return. He crossed his arms and leaned back against the stone wall of the sheepfold.

"Good morrow, lassies," Angus said, and though he addressed both girls, his eyes fixed on Cait. He smiled broadly, but the way his teeth fit together, it appeared a grimace.

"'Ello," the girls greeted, steeling themselves against a sudden frigid gale.

"'Ello, Una," Duffy said, his chin dipping shyly toward the hollow between his clavicles while his eyes darted from her to the ground.

Una forced a smile and stole a glance at Rindan.

Angus snickered beneath his breath at the exchange and said, "Well, Rindan Lennox, how fares the wee bairn you've been tending?"

"Fair, though not on account of you!" Rindan spat.

Angus chuckled. "Och, wheesht."

Rindan's eyes blazed yellow. "You've sought him out to torment him many times, without provocation. Believe me when I say it has to end, or I will see you remorseful."

"Leave it," Angus said with a sneer. "That lad needs to develop a thick hide. His delicacy makes me ill, and I seek to help him grow as hardy as this island requires."

"You tried to drown him the first moment you had him in your hands!"

Angus scoffed, watching Cait a bit anxiously as if to judge her reaction. When she met his eyes, he explained, "I had only offered my help, but Rindan and Indris became sore about it, 'tis all. I cannot help my strength. When I see something needs doing, I do it."

Rindan guffawed in disgust. "You've harassed and assaulted him at every opportunity. I cannot call that 'help'."

Angus shrugged.

"In the future," Rindan said between seething teeth. "You will leave Indris be or suffer the wrath of me and my father. 'Tis us and us alone that act as his guardians and we will see to his upbringing."

Angus threw his head back in mock laughter. "That so?" he asked, his face darkening into a glower. "I accept a threat as I accept a dare."

Cait and Una watched the exchange with wide eyes and loose jaws. Smiles played upon their lips as they shared a knowing glance and tittered. Though they were used to this display of male egos at battle, the constant drama Angus stirred up never ceased to entertain.

"He's a young lad," Rindan said. "Why do you wish to disturb him when he's been through torment and bides here so far from home?"

"Because he's weak," Angus replied without thought. "Teutatwen is only for the strong and those willing to work hard to survive. He doesn't belong here."

"That you've made clear enough," Rindan said, his lips clamping together in thought. "If you desire to prove your own strength and manhood, then prove it against me...on the cliffs."

Angus' face spread wide in a grin and while his focus remained on Cait, he said, "Aye, I suppose I can conquer you."

Cait rolled her eyes and threw her head back in disbelief. "Do you lads expect us to come watch you challenge one another like a pair of rams?" she asked.

"Have you aught better to do?" Angus asked, grinning at her.

"I'd rather pluck one hundred gannets underwater than see the likes of you scaling a cliff face," she replied smartly.

Angus snorted and turned to Duffy, "Come lad, let us fetch my rope."

"Not this moment," Rindan said. "A storm is on the rise."

Angus gazed up into the overcast sky and frowned at the thick clouds moving steadily with the gales. "'Tis the same view as any other day. Let us get to it before you lose courage."

"Nae, see how the sheep cower," Rindan said. "They ken better than us."

"We won't be long," Angus said. "Och, not I, that is. Simply a quick descent and return."

"Aye, let us be off then," Rindan conceded, growing more vexed with each passing moment. It was time to secure Angus back in his place beneath him. The lad never could remain there long, constantly coming up behind to nip at his heels like an island mutt challenging his alpha male.

Una stood up and stepped toward him. "You don't have to prove yourself, Rindan. You've shown many times in the past that you're the better climber."

"Aye, but he forgets," Rindan replied, his face turned away from her.

Competition seemed the remedy to smooth his edginess, and his desire for sport proved stronger than his desire for safety. To conquer the cliffs that he claimed as his and his alone would not only put Angus in line, but balm his frayed nerves. Trample his unquiet yearning.

"Both of you are imbeciles," Cait huffed.

Rindan glared at her, his gaze steady and stern. "I mislike the way Angus looks at you," he said.

Cait snorted. "Why should you care, Wee Brother?" she asked.

"Because he is beneath you," Rindan replied.

"Unlike Indris, I do not require your protection," Cait said. "But do not fash. Angus vexes me as much as he vexes you. He's not worth a thought."

Rindan's shoulders dropped back and he relaxed the tension in his stance. After nodding at the girls, he marched away to fetch his rope and supplies. As he walked, he looked back and noticed the sheep, huddled in mass. Storm or no storm, he would set matters right with Angus, or the lad would never stop. It was all to protect Indris, a child he saw as an irritating younger brother. He should not care, as Indris was a temporary fixture and would someday be out of their lives. But his sense of justice proved far too strong to allow Angus to go unpunished.

When he rejoined the group of youths on the slope, Indris was among them. The small child looked out of place, the delicateness in his features juxtaposed with the hard ruthlessness of the land-scape. He had taken his place with the girls, keeping a wide distance from Angus.

"We fetched Indris," Cait explained. "We told him you were to climb in his honor and thought he should be present."

Rindan chuckled sardonically. "The more to witness Angus' defeat, the better," he hissed.

"Wheesht," Angus emitted. "Let us be off then."

Angus and Duffy carried a length of rope between the two of them. Rindan carried his coil about his shoulder and the fact that he required no help in lifting it proved Angus' weakness outright. The rope hung heavy, composed of thick, tightly woven wool.

A few island hounds chased after them, their tongues hanging from their panting mouths as they ran up the incline. A sudden strong wind had them squinting, and they groaned, growing timid and unsure. They turned and clambered back to the safety of the dell.

"Even the hounds ken better than you two fools," Cait said, her voice uneasy through her humor.

"Wheesht, Sister," Rindan said. "It will be over soon enough."

He did not speak again, his mind focused on the competition before him. Adrenaline pumped through his veins and confidence flooded his system, prepared to make a fool of Angus. His muscles were stimulated and primed for battle. Justice would be served that day.

When the group reached the high clifftop of Àrdaill, the girls took one peek at the churning black waters below and stepped backward, shrieking. The gales blew stronger at the ridge and beat against them brutally, as if to carry them off. Indris, ever silent, stood back, shivering, his head bent and eyes squeezed nearly shut. It seemed the wind would sweep the frail form away, never to be seen again.

Rindan chuckled to himself at the thought. His life would certainly be easier without Indris. Despite carrying a note of tenderness and responsibility for the lad, it was through Indris' existence that Rindan now risked his life.

He examined the rocky soil for an adequate crevice to anchor his stake. Once found, he placed the point of the iron into the spot and drove it down with a hammer. He knotted his rope around the stake, forming a secure hold that he tested with his weight and found sufficient.

He happened to glance at Angus, who worked several feet away, and found him driving his stake much too close to the cliff's edge. Once the impetuous lad's full weight bore down on that iron, it would rip cleanly through the soil and send him plummeting into the sea.

Wordlessly, Rindan strode over to pry Angus' stake loose with his hammer. It dislodged easier than it should. In his haste, Angus had ignored the laws of safety. Angus opened his mouth to protest, but when he saw the result of his poor work, he clamped his lips shut. He let Rindan drive his stake, nodded humbly, and knotted his rope.

Cait and Una clung to one another, using their combined strength to pinion themselves to the earth as the fierce winds whipped through their long hair. Indris sat on the ground several feet back, huddled within his mantle as if he did not wish to be there. His large eyes watched Rindan with an icy stare, and something in the child's expression unsettled the older boy.

Brow furrowing in contemplation, Rindan focused on his rope. He tied its end around his waist and pulled the knot tight. Again, he leaned back and tested the strength of his knots. He waited while Angus followed suit, undoing and retying his knots with Duffy's help until they would bear his weight.

Rindan crawled backward down the slight slope and stopped when he reached the drop-off. Angus did likewise. They each bore their coils of rope over their right shoulders. Rindan turned to look down the cliff face, observed each ledge he would step upon, and mentally mapped out his descent. He did this out of habit, for he was so familiar with this climb that he could conquer it blindfolded.

He unwound enough slack from his coil to reach partway down the drop and gripped it in his left hand. With his right, he held onto the anchored rope. At last, each contender stood prepared at Àrdaill's edge, two sets of bare feet poised at the precipice.

Cait moved forward, bringing Una with her. The girls' knuckles were white as they clasped one another's hands in a tangle of thin fingers. Both wore consternation and eagerness on their faces.

"Ready, lads?" Cait asked, her voice thin and shaky in the buffeting wind.

Rindan gripped his rope with his calloused hands and looked at Angus. Both boys nodded to one another in a mutual signal. Cait regarded her brother with prolonged intensity, as if willing him to win. Then, with lips forming a thin line, she offered Angus the same note. Ripples of contempt smoldered in Rindan's chest. Angus responded with a smarmy grin. Rindan fumed, and his nostrils flared as he channeled his wrath into his ligaments.

"Alright then," Cait continued. "Steady now...be off!"

In one swift motion, Rindan propelled himself down the cliff face, leaning back as his long toes treaded the cracked gabbro. His last glimpse of the clifftop was of Indris' uncanny eyes peering through him. He dropped, his strong legs keeping firm contact with the rocks. His feet cycled his body down, down, down at a dizzying pace as his hands loosed his rope foot by whirring foot. Maintaining his stance against the force of the gale quickly burned his energy. The winds blew stronger and colder.

Midway, the cliff face cut back into an escarpment chiseled by eroding waters, and when he hung mere feet above the churning sea, the world pitched into darkness. The black billows that only moments before had rested far in the distance rapidly moved in to cloak the constant gray clouds, blanketing the island in dread. Biting spears of rain began to pelt his clothing and the bare skin of his hands and feet. Soon, he hung in the deluge.

He peered over at Angus and found him at the same level, about to make the ascent up the cliffside. They both struggled against the gale, bodies bobbing at the ends of their ropes while their feet fought for traction against the slick fortification. Rindan pulled himself up, gathering the rope as he went, and used his wide feet to walk himself up the escarpment, but the squalls beat him back. Several times, he nearly lost his footing, but his prehensile toes gripped the side. His muscles tightened against the cold and wet, emptying of all energy, but adrenaline pushed his body past its normal limits until he was halfway up the cliff.

Hearing screams from the girls, he saw Angus was still in line with him. How had the lad kept up? But when he looked past his shock, he noticed the wince of pain on Angus' face. Blood poured down his jaw from a large gash on his cheek and he no longer held his rope, but clung to the rocks with both hands and feet. He appeared disoriented and distressed.

Rindan could see Duffy's hands pulling on Angus' rope from the summit. It hardly mattered that his cousin offered aid. Angus' injury voided the competition. The saturated clothing of both competitors adhered to their bodies like a heavy membrane. Red ran in watery streams down Angus' face. Relentless rain cascaded down the rocks and washed away all traction. Angus could not help himself, and Duffy could not bear the larger boy's weight enough to pull him. Angus' grip loosened, and he fell. Dangled low from his waist and grappled.

Rindan imagined the fright of those on the summit above. He could not see them. Were they pinioned to the ground? He had to help Angus, no matter what dissent had passed between them.

Instead of working his way up, he used his last reserves to maneuver sideways. His tendons strained, and muscles burned with unfamiliar weakness. Callous winds beat him, and he felt sure his bones would snap. So cold, so stiff, he inched closer to Angus' rope. Angus swung wildly below. Rindan's right hand left its tether as he stretched. The tips of his fingers brushed the wet cord. He nearly had it, but a sharp gust whipped it from his grasp.

He sidestepped, laboring through the gale's resistance. At last, he grabbed Angus' line. Held it steady enough to give Angus the opportunity to regain purchase. The lad flailed like a fish on a hook as he reached for the escarpment. He slipped and skidded. At last he landed his hold, but his face lined with despair.

At the summit, a second pair of hands grabbed Angus' rope. Cait's hands. Soon Una held the rope too. The trio used their combined forces to pull him to safety. Their work went slowly, arduously. He could little help himself. His blood-streaked face was pale, and his eyes partly open. He weakly clutched his rope. Barely toed the cliffside while his friends struggled.

Rindan's right hand met his left. He angled his pull toward the anchor above. His legs were dead weight. Pain and exhaustion turned to numbness. Every tendon in his body risked overstraining, severing. He would become as limp as the dead sea fowl he used to carry on his belt.

He was daft to have followed his ego. Now he was in peril, toiling in a storm. How badly was Angus hurt? He could not tell, but they paid for their recklessness with suffering.

Rindan dragged himself near the escarpment's vertex. Agony wrenched his shoulders. Tore through his biceps. He lifted a foot toward a protruding ledge. It glided off the slick surface. He plummeted, his guts liquefying. His skull caught a jutting rock. White hot pain popped through his brow bone. Echoed through his body. He cried out with an inhuman sound. The insides of his head swam and shifted. Teeth rattled. He dangled helplessly. Violent gales whipped him to and fro. Bashed his body against the cliffside.

A tug on the rope forced his gaze to the summit. He dizzily observed a small pair of hands try to hoist him. Indris. Then Cait's strong hands joined. She had abandoned Angus' rope to help him instead. Reassurance mellowed the waves of misery pouring through him. Cait was tougher than she looked. He longed to weep, but wanted more to get off the cliff, to shelter, and reflect on his foolish ways.

He kicked toward the cliff face. Swinging his body like a pendulum, he tried momentum. Back and forth he swayed, but never drew close. Then, his rope lurched. His insides jolted. He looked up, his heart racing. The rope fibers had frayed in a section above, revealing his folly. Such swinging had sawed his tether upon a sharp crag. Flayed it of integrity.

He looked up in despair. A shaky pair of legs climbed down to the closest ledge. A little face winced in his direction. Indris was foolish too. He had removed his mantle and now flattened himself against the stone. Rindan opened his mouth to cry out for him to go back, but his voice ceased to function.

Indris' hands clung to the rope. Trembling, he stepped down each foothold. The wide eyes darted from his feet to Rindan. Had he witnessed the rope weaken and sought to get low enough so he could pull Rindan in?

Rindan strained to reach the cliffside. If he could only cling to the black gabbro, he could climb using his body alone. He needed to grab a ledge before Indris also became a casualty. But as he stretched one frantic hand, his weight sundered the last rope strands.

Indris had made it nearly halfway when gravity took Rindan. He plummeted. Watched the huge pair of eyes fill with horror as one tiny hand reached out helplessly. Pity consumed him. What would happen to the little lad when he was gone?

He entered the waves. The roaring sea drowned out all sound. Shock wracked his nerves. Frigid waters crashed, blurring his vision. Enveloped him.

In time, the pain disappeared. With it, the cold and desperation. The sea clutched him in its selfish embrace. He would let it have him. Tossed within the roiling swells, he felt nothing, thought nothing. Eerie peace overtook him. Restlessness, yearning, wanting–all washed away.

He sank deeper and deeper. His eyes opened to the swirling blackness. Once, he had assumed death to be painful. A body gripped by contortions and throes. But could not think of that now. His old life, his identity as Rindan of Teutatwen, faded. A new self was birthing. It peeled away. His battered remains descended toward the ocean floor.

TWENTY-FIVE

When Rindan's rope snapped, a jolt of fear and dread burrowed deep into Isolba's belly. She helplessly watched as the sea took him. His eyes connected with hers at the very last. Then he was gone, swallowed by black waves. Cait's cries pierced through the thunderous gales. Sorrow as deep as the sea blanketed the group at the clifftop.

Above her, Duffy and Una had Angus by the elbows, lifting him over the edge. He collapsed in their arms, wheezed and moaned, his long limbs hanging limply. Rain-diluted blood poured from a wide gash across his left cheek. No emotion registered on his ashen face. His eyes were closed, and he lay ignorant of the reality of the situation. Isolba could only hate him, the waste of human life he was. She focused on the crashing waves below, all air sucked from her lungs, and her belly clenched with nausea.

The beautiful boy was gone. The boy with the pure heart and kind face had been snatched away, consumed by the waters. She held the rope in the crook of her elbow. Her closed fists covered her ears to drown out Cait's screams.

She clutched the rock face helplessly. What else could she do but watch the waters crash against the cliffside, knowing he was down there? She had to do something. Was it not she the waters wanted? Not Rindan. It did not desire any soul but the sacrifice it demanded. That was her only identity, was it not? If she could save one soul now, it would be his.

She released the rope. Her body pitched backwards, stomach rising into her chest. She whipped through the airspace at a dizzying pace. When her body slipped into the cold water, the roar of the wind and sea deafened her. Abruptly stopped. Then, silence.

Pinioned in place by the force of the ocean, she opened her eyes and saw calm water. Swirls of blue and white surrounded her. Tiny bubbles raced around her fingertips and shot up to the surface. Mesmerized, she could see her stark white hands clearly in front of her, the joints moving languidly, her fingernails blue and translucent. Her delicate wrists bent, fingers swaying like in ritualistic dance. Suspended in space, time stopped, and her lungs did not burn for breath, nor did her blood crystallize with ice. There in the depths, untouched by freezing waters and lack of air, she could rest for eternity.

But he was also there. Sinking below her, his compact body descended soporifically, just out of reach. She dropped until she could wrap her arms around him and hold his lifeless form close. His face was slack, eyes closed, with microscopic air bubbles clinging to the dark fringe of his lashes. His thick brows furrowed slightly, and his bloodless lips parted, the rounded teeth visible between them. So beautiful.

What would it feel like to kiss that mouth? She longed to press her lips against his and hold them there. But she did not. Why steal something so sacred as a kiss? As she held him, a kindred bloom flowed from him to her, and she recognized their bond. She was now completely content to exist in that place, together with him. Death seemed not so bad now that she was dying.

She clung tight, rested her head on his shoulder, and waited for darkness to descend. Its approach held back, delayed while she entwined her legs with his, floating within inertia's sphere. All was soft and warm, and she held onto his solidity, her mind emptying of all thought.

A great pop burst in her ears, and the sea regurgitated her onto a shore. Warm sand sank beneath her fingertips, and she raised her head to see a green meadow before her. She looked around, searched the waters with her arms, but found Rindan nowhere.

In a short time, she recalled where she was. The Otherworld. A sense of peace overcame her. When she stood, her body seemed weightless and unencumbered, as if still floating underwater. The golden city lay in the distance, but did not draw her interest. Up ahead, a pinhole of light expanded as she walked closer, intrigued by its warmth, until it absorbed her.

Surrounded by this blinding light, she blinked away the brightness, and her eyes adjusted. She sat on a vast moor, the soft grass beneath her a lush green. The city had dissolved. Only the meadow stretched endlessly toward the horizon. An ambient glow emanated from all matter, from each blade of grass to the vast sky of blazing white.

Peering down, she discovered her dark hair hung past her waist in long, silky strands. She ran her hands through it, delighted by its smooth length. How she had missed it! Her hands were no longer child's hands, but long and slim with delicate, tapered fingers. She touched her face and found it the same, but what shocked her most were the mounds of breasts beneath her fine linen frock.

Her attention drew upward when she realized she sat in the shade of an enormous plant. Its brown stem circled wide and seemed composed of the same porous material that she knew as wood, used in the building of ships. It had hundreds of long arms that reached in every direction and sprouted oval leaves. Never had she seen anything like it.

"'Tis called a tree," a familiar voice noted.

Her heart nearly burst. Startled, she came aware of someone sitting next to her. The weight of their head rested on her shoulder. She stared at her companion in shock.

"Nareen!" she cried, but did not recognize her own voice. It was higher, with a feminine lilt.

Nareen lifted her head and offered a sweet, closed-mouth

smile. She, too, appeared older, prettier. Her light brown hair hung long and loose, her flawless skin glowing from within. She wore a white gown of a fine, sheer weave.

"I'm glad you've come!" Nareen said. "I've waited for you."

Tears formed in Isolba's eyes. "Where are we? Why are you here? Have you seen Rindan?"

"We are in the Summerland, the meeting place between earth and everything unseen. My mortal body is dead. That is why we meet here."

"Dead?" Isolba uttered, her voice weak and constricted. "But how?"

"I do not remember," Nareen replied. "My soul departed before the event of my body's death. I only ken what is helpful to you in this moment, naught more. I lived out my purpose in that body and the time had come for me to move on. I spent my earthly life serving you, and in this form, I can help guide you. But ken I do not have all the answers."

"Och, Nareen. I had hoped to reach Cormac so that he could rescue you and my mother, but the storms have hindered the safe passage by sea. I see that it's too late."

"'Twas not too late," Nareen sighed. "I died the day of your escape. You could not have saved me and 'twas in my soul contract to die that day."

Isolba collapsed against Nareen and squeezed her tight. "Is that why I saw you in the Otherworld? But you did not speak to me." Her voice was thin and shaky. She did not wait for a reply. "Is Mother here? Where is she?" she asked instead, pressed her palm into Nareen's, and squeezed. Her eyes implored, hungry for answers.

"Your mother remains with the living," the maid replied. "Escarans has not harmed her and will not hurt her. She is much too valuable because she is your mother. Do not fash for her. Your time with her has nearly ended. You must live your own life. Her path winds away from yours in a separate direction. Your life will differ greatly from the one you kent before."

The tears flowed freely down Isolba's cheeks. "And Rindan? Is he dead?"

"He is here as well, and is with his spirit guides. They are discussing whether he wishes to return to earth or enter the Otherworld."

"But he has to return with me." Isolba tried to leap up, meaning to search for him. "Where is he? I do not see him."

Nareen grabbed her hand and pulled her to the soft grass. "That decision is his alone to make," she replied, ever calm. "He needs this time to convene with his guides. Be patient, my Isolba, and sit with me awhile. You cannot see him because this is *your* meeting place. You may come here whenever you wish to see me or anyone else beyond the veil. But do not enter again through the water. 'Tis dangerous. Simply will it, and you'll see me."

"I do not understand. How do I have the ability to enter the sea and arrive in the Otherworld without dying?"

"'Tis one of your gifts, one you were born with," Nareen said with a smile. "But, as I spake, you cannot imperil your mortal body by entering the portal within the ocean. Your mother has similar gifts because her own mother was a priestess. Her mother spoke blessings over her while she formed in the womb. Yet Moira, having passed most of her energy to you, has suppressed that part of her. She's entrenched in the material world. You are at risk of doing the same, so I warn you to remain connected to the spiritual realm. Do not forget who you are."

"Mother did not tell me that part of herself and naught of where she came from," Isolba said sorrowfully. She recalled how Moira never once mentioned the land she traveled from before marrying Escarans.

"Because she is broken," Nareen replied. "You should look at her with caution and remember to remain strong against life's difficulties. Do not crumble as she did, awaiting death while enjoying the temporary delights of this world. You are different. What is inside you both intrigued and intimidated Baltair so much that when you failed to submit to his will, he could not allow you to change the future of Demoria. So he devised a new fate for you and foretold a prophecy, one he so believed in that he saw nae other outcome by your sacrifice than the one he predicted."

Isolba tensed. "What was the other outcome?"

"This one," Nareen said, chuckling lightly. "You were not meant to die that day on the altar stone, and 'twas my task to see you did not. Your life has greater value than you can imagine, milady. You will fulfill it as Isolba, not as the son Escarans wanted. Your legacy will be vast. You must stop doubting yourself and your worth. You alone are worth the world, but remember, you do not need a man to make you whole. 'Tis in your nature to be led astray by outside influences such as beauty and desire, so like your mother."

"I should not love Rindan?" Isolba asked.

"You may love him, but do not lose focus on who you are," Nareen said. "Nae matter if he chooses to stay or leave this world, you will be with him again. Men will play a meaningful role in this lifetime, but do not allow distractions. Never forget your gifts. You are young yet. Concentrate on your personal growth."

"I will try, though my love for him has become so strong that I long for him alone."

Nareen nodded knowingly and said, "I agree you cannot ignore your feelings, and you've a deep connection with him. But ken that he may choose to leave his life as Rindan, and you cannot deny him his choice. Despite your bond to him, he has his own will."

"But how could I return to Teutatwen without him?" Isolba asked. "His family needs him. *I* need him."

"If he decides to enter the Otherworld, his family will learn to go on without him, as will you," Nareen said. "He would not be truly gone, you ken this."

"Aye, I suppose," said Isolba. "But I could not bear it if I fail to save him. He must choose to come back with me."

"'Tis his choice alone to make. Your path without him will be different, but you will fulfill your purpose alone. Your souls are fused. That is why you are drawn to him. The two of you have chosen to meet in every life, whether briefly or for a lifetime. This life's meeting may be ephemeral, but only he decides that."

"I suppose I understand," Isolba muttered. "If he chooses to return with me, may I tell him who I am?"

"Nae," Nareen blurted. "Your secret identity is your protection. The isles are dangerous for you. You did well in trusting your instinct by allowing none to ken you are Isolba. The people of Teutatwen wouldn't understand, and their loyalty lies with Chief Escarans. If they kent they harbored his daughter, fear would strike their hearts, and they would turn on you. They would send you back. Tell none who you are and avoid anyone from Demoria."

"But I'm not his daughter," Isolba said. "Mother told me."

"His blood flows in your veins," Nareen said, speaking quickly as her eyes looked away. "Remember when Priest Baltair turned Escarans' heart? Baltair wished to see how far his loyalty extended. That loyalty remains. Escarans believes you are dead. If he kens you live, he would see you slain to fulfill the prophecy."

Fear filled Isolba's eyes, and her face fell into her hands. "What can be done?"

"You need do naught but wait. You are safe on Teutatwen as long as you remain in disguise."

Isolba's shoulders slumped, and she pushed her lower lip outward like a petulant child. She did not want to continue play-acting as Indris when she could not see an end in sight. She issued Nareen a cross look in hopes her friend could tell her a way out of her circumstances.

Nareen raised her arm and pointed toward the distance. Isolba squinted, and far away, made out the silhouettes of two small figures that stood hand in hand.

"Who are they?" Isolba asked.

"Those are your children," Nareen answered, beaming.

Isolba tried to discern their features, but they were too distant, small blurs on the horizon. As she looked at them, an all-consuming presence of love enveloped her, seeping through her skin until it melted into her bones. It coiled inside her womb.

"I do not have children," Isolba said, confused. She did not speak this so much to Nareen because Nareen knew this, but more to herself. She did not believe it. Yet, she could not deny the overwhelming warmth pulsing through her veins as she stared at the forms.

Nareen giggled, and the turmoil in Isolba's heart dissipated as the laughter recalled a simpler time.

"They are yet to be born," Nareen said.

"Who is their father?" Isolba asked, a deep yearning pulling at her heart.

"Their fathers are not yet chosen. Their souls are attached to yours and 'tis their will to be born of you."

"Fathers?" Isolba asked. "How can that be?"

"It depends on the decision Rindan comes to," Nareen said. "But I've told you too much and I shant go on. You should not ken too much of the future. The future is fickle. It can easily change. Some outcomes are absolute, while others are pliable and change by free will. Only ken that these souls are bound to you and will always be until the day we achieve oneness."

"Oneness?" Isolba repeated.

"Return to one," Nareen said. "'Tis human perception that divides us and places us in these separate forms, but we were once part of the Shapers and someday will be again. We are still connected to them and each other, but the human mind cannot perceive this. Now that I've left my human body, I experience this connection and hear the thoughts and emotions of other spirits. There is much I wish to tell you, but I've said enough. Your mortal body will perish if it stays beneath the water much longer. Time moves faster here, but you do not have forever."

Isolba shuffled through her thoughts. She had many matters to discuss, but found herself overwhelmed. When she opened her mouth to ask another question, Nareen stopped her short. "You must leave now. Rindan asks for you."

Isolba clasped Nareen's hands in her own. "Och, Nareen. I cannot bear to part from you again."

"I am always with you," her friend replied. "But you have to live your life. You've much to accomplish. Your memory of me and life on Demoria will fade because it was only your beginning. The soil where you sprouted does not hold you. Unlike that tree, you may pick up your roots and thrive where you choose."

Isolba threw her arms around Nareen and held on tight. Energy and warmth transferred from the maid to her mistress. Tears streamed down Isolba's cheeks and she closed her eyes, burying her face in Nareen's shoulder.

"Farewell, milady," Nareen whispered.

She was gone. Isolba's arms hung empty, and when she opened her eyes, she no longer resided in the meadow. She sat on a flat rock in a thicket of trees. Beams of soft sunlight spilled through the verdant canopy. Leaves rustled as twisted branches gently swayed and creaked in the breeze. A rippling stream flowed nearby. It gurgled around shiny boulders, humming notes of pleasure.

She examined her surroundings. Peered into the dense copse of fissured trunks and dripping foliage, and jerked in surprise. Across the stream, she noticed a man standing against a tree. He stared pensively into the void. The masseters of his cheeks protruded. His lips clamped in a grim line. Locks of brown hair hung over his forehead, creased in thought.

She gaped. A wave of recognition passed through her. The bond bloomed in her soul and nudged her in his direction. She bounded through the water, feet splashing, as she ran to him. Startled by the sudden noise, he raised his head. Light entered his sorrow-filled eyes at the sight of her. He cried out.

He looked older, a young man in his prime. He had cast off his boyish countenance, his features more defined. She had never witnessed such beauty.

"Rindan!" Her arms encircled his waist.

He held his hands up for a moment, stunned. Then he wrapped her in his embrace and rested his chin on her hair. She buried herself in his warmth, breathing in his sweet scent. Desperation overcame her. Sobs ripped from her throat. She clung to him tightly, as if she could hold him there by strength alone.

"Do not leave!" she begged. "Return with me."

"Methought you not to be real," he said, nearly in a whisper. "You endured only in my dreams. I never fathomed such loveliness to exist in the world."

"Yet I *am* real," Isolba insisted. "I am of the earth, and I beg you to return with me."

"That's what my guides have spoken," Rindan replied. "That you are human, not imaginary. I wanted to move on, yet they told me I may choose to return to Earth. They say if I go back, we will be together, but I shall suffer all my days."

"Aye, we *will* be together," she insisted. "But you must come with me now."

"They also told me we shall be together in the next life, but it will not be for three generations' time. I may avoid suffering by moving on, and we will be together at a later time."

She cried into his chest. He stroked her hair. Though he was so close, his mind seemed distant. A great decision weighed on him. She wanted him to stay with her in this life. The thought of meeting in some other time, some other place, seemed distant and foreign. It meant little to her in terms of what she understood. To return without him to Teutatwen was unthinkable.

"I beg you to come," Isolba said.

"And return to a life of uncertainty?" he asked, his voice full of pain. "I've lived all my youth on Teutatwen, and I see naught for me than what I've already lived. The storms have made life unbearable, and my people are starving. I stand by helplessly as my sheep perish, and when they are gone, naught will remain. Why would I wish to return?"

"I'm there," she said.

"But how will I find you?" he asked.

"You will not have to search for me," she replied.

"I do not ken your name."

"I am Isolba."

"Isolba? Isolba of Demoria?" he asked in surprise.

"Aye, I am she."

"Our Lovely Lass," he said softly. He smoothed her hair and examined her features, shaking his head in disbelief. A slight smile played on his lips, but faded.

"What's wrong?" she asked.

He looked away and clenched his jaw. "Isolba," he said. "I do want to be with you, but...but I nae longer wish to be Rindan Lennox of Teutatwen. I hear my grandparents calling me, and I long to follow."

"Nae, you cannot mean that," she said, her body shaking. "We are meant to be together."

Torrents of despair and desperation engulfed her. She lifted her head, peered into his eyes, and found an expression of resolve. It seemed he had made up his mind, but she could not let him go. In this place, her gender was not cloaked in mystery. He did not know her as Indris. She manifested as someone lovely, past the awkward stages of development. Here, she had allure.

With shuddering breaths, she pressed her lips to his, tasting sweetness. The returned pressure of his mouth on hers came willing and deep. Produced a headiness, a dizzy spinning in her skull. She weakened beneath his touch. His grip tightened and his body buckled.

Something nudged her feet from below. Forced itself between her and Rindan's legs. Her arms nearly detached from his waist. At that moment, all warmth and peacefulness departed. The green forest dissolved into the murky depths of the sea. She fought to hold on as waves sought to separate them. Something wrested her upward. Though her grasp remained unbroken, water swarmed around them.

Utter cold shocked her system, and when her head pierced the surface, she gasped. Frigid air filled her lungs with fire. Rindan grew heavy. His weight towed her back under, and she choked on burning salt water. A second push from beneath brought her head through the surface again. A solid form pressed amid their bodies. A furry, black head emerged. Yellow eyes blinked knowingly while a great pink tongue panted hot breaths against her icy skin.

She took in a gulping breath of disbelief. Collapsing against her black hound, she sobbed with pained relief. He buoyed himself amid her and Rindan, and paddled through the ocean swells. She struggled to keep his head above water, his body limp and helpless.

"Rindan!" she tried to shout, but the word strangled, her voice hoarse. She whispered frantically, "We're saved! We've been saved!"

He failed to react, even breathe. She cried out in anguish. Clung to him with all her might. His hair, slick and crusted with salt, matted to his head. She noted the deep purple bruise forming on his temple and the small abrasions covering his face. His skin was whiter than a pearl and tinged with blue. It resembled the belly skin of a baby seal. He was so colorless, so gray, that his straight nose with the round nostrils appeared cut from marble. Yet the network of blue-purple veins across his eyelids evidenced blood beneath the skin.

She closed her eyes and prayed to whatever god could hear her plea. Begged for Rindan's life. Above them, inky clouds churned, thunder growled and groaned. Cracked intermittently. The hound conquered each swell, swam across an untamed sea. Tantamount to her journey on his back months before, time accelerated and distance closed with rapid pace. They rounded the massive stac at the island's northeast edge and moved toward the bay.

She heard the surge before she saw it, a sound earsplitting and turbulent. It approached from behind like a rapacious beast. She turned to cower at the wall of black water as it charged. The hound could not ride out this swell. It was coming down upon them.

Her arms squeezed around Rindan. Eyes shut tight. The wave's force crushed her like a wall of stone, toppled over and piled its weight. The violence tore him from her arms. She somersaulted through the water. Pressure in her ears and nose threatened to pop her head open. Explode like a bittercress pod. As she hurtled, she reached for Rindan. Then, her body slammed into solid earth.

She lay motionless, certain every bone in her body had broke, and heard the water slosh its retreat back to the ocean. In her hazy existence behind her eyelids, she spun in circles, nauseated. She lay stunned for a long time, fighting the urge to slip away.

A persistent slapping noise echoed in her waterlogged ears. The sound multiplied by a thousand. Drumming upon her consciousness, it roused her from her stupor. She slowly peeled her eyelids up, squinted at the muddy earth before her, and saw blurred movements in her line of sight. Silvery shapes undulated the earth, smacking wetly. She raised her head by an inch, blinked until her vision cleared. She was within the bay. Around her flopped hundreds of fish, their eyes empty and mouths yawning.

She turned her face aside and relinquished the aspirated water. Her lungs screamed with expansion. Every haggard breath rattled her chest. Coughs erupted in a struggle to clear her airway. She crawled on hands and knees in search.

She knew the hound could not possibly belong to the mortal realm, and focused on Rindan. Desperate to find the lad she had nearly spent eternity with on the sea floor, she groveled between the fish, hacking and sputtering all the while. She shivered with cold. Her chest burned unbearably, and she longed to be back in the ocean's depths. Suspended in her warm cocoon with Rindan.

She noticed a limp arm splayed out from under a pile of fish. The swarm of mackerel, cod, salmon, and haddock stilled as they slowly gave up their spirits. Shouts from up the hill grabbed her attention, and she watched the lot of the islanders running to the bay. She frantically waved.

Whimpering, she picked the fish off him and flung them aside. She tried to scream and nudge him awake. Her voice drew out weak and raw. His eyes remained closed. He lay motionless, his skin cold and blue.

The islanders swarmed around. A pair of arms lifted her, but she reached for Rindan.

"Help him!" she squeaked, her voice thin and tremulous.

She collapsed against the person holding her. It was Askill,

Saithan's cousin. He sought to warm her. Her teeth chattered so violently, she could not control the shaking. Someone wrapped a plaid around her thin shoulders. Trembling yet, her eyes fixed on the motionless body, watched as Saithan and Beathag knelt over him. Though their voices were high-pitched with alarm, she heard no words.

Saithan turned Rindan onto his side. Pounded his back with force. Beathag rubbed his arms and legs, encouraging blood flow. His face hung lax and his chest did not rise. Their efforts continued a long time. Isolba's hope diminished. Sank deep. A sob escaped her lips.

He had chosen the Otherworld over a life with her.

She could not bear his death. How could she possibly go on without him when he was her true love? What of Saithan, Beathag, Cait, and all who depended on him? What of Rindan himself, his whole life before him, his desires yet to manifest?

She leaned far over to place her hand on his forehead, the skin over the hard skull cold. Her mind focused, her consciousness slipped behind a veil. Eyes closed, a heat radiated between them and flowed outward, directed toward Rindan.

Breathe, breathe, she willed.

Twenty-Six

He found the creature in his arms to be delicate, sensual, and a breed of woman that did not exist on his island. She had never come to him so vividly, and each sensation—electric, thrilling—pulsed through his nerves. Desire hummed in his head. Her touch became all-consuming, and his hands moved over her in eagerness. He badly wanted to feel her against him. She had him entirely in her thrall. He wanted more of her and ached for all of her, to have her in his clutch for eternity.

"Stay with me," she whispered, her soft voice full of longing.

He crushed his mouth against hers, tasted her sweet lips and knew a hunger he had not before. Urgency spurred him forward as if he had to take in all he could of her before she disappeared. All along, she was that missing piece, that vacancy in his life.

His fingers tangled in her fragrant hair and moved over the smooth folds of her dress, the planes of flesh and bone realized beneath his fingertips. Her arms were thin and toned beneath the sheer fabric. He squeezed her strong thighs in his palms, feeling her muscles tense to hold herself against his weight. Her soft hands slid over the back of his neck. Sparks of pleasure rippled down his spine.

This was no dream. In every dream or vision of her, she

remained just out of reach. A wisp hanging in the air and gone with the breeze. Here, she stood solid in his embrace and warm, so warm.

In a moment, she pulled away. Lowered herself to the ground on a bed of dried leaves and moss. She took one of his hands and coaxed him down to join her. They lay side by side and held each other close.

Her wide eyes stared into his as they misted with tears. "Do not leave," she begged, her voice thick with sadness.

"I'm not leaving you," he reassured as he stroked her dark hair. It was cool and slippery in his fingers. Why would he go? He could not remember wanting to leave. Who could depart from such entanglement?

"You seem uncertain," she said. A large tear pooled along the rim of her eyelid and flowed down her cheek.

He kissed her wet face, slowly, tenderly. "You are all I am certain of," he replied. "You are everything."

She brought her lips to his ear as if sharing a secret. "Come home with me. I need you to."

"Anywhere with you is home," he said and meant it. He tried to swallow the lump in his throat. Why did he feel such sorrow? He could recall nothing else. It was as though nothing existed before her. Nae, *he* did not exist before her. To be separated from her was death. Of that he was certain.

She was his. Had always been. His heart ceased to pine, the gaping wound healed over. She now occupied the dark pit of his soul and filled him with light. He wanted to live.

Rindan covered her mouth with his and immersed himself in sensation. The pressure of her pillowed lips. The faint salty, sweet tang of her tongue. The gentle gurgling of the nearby stream. His beating heart that eclipsed all sound. The soft give of her flesh under his touch. The heady scent of a woman in love, craving him alone.

He navigated her body like an ocean craft; crested swells, dipped hollows, and reveled in the majesty of her curves. Her beckoning fingers drew him beneath the water. His body weakened. A lethargy gripped his senses, and every movement was like pushing his limbs through sand. His heart now pounded against his chest wall like violent waves crashing into the shoal. Small explosions fired inside his head. Waves lapped up his throat and the sudden urge to cough sent water spurting from his mouth. A heavy weight rested on his sternum and he struggled for breath. He forgot how to inhale. His airway burned and yet he somehow managed a sharp intake of breath, one that ravaged his lungs with knife points.

"Good lad!" his mother's voice said, though the sound was faint as though it came from underwater.

"That's right, Rindan. Breathe, Son," he heard his father say, the notes echoing distantly in his ears.

He coughed and gagged on burning salt water. "Iso...?" he asked, but he could not utter her name. What was it? He had so soon forgotten.

When he opened his eyes, his vision blurred, and the figures swam out of focus. He would know his parents' faces anywhere, but where was the lass? He attempted to look about, but she was gone. He weakly tried to summon her visage, but the memory fractured, her features indistinct and muddy. She had merely been a character in yet another dream, and this time, he could not fully recall what his subconscious mind had rendered.

Incredible sorrow consumed him. Teutatwen bore no resemblance to home. It had become a foreign land with strange people. Home was some place far away, some place unreachable. He longed to go home, and it was as though he had touched it for a moment before he was thrust back onto Teutatwen. His body shook with uncontrollable sobs. His lips curled and quivered as cries erupted from between them, bearing unintelligible and tortured tones.

"'Tis alright," Saithan said. "You're alive."

But the word 'alive' offered no comfort at all. It repulsed him. Why did life carry such disgust? It was as though he was angry to find breath within him. A small hand came to rest on his arm and he recognized the little face of Indris looking down at him. The touch and the face provided sudden calm, and Rindan stopped shaking. Dear Indris. A little brother. A friend. He closed his red-rimmed eyes and fell into a deep sleep.

TWENTY-SEVEN

Exultant cries rang out. The islanders brought their baskets, crockery, and anything that served as a container. They scooped up fish and filled their vessels. Small children held vast armfuls, and women raised their skirts to stuff the limp, scaly bodies inside the folds. Youths tossed fish to one another in lighthearted play. They laughed as they struggled to catch the slick creatures with fumbling grasps.

No longer would they hunger. Everyone had plenty, with enough fish to dry out and store for future consumption. One by one, the islanders retreated from the bay to cook fish and feel the sensation of a full stomach. When the last islander left the shoreline, they left not a single fish behind.

Saithan carried Rindan home, laid him by the fire, and covered him in plaids. He slept so deeply that even the brief trip home and Beathag's constant prattling did not disrupt his slumber. In her incessant worry, she checked his breathing every few minutes. Her cheeks glistened with tears, and each deep breath shuddered, the fear still present as it gradually melted into relief.

"Mine own son. My lad," she repeated as she sat near him, rubbing his back and warming his limbs.

She stroked Rindan's hair and his face as if he were a newborn babe, her expression stricken with wonder and awe. Moments of calm lasted brief intervals. Her face contorted with powerful sobs, and she wept over him. She would eventually regain her faculties, only to again lose herself in tears.

Isolba remained by their side, silent, in a state of shock. She could not comprehend all that she witnessed. How much of it was a dream? She recalled speaking to Nareen and remembered everything that her maid told her, but retained little of what had occurred after. Her memory of Rindan ended with a kiss as she begged him to stay. If the experience was real, he had decided to return. The realization sent waves of warmth through her core.

Beathag, in a moment of calm, stretched out her hand and pulled Isolba into an embrace. The woman's racing heartbeats thrummed against her ear. Isolba closed her eyes, grasped for sensation, but a strange emptiness enveloped her.

Saithan knelt behind Isolba and wrapped her in extra plaids. Islanders crowded the doorway. Their excited voices and constant questions blended into confusion. Some brought cooked fish and offered it to the Lennoxes, but despite their hunger, they remained too shocked to eat.

Saithan directed his baffled voice toward Isolba. "Lad, will you now speak as to who you are? Can you explain how you saved my son?"

She shook her head and buried her face in Beathag's bosom. Her ears burned from the attention. How could she explain something that she could not understand? She longed to tell them of how twice she had visited the Otherworld, that the portal existed beneath the waves, and of the hound who lifted her and Rindan from the depths. But more than that, she wanted to divulge who she was, that she was a lass instead of a lad, the lost Isolba of Clan MacKay, and that she loved their son, the father of her unborn children.

But Nareen had advised against it. It was not the time to reveal her identity, but how could she bear it? Was she now to remain here on Teutatwen and not attempt to leave? Could she not try to save her mother? According to her maid, her mother was safe, but Nareen was dead.

The former angst and impulse to travel to the Argarves and seek refuge dissolved. Cormac became an afterthought. Nareen had not addressed his presence in her life. He ceased to exist, and all childish desires for a man she never met transferred to a boy known as her soulmate. It seemed absurd, but she decided that with all the strange events of the past months, she might as well believe in her journey. What more did she have besides belief?

Cait pushed through the crowd and into the blackhouse, bedraggled and out of breath. Her legs gave out beneath her, and she collapsed onto Rindan. He did not make the slightest twitch. She put an arm around Isolba, sandwiching her against Beathag.

"By Our Lovely Lass, my brother is alive, as they say, and 'tis all because of Indris! I'm obliged to you for saving him," she said through grateful tears.

Again, Isolba puzzled over the expression, though she had heard the islanders say it now and then. Perhaps it was one of their deities.

"Where've you been, lass?" Saithan asked Cait. "We didn't ken what became of you from the time you came to tell us Rindan was in the water." He choked on the last words, as if remembering the fear that gripped him the moment Cait had alerted the village.

"At Àrdaill with Una and Duffy," she answered. "I returned to help Angus home. He suffered a blow but should withstand it."

"Can you tell us what happened?" Saithan probed. "We wish to make sense of it."

"I can hardly explain it myself," Cait began. "The lads were competing on who could climb the fastest, but when the storm swept through, Rindan's rope gave way and he fell into the water. Indris jumped in after him. We watched him bring my brother to the surface. He was pulling him along. Una went with me to the shore, yet the waves rose and took them away. We feared them drowned. That's when I ran to the village to alert you."

Cait buried her face in the plaids covering Rindan and wept

fiercely. The neighbors had listened so attentively, and now rekindled their harried chatter and questions. The superstitious Grigor, who once confronted Isolba near the spring, stepped forward. Humility hung on his face.

"I was wrong about you," he said, looking at Isolba and then down at his hands in repentance. "I see you are powerful and nae doubt bound to a vow of secrecy. We will cease asking who you are and it's clear enough for me."

Should she correct him or allow him to think what he may? Despite Nareen's counsel, she felt no more powerful than one of the island hounds and could not pretend to know anything about the spiritual world. But had she not gone away, seeking to pull Rindan back from death's grip, and in that realm gain knowledge of herself and her future? Was the evidence of Rindan's living, breathing body not enough to convince her of her powers? Nareen told her she had strengths beyond her ken, but her belief in herself remained slight.

Grigor took Isolba's silence as validation. The neighbors huddled in the doorway and whispered shrilly amongst one another.

"Let us discuss more of this later," Saithan suggested. "Indris requires rest."

"We've decided to hold a prayer circle tonight," Grigor said quickly. "Though we are blessed with a bounty of fish–surely by the lad's doing–the skies remain overcast and the waters dangerous. Today's storm was a reminder that the blight remains upon us and the powers of darkness are gaining strength. Now is the time to drive another message to the Netherworld."

"I will join you," Saithan said and looked back to ensure Beathag could spare him to leave.

Isolba abruptly stood up and faltered in step. Though she was reluctant to leave Rindan's side, an inward nudge urged her to go. She would not be apart from him long.

She followed Saithan outside, where the islanders crowded together. They peered at her with wide eyes, their curiosity peaked more than ever. She did not think she was special, but the events of the day convinced her she was no insipid lass playacting. She was curious to know who she really was and what she was capable of.

The villagers walked a short pilgrimage to the moor and in the wide open area, spread out and joined in a large circle. Isolba stood between Grigor and Saithan with her tiny hands clasped in theirs. She looked into Saithan's kind face, with the smile lines deeply etched in his rough skin. She noticed tears brimming in his eyes and so shut her lips to quell the emotions flooding through her. She wished to call him 'father'.

When he closed his eyes, the tears released and slid down his cheeks. She looked around to notice everyone had shut their eyes. Someone was speaking on the opposite end of the circle and she could not hear. They spoke fervently for several moments and quieted. Someone else spoke, and their angry words spat and growled. The next person to speak blubbered and sobbed as their prayer was nearly intelligible.

Rain beat down again. It came first in tentative patters and grew to steady thrums. The others ignored it, but Isolba became cold and shivered, hoping the prayer circle would come to a close. Her open eyes focused on the ground and she realized with a jolt of surprise that she stood on a deposit of feldspar.

Saithan said, "Oh Shapers, we beseech you as humble servants to withdraw this scourge from our island. This day, my sons nearly lost their lives from a storm begat by this wretched curse."

Isolba's heart leapt at Saithan's utterance of the word 'sons'. Beathag had said so before, but she had disbelieved the couple considered her part of the family. Her own father had not hesitated to sacrifice her. Yet, Saithan and Beathag shared their precious rations without complaint, provided her with a warm place to rest her head, and defended her from all who spoke ill.

"Only you can lift the darkness so that we, your ever-faithful servants, may once again live our ordinary lives. You've granted us stewardship of this land, its flora, and its animals, but all will die as we will die if Father Sun is not restored. Yet if this is the true end of days, if it pleases you, collect us and take us with you so that we suffer nae more. We will join you in the fatherland and bow at your feet for all of eternity."

The islanders employed their collective energy toward a single focus. Isolba thought she saw a miasma of light radiate around their bodies, but shook her head, certain she had swallowed too much seawater.

"I've received a message from the Shapers," Grigor's voice shouted over the prayers and whispers of the group.

Isolba snapped her attention to the older man. His eyes were open and turned in her direction.

"Someone here kens who is responsible for the curse on our island," he continued. His hand broke from hers and he pointed an accusing finger at her. "You."

Her chest drew as tight as a drum and her stomach upended. Acid flowed over her tongue. "Nae...nae," she choked. "'Tisn't I who's caused this."

"Nae," he replied. "But you ken who has."

All eyes watched her intently as though she were on trial. Their attention singed her skin. She felt exposed as if they knew who she was.

"I do?" she asked, incredulous.

"Aye, someone in your former land. Someone in a position of power. Who could that be?"

Isolba thought of her father. He held the most power in Demoria. Yet she thought again. Did he truly, though? Was it not Baltair who offered Escarans counsel and advice? Escarans believed in Baltair's prophecy so much that he had condemned his only daughter to death.

"Aye," Isolba whispered at last. "I ken."

"Tell us who," Saithan said softly. "'Tis alright. You are in nae trouble. If you tell us, we can stop them."

Isolba trembled. If she told them, she risked giving up her identity. Yet if she remained silent, their world might never again return to normal.

"Very well," she spoke, her lips shuddering. "He is a dangerous man. 'Tis the druid priest in Demoria. I saw him manipulate the weather with mine own eyes. His incantations stirred the clouds and whipped the sea. His heart is as black as the night sky."

"Why does he do this?" Saithan asked.

Isolba sighed wearily, and her eyelids fluttered with exhaustion. "He kens his reasons alone, but I suppose he has aligned himself with the serpent and enjoys holding power over the people. He fears that when Clan McCloud absorbs Clan MacKay, he will lose his position."

"Dear lad," Saithan said. "Why could you not tell us this sooner? We could've prayed to suppress his powers."

"Because I am foolish and never connected the storms to him. I did not deliberately hold this information back."

"Perhaps if you had told us where you came from, 'twould have come to light," Grigor accused.

Saithan held his hand up to halt Grigor's words. "Enough. All comes in its own time. Do not fault the lad. He did not ken. And you are nae fool, Indris. You saved my son. Let us join hands once again and shatter this priest's curse. His name?"

"Baltair," Isolba croaked. Her throat constricted with shame and sorrow.

Escarans had loved her, but Baltair poisoned his mind. Baltair made the chief believe Isolba had no value in her current form. Why did he so despise her? Was it the power he saw in her and her unwillingness to take his guidance? She had the power to reach the Otherworld. Did she have the power to take down Baltair? Saithan was confident that their group had the means to dispel evil. She would try along with them.

Once everyone's hands joined anew, Isolba focused. Her pulse thrummed outward and matched the pulse of the hands clasped to hers. The energy they created in their closed channel circled infinitely, a profound loop of spiritual proportion. The warm stirring reached out to all living beings and attached to every particle in the universe. For a moment, she understood how everything came into being and existed on a grid-like pattern, built with texture and color. But explaining this to another person would prove impossible. No words could describe it without falling short of the true breadth of creation.

Cool drops of rain fell on her face and vibrated with life. The wind on her skin carried energy and intelligence. The soil beneath her feet throbbed with breath and sent seismic waves through her nerves, straight up to her skull, where they crackled and sparked.

Before her body hit the ground, blackness snatched her. She found herself splayed across the altar stone. Baltair's dirk dragged across the delicate skin of one wrist. Evil emanated from him. Isolba peered into his soul, and her theory rang true. She saw Baltair's body was no longer his own, instead overtaken by something that caused her bones to shake with dread. She tried to cry out, but found herself paralyzed and unable to part her lips.

The druids stood around her, looking down. Concern filled their eyes. She understood they disagreed with the direction Baltair had taken them. His corrupt teachings defiled their ways of healing, of lightness and discernment, of oneness with nature. He had come into his power wrongly and distorted the laws they followed.

In the next moment, Isolba stood next to the altar stone among the druids. Nareen laid in her place. The maid's eyes rounded with terror. The tendons in her neck stretched taut with dread.

Isolba met Baltair's empty eyes. "My people suffer because of you," she said, not to Baltair but to the thing inside him.

The edges of Baltair's mouth lifted into a wide sneer, his teeth bared like a growling hound.

"You have not won," Isolba said forcefully. "Stand down. Good is coming to overpower you, foul beast! You nae longer have dominion over these isles, nor our souls. They belong to us!"

He cringed, and his face altered. Pale skin darkened. Round pores squared into flat scales. His figure heightened and bulked to an enormous breadth. A thick, rough tail sprouted from his spine. His teeth grew long and sharp. Baltair stood high, transfigured into a black dragon. His shoulders hunched forward to fit beneath the ceiling of the cave.

"You are mistaken," he growled. His voice had shifted to gritty thunder. "I am not who you think I am."

Isolba trembled as she struggled to stand her ground. "You are a master of deception, and I will not believe a word from you."

"I am of the old gods," he said. His eyes glowed with fire as he craned his neck to be level with her face.

She would not cower, weep, or faint. She understood this as a spiritual battle and not a physical conflict.

So, she peered back at him without breaking eye contact. "For too long, we've sacrificed the blood of the innocent and gave you authority over us," she said. "But now, we–the Shapers' children, the true heirs of the earth–are reclaiming it."

"You have confused me with the serpent!" he barked.

"I ken that only the serpent demands bloodshed!" she bellowed. "You can be none other, and I demand you depart from this place. I am the heir of these isles, and in the name of the Father, the Mother, the Son, and the Maiden, I banish you!"

Agitated, he picked up his dirk with one clawed palm and sank the blade into Nareen's wrist. The metal struck the altar stone. Nareen's body lay there no longer.

"'Tis done," Nareen's voice spoke from all around, and her words burrowed into Isolba's soul.

The dragon crumbled to dust. As he dissolved, Isolba understood it was not truly the end. He departed for only a little while, to do his evil work elsewhere, and would someday return. As long as the Shapers' children resided in imperfect bodies, the serpent would tempt them into joining his army and trick them into giving up dominion of their land. Parcel by parcel, soul by soul, he planned to take over the world. He could never win, but that did not sway him from trying.

Isolba had to protect her islands and guard the shores. This vision played out with clarity. But how could she possibly fulfill this purpose?

TWENTY-EIGHT

Moira stepped across the rocky slope with care and purpose. She could barely see the robed shapes of the three druids leading her and Frang through the impenetrable darkness of night. Rain spat down, and though cold entered her bones, numbness overtook her extremities. Consternation rushed through her nerves.

The warm back of Frang's hand brushed against hers, then drew away. She longed to entwine her fingers with his, to fortify herself against the approaching confrontation, but such a touch was forbidden.

The terrain steepened as they found themselves in a craggy area and resorted to slipping single file through narrow crevasses between high rock walls. When they reached an opening, a druid turned and put a finger to his lips. He pointed farther down the slope, directing their attention to the faint glow of a faraway fire.

Moira nodded and pulled Frang along. Their steps came painfully slow. One stumble could create unwanted noise.

After a while, the druids stopped again.

"We mustn't go farther," one of them said. "He cannot ken we betrayed him."

"Aye," Moira replied. "We understand."

Her belly folded with dread. Outwardly, she held her head with confidence, as she was wont to do. She clenched her fists in readiness and crept forward, quietly, warily.

FIVE MONTHS BEFORE, she had lain in her bed, sickened with despair. A prisoner in her own chamber. Men at arms stood in the doorway and blocked egress by Escarans' orders. They would remain at their station for as long as her husband willed it.

She had failed Isolba. She had allowed herself to be captured by Escarans before she could reach her daughter. For her betrayal, he held her captive. She had never made it to their meeting place. How her poor child suffered. Ached with abandonment and desperation.

She had never had a plan for helping Isolba off the island. She wanted only to get her away from the altar stone and into hiding. A true escape was only possible with Frang's help–whenever the guards freed him. He was the only soul in Demoria she could trust with Isolba's life. She saw how poorly she had plotted.

Then, Escarans voice rang from the doorway. "The clever plan you had to save our daughter's life was for naught," he had said.

His heavy footsteps had crossed the room. His hot breath touched her skin as he leaned over and wrapped his thick arms around her shoulders.

"She threw herself into the sea when the search party nearly caught her," he continued. "She drowned. Her body was swept away. Now the entire island mourns."

Her vacant expression had drawn back into ugly contortions of grief. An inhuman sound formed in her throat. Her hands covered her face, and tears wet her palms. She wept fiercely. The fingernails drew red lines down her delicate cheeks. She pulled her hair. Such grief transformed human into animal, a reaction visceral and savage. A mind gone.

"I've consulted with Baltair. He assured me that the prophecy could yet come to pass. Our daughter sacrificed herself. With Isolba's soul so newly departed, we can create her new life. You will lie with me now."

She had tried to free her body from Escarans' grip. But he only held her tighter. Crushed her. She could not break free. She had clawed at him, but the exertion of his hands against her arms threatened to break bones. He forced his weight onto her. The men at arms stood expressionless outside the doorway. She had screamed for someone to save her. No one came.

HER EYES SQUEEZED SHUT as she tried banishing the memory. But how could she forget the moment she learned her daughter was dead? Escarans' coldness was only a small part of her anguish that day. But as she glared ahead at flames flickering before a black backdrop, her sadness turned to rancor. She would have revenge.

As she and Frang approached the fire, they discovered it nestled beneath an overhang, barely out of the wind and rain. Frang moved in front of her and ducked low. Shuffled forward. She followed, and could hear nothing beside her own pulse rushing in her ears.

They peered around a rock and found the area within the overhang empty. Frang pulled his body behind the slab and pressed his back against it. Moira leaned alongside him, understanding they should wait.

"I've expected you," a disembodied voice boomed through the darkness. It came from somewhere in front of them.

Frang's hand flew to the dirk at his waistband and he held it up. Moira crouched at the base of the boulder. They both looked about wildly, but could see nothing.

The sound of footsteps and rustling fabric drew near, and the shadowed form of Baltair stood before them, his facial features visible in the firelight.

"You've discovered my hiding place. I sensed I would receive an unwelcome visitor this night," he said. "You've come to kill me?"

Frang took a step forward, still holding the dirk in his hand. "Aye," he replied. "You've worked against the clan with your lies. You've brought the storms to our islands with your spells."

"All I have done was for the benefit of the clan."

"'Tis because of you that our daughter is dead," Frang shouted, his voice trembling with the words.

Baltair smiled. "Aye, so you now confess your sins in my hour of death? I ken almost everything, though I could only suspect your part in Isolba's existence. 'Tis nae matter. If 'twas not for you, Escarans would have nae heirs."

"And he still has none," Frang said. "Isolba was sacrificed to the sea, and yet the storms come, and a son is not born to Moira. You spake lies."

"'Tis because Isolba is not dead," Baltair said matter-of-factly.

Moira's chest swelled with possibility. But doubt snatched it away and sank it. "'Tis impossible!" she said. "Many witnessed her drown."

Baltair shook his head. "She is within these isles, I promise you. And as long as she remains alive, the fate of Clan MacKay is doomed. She will join Clan McCloud, and all that we have will turn to dust. All our history, our traditions–gone. I've continued the storms to prevent her from reaching the Argarves and Cormac from reaching her. How she escaped to other shores is beyond my ken. I did not believe she could survive out on her own in the wilds, but someone has helped her. In fact, her spirit has grown stronger, not weaker."

"I do not believe you," Frang said and took a giant step forward. "Every word you say is untrue! You deserve to die for your crimes against the clan!" He pointed the dirk at Baltair's throat.

The priest's hands lifted in surrender. "I demand you take me to Escarans to explain my case," he shouted. His emotionless eyes showed that he thought himself invincible. He did not think Frang could truly harm him.

"Nae," Frang replied. "You've twisted his mind. He believes every word you say. He performs every task you ask of him, even sacrificing who he believed was his only child."

"If you kill me, you will not find Isolba," Baltair bargained like a wheedling youth. "If you allow me to live, I will uncover her hiding place and bring her home to you."

"So you may sacrifice her? We cannot trust a single word you speak," said Frang. "You remain a danger to the isles and to our daughter. If you live, we'll all perish."

By this time, Frang had backed Baltair up against the boulder, as if prepared to flay him alive. Baltair's eyes shone dark in the night but blackened further. Looked from Frang to Moira and back to Frang. "If you take my life, you, your child, and your descendants will ken only sorrow all your lives. You will lament each day, mourn your existence, and cry out for death to take you. As you've done to me, death will be your one escape. So long as MacKay blood inhabits the earth, your happiness will become as elusive as the sun."

Frang withdrew his blade. He glared at Baltair with hatred. His features twisted in a pronounced scowl, but defeat cast a haze over his eyes. It seemed he held a slight belief in Baltair's words and became inactive, unsure of how to proceed.

"You threaten my family?" Moira said, gaining courage. Anger propelled her toward him, though Frang would not allow her to step between him and Baltair.

"They are not empty words," Baltair replied. "I am backed by the old gods who favor me. They will see your line destroyed. Allow me my life, and I will spare you from their wrath."

Moira peered into the priest's eyes and saw the darkness. Her soul quaked, and she trembled to find herself in the presence of evil. She retreated to step toward the fire without breaking eye contact with the priest.

"Nae!" Baltair shouted. He sprang forward, but Frang pushed his forearm against the priest's neck. Pinned him against the boulder. The dirk's point stuck into the skin of Baltair's throat. A drop of viscous blood appeared.

Moira's hands swayed over the smoke. Wrists rotated widdershins. The movement flowed to her elbows, her shoulders, and fluidly surged through her hips, knees, and ankles. Soon her entire body danced to the rhythm of the smoke in the gale. Deosil, she swung her feet around the perimeter of the fire. Whipped up the earth's energy to greet the sky.

The spirits drew in. Guided from the dark by her beckoning hands, they congregated. Understood her intent to quash the source of evil desecrating the isles.

An inhuman roar burst from Baltair's throat. His body stiffened, clenched in the grip of paralysis. Frang withdrew his dirk and stepped back. He gaped at Moira in disbelief as she plucked invisible strings. So immersed in her movements, she could not break focus to explain her methods.

Rain began to pour in a torrent and the sea surged. It shattered against the shore with an earsplitting crash. Winds buffeted their bodies. The fire hissed and reduced to embers. Still, Moira danced.

The priest's back arched, face contorted. He fell to the ground, writhed like a snake. His tongue flopped from a wide open mouth. He grunted and snarled, fingers clawing at the stony soil. The rain ended abruptly and the roar of the sea quieted.

Frang put distance between himself and Baltair. He stood slack-jawed at the wild, unpredictable movements. He readied his dirk should he need it. His eyes darted to Moira in fascination.

Baltair's teeth clenched. Scraped together so tightly they emitted an abrasive squeal. "Stop," he pleaded in a breathless rasp.

Moira's movements became more fervent. Droplets of rain covered her face in a vibrant sheen. Her delicate fingers wove a tapestry from threads of wind. Her feet trampled the earth in hurried desperation.

The priest let out a furious bray. His body twisted with such violence, as though his bones would break and his ligaments could snap. Frang winced at the sight, too intrigued by Moira's powers over the priest to look away.

Her hands waved over Baltair and tugged an unseen cord. She leaned into the effort and gritted her teeth against an incredible resistance. Baltair's eyes shut tight and, as his body defied her motions, his bellows recalled a wounded cow.

Yet, after pulling at the invisible force for far too long, her muscles fatigued. She frantically tugged at the evil. Grew weaker with each attempt at extraction. The bond between the priest and his possessor proved too strong. She staggered, unable to go on.

Baltair took the opportunity to lunge. He grabbed at her skirts, but Frang acted quickly. Dropped his dirk and flung his body onto the priest. In fury, Baltair wrapped his arms about Frang and flipped him on his back. His bony hands squeezed the younger man's throat.

Gaping in horror, Moira knew she could not spare Baltair's life. She had tried and failed. He was too far gone. She snatched the dirk and struck. It plunged deep into his side. He howled in pain. His hands released their grip on Frang's throat. Moira sought to withdraw the blade, but it stuck firmly within the thrashing body.

Frang rolled out from under Baltair. Shoved him a few feet down the slope. Moira recognized his intention and joined his side. Together, they wrested Baltair's frame over the sharp rocks. Pushing with all her might, Moira exerted every ounce of energy she had.

They watched him tumble downward. Each time his battered body came to a stop, they shoved again. And again. His bearded face gathered in tense folds of anguish. He cried with each push. Grunted with every kick. Moira's belly bubbled with nausea. She did not think it righteous to kill the man to extinguish his darkness. But she sought to liberate Baltair's soul, and that was the last shred of honor she could provide.

At last, they pushed him over one last ledge. He dropped into the darkness. His cries carried up through the night until a hefty splash sounded. All went silent.

Moira's chest burned from the effort. Her throat swelled with emotion as she struggled for breath. She flung her arms around Frang. He pulled her close. She lost all composure and wept in his arms. They had set the priest free.

"Baltair was right," she said. "Isolba is alive. The spirits told me so. I could feel her consciousness aid me, for that I could not do alone. I am reminded of who I am. Our Isolba is safe. But I cannot tell Escarans."

"'Tis nae matter. Escarans is not long for this world," Frang said. "These last few years have ruined him. 'Tis only because of my leadership that Demoria's people have not overthrown him—or killed him. We must continue on as before."

"I cannot go on that way," Moira replied. "That old man will never die. He'll remain alive to spite me."

He pulled back, completely releasing his touch. "We must. Escarans cannot ken how deeply I've betrayed him. He yet trusts me, and I will keep you safe."

"What shall we tell him of Baltair?"

"We say naught. We ken naught. 'Twas Baltair who fled and hid away when his prophecy failed. Escarans will anoint a new priest when he decides Baltair will not return."

Moira's heart wrenched. She could not bear to slip back into indifference. Yet she had performed well for all this time. For the sake of Frang and Isolba, she would continue the charade.

"Believe me when I say I desire naught more than to hold you in my arms, honestly and openly," Frang said. His voice cracked. "To continue what we had before you married my brother. But our loyalty to him comes first."

"I ken," she said. "Though I displeased Escarans for aiding our daughter's escape, he has forgiven me. Other than that one moment in time I do not regret, I've not broken my vow of faithfulness."

"'Tis why I adore you," Frang said with a slight smile. "And you are free to wander the island once again, not imprisoned in your chamber and barred behind guards."

She did not return the expression, but was thankful to regain some sense of autonomy. Escarans had loosened his grip on her as he turned into a frail, powerless man. Though he accused her and the other wives of preventing pregnancy, his anger soon turned to despair. He was deluded to think he would see the male heirs Baltair promised.

The priest had led him on for too long. Claimed the prophecy was yet to come. But when Escarans gave up his last stores of alcohol to appease his people, even gifting it to the crofters and fisherfolk in exchange for their loyalty, he lost all motivation. He could not live without the substance that gave him his personality, his good-natured humor, and the charming confidence that once won the hands of his wives.

The night lightened, and Moira peered up at the sky in awe. The dark clouds dissipated. Such splendor before her eyes froze her in place. She and Frang remained there a long while, lingering in each other's presence before they would return to reality and pretend that no affection existed between them.

Their long months of grieving came to an abrupt end. Isolba, the product of their love, lived on, somewhere within the isles. Moira was determined to find her and when she did, would send Frang to the Argarves and inform the chief. Moira would only be certain Isolba was safe if Clan McCloud held her in its fold, far from Escarans' reach.

TWENTY-NINE

Mournful laments entered Isolba's ears. Spirit Hound Cave faded from her sight, and she found herself in the Lennox's blackhouse.

Beathag wailed inconsolably as she held Rindan's limp body in her arms. The utterances sounded otherworldly and forlorn, unceasing, increasing. This vision faded, and Isolba roused. Her eyes fluttered open, only to shut against the blinding light filtering into the blackhouse.

The paralysis of deep sleep emptied from her limbs, but the mournful, howling cries continued. She lifted her head and looked about to find that the noise came not from Beathag, who lay asleep next to Saithan and Cait, all piled around Rindan near the embers of the fire. Isolba folded herself into a sitting position and rubbed her eyes. The howls came from outside. Her body went rigid with disbelief. She had to be dreaming, and willed herself awake.

Her body throbbed with bruises, formed by the relentless waves when they had slammed against her and hurtled her down to shore. Her heavy lungs ached, and her stomach echoed with a sore emptiness. Every hurt and abrasion lit up across her skin and drove into her bones. She resided not within a dream, as her awareness operated acutely. The agony within her soul proved deeper. Nareen had passed on, and her mother would no longer be a part of her life.

She stood on unsteady feet and staggered to the open doorway, viewing the night with shock. Before her, the moon rested low and massive, a colossal amber orb daubed with copper in a cloudless sky. Its glow rippled outward, lighting up the atmosphere in a fantastic display of white light. Every jutting stone, each stac and skerry, every sharp cliff edge, and the crests of the waves displayed a silver gild.

Isolba fell to her knees. Clasped her hands as she drank in the splendor. The waters rippled calmly, and the soft breeze caressed her face. Mournful howls filled the night, overwhelming the gentle lapping of waves, their power over Isolba's senses surpassed by the light alone.

When she allowed her eyes to wander from the moon to the ground, she discovered the source of the haunting wails. Dotted over the land sat the island hounds, their snouts stretched toward the moon. Each howled a plaintive hymn.

Beyond the village on a ridgetop, a lone hound faced the others, and from this promontory, he was a vocalist leading a choir. Moonlight outlined his dark silhouette. Solidly he sat in the night. Waters rippled the horizon behind him. By his size and distinctive features, he could only be her black hound. The howls resounded from deep inside him, a sonority and hoarseness to his voice unlike the others.

Shivers rippled up Isolba's spine and over her scalp. The hairs on her neck stood on end. Something miraculous had taken place. It was as if a great war had raged in another dimension and good had conquered evil, allowing peace to descend on the isles.

The weight of a hand fell on her shoulder, and she turned to find Saithan behind her. Beathag and Cait stood with him, their eyes wide as they peered into the open sky in disbelief. Around them, the other islanders stumbled from their homes, sleepiness disrupting equilibrium, and stopped short as they beheld the moonlit scene.

No one spoke. Who would wish to interrupt the song and the astounding breadth and light of the moon? All stood silent. All watched. The hounds howled for a few more minutes until, at the black hound's direction, they lowered their snouts. The island mutts dispersed, wagging their tails as they trotted away.

The black hound stood motionless on the ridge and regarded Isolba with his glowing yellow eyes. He stared for a lingering moment, turned his head, and squinting, sniffed the air as if finding some odor carried in the wind. Then he walked casually off into the darkness as though nothing out of the ordinary had occurred.

She knew that though he manifested from the spiritual realm, he was also part of her. His essence connected to her spirit and came to her in times of need. Perhaps he was part spirit and part mortal, an expert of the waters and allegiant to her. He retained knowledge she did not. He brought her to Teutatwen when he could have as easily brought her to the Argarves. He had taken her to Rindan—her soulmate—and pulled them both to safety.

But perhaps he was part of Rindan instead? A subconscious being that acted separately from him while working on his behalf? She longed to know the truth of the hound's existence.

Rindan. Her beloved. Warmth flooded through her at the very thought of him. She longed to tell him what he meant to her, but could not. Not yet.

Breathing in a deep gulp of cool sea air, she turned and smiled at the Lennox family, who remained in a stupor. She took advantage of the moment of solitude and reunited with Rindan inside the empty blackhouse. He resided in a deeply unconscious state, departed to somewhere out of reach.

She knelt beside him and covered him in an embrace. She touched her cheek to his. His skin was clammy. The dark lashes of his closed eyelids twitched, but did not flutter open. His hands folded across his chest, and she placed a hand over them. Tears spilled from her eyes and fell on his face as she willed him to revive. He would not hear her, surely, and she brimmed too full to hold back her words.

"Come back to me," she whispered. "I am forever yours. I am... Isolba."

Playlist

Chapter One – Isolba
"Her and the Sea" by Clann

Chapter Two – Rindan
"Where the Hills are Green" by Peter Roe

Chapter Three – Nareen
"The Last of Her Kind" by Peter Gundry

Chapter Four – Escarans
"Secret Religion" by BBC Scottish Symphony Orchestra

Chapter Five – Baltair
"The Gift of Sight" by Peter Gundry

Chapter Six – Grandfather Lennox
"Traditional Gaelic Melody" by Alasdair Fraser

Chapter Seven – Anticipation
"Love & Honour" by Celtic Woman